# THE CASE

# OF THE

# SECRETIVE

# SECRETARY

## by

## Cathy Ace

FOUR TAILS PUBLISHING LTD.

# PRAISE FOR THE WISE ENQUIRIES AGENCY MYSTERIES

'…a gratifying contemporary series in the traditional British manner with hilarious repercussions (dead bodies notwithstanding). Cozy fans will anticipate learning more about these WISE ladies.'
***Library Journal, starred review***

'If you haven't read any of Cathy Ace's WISE cozies, I suggest you begin at the beginning and giggle your way through in sequence.'
***Ottawa Review of Books***

'…a modern-day British whodunit that's as charming as it is entertaining…Good fun, with memorable characters, an imaginative plot, and a satisfying ending.'
***Booklist***

'Ace spiffs up the standard village cozy with a set of sleuths worth a second look.'
***Kirkus Reviews***

'…a perfect cozy with a setting and wit reminiscent of Wodehouse's Blandings Castle. But its strongest feature is the heart and sensitivity with which Ace imbues her characters.'
***The Jury Box, Ellery Queen Mystery Magazine***

'Sharp writing highlights the humor of the characters even while tackling serious topics, making this yet another very enjoyable, fun, and not-always-proper British Mystery.'
***Cynthia Chow, Librarian, Hawaii State Public Library in King s River Life Magazine***

'A brilliant addition to Classic Crime Fiction. The ladies (if they'll forgive me calling them that) of the WISE Enquiries Agency will have you pacing the floor awaiting their next entanglement…
A fresh and wonderful concept well executed.'
***Alan Bradley, New York Times Bestselling Author of the Flavia de Luce books***

## Other works by the same author

(Information for all works here: **www.cathyace.com**)

### *The WISE Enquiries Agency Mysteries*
The Case of the Dotty Dowager
The Case of the Missing Morris Dancer
The Case of the Curious Cook
The Case of the Unsuitable Suitor
The Case of the Disgraced Duke
The Case of the Absent Heirs
The Case of the Cursed Cottage
The Case of the Uninvited Undertaker
The Case of the Bereaved Butler

### *The Cait Morgan Mysteries*
The Corpse with the Silver Tongue
The Corpse with the Golden Nose
The Corpse with the Emerald Thumb
The Corpse with the Platinum Hair
The Corpse with the Sapphire Eyes
The Corpse with the Diamond Hand
The Corpse with the Garnet Face
The Corpse with the Ruby Lips
The Corpse with the Crystal Skull
The Corpse with the Iron Will
The Corpse with the Granite Heart
The Corpse with the Turquoise Toes
The Corpse with the Opal Fingers

### *Standalone novels*
The Wrong Boy

### *Short Stories/Novellas*
Murder Keeps No Calendar: a collection of 12 short
stories/novellas
Murder Knows No Season: a collection of four novellas
Steve's Story in "The Whole She-Bang 3"
The Trouble with the Turkey in "Cooked to Death Vol. 3:
Hell for the Holidays"

# PRAISE FOR THE CAIT MORGAN MYSTERIES

'…Ace is, well, an ace when it comes to plot and description.'
**The Globe and Mail**

'Her writing is stellar. Details, references, allusions, expertly crafted phrasing, and serious subjects punctuated by wit and humour.'
**Ottawa Review of Books**

'If all of this suggests the school of Agatha Christie, it's no doubt what Cathy Ace intended. She is, as it fortunately happens, more than adept at the Christie thing.'
**Toronto Star**

'…a mystery involving pirates' treasure, lust, and greed. Cait unravels the locked-tower mystery using her eidetic memory and her powers of deduction, which are worthy of Hercule Poirot.'
**The Jury Box, Ellery Queen Mystery Magazine**

'…a testament to an author who knows how to tell a story and deliver it with great aplomb.'
**Dru's Musings**

'Cathy Ace makes plotting a complex mystery look easy. As the threads here intertwine in unexpected ways, readers will be amazed that she manages to pull off a clever solution rather than a true Gordian Knot of confusion.
Cathy Ace's books always owe a debt of homage to Grand Dame Agatha Christie…the blend of "cozy" mystery, tragic family dynamics…
pure catnip for crime fiction aficionados.'
**Kristopher Zgorski, BOLO Books**

Dedicated to all those who understand the strength of community, and work to help it survive, and thrive. Thank you.

# 4ᵗʰ SEPTEMBER

# CHAPTER ONE

Henry Devereaux Twyst, eighteenth Duke of Chellingworth, was terribly worried about his cook. Word had reached him via Edward, his butler, that Cook Davies had requested a personal meeting with himself and his wife. A time had been agreed for the following day, so as not to clash with the already scheduled gathering of the Anwen-by-Wye Revitalization Committee, which was due to take place in just a few hours. Henry was far from happy, because both meetings were likely to be disastrous.

Seeking solace from his worrisome thoughts, the duke looked down at his precious son, Hugo, writhing in his adorable little onesie, and noticed a stain upon it which he'd been thinking was an oddly shaped blue dog. It wasn't. He tried to wipe it off with a cloth, but it smeared into an enormous mark. The penny dropped – he must have somehow managed to splatter a bit of gouache paint onto his son. Oh no…Hugo had some of it on his little hand. Oh dear…now it was on his face.

Henry panicked. His wife Stephanie had left Hugo in his charge, which was a highly unusual occurrence. Henry desperately wanted to prove he was a reliable father, so had welcomed the opportunity to show his mettle. But it seemed he had fallen at the first hurdle: he couldn't even keep Hugo clean, let alone safe.

He soaked a rag in water then wiped his son's face and hands with as much tenderness as possible, though he had to rub a lot harder than he'd have liked to get the paint off Hugo's cheek. No…cheeks. He noticed the color had managed to get under Hugo's tiny fingernails. *How on earth had that happened?* Then he realized Hugo would just end up in the same mess again unless he managed to somehow get the paint off his onesie – but all he managed to do was make the stain paler, yes, but now it covered almost all of Hugo's little body.

When his darling wife, Stephanie, entered the folly where Henry had his art studio, she first gazed down at their son with his blue fingernails, and his half-blue romper suit, then she looked at her husband.

Henry knew he was pink in the face, and hated it when Stephanie tutted quietly and rolled her eyes at him. It made him feel queasy. She seemed to do it rather a lot.

She smiled, then observed, 'I love what you've done with the sky in that painting, Henry. But did you really need to test the color on our son first?'

Henry thought, on balance, it was best to say nothing.

'I take it this paint is non-toxic, dear?'

Henry nodded with relief. 'Absolutely, and it's water soluble, so it will wash off. I'm sorry, I've no idea how I managed to splatter him like that. I did my best to get all the paint into the little pot things when I squirted out the colors, but it came out of some tubes a bit faster than I'd imagined it would. Especially the blue.'

Stephanie pulled a cloth from an invisible pocket and managed to remove the paint from beneath their son's perfect fingernails. Henry wouldn't have dared; he'd have been too afraid of hurting Hugo. Then she stripped off Hugo's little suit and replaced it with another which was – for some unfathomable reason – in the basket she'd brought from Chellingworth Hall which Henry had imagined contained only a picnic.

With Hugo looking as though the blue paint and he had never been so much as introduced to each other, let alone been such close companions, Henry allowed himself to relax and enjoy the sandwiches his wife had brought, and a cooling tumbler of lemon barley water – a flavor which, for him, was the essence of summer. It was an enjoyable break. He'd been battling with some new techniques on canvas all morning, as well as grappling with concerns about his cook, so was glad to be able to think of something else for a while.

However, his hopes were dashed when his wife asked, 'Have you any idea why Cook Davies wants to see us tomorrow, Henry?'

The duke sighed. 'I do not. However, since it's the only time I can recall her asking for such a "chat", I have to say I cannot imagine it's about something that's going to lift our spirits. And they'll need that after the meeting about the future of the village. Are you absolutely certain that my presence will be required for both meetings, dear?'

Stephanie prepared herself to feed their son. As his son was swaddled to his wife's breast, Henry did his best to conduct a normal conversation; the wonder of the mother-child bond was not lost on him, but he couldn't say he felt comfortable seeing it in action. He busied himself gathering up the detritus of their meal, attending to each item with great care. Then he checked that the basket was properly closed. Three times. As his son finally unclamped from his wife, Henry felt able to chatter more naturally.

As his wife tended to their son, she asked, 'How long has Cook Davies run the kitchens at Chellingworth, Henry, dear? Obviously I'm aware she was already here when I took up my post. My post as public relations manager for Chellingworth, rather than as your wife, I mean.'

Stephanie held Hugo to her shoulder as Henry stood, and began to pace about the plain, but functional, interior of the folly. He paused to look down the hill toward the impressive structure where the Twyst family had lived for many hundreds of years. All eighteen – and now nineteen – generations of them.

Henry muttered, 'Your *post* as my *wife*?'

'I'm sorry, dear,' she said pensively, 'I didn't mean that the way it came out. It's just that the Hall, the Estate…it's all a great responsibility, isn't it?'

Henry placed his arm around Stephanie's shoulders and smiled warmly at his son. 'Indeed it is. And you, more than anyone, know how that weighs upon me. But now we have Hugo, and I feel it's my duty to ensure that all the affairs of the Seat are in as well-ordered a situation as I can make them, during my lifetime…for my son's sake.'

'I know you loved your father, Henry. I never met him, of course, but I'm aware he had little faith in your abilities to run Chellingworth well. You only knew you'd become the duke after your older brother died, my dear. He was raised to believe the role would be his; you believed you'd be able to indulge your love for art, and your own artistic inclinations…not be called back here by your grieving parents to be trained for a role you'd never expected. I know that you've done great things here, dear, and will continue to do so.'

'Thank you, my dear. One does one's best.'

'Indeed you do, Henry. And thus – to answer your earlier questions – yes, you do need to be at the meeting with Cook Davies tomorrow. *And* you need to attend, and participate in, the committee meeting today, because the village of Anwen-by-Wye is owned by the Chellingworth Estate and it's an important part of your overall – sorry, *our* overall – responsibilities. Times are changing, Henry, and villages all over Britain are changing, too. Ours less than most, because of the control we exercise in terms of there being no privately owned dwellings or commercial premises here – especially since your mother purchased the Coach and Horses pub to bring it back under Twyst control. But now? Now we need to make decisions.'

Henry sighed. He knew Stephanie was right, but that didn't make the planning, or doing, that lay ahead an easier or more pleasant prospect. If only he could stay in his studio and paint, that would be wonderful.

Dissolving the vision of his fantasy life, Stephanie said, 'I shall return to the Hall with Hugo, and you can bring the picnic basket with you when you come down – how about that?'

Henry nodded. 'Of course.'

He kissed his son and his wife, and watched in awe as Stephanie walked elegantly, and seemingly effortlessly, along the gently descending path. She and her cargo were the most precious things in the world to Henry – though he was glad to get back to his canvas, because he was really enjoying trying out the gouache technique as a bit of a change from his usual watercolors…and he hoped that tending to the shading of one particular cloud would allow him to stop being quite so concerned about why on earth Cook Davies needed a 'chat'.

# CHAPTER TWO

Christine Wilson-Smythe tried to relax on the sofa in her small apartment, which was tucked into what had once been the loft of the converted ancient barn which now housed the business she and her three colleagues ran. She sipped her peppermint tea, and told herself that this was the day...the day she would tell them that she was pregnant. She'd been putting it off for weeks, but knew she couldn't do so any longer, though she was deeply concerned about how her news would be received.

Of her current colleagues, she'd known Carol Hill the longest; they'd met at one of those dreadful mixer things for women working in the City of London about five...no, six...years earlier. At the time, Christine had been an underwriter at Lloyds, which had allowed her ample opportunity to use her sharp brain and the extensive network of contacts that had been built up by her successful father, the Viscount Ballinclare. Carol Hill had been the head of computing systems and services for one of the world's largest reinsurance agencies, headquartered in the City. When Christine and she had met, they'd bonded over...well, Christine couldn't recall. It couldn't have been their backgrounds, because she'd been raised in the rarified social circles reserved for the daughters of titled families, whereas Carol had grown up on a sheep farm in Carmarthenshire. But they most certainly had bonded, and Christine had at first admired, then grown to adore, Carol, who was recognized as a true high-flyer in their male-dominated world. Christine had enjoyed seeing Carol fall head-over-heels for a man who had worked for her, and had then done her best to understand Carol's desperation, and determination, to have children.

At the remembrance of how very much Carol and her husband David had wanted to be parents, Christine smiled, then almost cried. Carol would probably cope with the news of Christine's pregnancy quite well...she'd be happy for her.

But what about Mavis? Hmm...Christine couldn't be sure about how Mavis would take her news. The oldest of the group, and their *de facto* leader, Mavis had been Matron at the Battersea Barracks, a sort of retirement home for ex-servicemen, when Carol Hill, and Carol's good friend Annie Parker, had gone there to collect Christine's late grandfather's belongings, following his sudden death at the facility. And…then they'd all ended up embroiled in a situation none of them had seen coming. Which was why they'd set up in business together as private investigators a few months later, when Mavis had retired.

Mavis might well be cross with Christine – as she might be with a child who'd not acted in a way that suggested they had more than two brain cells functioning. But Christine had been taking the contraceptive pill when she'd become pregnant, so it really wasn't her fault. Yes…she'd push that angle with Mavis.

As for Annie? Christine smiled as she thought of Annie Parker. If ever a woman had carved out a life for herself, when surrounded by those who thought she shouldn't, or couldn't, Annie was she. The daughter of Windrush Generation immigrants from St Lucia, Christine admitted to herself that she couldn't even begin to imagine the challenges Annie's parents, and even Annie herself, had faced. Although she didn't know Annie as well as she knew Carol, they'd been colleagues for a few years now, and Christine felt a warmth for Annie, whose grit she admired.

Annie was completely dependable and great fun to work with, too. And her ability to understand people was almost as legendary as her dry – sometimes seemingly scathing – wit. Mavis was in her mid-sixties, with two sons, and grandchildren; Carol was now in her mid-thirties and had Albert, who was almost eighteen months old – so they both understood motherhood. Annie? Single, in her early fifties, and only just now settling down with what everyone believed would be her mate for life – would she understand Christine's situation?

Christine stood, resigning herself to the fact she wouldn't know the answer to that one until she told her friends the truth. She smoothed down her dress; it was warm in her flat and the gathered, printed silk frock was appropriate for the time of year, but it wasn't the sort of thing she usually wore. She wasn't really showing yet, being only about three months gone, but she would be soon. Yes…it was time.

Alexander had offered to be there when she shared their news, but Christine had said she'd rather tell her friends and colleagues on her own. But now? Now she could have done with a bit of handholding, and Mr Alexander Bright was very good at that. Christine smiled as she recalled what he'd said before he'd left the flat that morning, on his way to the antiques shop he owned in partnership with Henry Twyst.

'Let them ask you whatever they want, Christine, and just answer them honestly. It's their business, too – and you being pregnant might mean that all their lives will change. Maybe not immediately, but quite soon.' He'd kissed her, and then had revved away in his Aston Martin to do an honest day's work in the village.

Christine knew it wouldn't be too much longer before she'd be unable to get into, or out of, Alexander's beloved car, because her trim figure was about to balloon, so it would be her Range Rover – her 'Chelsea Tractor' as Annie called it – from then on. And after that? Car seats, and bottles, and cribs, and pushchairs…

Christine told herself off: that was enough of that sort of thinking…she and her colleagues were gathering prior to meeting a potential new client – that was what she had to focus on for now.

Only after that could she break the news to Mavis, Carol, and Annie. And maybe even Althea, Henry's mother, the dowager with whom Mavis lived. Althea wasn't a private investigator, like the rest of them, but that small fact didn't stop her sticking her oar in. Often – Christine admitted to herself – in useful ways. The client they were meeting this morning was one that Mavis had brought to them, so maybe Althea would tag along with her housemate and companion; the dowager didn't like not knowing what was going on, especially when a case was closely connected to Mavis, which this one sounded as though it would be.

Spotting she'd have to get a move on if she was going to pop to the loo – again – and prepare the inevitable pot of tea required for the get-together, Christine headed toward her bathroom to gird her loins…whatever that meant.

# CHAPTER THREE

Mavis MacDonald was pleased to find Christine busy making tea when she and Althea arrived at the office. She was wondering when Christine would tell them all that she was pregnant, and thought it showed a slightly worrying level of naïveté on the part of the girl to imagine that none of them would have worked it out already. But she was only in her late twenties and might think that flowing clothing – something she'd never worn before – would cover any telltale changes in her figure. It wasn't the girl's midsection that was the clue, but her bosom, hair, and skin; dead giveaways, all of them. That was how Mavis's husband had known she'd been expecting their first child – at least, he had done when his mother had pointed it out to him. A widow now for the past too many years, Mavis was a little envious of her young colleague: she had it all ahead of her. Though how they'd manage as a business, she didn't know.

'Come along, McFli,' coaxed Althea sweetly as her aged Jack Russell seemed hesitant to enter the office.

Mavis observed, 'Ach, he'll be waiting for Annie to arrive with her pup Gertie, no doubt. I can hear Carol's vehicle approaching. Just wait here with him. He can be a stubborn one, when he chooses to hold his ground.'

Althea giggled. 'Everyone says that he and I are quite similar, Mavis, so I shall take what you've just said as a compliment. And you're right, we'll enjoy a few moments of this lovely sunshine before our meeting.'

Mavis sighed. 'It's *our* meeting, dear. You're here to observe only, as a friend. Remember? We agreed.'

Althea smiled so that her dimples puckered beneath her bright eyes; Mavis reckoned the smile always took a decade off Althea's more than eighty years. 'Of course I remember, dear. My memory is still quite sharp, thank you. Besides, you only reminded me two minutes before we got out of your car.'

With the arrival of Carol and Annie, a short chaotic interlude was endured by Mavis, as Annie's rambunctious black Lab pup Gertie, and

Althea's aged but still spry McFli, bounded and yapped around each other with much enthusiastic sniffing and licking. Then both dogs insisted upon greeting all the humans in much the same way, before the women of the WISE Enquiries Agency were finally able to all settle around the coffee table, to have what Mavis always liked to call 'a wee chat' before any potential client arrived.

Althea opened with: 'So what's the skinny on this dame, Mavis? Can we trust her?'

Mavis's heart sank. 'Have you been reading those hard-boiled books set in 1940s Los Angeles again? I keep telling you that's no' what it's like to be a private investigator in Wales, nowadays. And Frances Millington is no' a dame, she's a proper "Miss", you'll see.'

Annie kicked off her sandals, then stuck her feet back into them when Mavis gave her a sour look. Sheepishly, Annie asked, 'So you know this Miss Millington, Mave. What can you tell us about her?'

'Efficiency personified,' said Mavis, allowing herself to beam as she spoke. 'Frances Millington was secretary to the team of doctors we had at the Battersea Barracks. As such, we didnae work together, but we were both part of a joint effort: our shared duty was to ensure the best of health for our residents. She has a sharp mind, pays excellent attention to detail, and – of course – possesses an enviable understanding of medical terminology, for one who is not a medical practitioner. She hasnae told me why she wants to retain our services, but I have no doubt she'll tell us when she arrives.'

'So…no personal insights at all?' Christine sounded disappointed.

'She's nae' married,' said Mavis, 'as I told you. And as for her private life? We never discussed it. I understand she moved on from the Battersea Barracks not long after I retired, and I believe she now lives somewhere in the vicinity of Tenby, in Pembrokeshire.'

Annie chipped in, 'Is she Welsh, then? Because, otherwise, it's a bit of a coincidence you two both ending up in Wales having worked together in London. If she's Welsh, like Carol, that would make sense. And, yeah, I know I'm here and I'm as Cockney as they come, and Chrissy's Irish – though posh Irish, with a fancy pile in London too, so she's almost English, really—'

Mavis couldn't help but smile as Christine play-thumped Annie and exclaimed, 'Oi, you…I'm proper Irish, thanks, and don't you forget it.'

Annie grinned. 'Yeah, alright then – and we've got our resident Scot, in the shape of you, Mave—'

Althea smiled sweetly and added, 'And don't forget me. I'm a quarter of all four of each of the Home Nations.' She beamed, and patted McFli.

Annie sighed. 'So – yeah…why's she in Tenby, Mave? And where's she from?'

A clarion voice boomed, 'I was born and raised in Hove, and I live near Tenby because I missed the sea very much when I lived in London. The Thames is all well and good, but it's not the sea. Obviously.'

The five women looked toward the door, where they'd failed to notice the arrival of a small, neat woman who looked…

Annie said softly, 'Gordon Bennett, Mave, she looks just like you.'

Mavis stood to welcome Frances Millington and assessed the woman with fresh eyes. Yes, she was about Mavis's height – so, short; yes, she had a practical, neat gray bob – like Mavis; yes, she also clearly favored sensible, neutral slacks and shirts, and navy and beige always looked good together – in fact, Mavis was wearing a similar type of outfit that very morning.

As she moved toward Frances, Mavis said quietly to Annie, 'I don't see it myself.' Turning her attention to their potential client, Mavis held out her hand. 'Frances, how wonderful to see you. What's it been? Three years?'

Frances Millington replied in sonorous tones, 'Four, Matron, though you've not changed at all.'

Mavis hadn't been addressed in that manner for such a long time that it felt…wonderful, for a moment, then she realized she had to say, 'Ach no, it's no' Matron anymore, Frances, it's Mavis. Please.'

Mavis introduced all the humans, and both dogs; she was grateful that Carol had left her son Albert in the charge of her husband that morning – dogs could be disruptive, but could be disciplined, which couldn't always be said for bairns…nor for Althea, truth be told. Mavis hoped the dowager would be on her best behavior, though she always felt the woman was a bit like a jack-in-the-box, and you couldn't be sure what would set her off.

With teas all around, and biscuits within reach, Mavis decided to move things along. 'So, Frances, what brings you to see us? How do you think that a firm of private investigators can help you?'

Frances Millington took the time to make eye contact with each of the five women; Mavis understood why she didn't bother with the dogs, both of whom were lying quietly, and were best left – as everyone knew – undisturbed.

Frances hooked her bob behind one ear which – for some reason Mavis was unable to fathom – made Annie giggle. Mavis glared at her.

When Frances finally spoke, all she said was, 'I can't say.'

Mavis felt flummoxed. 'What do you mean, exactly?'

Mavis, and the entire team, had learned that sometimes a potential client needed time to get to the point. People felt awkward when they had to share what might, on occasion, be deeply personal information, or when it came to sharing their feelings toward someone they wanted investigated.

Frances replied, 'It's so many little things, that add up to either one big thing, or nothing at all. It could all just be a series of coincidences, but I fear not.'

Mavis felt her ex-colleague's response to be obtuse, to say the least. 'Might you be able to give us some examples of…the little things?'

'The lights – well, the electricity as a whole, really. The hot water. The cold water even. The blessed Wi-Fi. And then there was the rat.' Frances' face and tone suggested that what she was saying should mean something to the women.

Mavis could tell from her colleagues' expressions that they were as much at sea as she, herself, felt. She pressed, 'And the context for all these things, Frances?'

'The Lavender.'

Mavis guessed, 'And this is a house? Where, exactly?'

'It's a hotel. Just north of Tenby. Sits on a small point overlooking the sea, and Caldey Island. The monks there became famous for making perfume from the island's renowned lavender. The hotel is named for the flower because the man who built it claimed one could smell the flowers on the sea breezes. One cannot. But he built there, nonetheless. The hotel opened in 1929. It's remote, in the way a place can be when surrounded on three sides by the sea, though there are homes just a little more than a mile away. It is now owned by Toni Conti – with an "i", not an "e" as in the one-time prime minister of Italy. I am his personal secretary. He used to have a chain of cafeterias and ice cream parlors throughout Wales, but is now retired. The hotel was, at one time, his personal home. In his retirement, he has reopened it as a hotel. There are less than twenty guest rooms, and several of the so-called "guests" are really residents. So it represents more of a small community, in that regard. Mr Conti enjoys the company.'

Mavis thought it sounded like a peculiar arrangement, but asked, 'And these "little things" are problems you've experienced at The Lavender Hotel?'

'We who live there refer to it as The Lavender. And, yes.'

Mavis could tell that her colleagues were going to let her do the burrowing on this one, which she understood, so she set about doing it. 'And you think we might be able to help because…?'

'Someone has to do something. It seems that I cannot. I have expressed my concerns to Mr Conti, and he has said he does not share my point of view.'

'Which is what?'

Frances rearranged her shoulders. 'I'd rather not say. I would prefer it if a representative of your agency would come to see what's going on there. I've been told, in no uncertain terms, that I am imagining things. That I am making connections between occurrences that do not exist. I need a trustworthy third party to corroborate my suspicions. But, if I tell you what I "believe" is happening, then your objectivity might be called into question.'

Annie asked, 'Has anyone been hurt?'

'Not as such.'

Carol tried, 'Do you think that anyone staying there is in danger? Or would be?'

Frances hesitated. 'I don't believe so. I feel comfortable asking someone to stay there.'

Christine asked, 'Is there a pressing need for this investigation? I mean, why now?'

Mavis noticed Frances' cheeks grow pale. 'My…suggestions…have led to there being the possibility that I might not be able to retain my post, and would, therefore, also have to leave. I love The Lavender. I don't want to leave. It's my home.'

Mavis asked gently, 'How long have you been there?'

A smile crossed Frances' face as she spoke. 'Since I left the Barracks. Almost four years. I sold my flat in London, and receive my board and lodgings in lieu of payment for my duties. I am able to live within my means in other respects. It suits.' She paused, and her smile faded. 'But finding alternative accommodation, with a comparable location and lifestyle, at a rate I could afford, would be unlikely. And I do not deserve to be turfed out. As I believe an objective observer would be able to ascertain, and prove. That is how you can help me. And it has become a pressing matter. I…I have until the end of the month.'

Mavis considered her response carefully, but, as she was about to reply, Althea butted in. 'Mavis and I could come to stay at the hotel undercover. Is it the sort of place where two old biddies might be expected to fit in? Or would you need our youngest operative, Christine?'

The four women who were the *actual* professional investigators all stared at the dowager. Mavis felt quite miffed about it; she could see that Annie looked to be stifling a laugh, and even Carol was biting her lip, while Christine merely looked surprised.

'I don't think it's your place to suggest such an idea, Althea,' came out of Mavis's mouth, at precisely the same moment that Frances Millington said, 'That's a perfect plan.'

The two ex-colleagues shared a significant glance, and Mavis felt it behooved her to demur to the potential client. 'It's a direct approach that might get the job done within the short timeframe you have noted, Frances, and, of course, we have a personal history, so there'd be a set of "friendly rates" that I'm sure we could discuss. But we're professionals, Frances, who have to earn a living, so there would be a cost associated.'

Frances replied calmly, 'I have money in the bank, and am only here because I see it as better to invest in outsiders proving me to be right, than to hold onto it so I have more to fall back on if I lose my home.'

Mavis studied her colleagues' faces; all seemed to be in agreement. 'Very well then, though I have to say that, with as little to go on as you've given us, I'm no' as happy as I'd like to be about it. If you think that I would suit, I shall come. But, Althea, this is no' something you can be involved with. We've talked about this sort of thing before – you're no' a professional, you should stay at home.'

Frances spoke firmly. 'There is an unwritten rule about The Lavender accepting guests: they have to be approved by the owner, and Mr Conti is rather picky. A dowager duchess would sway his opinion, I believe. And he could easily be persuaded that a dowager would normally travel with a companion. Though I'd prefer that no one knows of our shared background, Mavis, if you don't mind. I don't think that would be a good idea.'

Althea giggled, 'Of course it wouldn't, because, otherwise, we wouldn't be undercover at all, would we? I'd just be being me, and Mavis would be being Mavis, which isn't much fun at all. I could be there for the sea air – something which Chellingworth is noticeably lacking. I'll make out that I'm suffering from ennui. I've always thought that sounds rather wonderful. Am I able to bring McFli with me?'

Frances shook her head. 'No pets, I'm afraid. That's a written rule. No exceptions.'

Mavis noticed that Althea rolled her little shoulders in apparent discomfort. 'Not even at the personal request of a dowager? McFli and I are very attached to each other, you know.'

Frances looked apologetic. 'Mr Conti's wife is allergic to…well, all animals, she says.'

Mavis heard Althea mutter, 'Preposterous,' under her breath, before she sat up and announced, 'Sacrifices must be made by those of us who seek the truth, I dare say. I'm in. Young Ian Cottesloe can see to McFli – though I'll have to speak to him about treats.'

Mavis knew that Althea's instructions to others about how many treats McFli was allowed bore no resemblance to the number the woman indulged him with herself, so she reckoned the dog might even lose a few pounds if they were away for any length of time. Which raised a question in her mind.

She asked, 'How long do you think we'd need to stay in order to experience enough "little things" to be able to come up with some evidence?' She felt a bit foolish asking such a woolly question, but Frances' choice to not explain further left her in a difficult position.

Frances gave the matter some thought. 'They come thick and fast, sometimes, so maybe only three days? But, if there's a lull, maybe longer.'

Mavis pressed one final time. 'And there's no more you feel able to tell us?'

Frances shook her head. 'Not at the moment, though I might have more…concrete information before you arrive.'

It was agreed that Mavis would email a contract to Frances later that day, so that she could read it through upon her arrival back at The Lavender.

Once they were alone, their newest client having taken her leave of them, Annie bustled with Carol to clear the remnants of their tea, while Althea tended to McFli. Mavis noticed that Christine was hovering, looking anxious. 'Something you want to say, Christine?' She thought she'd give the girl the chance to speak up.

Mavis was surprised when Carol added, 'Yes, come on, Christine.'

'Spill, Chrissy,' added Annie.

Althea said, 'What – hasn't she told you that she's pregnant, yet?'

Mavis glared at the dowager, who was examining one of McFli's paws.

Christine's gasped. 'You all *know*? How? Alexander hasn't said anything, he wouldn't.'

Mavis took pity on her. 'We're no' blind, Christine. You've got that glow about you, there's been the sickness in the mornings – which seems to have lessened, which is good. And the flowing clothes, though it's only up on top that you seem to need them at the moment.

And Alexander doesn't need to say anything, it's in his eyes every time he looks at you. How far along are you?'

Christine began to cry. 'Three months. Ish.'

Annie exclaimed, 'I thought you were supposed to know exactly. Isn't that important?'

Mavis and Carol both made to speak, but Althea got in first. 'They say so, but, honestly, it didn't matter in my day. One just had a general idea, and one went from there. Though they'll narrow it down with scans and so forth. Where will you be seeing someone, Christine? Here, or in London? I can give you recommendations, if you'd like.'

Mavis reasoned that the dowager had just experienced her daughter-in-law's pregnancy…and the wee woman had been all over that, as Stephanie herself had often remarked.

'If you'd prefer, you could talk to Stephanie,' added Althea.

'Or me,' offered Carol. Mavis noticed the warmth of the smile that passed between Christine and her chum. They hugged.

'Come here, Chrissy,' said Annie, joining the embrace.

'Thanks, Althea, and thanks, Carol.' Christine's voice was not much more than a whisper. 'I know I have decisions to make on that front…but we also have to talk about how me being pregnant, and then having a baby, might impact the agency and its work.'

Mavis could tell that Christine was past the teary stage, so decided to get right to the point. 'We need to make sure you're well employed with work that requires no physical danger while you're carrying the child, Christine. When you're a new mother? Maybe you should have a talk to Carol about that aspect of your professional life. She's most certainly got the hang of it.'

Carol nodded, and Mavis was glad that the two women shared enough of a friendship that they'd be able to have frank, and detailed, conversations about what Carol — and her husband — had to do to make things work. She didn't think it was the right time to ask about Alexander's possible future role, though suspected that would be an important component in any ongoing plans.

As she thought of that aspect, Mavis sighed; she was concerned by the knowledge that most of Alexander's business interests were in

London, and was only too well aware of how critical it was for Carol to have David as a full-time, on-the-spot parenting partner.

Mavis pushed aside her concerns, and moved to hug Christine.

'Thanks, Mavis. I knew you'd understand, really,' whispered Christine into her ear. 'I'll get myself sorted. And I will be careful.'

Mavis pulled back. 'Aye, no getting into situations like you did in Ealing, please. Agreed?'

Christine nodded.

'So steer clear of me, doll,' called Annie as she played with Gertie. 'We all know what I'm like on me plates, especially on them apples over there, and I certainly don't want to go fallin' on you while you're up the duff.'

Althea giggled. 'You're not good on your feet, especially on the spiral staircase, and you don't want to endanger Christine while she's pregnant? I love a bit of Cockney rhyming slang. It takes me back to my days on the stage.'

Mavis replied, 'Shall we get on? I've this contract to finalize; I know you and Carol are working on that background check for Carol's old company, Christine; and you, Annie, you're finishing up that paperwork for our invoice that I've asked Carol to get off to Rhodri Lloyd for the Case of the...what was it you decided upon? That chap in Birmingham who was hiding his money from his wife when they were getting divorced, I mean.'

'The Case of the Miserly Administrator,' replied Annie. 'He was in the admin department of that plastics firm, so I went with that.'

'I still can't believe he had that much cash to stash,' commented Christine.

'Which we wouldn't have found, if it weren't for you being so good with financial records,' said Carol.

'And I wouldn't have known where to go to catch him red-handed, so to speak, if it hadn't been for you trawling through as much as you did online, and spotting that pattern about someone who kept winning big at the bingo, Car,' replied Annie. 'I haven't played bingo for such a long time. That was fun, doing that. Eustelle and I used to go together, sometimes. Dead embarrassing she was, leaping up and screaming her head off if she won. But there, you can't choose your mum, can you?'

'What a weird secret life to have,' observed Christine. 'Playing bingo when he said he was volunteering at a soup kitchen. And then hiding his winnings. Twenty years' worth of them. Odd. You could have called it The Case of the Bonkers Bingo Player, Annie.'

'Or the Jammy Jackpot Winner,' offered Carol.

'An excellent team effort,' said Mavis, 'but I'd prefer to call it The Case of the Client Who Was Invoiced In A Timely Manner, thank you. Now onwards, and upwards. Let's get going. Althea and I have an appointment at Chellingworth Hall in an hour, so I need to get this done quickly.'

'Yes, we mustn't be late,' noted the dowager. 'Stephanie's quite particular about meetings starting on time.'

'Not enough alliteration in that case title, Mave,' called Annie as she and Gertie headed to her desk.

'I prefer a bonnie bank balance over amusing alliteration, as you all know,' said Mavis, smiling at her own quip as she took her seat.

# CHAPTER FOUR

Stephanie Twyst, Duchess of Chellingworth surveyed the room. Yes, everything was as it should be. 'Thank you, Edward. I appreciate your efforts, as always.'

'Your Grace.'

'Please send everyone in as they arrive. No need to escort them, they've all been here before. And keep the tea coming. I think three pots at a time should suffice. And we'll serve ourselves, thank you. I'll ring if we're running low on anything.'

'Your Grace.'

Before she released Edward to his other duties, Stephanie dared to add, 'I don't suppose you know why Cook Davies has asked for a private meeting with myself and His Grace, do you?'

Stephanie noticed how the Twysts' beloved butler hesitated before he replied. 'I couldn't say, Your Grace.'

She judged him to know exactly what was going on, but wasn't surprised by his answer. 'Thank you, Edward. Though I hope you understand that, while I would never wish to pry, I'm always here to listen to issues of even a personal nature which might be challenging the smooth running of the Hall and the Estate.'

'Indeed, Your Grace.'

She knew he understood this to be true, the WISE women having recently investigated the difficult situation surrounding the death of his own brother.

'I shall remain here, Edward, to check through the minutes of the last meeting. You may leave the door open, thank you.'

Finding herself completely alone, which wasn't something she had been accustomed to since the birth of her son, Stephanie flicked absently through the printed minutes on the table in front of her – though her focus was elsewhere. She'd been at Chellingworth Hall for years, but had only been its mistress for a little less than eighteen months, since she'd married Henry. Within that time, she'd had to work out her duties, then 'become' a duchess, and now she was learning what it was like to be a mother – another steep curve. Surprisingly, she discovered she was now also expected to be something of a town planner, when it came to deciding the future role of various buildings in Anwen-by-Wye.

She hoped that her insistence that Henry participated – actively – in the village revitalization committee meant he would, in fact, contribute in some way. But she doubted it. She loved Henry; he was a gentle soul, possibly born out of his time, who was kind, and didn't have a spiteful bone in his body. He never bore grudges, and did his best to not be too judgmental – though that wasn't always something at which he excelled. As she'd suspected he would be, he was a devoted father to their son, and loved him with a tenderness that bordered on…well, Henry always looked as though he were afraid he might break Hugo when he held him. But, for all his faults – and even Stephanie had to admit he wasn't short of those – her love for him was strong, and deep, and she knew it would endure, even if his lack of a spine made her quite cross on occasion.

'Ah, here you are.' Henry appeared at the door, with Hugo in his pram. 'Am I parking him beside you?'

Stephanie smiled as her husband and son approached. All she could see of her offspring was one little arm, which was reaching toward Henry, whose face was pink beneath his tousled hair and above his half-undone bow tie; Hugo enjoyed pulling at his father's hair almost as much as he delighted in grabbing at his ties.

'Yes, here, please, where I can reach him easily if he frets. Thank you, Henry.'

Henry fussed with the pram's position, then set the brakes. 'You're quite sure you want him here? I could keep him up in our rooms, so you could concentrate on…this.'

Stephanie easily spotted her husband's clumsy attempt to wriggle out of attending the meeting. 'Thank you for such a selfless offer, dear, but I want Hugo to grow up within the fabric of all that Chellingworth means. Today's a big day, Henry; what's decided will impact the future version of the Seat that Hugo will inherit. Though, of course, we both hope that will not be for many, many years to come.'

'Indeed,' replied her husband with feeling.

'You'll need to attend to your tie, Henry.'

Henry fiddled at his neck. 'Oh gosh, those little fingers of yours, Hugo,' he said, beaming down at his son. 'I'll just pop upstairs to use a mirror. Please start without me, if needs be.'

'Don't be silly, dear.' Stephanie stood. 'I'll do it for you, then you won't need a mirror.' She noticed her husband's shoulders sag, just a little.

The duchess wasn't surprised that Tudor Evans was the first to arrive, nor by his jovial words upon entering the meeting room. 'How's my godson doing today?'

Stephanie always found Tudor's appearance to be comforting; true, he wasn't a man who'd ever be likely to be referred to as 'handsome', but his tall, broad-shouldered body, his large head, and craggy face reminded her of a human version of Bagpuss, an animated character she'd enjoyed watching on TV who'd been described as 'a saggy, old cloth cat, baggy, and a bit loose at the seams'. That was how she saw Tudor. The fact that he, like her husband, favored wearing a waistcoat, shirt and bow tie, meant she couldn't help but compare them when they were together. Henry's chin aside – he had the prominent, Chellingworth Chin – the two men were not totally dissimilar, though one would never mistake them for brothers. Tudor was a distinctly positive, action-oriented person who was large, but not flabby; Henry, on the other hand, vacillated so, and his girth was mainly due to his love of good food, rather than achieved by lifting and carrying heavy objects like barrels of beer.

As Tudor took his chance to indulge in his role as godfather to Hugo – a role to which both Stephanie and Henry agreed he was eminently suited – Stephanie forced herself to push aside the trepidation she was feeling about the meeting. The room was about to be filled with a group within which, as she knew only too well from bitter experience, there was likely to be little consensus. She had to run the meeting to gain agreement about direction, and ensure that action points were agreed upon – then ensure that action actually ensued, and was completed.

She sighed. Heavily. Yes, it would be a challenging meeting, but – even if it went well – it was just the beginning of a potentially massive undertaking.

'Everything alright, Stephanie?' Tudor always used personal names when no one other than the duke and duchess were present – his godfatherly relationship with them allowed for it, it had been agreed.

'It's an important meeting, Tudor,' admitted Stephanie. 'What we decide today, or fail to decide today, will have long-term ramifications for a good number of people. Possibly the entire village. Henry and I feel the weight of the responsibility.'

Tudor nodded. 'Just reading the agenda gave me shivers. I have my own ideas, of course, but haven't talked to anyone except Annie about them. That's what this meeting's for. Besides, I don't want any arguments in the pub, do I? We need to attract people in, not make them think there's going to be a right old barney there every time they pop in for a half of mild and a pasty, right?'

Stephanie chuckled. 'Thanks for that, Tudor – now I fancy a pasty.' Stephanie winked, then straightened her back and stuck out her chin as Marjorie Pritchard arrived with Iris Lewis in tow. Iris was grinning, as she usually was, but Marjorie had a face like thunder. Stephanie felt her spirits droop. *What now?*

Forcing herself to smile, she crossed the room with her hand outstretched. 'Hello Iris, please take a seat. Something the matter, Marjorie? You don't look too happy.'

'The lane from the village is in a pitiful state.' Marjorie's tone suggested a scandalous situation. 'I know we had unusually heavy rains in July, so some damage might be expected, but I'd have thought it would have been remediated by now. Iris and I had to keep hold of each other as we walked here, or I'd have gone for a burton, I'm sure. Has no one reported it? Because, if not, take this as me doing so.'

Stephanie looked at Marjorie's stout, capable body, then at Iris Lewis…who was over eighty and half the size of Marjorie – the woman most folks often thought of in a less than kindly way, due to her overbearing nature. Stephanie couldn't imagine that hanging onto Iris would have helped much if Marjorie had taken a tumble.

The duchess replied as evenly as she could, 'I'm not sure what's happening with the lane, Marjorie, but thank you for bringing the problem to my attention. I'll speak to Bob Fernley about it…ah, there he is now, but I'll do it after this meeting, if you don't mind. We have rather a lot to get through today.'

'I know,' said Marjorie, taking a seat. 'I've come prepared.'

Stephanie was horrified to see the woman pull two ring binders out of her plaited straw shopping basket.

'Please, help yourselves to tea,' said Stephanie as she greeted Sharon Jones, who ran the shop in the village. Sharon was a relatively new addition to the committee, and had been brought onboard once Iris Lewis had signified she'd like to step back in the not-too-distant future.

Almost everyone was there – only Mavis and Althea were yet to arrive. Those in attendance were all chatting nicely, taking tea and cake for themselves, and Stephanie found – to her surprise – that she was sweating. Yes, it was a warm day, but the meeting room was large and airy. She told herself to stop being silly; in her time as a PR executive, she'd presented to large groups of influential stakeholders of many types. Indeed, on many occasions, she'd had to tell classic alpha males just how they should run their companies in order to prove to the world that they cared about something other than profit. Now all she had to do was lead a gathering of locals toward the end she desired – surely that was within her capabilities?

Taking her seat at the head of the table, with her son's pram to her left, she noted with some dismay that Henry, Bob Fernley – the Chellingworth Estates Manager – and Tudor, the man who ran the Chellingworth-owned pub in the village – were all sitting along the right-hand side of the table, with Sharon, Iris, and Marjorie facing them. It looked…alarmingly confrontational.

Stephanie dared, 'Henry, dear, would you mind terribly if you changed seats with Marjorie, please? Marjorie, if you wouldn't mind? That would mean that Henry will be able to tend to Hugo, should he need attention. Thank you both.'

Marjorie harrumphed her agreement, and Henry helped with what were – apparently – quite heavy ring binders.

Stephanie felt a little better: at least Marjorie Pritchard couldn't glower at Tudor without some effort, and they had Bob between the pair of them, which might prove useful. Of course, the woman was now right beside Stephanie herself, so she'd have to deal with that if the need arose. Which she hoped it didn't.

Mavis scuttled in. 'Apologies for being late. Althea insisted upon bringing McFli, and he didnae want to come. I don't know what's got into him today. He's no' usually this stubborn. Ach, there you both are.'

Althea trotted into the meeting room, spotted the cake, plonked herself into a seat and grabbed a plate. 'Come on, McFli, it's Victoria sponge, you like that.' McFli skittered across the ancient wooden floor and took up a position beside Althea's chair, with an expectant look on his face.

Mavis sat beside Tudor Evans, across from the dowager and her dog. 'Ach, there's nothing can get him moving like the promise of a treat.'

Althea grinned. 'It's the same for humans, Mavis. I'm only here for the cake, myself. Don't let me stop you, Stephanie, dear, on you go.'

Stephanie nodded. 'Thank you all for being here. As you know, we're here to discuss the future of Anwen-by-Wye as it, and all of us, face new challenges. We're all aware that we have almost no children left in the village, and even the education authority has come to the conclusion that's not likely to change. At least, not sufficiently for them to ever need to reopen the school again. As we all know, they "own" the school, insofar as they built it upon land they lease from the Estate. They will not be renewing the lease, so now we have to decide what to do with the building itself, which the Estate has purchased for an extremely favorable price. Bob – over to you, I think.'

Bob Fernley nodded. 'I sent out the report with the papers for the meeting. As you can see, the building is structurally sound, except for the roof, which – though it's got a few years left in it yet – could, in my opinion, in any case, do with being renewed. The rest of the building's been checked, but it wouldn't be fit for any purpose without the electrics being updated and some sort of refit of all the toilet facilities. Now, obviously, what it's going to be used for in the long run will dictate how we'd proceed in those two, critical directions. Once the decision regarding purpose has been made, I've been told that renovations would probably take about six months. That would allow for the roof, electrics, necessary upgrades, general decorative requirements and a bit of landscaping to be done, too – though, again, what use would be made of the area that was once the playground would dictate how we approach the exterior space. I'm sure it's not escaped anyone's notice that what was once a good, flat, tarmacked yard has been compromised, with vegetation poking through the surface in many areas.'

'Thanks, Bob.' Stephanie nodded. 'As you all know, I asked for ideas regarding the future use of the facility, so the floor is open.'

Stephanie wasn't surprised when Marjorie's hand shot up. She did her best to sound cheery as she said, 'The chair recognizes Marjorie Pritchard.'

Marjorie beamed – quite alarmingly – and opened a binder with a thump. 'I propose we use the old school as an arts center. Not just a gallery – though there should be an area for that – but a center where things are actually created.'

Stephanie waited for more. There was bound to be more – this was Marjorie, after all, who loved nothing more than the sound of her own voice. But the woman said nothing.

'I say, I like that idea,' said Henry.

Marjorie smiled slyly. 'I thought you would. It's because you're an artist yourself, Your Grace.'

Henry beamed at Marjorie, and she beamed back.

Stephanie wondered if she'd fainted, and this was all some sort of fevered hallucination.

Iris Lewis sounded excited when she added, 'Yes, we could have a gallery there, and use parts of the facility – sort of cordoned off – for other types of artisans, too. Silversmiths, people who make things with stained glass, or leather, do upholstery, that sort of thing. Not just all painters or sculptors.'

Sharon Jones added, 'They could have little workshops, and there could be an area where lessons could be given, that sort of thing.'

Bob Fernley was all smiles when he said, 'And what about a shop, too? People like to buy bits and bobs…especially when they've seen how they're made, and have possibly had a chance to chat to the person who made them.'

Stephanie jumped when the dowager added, 'My darling daughter Clementine and her new husband Julian are taking up residence at the house in Scotland. Surprisingly, she's informed me that the smithy on the Estate there is ideal for her husband to continue his work as a blacksmith, and he says there's great demand for blacksmithing lessons – if that's the right description. I suspect this means there might be the demand for tutorials and even longer courses of study of crafts and artistic endeavor in this general area too. You could teach people how to paint, Henry; you spent enough years learning at the feet of artists yourself.'

Tudor added, 'If people were coming for courses, they might need to stay overnight, and we'll have those four rooms ready at the Coach and Horses before you know it.'

'But what about musicians?' Iris Lewis was waggling a hand. 'As I know from my granddaughter Wendy, who studied music in Cardiff, there's a small but growing requirement for piano lessons in the wider area. Maybe we could think about other types of musical instruments being taught, too. But…how would that work with all the artisans there – would it become annoying? And there wouldn't be room for a performance area at the old school, would there?'

'There wasn't a stage at the old school, just a hall for assembly. But we've got the village hall for that, Iris,' offered Marjorie. 'It's not used for Brownies or Guides, nor Cubs or Scouts any longer, and that judo thing never took off, did it? The hall's hardly ever used in the day – and it's got a decent-sized stage. Though the seating's a bit dilapidated, and we all know the stage lighting doesn't work properly.'

Stephanie felt like Alice, discovering herself to be in Wonderland. What on earth was happening? She held up her hand to try to regain control – of herself, as much as the meeting.

'What wonderful ideas,' she said, reeling a little. 'Did you manage to get all that down, Mavis?'

Because Althea had insisted upon Mavis being with her when she came, Mavis had agreed to take the minutes of the meeting and to circulate them afterwards, thereby allowing Tudor, who usually did it, to have a bit more time to get himself sorted at his new pub.

Stephanie could see the panic in Mavis's eyes. 'I wasnae expecting there to be so many ideas coming at me all at once,' she said, sounding helpless.

*You and me, both*, thought Stephanie, though she said, 'Well, let's just revisit some of them, then, shall we? Let's start with the general idea – that of the old school becoming a sort of sanctuary for artists. Is everyone in agreement on that point?'

A chorus of 'Ayes' rang out around the meeting room, leading Hugo to stir in his pram – which was the last thing Stephanie needed.

'That's a wonderful thing. We have a plan. An agreement.' Stephanie had hoped for one such decision to be made at the meeting, so felt elated, and yet a little unsure of where to go next. 'And the general idea that workshop areas would be designated, and presumably rented out to artisans who need a base, as well as a more flexible area, or maybe more than one, that would be rented out separately to allow for groups to attend something along the line of "lessons" given by either the resident artisans or others who just wanted to use the place for the odd session. All this is agreed?'

'Aye.'

Stephanie felt compelled to move on. 'And the village hall – if it were renovated to allow it to be fit for purpose – would have a focus on the musical and performance arts? Music, dance, theatre, that sort of thing?'

'Aye.'

'With a couple of provisos,' said Tudor, raising a hand.

Stephanie sucked in air. 'Those being?'

'That we give priority to Welsh culture – you know, the people themselves being local, or Welsh, or at least producing things that are aligned with local and Welsh culture. I suppose if we can't find enough of those sorts we could allow in others – but I feel we should tend to our own first. I hope that doesn't sound overly nationalistic, but there's a need for Welsh culture, in all its forms, to be cared for, and encouraged, I'd say.'

'Hear, hear,' said Althea loudly.

Another round of loud 'Aye's followed.

Stephanie looked across at Mavis, who nodded her head even as she was still scribbling notes, then she gazed around the table at every face; they were all smiling back at her.

Stephanie realized that her entire body was vibrating. 'Well, I must say, I wasn't expecting that. It's almost as though you've all had a think about this before we met here today, and you have a clear, shared vision for the direction you wish Anwen-by-Wye to take – as a destination for local, and Welsh, artisans, artists, and performers. I'm so incredibly pleased. Of course, none of us wants Anwen-by-Wye to become transformed into something that's not authentic, and we absolutely don't want it to be turned into some sort of themed village. But I do believe that a thoughtfulness about what it offers to the world – how it presents itself to the world – is important. We don't want it to die, without purpose. Attracting people to it can bring fresh energy and perspectives. We already have a wonderful community spirit within it, and we want that to continue. But I had feared that might falter, without fresh ideas to give it an opportunity to develop, and grow, as we face the future which, of course, no one can foretell. I…I concur with your suggestions. We both do, don't we, Henry?'

She turned to her husband who was glowing with delight. 'Indeed I do. As Marjorie so graciously recognized, I am an artist myself, and I can think of nothing I'd rather do than support the efforts of those who might not be able to pursue their artistic career if not for the availability of a suitable, affordable workspace. I know how my own artistic endeavors have thrived since you had the folly done up for me; I'd hope others might find the same in a specially designated space within which they can develop their skills. And the chance to belong to a community of like-minded individuals would be beyond price. I absolutely agree with today's recommendations.'

Stephanie glowed. 'Bob, what would this mean in terms of timescales, and costs?'

Everyone stared at Bob Fernley, who Stephanie could see felt he'd been caught out.

'Well, that would be something I could look into, Your Grace,' he muttered. 'As you know, my schedule's already quite full, but I'll make it a priority.'

Stephanie did, indeed, know how stretched Bob already was, and was immediately concerned that taking on what was bound to be a great deal of work might bring him to his snapping point.

Althea piped up. 'Why not ask Alexander Bright to take a look at it? He's already in business with you, Henry, with the antiques shop in the village, and he's a property developer, so he'll know people who can work out costs, and probably even do the work needed. Bob, you're a wonderful Estates Manager, but this is now moving into areas that are quite different than those you usually handle. It's not about remediating the problems that arise in all the old buildings the Estate has a responsibility to care for, it's about getting big renovations done, and quickly, too.'

Stephanie hated to admit it, but her mother-in-law was right, and the idea of getting Alexander involved seemed like a good one; she and Christine were quite close, and – having been told just an hour ago, by Althea on the phone, that Christine was expecting – she suspected that Alexander Bright would be spending a good deal more time in the area than he had done up until now. 'I'll approach Alexander,' she said. 'If no one has any objections.'

'None,' was the chorus, which included Bob Fernley.

Still feeling as though something was going on that she couldn't quite put her finger on, Stephanie looked down at her agenda. They'd ripped through it. 'Local housing needs?' That was all that remained.

Tudor raised a hand. 'The Hughes family is leaving the village, I hear. Sarah's got a teaching job that means they'll all have to go, so that's her two boys gone. We won't have many children left at all very soon. Isn't there something we can do to attract families back to the village?'

Stephanie looked at Bob. 'Did we know about the Hugheses leaving?' Bob nodded. She must have missed that. 'Have we any candidates for the house?'

'Not yet. I was only informed last week,' said Bob, his neck flushing pink.

Stephanie didn't want to put the man on the spot – again – so said, 'Why don't you and I take that forward after this meeting, Bob? It's a good-sized home that might attract another family into the village, Tudor. Though if we're developing facilities aimed at appealing to artisans, we might need to be able to offer smaller places too.'

'Annie's out of her cottage now,' said Tudor. 'A couple could fit in there, and maybe if they had a baby too? But it's small, as you know.'

'I barely fit in mine, and Iris in hers,' observed Marjorie, 'and they're all basically the same as each other. To be honest, Tudor, I think Annie's old place would suit a couple, and that would be it. Babies take up so much space.'

Stephanie knew this to be true; the cottages wouldn't be practical for anyone with children. 'We only have limited funds to spend, and you've all made it quite clear that you believe an investment in facilities with an aim to attracting the artistic world to our door is the way we should go. That's going to mean we have no ability to create new homes for folks in the area.'

Stephanie noted the silence.

Eventually, Iris Lewis said, 'If people pay to work here, and provide an attraction that makes other people want to visit to watch them work – as well as spending time here at Chellingworth Hall, when you're open to the public – then the village would become more vibrant, and the Estate could end up actually making money from the village, not just having to spend it all the time. Then you could invest in more housing.'

Stephanie was aware of Iris Lewis's career in the field of education, but hadn't ever thought of her as a strategic planner before.

'Excellent point, Iris,' she said. 'Maybe you and I can go over the current tenant status details after the meeting, Bob?' Bob nodded.

Stephanie asked, 'Any other business?' All heads shook. 'Very well then, I'll let Mavis know how things go with Alexander, and she can add that information to the minutes of the meeting before she sends them out. Meeting adjourned.'

Stephanie couldn't believe it had gone so well.

As chairs scraped and people started to chatter, she noticed Althea cozying up to Tudor, and thought she overheard her mother-in-law whisper something like, 'Thanks for letting us all use the pub to sort this out last night, Tudor – all well worthwhile, as you saw.'

Stephanie chose to believe she'd misheard the dowager.

*Althea wouldn't have gone that far to get her own way, would she?*

# 5<sup>th</sup> SEPTEMBER

# CHAPTER FIVE

Annie was still getting used to the kitchen in the flat where she and Tudor were now 'living the life of a real couple', as her mother had put it; she'd burned the first lot of toast, and couldn't get the eggs to scramble, or even cook. She turned the toaster down, and turned the new hob up, hoping she'd have better luck – only to end up with what was essentially warm bread and an omelet. It would have to do.

'It's on the table, Tude,' she called.

Tudor ambled up from the pub below, where he'd been doing odd jobs since about seven. It was now gone eight, and she knew she had to get started on her own tasks for the day – which included making all the décor decisions for the guest rooms – or she'd not have any time for actual paying work, for the agency.

'Got enough hot sauce on that?' Tudor chuckled as he poured a tiny bit of brown sauce onto his plate, beside his eggs, whereas Annie had slathered her whole meal with her favorite condiment, the St Lucian brand her mother sent from London in boxes, which it was impossible for Annie to get online, or locally.

'I'm gonna need it today, Tude. Full head of steam required, and no mistake. You alright down there in the pub, or do you need a helping hand?'

Tudor shook his head, for which Annie was immediately grateful. Her phone rang in her pocket. It was Marjorie Pritchard. She showed the screen to Tudor who rolled his eyes and mouthed, 'Good luck,' as she answered.

'Hello, Marjorie. Sorry, eating breakfast – can this wait?'

'No. I want to report a theft.' Marjorie was using her really annoying stroppy voice, which always got right up Annie's nose.

'Sorry, Marge, that would be what the police are for. If it's not urgent, phone the Brecon station. They'll do theft.'

'I have done, and they said they can't help.'

Annie sagged. 'Oh dear. So…what's gone missing?'

'Kevin.'

'Kevin? This is a kidnapping?'

'Kevin's my gnome. You see him every day. He's by my front step. But now he's not. Someone's stolen Kevin.'

Annie stood and walked to the window – she couldn't cope with the faces Tudor was pulling without laughing, and she could tell that Marjorie was distressed. 'Tell you what, Marge, I'll come over as soon as I can. In about an hour, alright? I'm not even dressed.' She was, but she didn't want Marjorie to know that.

'Well, you look dressed to me.'

'How d'you mean?'

Marjorie snapped, 'I'm down in your beer garden looking up at you standing in your front window. You look dressed to me. I'll come up.'

Annie decided to put her foot down. 'No, Marge, you won't. Yes, I've got clothes on, but they are my "this is what I pull on when I've got out of bed but before I've had my shower" clothes. I'll come over to yours in an hour. Now, go home.' She disconnected, managed to stop herself from poking her tongue out at Marjorie, and flounced back to her cold eggs.

'Remind me that I mustn't stand in front of that window until the curtains are up, Tude. Marjorie flamin' Pritchard could probably see my tonsils from the beer garden. And when's the rest of the furniture for that going to turn up, I'd like to know, and the gazebo thing they said they'd put up. That Bob Fernley doesn't seem to be on the ball at all when it comes to getting stuff here that we need.'

'What did she want?' Tudor had almost finished his eggs, and his coffee.

Annie sulked as she ate. 'Who?'

Tudor chuckled. 'Marjorie. Did I hear you mention kidnapping? Isn't that something for the police?'

Annie stuffed a last, massive mouthful into herself, and chewed, silently fuming. When she could, she replied, 'She reckons someone's nicked her Kevin. Which – before you ask – is her garden gnome.'

Tudor nodded. 'Oh yes, Kevin. He moved in before she did, you know. Put him in the front garden before she even got her stuff into her cottage. Kevin's been with her for a long time, Annie. She'll not rest until she finds him. Will you charge her?' Tudor stood and arched his back with a groan.

'Charge her for what? I haven't got time to be looking for gnomes, Tude. But...if I did, yeah, I'd have to charge her. I mean, I know we've done favors for her in the past, Carol, especially...but a missing gnome doesn't sound like a Carol job, does it? Can't imagine gnomes have a digital footprint...nor are there likely to be secret dealers in stolen gnomes that she might flush out with all her online sleuthing. Nah, not a Carol job, that. And I can't see Mave going for a freebie for Marge these days – it's all hands to the pumps, as per.'

Tudor spoke gently. 'I know you two don't usually see eye to eye, but Marjorie isn't as bad as people think she is. And Kevin's been with her a lot longer than you've had Gertie and I've had Rosie, and you can imagine how we'd feel about losing them.'

Annie looked across the large table at the man she loved, then down at his yellow-furred Rosie, and her black-furred Gertie rolling together on the rug beside the sofa. Yin and yang – a bit like her and Tude, she thought.

'They're alive, Tude, not a bit of plaster, or plastic, or whatever,' she said, with a wink, 'but I get what you mean. Yes, I'll go and see her. But first, I need to get myself clean and *properly* dressed, then get these two sorted, then try to pin down exactly how floral I want to go with the decorating in our guest rooms.'

'Let the last thing end up with "not very" in there, and we'll be fine, Annie. Remember, we talked about this, and you agreed that not everyone staying here will be in love with flowers, or even color – neutral is best.'

'Yes, Tude,' she called as he disappeared downstairs, then she muttered to the dogs, 'but neutral's so boring, innit?'

They both agreed, with yaps.

Annie checked her watch as she knocked at Marjorie's door – it was exactly an hour since she'd promised to arrive, so she at least felt good about that. However, the bare patch beside Marjorie's front door bore testament to the fact that Kevin wasn't there, on duty, so Annie reckoned he really had gone.

When Marjorie opened her front door, Annie's heart melted. 'You've been crying haven't you? This has really upset you, doll, hasn't it?'

Marjorie nodded, and stood back, silently, for Annie to enter. As at the cottage Annie had just moved out of, the front door opened directly onto the main room of the interior. As she walked in and took a seat, Annie immediately knew what Tudor had meant when he'd said that not everyone liked floral décor, because Annie realized with a jolt that she was just such a person.

Marjorie had opted for floral wallpaper, floral upholstery, floral lampshades, floral blinds – which were half-closed, thereby robbing the room of much-needed light – and, of course, floral curtains, not only at the windows but also covering the entrance to the kitchen. And *everything* matched.

Annie felt as though she were inside a cushion from which she needed to escape before she suffocated.

*Get the job done, and get out,* she thought. 'So, when did you notice that Kevin had gone, Marjorie?'

'Joan Pike knocked on my door to tell me at about half six this morning.'

Annie knew that Joan liked to push her wheelchair-bound mother around the village green every day, and that – if the day promised to be a hot one – she liked to do it early. Indeed, she'd often exchanged friendly waves with Joan and her mother, Gwen, when she'd been out and about with Gertie of a morning. But for Joan to knock on Marjorie's door because of a missing gnome? That seemed a bit extreme.

'That was early,' she replied.

'Joan knows how much he means to me,' said Marjorie tearfully. 'I've had him for forty years.'

'Forty years?' Annie's surprise was genuine. Other than body parts, Annie couldn't think of a single thing she'd owned for forty years. She squared her shoulders and put on her professional head. 'Right – tell me where you've looked for him already.' She knew Marjorie must have done some hunting about, if Kevin were that meaningful to her.

Marjorie sobbed. 'I've looked everywhere.'

Annie bit her tongue, then said calmly, 'Could you be more specific?'

Marjorie was, and Annie was sorry she'd asked.

When Marjorie got to the end of the list of places where she'd searched, Annie asked, 'Then you phoned the police?' Marjorie nodded. 'And then you came to the Coach and Horses?' More nodding. 'Anything else?'

'There were no shards of broken plastic anywhere in my little front yard area, so I suppose there's hope?'

Annie felt that the absence of shards was akin to the absence of blood in Marjorie's mind. 'There's always hope, Marjorie,' she said warmly.

Marjorie managed a weak smile. 'Thank you so much. You're very kind. So…what should we do?'

Annie considered her response carefully. 'Do people around here know how much Kevin means to you?'

'Oh yes, I speak of him often.'

Annie dug deep to keep a straight face. 'In that case – and I don't want you to get upset when I say this…'

Marjorie nodded, looking intense, and earnest. 'I can cope – go on.'

'Do you think someone local might have kidnapped Kevin, rather than having stolen him? Have you received anything like a ransom demand, for example?'

Marjorie's eyes grew round. 'Oh…that hadn't occurred to me. But you're right, I'd pay a lot to get him back. But there haven't been any notes under the door or anything like that.'

'How about via email, or through any social media you might use?' Annie couldn't imagine that Marjorie spent much time online, but thought it best to ask.

Marjorie grabbed her phone and started scrolling. It took what felt to Annie like a lot longer than it needed to. Finally, Marjorie looked up. 'Nothing at any of my email addresses, and no messages on any of the boards I use, nor in any of my inboxes.'

Annie grappled with the idea that Marjorie Pritchard might have a much more active online life than she'd imagined. Professionally, that was interesting.

*Maybe not a local, then?* 'Do many of the folks you mix with online know about Kevin?'

Marjorie looked at Annie as though she were a person with few functioning brain cells. 'Everyone does. He's my avatar.'

*Of course he is,* thought Annie. 'How lovely,' she said. 'But that could mean a lot of people know how much he means to you. Do many of the people you mix with online live in the area? Close enough to make it possible that they could have taken him?'

Marjorie didn't reply. For about a minute.

Annie was about to speak when Marjorie said, 'Don't…shush…I'm thinking.'

This time Annie almost drew blood when she bit her lip.

'Quite a few, yes. Many dozens,' said Marjorie, eventually.

Annie was torn…she now wanted to know who all those people were, because she couldn't begin to imagine a scenario where Marjorie Pritchard had that active an online life – but she needed to focus on what might help her come up with a way to try to track down Kevin.

'Okay, this is what I need you to do for me, Marge, alright? I need a photo, and a full physical description. Any distinguishing marks or characteristics. Photos of them too, if you have them. Write up the list of where and when you searched. Write up a list of anyone you can think of who's said derogatory things about Kevin, or you – you know, enemies of either of you who might want to put you through the wringer a bit. Local residents, who see him on a daily basis, and others you know only online. Then think about anyone who might have mentioned they're short of money – someone who might know how much he means to you and think you'll pay up to get him back. Then email all that to me. When I've got that, I'll get Mavis to draw up a contract, and – if you agree – we'll come up with a plan of action. How does that sound? It might mean having to lay out a bit of money, though.' She wanted Marjorie to know she was taking the whole Kevin thing seriously.

Marjorie beamed. 'Of course I can do all that. And I'd rather pay your lot to find him and bring him home safely, than pay any sort of ransom. My home isn't really my home unless he's here, you see.'

Annie patted Marjorie on the shoulder. 'Email it all to me here,' she held out a card, 'and I'll get going with a few other things I've got on my plate while you do that.'

'Thank you, Annie. I appreciate you treating this like a proper case, because it is to me.'

As Annie crossed the green to the Coach and Horses, she wondered to herself what she'd call the case…if it really became one. *The Case of the Gnome Who Left Home? The Case of the Roaming Gnome?* It would come to her.

# CHAPTER SIX

Mavis had faced the challenge of packing efficiently for a visit of unknown length to the Welsh coast and felt she had won…but she stared in horror at the three large suitcases Ian Cottesloe was struggling to wedge into the rear of her Morris Traveller. *Althea!*

'We're no' going for a month, just mebbe a week,' she observed as Althea supervised the stowing of her bags.

'I have no idea what I might need while we're there, dear, so I've made judicious choices to allow for most requirements.' Althea didn't sound at all apologetic, despite the fact that even Ian looked warily at the tires as he closed the rear doors of the vehicle. There was no question the bags were heavy.

Mavis sighed and accepted she could do nothing about Althea's penchant for changing her outfit several times a day, so the pair set off toward Pembrokeshire at a slower pace than Mavis had originally planned or hoped.

For quite some time, the journey progressed in silence, and Mavis was grateful for it, because, if she were true to her usual *modus operandi*, she suspected that once the dowager began to chatter, she wouldn't stop.

'Have you ever been to Tenby?' Althea's question sounded innocent enough, but Mavis dreaded what might follow her answer.

'I've no' had the pleasure.'

'I'd say we could pop there on our way – even though it's farther than we need to go – but I fear it might be busy. I know the schools have gone back, but it's such a popular place for tourists, and the weather's so good, that we might not be able to drive around it easily.'

Mavis dared, 'That's a shame.'

Althea gushed, 'Indeed it is, Mavis. It's quite a wonderful place. The medieval walls are some of the best in Britain, you know, and, of course, they have a special significance for the Twyst family.'

Mavis sighed, and indulged her friend. 'And why's that, dear?' She hoped it would be a brief explanation, but doubted it.

'Because in the 1450s, Jasper Tudor, the uncle of Henry Tudor, made the walls the responsibility of the Mayor of Tenby. The walls had been there since the middle of the 1200s and hadn't been well maintained, so the locals reinforced them.'

'And why is that so special for the Twysts?'

'Because of the Wars of the Roses, of course.'

Mavis honked her horn at a driver who didn't deserve it. 'I'm sorry to say that my history lessons were delivered in a monotone voice by a wee man with the personality of a dead fish, Althea, so I didnae get as much out of them as I might have done.'

Althea sighed heavily. 'Well, you live at Chellingworth now so you should know these things. Henry Tudor was in danger, and he escaped from Tenby to Brittany. He was born in Pembrokeshire, you see. Anyway, when he came back to fight for the throne, and won, that's when he gave the land we have to the family. So – Tenby kept him safe, and, in the long run, we benefited. Thank you, Tenby from the Twysts.'

Mavis saw the light. 'I see dear, without Tenby there'd be no Chellingworth.'

'Exactly.'

'Well, good for Tenby, then. Is it a nice place?' Mavis regretted the question almost as soon as she'd asked it.

'It was. Haven't been there in…oh many years. It's had its ups and downs, of course. It's been an active port since before the Normans arrived in all their bloodthirsty glory in 1066, so one would expect a seaport that's existed for about a thousand years to have had a few heydays, and a few difficult times. But, other than the medieval walls, and the Tudor Merchant House – oh, and there's a lovely twelfth century church not far away – other than *that*, a lot of what one sees today was built during the Georgian and Victorian era. It wasn't terribly popular as a fishing town or as a port at that time, then a chap named Paxton built some delightful houses, and roads, and paths, and theaters and suchlike, and managed to get it known as a spa town.'

'You mean all the buildings around the harbor that are painted in pretty pastels? I've seen those in pictures of the place. Is that right?'

'Exactly,' replied Althea. 'Didn't someone say something like, "If you build it, they will come"?' Mavis shrugged. 'Well, if they didn't, they should have done, because it's so often true. In the case of Tenby, Paxton – and then others – built the swish houses, and the elevated roads, and they brought in fresh drinking water. Then they made walks through some lovely gardens, descending to the beaches, especially designed for women wearing crinolines – lovely wide paths all around the seafront there. Then the people came.'

Mavis was half listening, and half thinking about how she could stop the torrent of information pouring out of Althea. 'Have you taken the waters there, dear?'

'No, but Chelly and I visited many moons ago. We even took the ferry over to Caldey Island to see the monks. They make perfumes there, you know. Oh yes, of course, Frances mentioned that, didn't she? Cistercians. A lovely monastery. Really quite modern, relatively speaking. But there was almost a disaster – not that day, but another. Chelly almost got caught by the tide. He insisted upon walking out to another little island just off one of the beaches there – no more than a large rock in the sea really…St Catherine's, I think it is. It has one of those Palmerston forts, those hideous things they built all around the coast during the Napoleonic Wars. Anyway, you can walk out there at low tide, but he fell asleep in the sun, and almost couldn't get back. Silly man. I'd stayed at the hotel to nap. We were young at the time, and had endured a rather late night, meaning I needed a rest and knew it, and he needed one too, but was in denial. Oh dear, I do miss him so, Mavis. We did some wonderful things.'

Mavis was grateful for the fact that Althea stopped chattering, and took her chance to enjoy the verdant scenery they were passing through. It really was very picturesque, though the road wasn't without its challenges. She was hoping that driving directly to The Lavender was on the cards, because the trip was taking much longer than she'd planned, and she didn't want to let Frances down: there was a case to get on with, for heaven's sake.

Althea mused, 'It's funny how buildings make places what they are, don't you think?'

Mavis was lost. 'I'm sorry, dear. How do you mean? Surely buildings *are* a place.'

Althea was quiet for a moment, then said, 'I'm not putting it well. What I mean is…like the Paxton man building places that people with money, who did the Grand Tour, would be happy to buy. They had to be a certain sort of building to attract a certain sort of person.'

'You mean posh?'

Althea demurred, 'Well, yes. In that example. But there are cottages and shops, and inns, and theaters, and pubs that all came because of those houses. Do you see what I mean?'

'It sounds a bit like the chicken and the egg, dear. There must have been people in Tenby before that man built those houses; you said it had existed since before the Normans arrived, and I'm assuming the population didn't all go away. And the posh new houses only sold because of where they were, and what he surrounded them with, in terms of delightful gardens and so forth…so the place without the houses had a community in it already, then he changed the houses and the community changed…but it might have changed anyway, if the place was what made it special – you know, restorative waters and all that.'

Althea replied, 'In that instance, I'd be a chicken person then. Because eggs are quite passive, whereas it's the chicken that makes a difference. So I don't think Tenby would be what it is today if the Normans hadn't gone there, then the walls hadn't been built, then the Paxton thing hadn't happened, and so on. I mean the place would be there, and people would have lived there. It's had its share of famous sons and daughters, you know.'

Mavis bit…suspecting she'd regret it. 'Such as?'

Althea hmm'd a bit, then said, 'A man named Robert Recorde was born there, in the early 1500s. I understand he invented the equals sign…which seems like such a simple thing that it wouldn't need to be invented, but it did, and he was the one who did it. We'd be lost without, wouldn't we? And that wonderful artist Augustus John was born there. His sister, Gwen, was born in Haverfordwest, but she lived in Tenby. I always think it's such a shame that she's remembered more for being one of Rodin's models than as an artist in her own right. And, of course, the marvelous Richard Stanley Francis was born just about ten miles away.'

Mavis dared a glance at Althea, who was dimpling. She sighed. 'Go on then – who's he, when he's at home?'

Althea giggled. 'Dick Francis, of course. He was a brilliant jockey; one can imagine how he and the dear old Queen Mum must have enjoyed him being her jockey. But the poor thing came off that horse of hers with such a crash that he had to find something else to do. You know how I've always loved my horses, so you can't be surprised to know that I adore his thrillers. I've brought several to reread while we're not actively investigating. I say, you don't think we'll find ourselves in peril, like all his young heroes do, do you?'

Mavis had read and enjoyed many of the books Althea was referring to. 'I most definitely hope not. Besides, I'm a professional, whereas all his lot are ordinary people to whom something happens so that they end up having to work it all out for themselves. I have a client, and a contract – and a professional case to focus on, dear. So, no, I don't foresee any threats to our safety, no' in a wee hotel near Tenby…however historic it might be.'

'Good. But, you do see what I mean, don't you, Mavis? Tenby is something of a special place. And it means something to we Twysts. It's more than just a name on a map.'

'Speaking of maps,' said Mavis, hoping she could change the subject, 'I'll just take a moment to check the GPS, dear, if you don't mind. Ach…there's my phone pinging. Would you please check my messages, Althea?'

Mavis handed her phone across the car and Althea poked at it. 'It's Annie. She's asking…hang on, I'll read it out: "Marjorie Pritchard's Kevin's gone missing and I'm on the case. I've got a contract sorted. Just FYI." Oh dear, poor Marjorie. She'll be devastated.'

Mavis snapped, 'Who on earth is Marjorie Pritchard's Kevin?'

'Garden gnome. Very important to her. He's her avatar, you know.'

Mavis didn't dare take her eyes off the road. 'How exactly do you know what Marjorie Pritchard uses as an avatar?'

'I belong to a few online things with Marjorie. What do you imagine I do all day, when we're not…you know, running an undercover operation, or something? I have people I connect with all around the world for various reasons. I have interests, you know.'

Mavis was puzzled. 'So go on, tell me…what online groups, or whatever, are you and Marjorie both involved with, then?' She truly couldn't imagine.

'Well, you know I enjoy listening to *The Archers* on the radio?'

'Aye.' Mavis had never seen the appeal of the lives of the folk who lived in the fictional village of Ambridge, and marveled that it had been on the air since 1951 because it seemed so terribly unrealistic to her ears. Not that she'd given it much listening time. However, she was aware that Althea was all but addicted to it.

Althea said huffily, 'Well there's a large, and extremely active, online forum about it. More than one, actually. And we all talk about the characters we like, and what they're getting up to, that sort of thing.'

'Like they're real people, you mean?'

'They are, to some of us, dear. I miss Phil Archer dreadfully, though at least we still get a bit of Jill. She's been in it since 1957. Anyway, Marjorie's a fan too. Though we disagree vehemently about the way some of the newer characters behave.'

Mavis knew she shouldn't say anything.

A moment of silence followed, then Althea added, 'And Kevin is Marjorie's avatar. He's rather precious to her. And here's Annie saying he's gone. But the text means she's looking for him, so that's good. Though, if he's gone, that means he must have been taken, and I cannot help but wonder why. Do you think he'll be held for ransom?'

Mavis was delighted to see that they were only a few miles from their destination. 'Tell her that you and I are almost there. Tell her thank you for letting us know. Could you do that?'

Althea wriggled and smiled. 'Of course. The car's jiggling about so much that I'll do my best, anyway. And I'll wish her good luck, too. A bit of good luck never hurts, does it?'

'Indeed not.' Mavis couldn't cover the last few miles fast enough.

# CHAPTER SEVEN

Henry and Stephanie were waiting in their private sitting room for Cook Davies with Hugo nestled comfortably in his pram, which sat between them. They were both worried about what the request for a private meeting might mean. Given that Edward certainly knew that Something Was Up, but wouldn't speak of it, they were both feeling nervous, as well as worried.

When Cook Davies finally arrived, even Henry could tell that she'd put on a clean apron and tidied her hair, because she never looked as bright and shiny whenever he saw her down in the kitchen.

He straightened his shoulders, and opened with: 'Please, Cook, take a seat, and tell us what's bothering you.'

Cook Davies was probably somewhere in her sixties, had been at Chellingworth Hall for about thirty years, and was Edward's right hand when it came to running the household. Though she was – technically – supposed to report to Edward, Henry understood their working relationship to be more that of two equals with different areas of expertise who worked toward a common goal: the satisfactory delivery of services required by the family and the Estate. He'd never been aware of any problems between them…but maybe now? He sighed. He'd know momentarily.

Cook Davies settled herself on the easy chair, stuck out her chin, and said quietly, 'I wish to tender my resignation. Effective immediately. I haven't had a holiday in over a year, so, with six weeks' notice, I believe that means I can leave next week.'

Henry was flabbergasted. 'Good grief – that's the worst possible news. Whatever is the matter? What's happened to make you say this? Are you…oh dear…are you unwell? If you are, we'd support you through whatever…um…treatment might be needed, wouldn't we, my dear?' He looked to Stephanie for moral and practical support, and was delighted when she jumped in.

Stephanie smiled in only the way she could, with great warmth, and said, 'What His Grace means to say, Cook, is that we value your presence here at Chellingworth a great deal, and we would hope that – rather than taking such a precipitous course of action – you might take this opportunity to speak absolutely freely, to allow us to understand what has led you to reach this decision.'

Henry looked at Cook Davies, and she looked at him, then Stephanie.

She said, 'I can speak freely, you say?' Henry nodded vigorously. 'Very well then, I shall. It's the baker you've brought in. He's a thief and a liar, and I won't work with him a minute longer than I have to. There. I've said it.'

Henry didn't quite know how to react. He honestly had no idea what the woman was talking about. 'The new baker…?' He thought it best to start there.

Stephanie replied gently, 'You recall we agreed we'd need some extra help when the tearooms opened in what was the Lamb and Flag pub in the village. Cook Davies herself, Bob Fernley, Tudor Evans, and Mrs Jackson, the person we took on to run the tearooms, were all here. It was not more than four weeks ago. The tearooms have only been open for a week. And you say there's some problem, Cook? With Mr Baker?'

Henry turned to his wife. 'We have a baker actually *named* Baker working for us? Or are you using the term generically?'

'Yes, dear, the baker's name is Baker. Paul Baker.'

Before he knew he'd done it, Henry muttered, 'How frightfully odd. Just as well you didn't marry a chap named Cooke, eh, Cook?'

'I never married,' replied Cook Davies, a little sourly, thought Henry.

Henry wasn't aware he'd known that Cook Davies had no husband, then realized he'd be living at the Hall with her if she had one, and he'd never met such a person, so she had to be right about her marital status, which – of course – she would be. He smiled as brightly as he could while he thought all this.

The cook's eyes glittered with what Henry took to be pure hatred as she said, 'Baker he might be named, but he's a thief and a liar, and he shouldn't be here at all. Shouldn't even be in a kitchen, if you ask me. Which you are, which is why I'm telling you.'

Henry looked at his wife who said calmly, 'You think he's not equal to the role we've employed him to fulfil? I have to say, Cook, this is the first we're hearing of this. Mrs Jackson hasn't advised us of any problems at the Lamb Tearooms.'

'Have we dropped the flag?' Henry had to ask. 'Um…that didn't come out quite right…you know what I mean.'

Stephanie almost glared at him. 'Indeed. If you recall, we decided that the Lamb and Flag Tearooms sounded too much like a pub.'

Henry replied, 'But it was a pub. It's always been a pub.'

His wife smiled sweetly. 'Exactly, dear. Hence the use now of only a part of the original name. It's likely that you haven't seen the new sign outside the building itself, because I know you've been rather busy here with your duties – but maybe you remember that lovely rendition of a fleecy, sweet lamb we decided would be suitable? And Mrs Jackson's been working with me on the use of the design for various memorabilia to be sold at the Lamb itself. Mugs, tea towels…and so forth.'

Henry peered back into the mists of what had clearly been quite a busy meeting. He vividly recalled the sandwiches, because they'd been Coronation chicken, one of his favorites…which his mother always poo-pooed as either not spicy enough or too spicy…but, beyond that – nothing.

'Of course,' he said as brightly as he could. He turned his attention to Cook. 'So he's not a good baker?'

Cook Davies studied her fingernails, which Henry could see were gleaming, then looked up as she replied, 'I suppose I wouldn't go as far as to say that. His fancy cakes are – well, you know the fashion these days for those cupcake things, and he manages to make them look very appealing, if you like that sort of thing, I suppose. And his breads? Good texture and color, and the flavor's not too bad, though he's got a long way to go to match my own seeded buns, I think. That's all about knowing your ovens, though, so I dare say he might get better at judging those. No, what I mean is…well…' The woman stopped speaking and returned her attention to her nails.

Stephanie leaned forward and smiled sadly at the small woman. 'Come along, Cook, you can tell us.'

Disgust glittered in Cook Davies's eyes as she spat out, 'He's gone and stolen things from my pantry, so when I go looking for them, they're not there, and then I have to change my plans and that's not a good way to run a kitchen.'

Henry also leaned in. 'What did he steal?' He couldn't imagine.

Cook sniffed. 'First off it was my currants. I'm very particular about my currants, as you have to be. I ended up having to use sultanas in my last batch of Welshcakes for the Hall tearoom. Can you imagine that?'

Henry could tell by the way she asked the question that the answer had to be a very strong: 'No. Really?'

He felt rather pleased with himself when the cook looked at him with a clear glint of vindication in her eyes. 'Exactly.'

'And he lies about...?' Stephanie spoke gently.

'Said he'd never so much as seen my currants, and he wouldn't want them for anything he bakes, anyway. Says sultanas are a better choice in any circumstance – which set us off on a bit of an up and down, I can tell you. And that's another thing. He thinks he knows everything. Which is *twp*, because he's only in his late thirties. How can anyone be expected to know everything there is to know about baking when they've only been doing it for two minutes?'

Henry felt quite confident in being able to agree with Cook on that point, 'Ridiculous,' he said.

Another warm glow flushed through him as Cook said, 'Thank you, Your Grace. Exactly.'

Stephanie prodded. 'But nothing other than the currants?'

Henry waited, agog.

'He's...he's been talking to my flour supplier. Directly, mind you. And now I think they've gone and made an arrangement behind my back. Which is not how my kitchen works at all. As you're both well aware, choosing suppliers, negotiating prices, quantities, and deliveries is my responsibility. I took all that out of Edward's hands years ago, and it's worked for us ever since. The idea of anyone at the Hall talking to my suppliers, about anything, is absolutely unheard of. My flour man tells me that this so-called baker has asked for his own blend to be mixed. "His" own blend, if you please. And he lied when he did it – said I knew all about it. How's that going to work, is what I want to know. He could be making all sorts of deals and saying all sorts of things about me that I know nothing about. I can't work like that. So I'm off. I don't need that sort of aggravation on a daily basis.'

'Who would?' Henry was shocked to hear such a litany of wrongdoing. If Cook Davies left, who would make all the cakes and scones and pastries he enjoyed so much? And it was she who was responsible for overseeing all the menus for every meal at the Hall; this was serious. He also thought this chap Baker sounded like a bit of a bounder.

'We should do something, dear,' he said to his wife, who – he noticed too late – was flaring her nostrils at him. That was never a good sign.

She said calmly, 'What would we have to do to get you to reconsider your decision to leave, Cook Davies? We certainly don't want to lose you, and we don't want you to be unhappy in your work here, either. But – and please don't take this the wrong way – it might prove rather problematic to fire someone because they took some currants, you see? Maybe there's a way around this?'

Cook Davies crossed her arms. 'Thank you. I had hoped you might say something like that, so I've been giving it some thought. I checked his references, of course, before I recommended him, and there was nothing amiss there. Though I have to say that no one warned me that he was such cocky one. But, well, I know that Her Grace the Dowager's friend Mavis, and her lot, helped Edward out when his brother died, and I wondered if they might be able to have a bit of a dig about into the man. You know, a bit more than three references goes. See, I can't imagine it's the first time he's been like this. Theft and skullduggery don't appear in a person overnight, do they? He's a battler, though, and he won't tell me a thing when I ask him – just denies it all, then goes off at me. It's *my* kitchen he has the run of. I know it's only the side kitchen, the baking kitchen, but still, it's mine. And don't let him try to tell you that I've held the fact that he's English against him; I make a special effort to not allow that to color my thinking about him. Liverpool's quite close to North Wales, really.'

Henry's pulse slackened a little when his wife replied, 'But of course, Cook. I dare say Paul Baker's references are in the Estates Office, so I'll get those to the women at the WISE Enquiries Agency as a matter of urgency. I shall, as you have requested, retain them to investigate the matter. As you know, they are consummate professionals, so maybe we'll trust them to take it from there? But, please, let's not speak of your leaving. It might take them a little while to get to the bottom of things, so why don't we set aside that possibility, and give them a couple of weeks' grace?'

Henry tried to work out what Cook Davies was thinking. Her screwed-up face conveyed nothing but anxiety. *Oh dear.*

'You'd have them do it like a proper job? You know, not just a bit of a favor, so it would end up being a slapdash affair?'

His wife nodded. 'But of course.'

Cook's shoulders became unhunched. 'Alright then. Two weeks. But I'm going to write down everything he says or does that's not right in the meantime.'

Stephanie gushed, 'Please do, and please pass such notes to me, Cook. Indeed, I'd ask you to provide me with any information you think might help a firm of *confidential* private enquiries agents with something to go on – beyond what you've told us today, which we'll pass on. Won't we, dear?'

'Absolutely.' Henry knew that had to be the right response.

Finally alone, and having spent some time attending to their son, the duke and duchess were, once again, able to relax as a husband and wife.

'You handled the situation marvellously, dear,' observed Henry, knowing he'd have ended up in a terrible pickle if Stephanie hadn't been there to pour oil on troubled waters.

'Thank you, though now we'll have to talk to the WISE women about it. It's a shame that Mavis and your mother aren't here to help – this would have been right up Mavis's street.'

'Why aren't they here?' Henry had no idea.

Stephanie rolled her eyes, sighed, and went a bit pink around the gills. 'They've gone away to work on a case for someone Mavis used to know. Your mother told us at dinner last night, Henry. I sometimes think you're so wrapped up in your own little world that you really don't take notice of anything that goes on around you.'

Henry felt hurt. He did notice, he just wasn't terribly good at remembering. Dinner? Last night? Roasted goose with that zingy orange dressing, roasted carrots, and a creamy polenta. He recalled it all in great detail. And his mother had been talking about packing, which he had imagined meant she was getting rid of some of those dreadful outfits she insisted upon wearing. Maybe not?

'Such a lot happened yesterday, dear,' he said feebly. 'I'm sorry. But...does that mean that mother is *working* with them. *Officially*?'

'She was, apparently, critical to the success of a plan Mavis had for some undercover job. Althea used her charm, and her title, to get the pair of them into an hotel in Pembrokeshire. She said they might be gone for as long as a week.'

'Sounds like an odd sort of hotel if one requires a title in order to become a guest there.'

'I know only what Althea shared last night, dear. But she and Mavis have gone, so we can't ask for more information from Mavis. We both know how terribly busy Annie is, helping Tudor get the Coach and Horses sorted out, and then Christine's expecting now, so—'

Henry interrupted. 'Sorry, dear, what? Christine Wilson-Smythe's having a baby? When did this happen?'

Stephanie was smiling, a good sign. 'I can't be sure of the exact date or circumstances, dear, as one might imagine, but she's a few months along.'

Henry felt hot. 'Ah. I see. Of course not...I mean, of course. There's Carol. She's the one who does everything with computers, isn't she? I bet she could help. They do say that a person's entire life is recorded somewhere on a computer these days, don't they? I bet she could find out about the baker.'

'Good idea, Henry.'

Henry glowed.

# CHAPTER EIGHT

Mavis MacDonald pulled to a halt in the car park behind The Lavender. She'd expected the building to suggest the period when it had been designed and constructed, so had been looking forward to an art deco confection. Instead, it was apparent that the man who'd caused it to be built had favored a neo-Gothic approach, which meant the place looked a little ominous. At least she enjoyed the symmetry of the central portion of the building and the two wings which stretched their arms wide, toward the sea. However, she wasn't impressed by the lack of any greenery, as such. It was all a bit stark for her liking.

'Oh, I say, it looks like a big old, haunted house. Though I bet the views are spectacular,' observed Althea as she straightened herself. 'Oh dear, I'm a bit stiff.'

'I'm no' surprised,' replied Mavis as she held out an arm for the dowager to grip. 'If we'd stopped half an hour back, you could have unfolded yourself a bit then. But, no, we had to push on, you said.'

'It's only been a few hours, but your Morris Traveller isn't as comfy as my old Gilbern.'

Mavis tutted. 'Ian Cottesloe was right – that old thing's no' reliable enough to make a trip like this. He's managing to keep it going for local journeys around the village and so forth, but those were some challenging roads. And my Morris is more than up to it, even when the poor thing is stuffed full of heavy bags.'

'Well, I think you need to have your suspension checked,' snapped Althea.

'I'll volunteer for that.' The voice made both Mavis and Althea jump, then a head popped up from behind one of the neatly clipped box hedges, which turned out to be much taller than Mavis had imagined – no, there must be a dip beyond them.

Circumnavigating the hedge, and ascending a couple of hidden steps, the man who owned the voice approached. He removed a large straw hat as he walked, and wiped a hand on his trousers…which he then held toward Althea, who shook it vigorously.

'Good morning – or is it afternoon already?' He checked a wristwatch that he pulled from a pocket. 'No, still morning for a while yet. Now, which of you two is the Dowager Chellingworth?'

Althea dimpled and replied, 'You have me at a disadvantage.'

The man bobbed his head. 'Dennis Moore, at your service.'

Mavis was taken aback when Althea let out a little scream of: 'No! Dennis Moore? Oh my goodness me, I've been hoping to meet a Dennis Moore for decades. My pleasure.' She grabbed the man's hand again and shook it until Mavis thought it might drop off.

The man's green eyes sparkled with delight. Mavis put him at about her own age – mid-sixties, maybe – though he still had a full, and quite impressive, head of hair that was sort of hazel-colored. She noted that his face was wrinkled in the way it would be if one smiled a great deal and was also – for want of a better description – hazel, due to the effects of the sun, Mavis presumed. Given his general attire, and where he'd been when they'd arrived, Mavis assumed he must be the gardener – with little to do but trim some rather austere hedges in this area.

Eventually, when Althea released his hand, Dennis Moore said, 'Delighted to make your acquaintance, Your Grace. So this must be…?'

'My companion, Mavis MacDonald. Used to be a nurse, so there'll be no problem with my needing any external care should I take a turn while I'm here. The doctor says sea air will be good for me, you see, which is why we've come on rather short notice.'

Mavis wanted to remind Althea that – as they'd discussed on the way – there was no need to shove a cover story down the throats of those one was wishing to deceive. Instead, she nodded at the man, who wrinkled a smile back at her, displaying a perfectly aligned set of teeth. False? No…real, but well-tended.

'Miss MacDonald.'

'She's a Mrs, but a widow,' said Althea, with what Mavis only too-readily recognized as an impish grin.

'Ah…a *merry* widow, by any chance?' He beamed cheekily at Mavis.

'A widow who lost a good man far too soon. Responsible for this one, now,' said Mavis, deciding the gardener shouldn't be encouraged.

'I'll pop inside and see if there's someone available to fetch your bags from your car,' he said, suddenly somber. 'Someone would usually be here by now, but we've had…well, it's been a bit of a busy morning. It's nothing for you to worry about.' He beamed again – this time at Althea. 'You just make your way inside. I expect there'll be someone at reception who can get you sorted. I hope so, anyway. Though Pippa was a bit…well, you know.'

Mavis didn't know, but didn't want the man to chatter any longer, so took Althea's elbow and began to steer her toward the double doors that stood open ahead of them. 'Take your time on this gravel, dear. We don't want you taking a tumble, not with that new hip of yours.'

Dennis took himself off in the direction of a side door, as Althea and Mavis headed inside. 'My hip's perfectly fine, thank you, Mavis, as you know.'

'Aye, well, we want them to think you're more doddery than you are, don't we? As we discussed. And do try to no' babble, dear. We don't want people to think we want them to know all about us – we'll just let it come out in conversation, as we agreed. Now, let's get our rooms sorted out, then we can casually bump into Frances at lunch, as we also agreed, alright?'

Althea removed her elbow from Mavis's grasp and snapped, 'Yes, Mavis.'

Contrary to Dennis's assurances, the reception desk was deserted, as was the rest of the place. However, Mavis and Althea didn't mind, because as Althea said, 'This hall, and that view, are magnificent.'

Mavis had to agree. The hall itself was a symphony of every architectural device from the Gothic Revival era, with pointed arches, soaring columns, and a ceiling boasting carved ribs. And the view beyond the hall was, indeed, quite something. The two women walked through the main entry lounge, then through what was obviously a dining room. From their new vantage point, it was clear to Mavis that The Lavender was on a promontory, on top of high ground, which meant the sea hugged the building on three sides. However, because the land didn't fall away, there was an undulating terraced garden which wound its way downward, meaning that it looked as though the entire world consisted of the hotel itself, flowering plants and shrubs, and the sea and the sky beyond.

'That's Caldey Island,' announced Althea, nodding toward a bump of a rock some miles away. 'It's highly unlikely one would be able to smell lavender growing there all the way over here.'

'Ah, but you can, especially on a warm summer evening, when the breeze blows in the right direction.'

Mavis and Althea turned to see a tall, broad man with suspiciously dark hair for his age, and a twinkle in his unusually blue eyes that made Mavis think of the marbles she used to play with as a child.

He added hurriedly, 'My apologies, I didn't mean to startle you. Toni Conti, your host, at your service, Your Grace.' He nodded at Althea. 'Mrs MacDonald.' He nodded again, then almost completely ignored Mavis as he extended a hand to the dowager and steered her back to the main entry hall, then toward a bench beside the intricately carved and ecclesiastically-inspired reception desk.

Conti opened with: 'Dennis informed me of your arrival. My apologies – again – that there was no one at the desk. We've had a bit of an upset today, and my wife, who usually greets our guests when our receptionist is off duty, is feeling a little unwell, so she's having a bit of a lie down, which means you've got me instead, and I'm not good with things like this, but I do know where your rooms are, so – if you'd allow me – I'd like to take you there, now. As soon as he can, Dennis will bring your luggage up. Young Simon's also gone home for the rest of the day.'

Mavis didn't hesitate. 'That sounds like rather a large upset, no' a wee one, Mr Conti. Is everything alright?'

Toni Conti sucked his thumb. 'Well, no, it's not. A valued member of my staff, and a resident here, too, has left us. Rather suddenly, as it happens. Quite unexpectedly. I…I find myself in need of a secretary.'

Mavis was on full alert. 'Your secretary has left you? Without warning? Today?' She told herself off for unintentionally sounding so surprised; she didn't want to give away the fact she really was surprised. Why on earth would Frances beg her to come to the place, then up and leave it herself? And without even warning Mavis?

'I fear that's the case,' replied Frances' now-former boss.

'Ach well, I dare say she might come back,' said Mavis, hoping the remark was something a stranger might say, while wondering if something 'big', as opposed to 'little', had finally happened, and Frances had thought better of staying.

Toni looked puzzled. 'I…I don't think that's going to happen. Maybe I didn't make myself clear – we're all so accustomed to euphemisms, aren't we? My secretary, a Miss Frances Millington, died in her sleep last night, ladies. Nothing for you to worry about, of course, and the sort of thing I dare say most of us would hope would happen…when our time comes. But, for those of us who knew her, she will be greatly missed.'

Mavis and Althea exchanged a panicked glance, which Conti obviously noticed, but misinterpreted.

'I'm sorry, I didn't mean to put you off staying. You will stay, won't you? I tell you what, how about a brandy from the bar before I show you to your rooms? On the house, of course.'

Mavis nodded her head, doing her best to hide her shock. Althea, she noted, had decided to cover her feelings by wittering uncontrollably as they crossed to the bar at the end of the lounge.

'Now where's that accent of yours from, Mr Conti? I can't quite place it,' Althea was dimpling as she allowed the large man to accompany her to a pale lavender velvet sofa.

'Ah yes, it's a bit tricky, isn't it? Abergavenny, originally, but I lived in Cardiff for a good number of years, so I do tend toward a bit of the Cardiff now and again.' Conti ensured that the dowager was comfortable before bustling behind the bar with bottles and glasses, finally presenting a brandy bowl to each of the women.

Althea swirled the large glass in her tiny hand, and Mavis followed suit. She'd have preferred a Scotch, but wasn't going to look a gift horse in the mouth – and she needed a stiff drink. However, when Althea downed her drink in one, Mavis felt it better to sip.

'Had Miss Millington been with you long?' Mavis's mind was in a whirl; she knew she had to find out what had happened, but without appearing to be too ghoulish.

Conti perched on a high stool, on the guests' side of the bar, swirling his own balloon of brandy. Mavis thought he seemed quite at ease with the glass. 'Coming up to four years. Long enough for me to have developed a great respect for her work ethic, and to have come to rely upon her in so many ways.'

Althea placed her empty glass on a marble-topped table. 'So was it a heart attack? Or did she have some disease you knew nothing about? You said it was unexpected – but had she been ill? Was it – you know – a blessing, in disguise?'

Normally, Mavis would have glared at Althea, but she could see that the dowager's obvious glee at having a sudden death to discuss might be exactly what Conti would expect of an octogenarian who didn't get out too much. Mavis hoped that's what he'd see, in any case – rather than an amateur sleuth, keen to gather clues, which she knew was exactly what Althea was doing.

'No illnesses, though she'd been a little…unsettled here, of late. She'd been fulfilling all her duties as usual, even took herself off to meet up with an old chum of hers from London a few days back. Which makes me think…oh, please forgive me, but, you see, we all knew that Frances had no family, but if she did go to visit an old friend, then maybe we should try to find out who that was, and inform them of her passing.'

Mavis jumped in with: 'She might have had lots of friends. Wouldn't it be better to make sure that her death is announced widely – newspapers, online sites, that sort of thing? That way the word would reach far and wide; one person who knew her might see it and be able to tell whole groups of friends, acquaintances, even old colleagues.'

Mavis didn't want anyone digging around in Frances' past and discovering their connection, because she was already quite sure in her own mind that the fact that the poor woman had come to Mavis asking for help, and had died less than forty-eight hours later, was not a coincidence…there had to be foul play afoot, and she was immediately determined to root out the reason, and unmask the perpetrator.

# CHAPTER NINE

Carol had missed lunch, so she was sitting at the dining room table with two laptops open in front of her and her son playing on the floor. Her calico cat, Bunty, was walking back and forth outside the gate Carol had placed at the dining room door to stop Albert from escaping; she very well knew that all Bunty had to do was make a slight effort to get over the thing, but the expression on her beloved cat's face told her that she'd decided to sulk instead of leap. Carol was holding a banana in one hand and a lump of cheese in the other. And she couldn't think. At all.

*I'm losing my mind. I cannot think why I created that spreadsheet that way. It makes no sense.*

As she stared at the titles of the columns on the screen to her right, she could see that they didn't tally with those on the screen to her left. And she'd been trying to work out, for half a banana, why that was. But she couldn't spot the problem.

Just as she considered turning herself off, then turning herself back on again, her phone rang. It was Christine.

'Is this urgent? I'm a bit tied up at the moment.' Carol hadn't meant to snap. 'Sorry – yes, Christine, what's up?'

'Umm...not urgent, but it is work. Does that help?'

'Fire away.'

Christine explained, 'I'm up at the Hall, with Stephanie, and we wondered if we could get you on video. It's better than just voice, don't you think? But you weren't expecting me, so I thought I'd better check on the phone first.'

Carol laughed. 'If you two can cope with taking me as you find me, yes. I'll connect with you from my laptop, though, it's easier at this end. Will you two be on just your phone?'

'No, I've got my tablet. Connect with me there. Thanks, Carol. See you in a minute.'

When her screen sprang to life, Christine and Stephanie were huddled in what was clearly Stephanie's massive bedroom.

'Hello Carol,' said Stephanie, 'Hugo's napping in the next room. That's why we're here. It's a really busy day at the Hall today – so many visitors so that nowhere other than this is really quiet. Thanks for this. It's all my fault. We've got a bit of thing going on here at the Hall, and I need your help. Well, all of you, but maybe you to start with. Though I've talked things through with Christine already. She came for lunch, and is still here.'

Carol couldn't help but imagine what it might be like to have people to cook and clean for her, and present her with a lovely lunch at a beautifully laid table in a stately home every day.

'Well, you'll have to cope with me eating my emergency rations while we talk.' She held the stump of her banana and her lump of cheese in front of the camera. 'Albert's playing nicely, so I'm grabbing this while I can. You talk, I'll listen.'

'Is that jam in your hair?' Christine sounded surprised.

Carol didn't even bother to check. 'Highly likely. And this is Marmite on my right boob. Nothing kinky, just today's Stain of the Day, which will become tomorrow's Laundry Challenge of the Day. And yes, before you ask, these are dark circles under my eyes, because this one's decided that four hours' sleep is enough for anyone. So, please…talk while I eat – hopefully I won't drop off.'

By the time Stephanie had told Carol about what Christine suggested should be referred to as The Case of the Battling Baker, Carol had finished her cheese, and had stuffed the last bit of banana into her mouth, having saved it up so it would feel like dessert.

'Have you talked to Mavis about this, Christine?' Carol knew it had to be her first question because she understood only too well how long a deep background dive could take, and that there were costs incurred when she did one. It was the sort of work they were – thankfully – charging her old firm in the City a pretty penny for.

'I've left a message for her, and have texted her, but she hasn't got back to me. Which I know is odd,' said Christine, 'so I thought we could at least have this chat about the case while we wait to hear from her. Though we can accept cases on our own, without her say-so, can't we? I mean, we're all equals. And you know all about our charging structure, and Stephanie says she'll pay. Well, the Estate will pay. But you know what I mean. Thing is – it all depends on whether you have the time. Or, if not, if you think I'm up to it on my own. This is your area of expertise, Carol, I know that.'

Carol sucked in air, and replied, 'Yes, you're up to it. No, you don't need me. I accept it'll take you longer than it would take me, but that's because I do so many of these things that I'm used to crunching through the steps to gather the information. But I *am* a bit busy at the moment; I'm doing two deep dives, one being financial, and it's not adding up. Which is driving me nuts.'

Christine looked pensive. 'How about we swap? I'll take the finance one off your hands – fresh eyes and all that. And you could get going with this one. Sound fair?'

Carol knew it did, but didn't like the idea. She hated not finishing any job she'd started. But she knew she had to be practical. 'Why not? I've hit a roadblock. Can't see the wood for the trees…all that sort of thing. Blah, blah, blah. You know? I'll send you everything I've done so far. Hopefully you'll take one look at it, spot my stupid mistake, put it right, and we'll all be tickety-boo. And you can send whatever notes Cook Davies has prepared to me. I'll read them up as soon as I finish this other personal profile I'm doing.'

Carol saw Stephanie and Christine exchange a significant glance – which worried her. 'Something wrong?' She knew there was.

'All Cook Davies's notes are handwritten.' Stephanie looked embarrassed. 'It didn't occur to me that she'd do that, but…well, not everyone is keyboard savvy. I could take photos of them and email them to you.'

'Or I could drop them off at your house,' suggested Christine.

Carol nodded. 'Originals would be favorite, thanks. I'll take copies so I can make notes on them. It might help my frazzled brain cells to have a break from screens and work with a pen and paper for a while.'

'They say a change is as good as a rest.' Christine was trying to sound cheery.

Carol wondered why it seemed that was such an effort for her. 'I tell you what, Christine – and I bet Stephanie will back me up on this one

– when you become a mother, you're glad of any change at all from the routine that your life becomes ruled by. Babies need routine, and parents grow to hate it. That's the way it goes.'

Carol saw Christine's chin pucker, her nostrils flare, and then her face disappear into her hands. Stephanie put her arm around her as she sobbed. Carol's heart sank.

*Hormones. Terror. How could I have forgotten?*

All she could do was wait while Christine composed herself, sniffling into a wodge of paper hankies. Eventually, she managed to say, 'Is this normal? Is this how you two felt when you were pregnant? Like the smallest thing could set you off and there was nothing you could do about it? It's as though some pathetic wimp has taken over my emotions and I can't do anything about it. I hate it. Will it stop?'

Carol tried to answer. 'Yes…but…'

Stephanie stepped in. 'It doesn't stop with the birth, I'm sorry to say, Christine. At least, it didn't for me. I wanted to decapitate Henry whenever he opened his mouth until quite recently, and I still do, sometimes – but maybe that's just me. And him.'

Carol laughed. 'Yeah, ask David – I might have ripped his head off a fair few times, too. It's not something you can control, Christine. Tears. Temper. Tight skin. Your life for the next several months, sorry. Yes, it does get better – but not as soon as you've had the baby, as Stephanie said. Even after the birth your hormones will be raging for a while. And this is what happens. Though I'm sorry if it was me who set you off.'

Albert smacked Carol's leg with the corner of a large plastic building block. She let out an, 'Ow,' before she could stop it, which frightened her son, whose face melted into a mask that told her he was about to bawl as though the end of the world was two minutes away, and only he knew. It was time to go.

'Look, I'm sorry, but Albert's about to explode, and he needs his mum. Bring the notes to me, Christine, I'll email the finance stuff to you, and don't worry – it won't always be this way. Bye.'

As she clicked off with one hand she reached for her son with the other, then bent to gather him onto her lap. As she tried to console her seemingly inconsolable child, she was pleased she'd managed to not tell Christine that the first few months of pregnancy would seem like halcyon days when she was another two years further along the road of motherhood.

She kissed Albert's wet cheeks and whispered, 'And I wouldn't have it any other way.'

# CHAPTER TEN

Annie shouted, 'You want to come out with me and the girls, Tude? We're off around the green. You're on your afternoon break, right?'

Tudor replied, 'How about I make us a snack, and you come back in twenty minutes to help me eat it?'

'Alright then. Back in twenty. Put your feet up for at least ten of them. But no baked beans on toast for me. You know what they do to me.'

As she followed the dogs down the stairs, she heard Tudor shout, 'They do the same to everyone, it's just that some folk choose to manage the effects, and not draw attention to them with a grin and a request for praise.'

'I only did that once, when we were alone.'

'One too many times, my love. Mystique is a concept you never grasped, did you?'

'Nah, Tude, us working-class numpties haven't got time for anything like that. Twenty minutes. No beans. Bye.'

She did her best to control the dogs, though – as they grew in strength, size, and determination – she was finding that more difficult. With a lead in each hand, she found she didn't get tangled up too often, though she was constantly uncrossing the leads as the dogs enjoyed the scents on the grass and each searched out the perfect spot to perform their ablutions.

Surprised to see Joan Pike and her mother so relatively late in the day, for them, they exchanged greetings.

'Haven't seen you for a bit, Annie,' said Gwen Pike, shielding her eyes from the sun as she looked up from her wheelchair. 'How are things going at your new place? All settled in now?'

Annie grinned, and twirled, as the dogs pulled at her. She managed to not fall over as she replied, 'Still a lot to do, but we're getting there. Joan's been a great help.' She smiled at Joan, who blushed. 'She and Aled make a great team. Thanks for managing without her when you can.' Joan flushed even more deeply.

Gwen Pike turned toward her daughter, as much as she could. 'I'm having a bit of a better time of it at the moment, aren't I, *cariad*? This multiple sclerosis is a tricky devil; it flares up when you least want it to, but there are times – like now – when I can manage a bit better on my own. Can't walk around the village, or anything, but I'm not too bad inside the house at the moment. And it's nice for Joan to be able to get out and…you know…meet people.'

Annie wasn't sure if anything romantic was going on between Joan and Aled. She'd noticed that Joan had been helping him out at times when there were special jobs to be done, but, other than that, wasn't certain if they were seeing each other anywhere but inside the pub. There again, she realized she had no idea what sort of life Aled lived, except for the fact that he had a little place of his own now, finally away from his mother, who was doing well without him.

Joan sounded scandalized when she said, 'Did you hear about Marjorie's Kevin, by the way, Annie? He's been kidnapped, she thinks.'

Annie almost fell again when Gertie yanked at her lead. 'Yes, she told me, and I'm on the case. Look, sorry, I can't stop too long – these girls have other ideas. You two didn't see anything, did you? No strange people hanging around outside Marge's house at all?'

'No,' replied Joan. 'Shall I ask around?'

Annie grinned as she was led away by the pups. 'That would be lovely, Joan, ta. Bye, Gwen. See you later.'

After eating far too much of Tudor's delicious 'snack' of a doorstep of a ham sandwich followed by a massive custard slice, Annie prepared herself to get going with the job for Marjorie. She was used to long days, and applying herself: she'd left school at sixteen on a Friday and had started work in the City of London the following Monday, and she'd worked ever since. In fact, working for the enquiries agency in Wales had given her something she'd thought she'd never have – a flexible work schedule where her aim was to complete tasks, not be on duty at a reception desk and switchboard from one set time until another.

Today she'd decided to put off the arrangements for the guest rooms so that she could put in an extra couple of hours trying to help Marjorie

Pritchard. She'd got Carol to draw up a contract – at stupidly low rates – but it meant she was working on a real case, and Marjorie deserved at least that. She'd read through all of Marjorie's notes, and had come to the conclusion that the woman was a Dark Horse; Annie couldn't imagine how one person could belong to so many online communities and still have time to eat and sleep, or maybe even breath. It certainly made her wonder how Marjorie seemed to have the time to be significantly involved with so many activities in the village. Maybe she really didn't sleep?

Given that Marjorie's Kevin was – apparently – known about literally around the world, Annie judged that the online community was the wrong place to begin. Working on the basis that petty, and opportunistic, theft tended to happen where the thief felt comfortable, she decided to start by asking everyone who lived around the green if they'd seen or heard anything unusual on the night and early morning in question.

She'd already spoken to the Pikes, and was delighted that Joan had offered to ask around too, but she was a professional, and wanted to do things properly for Marjorie. She settled the dogs back at the flat, grabbed a clipboard and some paper, and left the pub by the back door, shouting that she was off for a couple of hours loudly enough so that Tudor could hear her from the kitchen, where it sounded as though he was rehearsing for a steel drum extravaganza.

She decided to work her way around the green in a clockwise direction: she walked across the large beer garden at the front and side of the Coach and Horses, crossed the road, and walked along the row of small cottages – one of which had been her home. She didn't need to talk to Marjorie, so she knocked at Iris Lewis's door, knowing she'd be at home.

When Iris opened the door, she beamed. 'Oh Annie, how lovely to see you. It's been ages. I've just made a pot of tea, you'll have a cuppa with me, won't you?'

Annie had feared this might happen, hence the clipboard; she found they always gave the carrier an air of authority, and she needed to work, not chatter all afternoon. Though she really did fancy a catch-up with

Iris – it had been weeks since they'd had a natter.

Annie stuck to her guns. 'I wish I could, Iris, but I'm working. Sorry. But – just quick – are you doing alright? You look well. I've never seen you…well, those shorts are a new thing for you, aren't they?' She'd always imagined Iris had legs, but couldn't be sure they existed above the calf, which was all she'd ever really seen.

Iris stared down. 'Too much? It's a hot one today, and it's going to continue this way…so they said on the news, anyway. Not that you can give what they say much credence. And I found these in a cupboard. I think I bought them…oh, it's got to be fifty years ago. And look – they still fit.'

Annie managed to keep a straight face. 'Ah yes, the age of the hot pants. Still, as long as you're comfy and cool, eh? Now, look, I'm sorry, but like I said – work. You heard about Marjorie's Kevin?'

Iris rolled her eyes. 'Who hasn't? All round the village in a flash, that was. And if you're asking did I see anything, I already told Joan I didn't. Nor did I hear anything. Nor did I smell anything. She's very thorough, Joan, isn't she? Nice girl. But thorough. Is she working for your lot, now? I dare say you'll need some help if Christine's leaving.'

Annie said, 'Chrissy's not leaving. Who said that?'

'Who do you think?' Iris nodded toward Marjorie's cottage. 'Her and Sharon at the shop? If they'd had those two at Bletchley Park in the war, they'd have cracked those codes in a week, because they'd have heard the solution whispered about somewhere in a pub in Germany, all the way over here. She is pregnant though? Christine.'

Annie nodded. 'Yeah, but that's not an illness, is it? She'll be able to work for ages yet. None of us have talked about her leaving. I mean, Carol's got her Bertie and she's still one of us.'

Iris nodded. 'Exactly what I told her.' She indicated Marjorie's cottage again. 'And her.' She nodded toward the shop. 'Oh, and it looks like they've brought in reinforcements, too. Have you met Mrs Jackson at the newly named Lamb Tearooms yet?'

'Nah, I haven't been in there since it stopped being a pub.'

'Too raw? I understand.'

'Haven't had the time, Iris. But I'll go there a bit later to see if she can help…so thanks for the tip-off, because I'll watch what I say.'

'Best you do. Anyway – you should have come in – you'd have drunk a cup by now, and had a biscuit.'

'No biscuits for me, Iris. Tude's spoiling me.'

Iris leaned forward. 'Enjoy it, Annie. He's a love, is Tudor.'

'He is, Iris. I'll make a point to come over so we can share a pot soon. Ta-ra.'

Iris giggled, and went back into her cottage, taking what Annie could somehow only think of as her 'naked', rather than 'bare', legs with her. She had to admit they were pretty good for someone in their late eighties…but not actually pretty.

She passed the Pikes' cottage, crossed the road, and decided she didn't reckon that the Reverend Ebenezer Roberts would be of much help: he lived in his own little world, and the Rectory was set way back behind the church, near the church hall, so he'd have been unlikely to have seen anything going on at Marjorie's cottage in any case. She passed the lychgate at the entrance to the church grounds, and could see that someone was inside the church doing…something. Then she caught the sound of the organ playing. It had to be Wendy Jenkins, Iris Lewis's granddaughter; Annie had planned to catch her at her little flat above what had once been an old teashop, that now stood empty, further around the green, so wandered along the path through the graveyard to the church door, and peered inside.

Annie liked the smell of old churches; all the candles that had been snuffed out in St David's since it had been built hundreds of years earlier had left the air full of their memory – at least, that was what Annie thought. Yes, she could see Wendy at the organ and there was Sarah Hughes, polishing the brass part of the lectern that held the Bible. Good, Annie wanted to see her too.

Rather than disturb Wendy, who was playing something Annie liked, but couldn't remember the name of – *Paco-somebody's something or other?* – she waved at Sarah who beckoned her over. As Annie approached, the smell of Brasso took her back to her childhood, when her mother had always let her help shine up the few bits of brass they'd had.

Sharon paused in her task, a blackened cloth in one of her rubber-gloved hands. 'Hello, Annie – we don't see much of you in here. In fact, not since Hugo Twyst was christened, and that's a few months back, now. But there, you won't be seeing anything of me here before you know it. That's why I'm doing this. I want it to look as good as I can before I leave. We're off at the end of the week.'

Annie assumed a late summer holiday for Sarah, Steve and their two boys, Owain and Rhys…but weren't they back in school now? She asked, 'Going somewhere nice?'

'Abertillery.'

It didn't sound like much of a holiday destination to Annie – though she had to admit to herself she didn't really know where it was, just that it existed. 'On holiday?'

Sarah laughed. 'That would be just a day trip, I should think. No, we're moving there. I've got a position as headteacher at a primary school, and the boys will be at a school that's literally next door to mine, so I can drop them off on the way. Their last place, and mine, were miles apart. It'll make life a lot easier for all of us, especially now that they're getting to the age when they have things before and after school. But I'll be sorry to leave Anwen-by-Wye. Lovely village, isn't it? And this place? You can feel the history, can't you? Love it, I do.'

Annie didn't want to get sidetracked, so waved the clipboard between them. 'Well – the new job will be wonderful, I'm sure. And you'll be great at it. But – before you head off into the sunset – can I ask: did you hear or see anything unusual the night before last? Anywhere around the green? You're on the corner, just past the church here – so you'd have had a good view of Marjorie's cottage if you'd been looking out of the front of your house.'

Sarah tutted sadly. 'This is about Marjorie's Kevin, isn't it?'

'Yes. He's gone.' Annie hated the fact that she'd just referred to a garden gnome as a 'he', not an 'it', but admitted to herself that she'd begun to think of Kevin as a person. Which annoyed her even more.

Sarah shook her head. 'I didn't see anything. I told Joan Pike half an hour ago – ask her. She talked to Wendy just as she arrived, and she hadn't seen, or heard, or smelled anything, either. Though we both said when Joan had gone that we thought that was a very odd question to ask. Working for you now, is she? Replacing Christine?'

Annie sighed. 'Christine's pregnant, not leaving, and no, Joan's not working for us. But if she talked to you and Wendy, I'll get going now. Ta. Best of luck with all those kids. Knock 'em dead. Well...not literally, you know? Ta-ra.'

Annie escaped and was glad that the first building beyond the church was Sharon's shop; she was already thinking through how she could best convey her annoyance at the gossip about Christine that Sharon was spreading. Annie bridled; hadn't Sharon learned anything from all that trouble her mother had got herself into? Apparently not, but Annie was looking forward to putting her straight on a thing or two.

When Annie pushed open the door to the shop, the little bell tinkled, and Sharon emerged through the curtain made of multi-colored strips of plastic that gave the rooms beyond the shop at least the illusion of privacy.

The first words out of Annie's mouth were: 'And what have you been doing telling anyone who will listen that Christine Wilson-Smythe is leaving the WISE Enquiries Agency? First of all, you're wrong, and – even if you were right – have you learned nothing from your mother's example that might encourage you to not spread wild rumors?' She knew she had to get it all out before it choked her.

Sharon stepped back. 'Down, Annie. Down. I haven't said any such thing. It was Marjorie who told me that Christine was pregnant and that she'd be off to London to live. She isn't?'

'Is pregnant, yes. Not leaving, no.' Annie felt the horribly familiar warmth at the back of her neck as she realized she was running about, doing a favor – well, a cheaper-than-it-should-be job – for a woman whose gossip was caustic. She hoped the hot flash wouldn't amount to much. Then immediately realized it would, whether she wanted it to or not. She stared longingly at Sharon's refrigerated display cases.

She allowed herself a big sigh, then added, 'Right, well, I'll talk to Marge about it, then. How is your mother, by the way?' She felt she had to ask. Mair Jones had upset her daughter a great deal, she knew.

Sharon's reply was tart. 'Moved to Rhyl, of all places. Staying with a cousin. Trying to sell her cottage. No one's biting. Too out of the way.

But there…she made her own bed.'

Annie's heart went out to Sharon; she and her mother had always acted like friends, rather than like a mother and daughter, and she'd just come in and torn Sharon off a strip…now she could see she was feeling down. She opened one of the chiller cabinets and stood with the door open, pretending to decide which can of fizzy drink she wanted. As the cool air hit the sweat on her scalp, she felt relieved enough to say, 'Sorry, Shar. I know you must miss her. And sorry I shouted. I'll have this one, please…and has Joan already been in here asking about Marjorie's Kevin?'

Sharon took the money Annie produced from her handbag. 'Yes. I didn't see anything. I know I'd have woken up if there'd been any funny noises. Like the grave it is around here at night, and I'm a light sleeper. Wake up every time a blessed dog barks. Oh!' She blushed. 'I know you and Tudor have Rosie and Gertie and, of course, dogs do bark…so that wasn't a criticism. They're very good, your two. I don't hear them often. Mind you, I'm surprised you weren't up with them yourself the other night – one of yours went off on one for a while, didn't they?'

Annie knew she usually slept well, but also knew she usually woke if Gertie was making a fuss. Maybe it had been Rosie making a noise, and she wasn't as attuned to her distress yet? 'No, I didn't hear anything, which is annoying.'

'Maybe Sarah?'

'No, I saw her at the church. Ah well, I'll pop into the Lamb Tearooms to see if whatshername there heard anything.'

'Jackson. Janet Jackson.'

Annie felt her eyes widen. 'Really?'

Sharon grinned, covering her mouth. 'I know. Poor thing. Married the name. Must have loved him, I suppose. Widowed now, I hear. I'd have changed it back to whatever I was before, if that was me. But, there, she must be used to people asking her about it. Didn't turn a hair when I did.'

'You've met her?'

'Yes. Well, setting herself up, isn't she? Is it weird to think of her living in Tudor's old flat? I know you spent a lot of time there.'

Annie shrugged. 'Nah. It's just a place. The Coach is nice. Much bigger, and we've had it done like we wanted it. Almost, anyway. Right-o, off I go to see Janet Jackson. Nice, is she?'

Sharon smiled. 'She's…no, I'm not going to say it. Meet the woman for yourself and make up your own mind about her. I'll see you when I see you. Want to open the fridge and stand by it for a minute before you go?' She winked.

'Ta – but no. Bye.'

Annie walked to the front of the Lamb and Flag and gazed up at the brand-new sign swinging from the iron arm above the door. Gone was the weathered board showing a very literal interpretation of a lamb and a flag, now replaced by a brand-new sign that showed a cutely woolly sheep, drawn as if by a child, on a half-green and half-blue background – as though half the world were green grass and the other half blue sky…which, as Annie looked across the green, it was at that moment. She sighed. She didn't hold with the infantilization of so many things in life that seemed to be going on these days – but maybe young people couldn't cope with a bit of history slapping them in the face when they fancied a cup of tea.

Inside, nothing much had changed: the beer taps had gone from the bar, of course, and the shelves behind it were filled with teapots and tea-related *objets*, rather than bottles of spirits. The chairs were new, and the tables were all covered with blue-and-white checked cloths…and there was no shortage of blue-and-white china in the place, too. It looked fresh, and pretty enough, though Annie reckoned she could still catch a whiff of stale beer now and again. But, there, it had been a pub for hundreds of years, and it had only been a tearoom for a week – what could you expect?

'Can I help you?'

The voice came from behind Annie, so she spun around and caught her first glimpse of Mrs Janet Jackson. In a way, Annie was sorry that Sharon Jones had chosen to say nothing about the woman, because at least that might have prepared her for the sight that met her eyes. Janet Jackson looked as though she'd stepped out of a 1960's film about a diner in some small American town. She had a tall beehive hairdo – that was suspiciously black for a woman of her years – was dressed in a blue gingham frock that was a little too short and a little too tight for the current fashion, with the addition of a blue gingham apron that had just a little too much lace frilled at its edges. She'd also clearly decided that frosted pink was a shade of lipstick of which one could never wear enough.

'Pick anywhere, and have a seat,' she said pleasantly. 'I'll be with you in a tick.'

Annie noted the English accent at once. 'Are you from Liverpool?'

Janet Jackson tilted her head and laughed. 'A lot of people think that, but, no, I'm from Wrexham. First language Welsh, me. Learned English in school. But I know what you mean. You're not from around here, though, are you?'

Annie paused…Janet's comment had stung, and she found that curious. 'Originally from the East End of London, proper Cockney, you know? Now? Me and Tudor Evans are over at the Coach and Horses. Used to be here.'

Janet's eyes grew round. 'Oh, Annie Parker. I've heard so much about you. But no one mentioned you were…so tall. You'd think they'd have mentioned that, wouldn't you? Lovely to meet you.' She wiped her hands on her apron, then stuck one out.

Annie smiled down at the woman, who was probably about six inches shorter than her six feet, as they shook hands. 'Yes, I'm very…tall.'

'You haven't left something behind that you forgot, have you? I haven't come across anything that I would have thought of as personal – though I've only been here two minutes, really, and I haven't even opened all my cardboard boxes yet, so I dare say there are some corners I haven't found.'

Annie had become used to how fast the locals spoke, especially when they were talking to each other in Welsh. This woman? She sounded as though she were a record playing at half-speed. It was something she'd have to get used to; a surprisingly deep voice, with a slow delivery. It made Annie decide to speak quickly so she could get on –

now wasn't the time to linger.

'Pleased to meet you. It's Janet, right?' Janet nodded. 'I'm sure we'll have a proper chance to get to know each other, but I'm working at the moment, and I wondered if I could ask you a couple of questions. I know you're working, too, but I promise it won't take long.'

Janet nodded at Annie's clipboard. 'Survey, is it?'

'No, I'm a private investigator.'

Janet grinned. 'No, you're not.'

Annie sighed. 'Yes, I am.'

Janet's expression shifted to one of suspicion. 'Out here? In a little place like this? You're having me on.'

Annie dug around in her shoulder bag for a business card and handed it to Janet. 'The WISE Enquiries Agency. There's four of us. Office out on the Chellingworth Estate. I'm surprised no one's told you.' She was. Especially if this woman had palled up with Marjorie Pritchard to the extent that Iris Lewis had spotted it.

'Well, so am I. That's a lot I haven't been told about you, isn't it?'

'I bet Marjorie's told you about her Kevin going missing though, hasn't she?'

Janet looked shocked. 'Her who? Going what? Who's Kevin?'

Annie began to think that Janet and Marjorie weren't quite as close as Iris had suggested. But, even so, she was amazed that the news hadn't reached the woman via Sharon.

Annie explained the situation to Janet, whose puzzled expression remained fixed throughout. Eventually Janet commented, 'I haven't really been here long enough to know what's normal and what's out of the ordinary. And I do sleep well. I've it earned it by the end of the day in this place. But, other than having worked out that there are dogs in the village, and that a car passing after midnight is something that's really very unusual, no, nothing weird. I'll have to ask Marjorie about that if I see her today. She came in the first few days I was open, but I haven't seen her for the past day or two. Maybe that's why, if she's as upset about it all as you say. Strikes me as a very intense person, wouldn't you agree?'

*Ah.* Annie replied warily, 'Marjorie's Marjorie.' She wouldn't be drawn into any sort of characterization that might, one day, be mentioned as something she'd 'said'. She'd been down that road before, and Iris's warning had at least prepared her in this respect. She continued, 'Thanks for your time. Like I said, I'm on the clock, so I won't stay. But I dare say I'll be in at some point for a cuppa. I can see you've got a good selection of teas, and those cakes look very tempting. I'm glad you and Tudor got that all sorted.'

Janet smiled, then frowned. 'So am I. Got what sorted?'

'That we won't sell anything sweet, other than desserts, at the Coach, and you won't sell anything savory here. And you get the ice cream in the village.'

Janet looked surprised. Again. 'I don't recall any such thing. And Paul's bringing pasties here tomorrow.'

'Paul?'

'Paul Baker. The baker at Chellingworth Hall who does the baking for here.'

Annie had no idea who Janet was talking about. And pasties? Tudor would lose it if he heard that. If people thought they could get a pasty at the tearooms, they might not come to the pub for one, and they'd both agreed that lunchtimes could make or break them. Deciding that wasn't a battle she had the time to fight at that moment, Annie decided to stand down.

'Right-o, well, don't let's worry about that for now, eh? I'll be off, and I dare say Tude will get in touch. Ta-ra. Nice to meet you.'

When she stood outside the Lamb Tearooms, Annie felt as though she'd escaped. Such an odd feeling.

'Are you alright? You look a bit...shaken.'

Elizabeth Fernley was adjusting the A-frame noticeboard outside the antiques shop she managed on behalf of the duke, Alexander Bright, and his partner Bill Coggins. When the decision had been made to call the place 'Anwen Antiquities & Curiosities, curated by Coggins and Chellingworth' Annie had thought it was a bit of a mouthful. Seeing it painted on a board didn't change her mind, though it looked alright across the top of the shopfront, where there was more space.

'Thanks, Elizabeth, fine.' Annie knew better than to refer to

Elizabeth as Liz – the woman was a tartar for using her full name. Painfully aware that time was rushing past, Annie immediately asked, 'You didn't see anyone walking off with Marjorie's Kevin, did you? I know it's unlikely because you live out at the Hall, but I'm asking everyone.'

Elizabeth shook her head. 'I know about him having been kidnapped, of course, but no, you're right, I'm away from here by five or six at the latest, so I wouldn't have been around at the time. I think Bob came into the Coach for a pint that night, but he'd have been away by nine-ish himself. Sorry. I did tell Joan all this.'

Annie sighed. *Ah yes, Joan.* 'Right-o, ta. Just thought I'd ask. Won't stop. Going well here though, is it?'

'Run off my feet, I'm pleased to say. Time goes faster that way. I never thought things would be this busy. Just goes to show that people like to buy stuff they know has been picked by a duke and a posh London antiques firm. They'll pay more knowing that, I've found.'

'Think of it as recycling…you know, reuse instead of buying new. All good,' said Annie as she headed across the road toward Carol's house, where she hoped there'd be a pot of tea on the go.

Knocking on her friend and colleague's kitchen door, Annie shouted, 'It's me, Car. Can I come in?' There was no answer, so she phoned Carol's number.

'Hello, Annie. What can I do for you?'

'You can tell me it's safe to open your kitchen door.'

'It's safe. Bunty's in the sitting room with me and Albert. I've brought a cuppa in here, for a change. Come and join me.'

'Alright, see you in a sec.'

Annie dumped her bag and clipboard on Carol's kitchen table and grabbed herself a mug, then joined the family group in the comfy sitting room, which had a lovely view of the village green.

She announced, 'All round the village I've been. And no one saw anything that can help me with Marjorie's Kevin. The Case of the Roaming Gnome has not progressed, though I did meet Sarah Hughes at the church – did you know she's leaving? And I met Janet Jackson at the Lamb Tearooms. She was on about someone making pasties for her out at the Hall. Tude's not going to like the sound of that.'

Carol nodded. 'That would be Paul Baker. Christine, Stephanie, and I were talking about him. I'm going to start a deep dive into him today. The Case of the Battling Baker.'

Annie paused as she poured her tea. 'Oi, you – what's this? You lot can't go naming cases without me. So tell me all about it, Car. And explain what the so-called "Battling Baker" thing is all about, because this is something Tude and I might need to get to the bottom of, too. We can't have a sweet versus savory war going on in the village, can we?'

'A what?'

'No, you go first. Paul Baker? And he's a baker? This should be good.'

# 6th SEPTEMBER

# CHAPTER ELEVEN

Mavis opened the door of her room just a crack, and listened carefully…just to be sure that everything beyond it was as quiet and deserted as she'd hoped. Nothing. She stepped out into the hall, grateful for the plush carpeting that would deaden the sound of her footsteps, and closed her door as quietly as she could. It was just gone three in the morning – everyone should be asleep. At least, that was what she hoped.

Since she and Althea had arrived, she'd done everything she could to prepare for this sortie. Luckily, the hotel was old and quirky enough that each room had a pigeonhole allocated to it behind the reception desk, and a key hanging up if the room was not in use, or if the occupant was not on the premises. She'd seen the key to room sixteen being replaced in such a somber way that she knew it had to be poor Frances' room. Now all she had to do was get the key from behind the reception desk and get into that room so she could look for…whatever she could find that might help her work out what had happened to cause the death of her onetime-colleague, and client.

Ignoring the lift, and using the grand staircase instead, Mavis cursed Frances for being so secretive. If only she'd given Mavis more information…but she'd been intentionally opaque, and that wasn't much help now, because the poor woman was dead. And how had she died? Of what? That was what Mavis really wanted to know, but no one had been able to tell her. Not that she and Althea had exactly 'mixed' that day.

In fact, to say that it had been an odd day at The Lavender would have been understating it.

They'd been delivered to their rooms by Toni Conti himself and, once Mavis had got over the shock of the news of Frances' death, she and Althea had opened the connecting door between their rooms and had whispered about what it might mean. It was all 'very fishy' – Althea's words. Mavis had to agree, and they both also agreed to stay on at The Lavender, to try to – somehow or other – honor Frances' request for help…and find out what had happened to her, of course.

With nothing but 'she died in her sleep' to go on, Mavis couldn't be sure that Frances' death had been helped along in any way, but she knew she'd be ignoring her every instinct if she didn't try to find out more – indeed, she intended to unearth the whole truth of the matter.

Lunch had been a casual affair of sandwiches served on the terrace which overlooked the garden and the sea. None of the other guests had put in an appearance since Althea and Mavis had arrived. In fact, the only people they'd met were Dennis the gardener and the owner himself, so Althea and Mavis had played their parts of a dowager in desperate need of the recuperative powers of the sea air, and her doting nurse-companion, to a tiny audience all day. Then, when it came to dinner time, they had dressed and descended to the bar, only to find themselves alone, again, with their host.

With more apologies – he'd let as many staff go for the day as possible due to the upset – Toni had served their aperitifs himself, and they'd selected their meals from what he'd referred to as a 'special menu'; 'special' because it offered only two options for the main course, and none at all for the others. Hardly in a position to complain, Althea and Mavis had eaten cheese souffles with parmesan crisps, then an excellent trout almondine – neither of them fancied the alternative of a ham salad – followed by a light and fluffy zabaglione. It had all been delightful and, apparently, prepared by the owner's still-invisible wife. They'd been in a position to repair to their rooms before nine, to which Toni Conti personally delivered their requested Madeira.

Yes, an odd day, to be sure. Though Althea's constant twittering had allowed the time to pass quickly, if a little annoyingly.

Mavis had managed a few hours' sleep; years of strange shift patterns, and having to be able to snatch a nap whenever it was possible, meant Mavis had woken refreshed. She'd washed her face, pulled on her navy slacks, and her navy cardigan, grabbed her phone, then set about putting her plan into action.

The stone staircase didn't, of course, creak, as she crept down it – for which she was grateful – and she managed to get the key she wanted and get back to room sixteen without much ado. Taking care to unlock the door as silently as possible, Mavis hoped it wouldn't groan on its hinges; it didn't. Then – she was in.

Her eyes having already adjusted to the darkness, Mavis allowed herself a chance to get her bearings in the room. It was laid out in much the same way as Althea's – a mirror of her own – but there were pieces of furniture in it that weren't in the dowager's room, possibly owned by Frances herself and installed as part of her agreement with Toni about her living at the hotel, as opposed to being 'merely' a guest.

The bed was in disarray, that much was immediately clear; linens were discarded on the floor, as well as heaped upon the bed itself. A lamp that had once been on the bedside table was also on the floor, and broken. Beside it lay a water carafe and a glass. Only the glass was shattered. Between the two windows which would – in daylight – offer an enviable view of the gardens and the sea beyond, stood a more personal version of the desk in Althea's room. This one had a rolled top, and was closed. Mavis tried the lid. It moved. She was elated. Knowing Frances' reputation as an excellent record keeper during her time at the Battersea Barracks, Mavis had high hopes of finding something that might prove illuminating in the woman's desk.

She inched the top open, cursing the scraping noise it made, then, finally, was able to sit on the seat in front of it to assess the situation. A leather-covered writing pad gave way to two layers of wide, shallow drawers, above which there were narrower drawers, then a set of cubbyholes. Mavis set her phone on its little easel, turned on the torch app, opened the bottom drawer first, and lay everything from it on the writing pad.

Nothing – just stationery supplies.

She repeated the task for each of the large and small drawers, then for the cubbyholes. Everything was useless, except for Mavis to be able to deduce that Frances had been a bit of a stationery hoarder. Turning to get up, her foot hit something. Looking down she could see it was part of a power cable for a laptop. Excellent. She searched the room, looking for the laptop, but to no avail. What she did find was a small printer, tucked out of sight on one of the windowsills. She couldn't imagine that was a good place to keep a piece of electrical equipment, but could see it had a cable dangling from it that would have reached as far as the desk. It should have connected to the missing laptop.

Mavis paused. She'd dug about in the wardrobe, the chest of drawers, and the drawers in the bedside table – there was only one. Finally, she checked the bathroom. In there, she found a bottle of painkillers, and some over-the-counter sleep aids – nothing that could have proved harmful, if taken in the correct dosages. It also appeared that, beyond her love of stationery, Frances had enjoyed trying out many, varied body lotions.

Then Mavis heard a sound…a hint of a sound. She froze.

Someone was opening the door to Frances' room. Standing in the bathroom with the door half-closed, Mavis hoped whoever it was hadn't seen the light from her torch, which she immediately turned off. Plunged into darkness, she listened as hard as she could. She realized that the person was doing what she had done – they were trying to open the roll-top of Frances' desk, but they were making quite a racket doing it.

The unknown person muttered, 'Stupid thing,' and Mavis made a snap decision. She opened the bathroom door and hissed, 'Is that you, Althea?'

A little whimper told her it was.

'Don't make a sound when I turn on my torch.' When she did, she was shocked; Althea was in a full-length, dusky-rose cotton nightdress, her hair wrapped in a scarlet scarf, and her face was covered in something green and patchy and…cracked in places? A mud mask?

Mavis hissed, 'Good grief – what are you doing here? And why do you look like…that?'

Althea simpered, 'I wanted to see if I could find any clues. As soon as I saw that the key had gone – we both noticed Toni putting it back on that pigeonhole's hook this afternoon – I knew you'd had the same idea. The door was unlocked, so I came in, but you weren't anywhere to be seen. And I'm dressed like this because I thought that if someone saw me, I could act confused and say that I sometimes don't know when I'm wandering. You, on the other hand, look as though you're off to the shops. Who wears a cardi to snoop around a dead woman's room in the early hours?'

Mavis fumed silently for a moment, then grabbed Althea's elbow. 'I've searched the room thoroughly. There's nothing here. Not even a laptop, which there should be. There's a printer – there should be a laptop.'

Althea pouted. 'Is it plugged in?'

'What?'

'The printer.'

'Aye, by the looks of it.'

'Then we could see what she printed last. Just tell it to print the last document again, and it will. It might even have a queue that it will print, though probably only the most recent document.'

Mavis was amazed. She knew Althea was right – though she had no idea how the woman knew such a thing, and didn't intend to have that conversation at that precise moment. But she was also annoyed with herself that she hadn't thought of it.

'It'll make too much noise,' she hissed back.

Althea stuck out her chin. 'It might make a little noise, but who would imagine a printer to be in use at this time of night? If anyone hears it, they'll rationalize so they think it's something else.'

Mavis hesitated. She hated it when Althea made a valid point. 'Aye, well, we'll give it a go.'

Mavis took a moment to acquaint herself with all the printer's buttons, then pushed one, and it woke up. She only hoped none of the guests did. It swooshed and whirred, but it didn't clatter, and a sheet slid out of it. It was a spreadsheet. Then another sheet slid out, then another…Althea kept getting more and more excited, while Mavis hoped there was enough paper to finish printing what was obviously a large document.

When the machine stopped whirring, Mavis grabbed the pile of papers. 'Let's go. Me first – I'll check that the coast is clear.' Mavis could see the excitement in Althea's eyes – which was about the only part of her face visible beneath the khaki, caked mask, which was starting to flake off.

Eventually urging Althea to follow her, Mavis locked the door, and popped the key into her pocket. Her plan was to get Althea back to her room, then take the key back to reception.

With Mavis taking the lead, the pair crept along the corridor toward their rooms in the wing which mirrored the one where Frances had lived. As they were crossing the top of the staircase Mavis heard a little cry, then an almighty thud, and a crash. She turned to see Althea on the floor. The dowager had managed to knock into a spindly tripod stand and its pot of orchids as she'd fallen. The ceramic pot had smashed as it had landed on the only part of the upstairs corridor that wasn't carpeted. Mavis rushed to the dowager's side.

'I got my foot caught in my nightie,' said Althea quietly. 'Sorry.'

'Stop apologizing. Are you alright? Does anything hurt?'

'My pride. That's it. But I could do with a hand up. I think my toe is stuck in the broderie anglaise trim.'

Mavis unhooked Althea's toe and the pair had just managed to right themselves, when the door nearest them opened and a head popped out. As soon as the person saw Mavis and Althea, they screamed,

'Help! Help! Murderers!' It was a woman's voice. She slammed her door shut.

Another door opened, and light spilled into the hallway. 'I'm armed. Move no further. The police are on their way.'

Mavis could feel the panic roiling in her stomach. She had to act, or the situation could spiral further. She stuffed the sheaf of papers down the front of her trousers and pulled her cardi down over them. 'It's alright. It's just me, Mavis MacDonald – a guest here – seeing to the dowager duchess. She's gone walkabout. She had an accident. Sorry.'

The head of the man who'd shouted emerged from his room, as did the head of the woman who'd screamed. At the same instant, the whole scene was illuminated by the massive chandelier which hung over the staircase, and Toni Conti appeared through a door Mavis hadn't noticed before, beside the lift. He was wearing striped pajamas, and brandishing a brass poker.

He barked, 'What's going on?'

Mavis could tell by the expression on his face, as well as those on the faces of the unknown man and woman who were both now staring at Althea, that it was the dowager's appearance that was causing alarm and confusion.

Mavis did her best. 'Ah, Mr Conti – our apologies. I'm afraid that the dowager gets confused, sometimes. She must have awoken, decided to…use a face mask as part of her beauty regime, then went wandering. As you can see –' she indicated her own fully dressed form – 'I am always ready to be able to help. On this occasion, I'm afraid there's a casualty – your orchid. When she's come to her senses she'll be mortified.'

Althea rallied. 'Where am I? Oh no, I'm crumbling away to nothing – look, my skin's coming off in my hands…' She pulled at her mud mask and a big chunk fell to the floor. 'Mavis…what's happening, dear? Where's Henry? My Hugo?'

Mavis explained, 'Her son, the duke, and her grandson. I think I'd better get her back to bed.' She still didn't know who the man and woman were, but managed to add, 'I hope you didn't really call the police,' as she steered Althea to her room.

'I did not. Nor am I armed. Though I could be, if it became necessary,' called the man, then he closed his door.

The woman shouted, 'Not the sort of guests one expects at The Lavender,' more for Toni's benefit than hers, thought Mavis.

'May I be of assistance?' Toni Conti was at Mavis's side.

'Not at all. The dowager's doctor thought that the sea air might ease her tension, which leads to the wandering, he says. She's just no' had enough of it for it to have worked its magic yet, I expect,' she replied fulsomely. She bundled Althea into her room, grinned in what she hoped was a friendly, not manic, way, then shut the door with a thud.

Althea trotted across her room, turned on the bedside lamp and wriggled her way onto the bed. 'Oh that was fun. Wasn't it fun, Mavis? Sorry about the plant, though. That was a genuine accident.'

Mavis chose her words carefully. 'You put us both in danger of being found out, you…you shouldn't have followed me.'

'I didn't follow you. I thought of it all on my own, and you happened to have got there first. I'm old. Everything takes me longer.' She dimpled at Mavis, who wasn't having any of it.

Mavis pulled open the door that connected their rooms. 'Well, now you're going to have to pretend you're a confused old woman for the rest of the time we're here, or they won't buy our story tonight. Though maybe that'll no' be too much of an act for you.'

'I'll do my best,' said Althea sweetly.

'And take that stuff off your face before you get it all over their pillows. That's no' fair to whoever has to do the washing.'

'Of course, dear. Night, night. Down for breakfast at eight?'

'Aye.'

Mavis closed the door and stomped across her room. She knew her plan to creep back down to the reception desk to replace the key to Frances' room was scuppered for the time being. However, it had to be done…she hoped she wouldn't disturb anyone – again – if she waited for an hour or so before she left her room. Meanwhile, she pulled out the papers from her trousers, uncrumpled them, and sat at the little desk between her windows to read whatever it was that Frances Millington had last sent to her printer.

# CHAPTER TWELVE

Mavis MacDonald felt as though she were a hundred years old as she hauled herself out of what was, admittedly, the extremely comfortable bed at The Lavender. It wasn't the bed that was to blame. No, it was her own fault that she was starting the day feeling more than her age. She'd been unable to stop herself from spending longer than she should have done poring over the papers she'd managed to obtain during her sortie in the wee hours to the room where poor Frances Millington had lived...and died.

Now she was regretting having given in to her curiosity – not least because she wasn't any the wiser about what all the spreadsheets meant, except to have worked out that Frances had been recording 'occurrences', of some sort, on a calendar of her own devising. The trouble was, the woman had been using a code, which Mavis had been unable to crack. Though why the woman would have done such a thing was beyond her.

Hoping a shower would revitalize her spirits as well as her body, Mavis ended up having to dress in a hurry, because she'd lingered under the delightfully strong current of hot water for just a little too long.

When she heard a knock at the door which connected her room to Althea's she knew she was five minutes late – which annoyed her. Punctuality was one of her main tenets in life.

She pulled open the door ready to apologize but was taken aback by Althea's appearance.

'If that's what you're wearing for breakfast, what on earth will you do if we're suddenly summoned to attend a ball?'

Althea was kitted out in a long, flowing tangerine silk gown, and had draped a pink pashmina across one shoulder. Mavis had seen the pashmina several times before, so knew it was a genuine Indian one: Althea had proved it could be pulled through a wedding ring on several occasions; Mavis hoped she wouldn't perform that particular party trick over the scrambled eggs and porridge.

Althea sniffed. 'If you want everyone to think I'm batty, then I'll act as though I am.'

Mavis knew very well that Althea wasn't dressed all that unusually for her, but felt she had to mention one thing. 'I can understand the yellow plastic clogs, because they'll be useful if we go out to the terrace later on, but do you really think it's a good idea to wear the diamond necklace as a headband, dear? It's a bit much for breakfast, do you no' think? Best kept for the evenings, mebbe?'

Althea reached up to feel the sparkling stones. 'Hmm…the pendant is a bit big, isn't it? I don't want it plopping into my porridge. Yes, maybe I'll save that for later.'

Mavis couldn't understand why the dowager had even brought the necklace on their trip; she knew it was one of her favorites, then realized – with quite a jolt – that Althea rarely dined out any longer. In fact, upon reflection – which was what she had time to do as Althea removed the headband which, of course, got tangled in her hair – she could only think of a very few occasions when she and Althea had dined anywhere but Chellingworth Hall.

'There, that's…better,' said Mavis eventually, eyeing the lime green silk scarf Althea had managed to wind around her hair in a trice. 'You've brought a lot of those scarves with you, have you, dear? The red one last night, now this green one. They're quite, um, interesting.'

The pair made their way to the lift. As they descended, accompanied by the groaning of the mechanism, Althea explained, 'My hair's getting thinner, Mavis. I don't care for it. It's better to dress it up with a bit of color than have everyone feeling sorry for me because they can see my scalp. Scalps were not designed to be seen. We're supposed to be hairy beasts. So I shall adorn myself as I choose, thank you.'

After they'd shuddered to a halt, Mavis grappled with the tricky iron gate, then pushed the heavy wooden door which opened to the main reception area. Compared with the way she'd seen it since their arrival, Mavis felt it was congested; there were people wandering about the place, two were chatting at the reception desk with a white-haired woman who was looking stressed, and several were heading toward, or milling about in, the dining room.

Mavis hissed at the dowager, 'Right, remember what we agreed: don't push the cover story; do gather intel on Frances; do pick up on any mention of odd things happening here. Got it?'

'Roger. Out.'

Mavis couldn't keep up with the dowager as she shot off toward the dining room. Her little legs, and even her feet, were hidden by her long dress, giving the impression that Althea was on wheels. Which was an alarming thought – she was dangerous enough as it was. As if to prove Mavis right, just as she passed beneath the pointed arch which divided the dining room from the main, open lounge area of the hotel, Althea collided with a tall, well-built man. He was sporting a striking orange short-sleeved shirt that was almost as eye-wateringly vivid as Althea's frock.

He remarked to Althea gruffly, 'You again? Watch where you're going, will you?'

Given the nature of his greeting, Mavis assumed this was the man who'd threatened gunplay and a police presence in the early hours. Wanting to calm things down, she scuttled to Althea's side and said, 'Thanks for your understanding last night. Well, earlier this morning, really. I hope you were able to get back to sleep, Mr…um?'

'Lee. Malcolm Lee. And it's Sir. Who are you?'

Mavis felt the hairs on the back of her neck prickle. How she hated stuffed shirts. 'I'm Mavis MacDonald. This is Her Grace, the Dowager Duchess of Chellingworth. Your Grace, this is Malcolm Lee. He's a Sir, apparently.' Mavis made a point of giving the man a good look, up and down.

Althea played her part by peering at the man, haughtily. 'Why?'

The man spluttered, 'I beg your pardon?'

Althea continued her examination of the man, now paying particular attention to his shoes. 'Why are you a "Sir"?'

Sir Malcolm Lee puffed out his chest within his straining shirt. 'Knighthood four years ago. Services to gardening.'

Mavis did her best to mask her surprise.

Althea didn't bother. 'Services to gardening? What on earth does that mean? Or should I ask, what *in* earth does that mean?' Althea giggled.

Mavis worried for a moment that Althea was overdoing things a bit.

'Owned a large chain of garden centers up and down the country. Lee's Garden Emporia. Maybe Your Grace has heard of them?'

Althea sniffed. 'I don't think I've ever been to a garden center, though maybe my head gardener, Ivor, has done so, upon occasion. I shall ask him when we return to Chellingworth. But I must have my sea air before I can go home, and before that I want sausages. Come on Mavis, let's see what they've got for us.'

Mavis watched as Althea swooshed her skirt, lifted her little chin, and walked into the center of the dining room as though she'd been formally announced. Mavis followed, leaving Sir Malcolm Lee staring after them.

'Sir, "I've called the police and I've got a gun" indeed,' said Althea. 'That was fun. I think I'm going to enjoy being batty and haughty.'

Mavis sighed, fearing a long day.

Once they'd finished their breakfast, and had exchanged polite nods with all the others who were also enjoying theirs, Althea announced, 'I'm going to talk to that woman over there. She's alone and looks like she's a bit nosey. She's been staring at us for the past twenty minutes. If there's anything to know she might know it. But let me do it alone, dear? Go to the lavatory, or something. No…I know…'

Surprising Mavis, Althea stood and said loudly, 'They're in the little table beside my bed. I can't believe you didn't bring them. They must be taken immediately after I've eaten. I'm going to meet people now – off you go.'

Mavis flared her nostrils at Althea, bobbed her head, and left the dining room. A backward glance showed her Althea sidling toward the lone woman sitting beside the window. She decided to take the stairs rather than wait for the clunky lift – she couldn't afford to leave Althea to her own devices for too long.

By the time Mavis returned to the dining room, Althea, the unknown woman, an unknown man, and Sir Malcolm Lee were all sitting at the table beside the window, and laughing at…something. The table had been cleared and…were those glasses of sherry?

*What's she up to now?*

Mavis handed a tiny mint to Althea. 'There's your tablet. Lots of water, remember – and straight down.'

Althea looked at the mint, pulled a face, then said cheerily, 'Ah well, down the hatch.' She popped the mint into her mouth and drank down the whole glass of what Mavis was now certain was sherry. She could smell it.

Althea's tablemates roared with laughter.

Sir Malcolm even gave her a round of applause, then said, 'Althea here's been telling us about how a glass of sherry first thing in the morning is the best pick-me-up she's ever discovered. How clever of you to have told her about it. All that battlefield experience as an army nurse must have led you to discover some quite interesting facts as you served.'

Mavis could do nothing but follow Althea's lead. 'Aye, well, you're right about that, I dare say, Sir Malcolm. Though drinking before reporting for duty is no' the norm, neither on nor off the field of battle. But, when taken in moderation, a small snifter can prepare one for the day – as long as one's not going to be behind the wheel, of course.'

'None of us will be, today, eh?' Sir Malcolm raised his glass toward Althea, the man and woman raised theirs, and all three drank down their sherries. Mavis hoped none of them were on medication that would interact adversely with alcohol – all three were of an age where they were likely to be taking any number of pharmaceuticals on a daily basis.

Mavis was still hovering when Althea said, 'Do come and sit, Mavis – you're making everything look untidy. And while you settle yourself, allow me to introduce my new chums. You've already met Sir Malcolm, of course. This is Uma Chatterjee, who retired from being the receptionist at a local newspaper in Brighton. And you'll never guess what – she was an old school chum of the woman who died just before we arrived here yesterday. I'll have to tell her all about Sharon Jones who runs the shop in our village, because they're very much alike, in some ways.'

Mavis was surprised that Althea didn't add a massive, comedic wink or tap the side of her nose as she spoke.

The dowager continued, 'And this is…now, let me get this right: Sigismund Horatio Welbeck. Siggy, to his friends, amongst whom I am now honored to be numbered. And I bet you can't guess what Siggy did before he retired.'

Mavis wanted to kick Althea – just gently – under the table. 'I dare say I'll no' guess, Your Grace.'

'No. You won't. He "worked for the government".' Althea made exaggerated bunny ears signs with her fingers as she spoke. 'That means he was a spy, doesn't it? We all agree, don't we?'

Siggy's voice was musical, his accent clipped – upper-class English. 'As I said, I wasn't a spy, Althea. I worked at the Foreign Office. Rather low-level admin stuff, if I'm honest. Nothing glamorous. But a decent pension, which is why I can afford to live here. For which I'm grateful. Nice to have a soft landing…even if it's only from a desk job.'

Uma nodded. 'A soft landing? What a lovely way to put it, Siggy. It's alright if I call you Siggy, too, is it? I wouldn't want to presume.'

Siggy smiled. 'But of course…Uma?' Uma nodded. 'My pleasure to hear you say it.'

Mavis asked, 'So you live here, Siggy, but you're just visiting, like us, Uma?'

Uma smiled coyly. 'Oh no, I've been here for about four months already. I live here, too.'

Mavis was confused. 'But it sounds as though you two have never spoken to each other before now.'

Siggy said, 'We've not done so. Though I have to say I regret that. Althea gently bullied Sir Malcolm and myself into joining her and Uma. She…um…she told us a few rather entertaining stories about you, Mavis, and about her wandering last night, and then about the sherries and…well, here we all are. Getting on like a house on fire.'

Mavis felt as though she'd tumbled into a world that only existed in black-and-white films. How could people share a hotel dining room for months on end – live within yards of each other – and yet not speak? Was it still 1953 at The Lavender?

Still, at least Althea had found a spy and an entrepreneur to take a tipple with – as well as a woman who was from the same neck of the woods as Frances Millington. Althea had said the two women had been school chums; Mavis hoped they'd find a way to get Uma on her own.

At that moment, Toni Conti appeared beside Althea. 'Quite the little gathering we've got here. So pleased to see it. As a person who knows he thrives in company, I have to say that it warms my heart when those who have previously existed as lone islands in the churning sea of life come together to form a more substantial bulwark against its rigors. Frances Millington will be missed by us all – me, more than most, because of our working relationship. I hope you'll all take comfort in the company of others as you grieve. You've been…um…toasting the departed? At breakfast?'

Mavis saw Toni's surprise at seeing four empty sherry glasses on the table.

'Little toast to Frances, yes,' said Uma Chatterjee quite cheerily.

Mavis noted that there wasn't a hint of deception about the woman's tone or demeanor – which she found fascinating.

Conti squared his shoulders. 'Right then, well, have a lovely day. It's going to get relatively hot for the time of year, they said, so enjoy the breeze while you can. I intend to. And I'm hoping my dear wife feels up to joining me for a walk. Thanks for all bearing with us yesterday. Obviously, it was a far from normal day.'

'What did she die of?' Althea spoke directly to Toni. 'The woman who died. Frances. What did she die of?'

Toni looked trapped. 'We're not sure. They mentioned "natural causes", and the doctor who came said her heart had stopped beating – so cardiac arrest?'

Althea waved a hand. 'Everyone dies of cardiac arrest. That's what being dead is. But what made her heart stop? That's the question.'

Sir Malcolm piped up with: 'Yes, nothing catching, I hope.'

Toni blanched. 'No. Nothing catching, I'm sure. They'd have said so, if that had been the case. Not that I saw them myself, but Maria did. She told me.' He paused then addressed Althea directly, 'Maria's my wife, by the way. She's at reception for now, but you'll have a chance to meet her properly later on, I'm sure. She enjoys meeting all our new guests almost as much as I do.'

Mavis was just about to say how much she looked forward to that, when Siggy reached behind her and pulled at Toni Conti's jacket sleeve. 'Look up, old chap. It's happened again.'

The entire group looked up. All that Mavis could imagine Siggy was referring to was the row of ceiling fans above their heads. They were designed to look like long, narrow, pointed arches, and they were turning slower…and slower. She also noticed that the brass lamps that had been – unnecessarily, to her mind – illuminating the paintings on the walls had also gone out.

Toni sagged. 'Oh drat. The electricity's gone again. Excuse me, please, would you? I'll go and sort it out now.'

'You'll need another shilling in the meter,' called Siggy playfully as Toni headed off.

'Does this sort of thing happen often?' Mavis did her best to sound worriedly curious, in the way a normal guest would – rather than sounding intrigued, which was how she was feeling.

The glances exchanged between the three residents of The Lavender told her that they were all – silently, and without knowing each other well – trying to decide how much to say.

In the end, it was Uma Chatterjee whose comment opened the floodgates. 'It happens too often, and other things do, too. Sometimes I think this place is cursed…or haunted…so many things go wrong.'

Althea nodded. 'I said to Mavis when we arrived that the building looked like a big, old, haunted house. But she poo-pooed that idea, of course. Mavis is very practical.'

Siggy said, 'I agree that having the electricity cutting out can be exceptionally annoying, depending upon what one might be doing at the time, of course, or on the time of day. A great deal more annoying when it's dark outside. I wouldn't be surprised if the place burned to the ground, one day. I dare say I'm not the only person who has a stock of candles ready to use, should they be required.'

Sir Malcolm shook his head. 'Oh, I don't know. I think you'd have to go a long way to beat the hot water going cold when you're having a shower. I've been caught that way a few times. And sometimes there's a right old pong around this place…not pleasant at all.'

Uma sniffed. 'Well none of those things are as bad as seeing a rat run across your room, and that's what happened to poor Frances. But Toni wouldn't listen to her, would he? Oh no. Told her to shut up, or else get out. Well, he's got what he wanted, hasn't he? She's shut up, and she's gone forever.'

Uma burst into tears. Sir Malcolm patted his pockets. Siggy provided a linen square for Uma to sob into, and Althea looked at Mavis with an expression of such joy and excitement that Mavis thought she might burst.

# CHAPTER THIRTEEN

It was still surprisingly warm for the time of year, so Annie risked setting off to the office without a jacket. She'd managed to escape Tudor's threat of a massive breakfast by saying she needed to put in some proper computing time, which she did, even though she didn't really want to.

However, by the time she got to the barn her tummy was rumbling and she was imagining a plate of sausages. Gertie had seemed less than pleased to leave Rosie behind at the Coach, so she wasn't in a particularly good mood, either, and Annie had hoped that Christine would be at the office when she arrived, but she found herself alone.

With a grumpy Gertie. And a cupboard full of biscuits.

She put the kettle on even before she'd kicked off her shoes.

Cursing the fact that she seemed to be forever entering totals from receipts into spreadsheets so that Carol could send out accurate invoices, Annie plodded through a couple of hours' work before she dared make a second pot of tea. Which led her to open another packet of Garibaldis, as she'd known it would. At least Gertie was placated by the tidbits Annie shared.

Stepping outside to give both her back, and Gertie, a bit of a break, Annie was scrunching her way happily along the pea-gravel drive outside the barn when her mobile phone rang in her pocket. It was Sharon at the shop.

'Hello, Shar, you okay?'

'No, I'm not. You're dealing with Marjorie's Kevin, aren't you?'

Annie was taken aback by Sharon's tone. 'I'm doing my best to locate him, yes. Why?'

'Felix and Fliss have gone. I need your help.'

Annie paused. Gertie sat down and looked up at Annie, as if waiting for a cue. 'Okay, I'll bite,' said Annie. 'Are Fliss and Felix your cats?' She didn't recall Sharon having any cats, but the name Felix suggested as much to her.

'No. I haven't got any cats. They're my flamingoes. From Cyprus.'

Annie looked down at Gertie, who looked up at her, offering no help whatsoever. 'Umm…okay…and they're not real, right?'

Sharon tutted. 'Don't be *twp*. They're plastic. On bendy metal legs you stick into the ground. Got them when I went on a ten-day package to Limassol. Picked them up at Larnaca airport. Two of them. Obviously. Brought them back on the plane with me. Not an easy task, I can tell you. They don't weigh anything, really, but their bodies are over a foot long, and I wasn't the only one on the plane with them. The flight attendant made a right fuss about them. Didn't say anything about the woman with a massive sombrero, did she? Though what sombreros have got to do with Cyprus I don't know.'

Annie started to wander back to the office. She suspected she might need another biscuit. 'And…?'

'They've gone. Both of them. There when I locked the back door last night, gone this morning. And no, I didn't hear anything odd. And yes, I do think the same person took them as took Marjorie's Kevin. So, yes, I do think you should come and take a look at where they went from. And no, I haven't trampled all over the back garden. I learned my lesson about that when all those jars of pickles went missing from my shed and your Carol came to help.'

Annie felt she should draw breath on Sharon's behalf. 'I'm out at the office at the moment, but I should be back in the village before lunch. How about I pop in then? That alright?'

Sharon sounded relieved. 'Aw, thanks, Annie, that would be lovely, ta. Do you want me to do notes and give you photos like Marjorie did for Kevin? I've got lots of pictures of them…well, more of Fliss than Felix, because he's not as photogenic as her.'

Grappling with the idea that one plastic flamingo could appear more attractive in a photo than another – as well as the concept that there were gender differences to take into account – Annie thanked Sharon for her suggestion, agreed it would be a good idea, promised to be there soon, and disconnected.

Finally back inside the office, Annie filled the kettle and spoke to Gertie as though she were a person – which, of course, she was. 'You know what, Gert, there's some folk who might think that being a private investigator is all glamor, danger, and great deeds of derring-do. But it's not. I don't think plastic gnomes and flamingoes feature much in the novels of Dashiel Hammet or Raymond Chandler, but, there you are, that's what's on today's To Do list, Gert. So, what do you think of that?'

Gertie's yelp suggested she was more interested in the custard cream that Annie had in her hand than anything else.

Just as Annie was locking the door behind her, Christine arrived, the wheels of her Range Rover spitting pea-gravel as she braked hard.

Annie unlocked the door again as soon as she saw the look on Christine's face. The fact that her friend and colleague shouted, 'Loo,' as she ran past her confirmed Annie's suspicions.

When Christine emerged again, Annie couldn't help but comment. 'Is this something to do with being pregnant? You're not even showing, yet – what are you going to be like when you're nearly due?' She couldn't remember Carol having gone through anything like this when she'd been expecting Albert.

Christine laughed. 'I know what you mean, but no, it was my own stupid fault. Drank too much tea with Stephanie up at the Hall, offered to come back here to get some papers Alexander had left upstairs in the flat, and didn't realize I'd need the loo so much. Anyway, it was grand of you to open the door – those extra seconds? Critical. Lesson learned.'

Annie chuckled. 'Yeah, Car's always telling me to go before I go…like my mum she is, sometimes. Anyway, I was just off to the village to see Sharon about her flamingoes. Don't ask. But if you're going to the Hall, I won't ask for a lift. The walk'll be good for me and Gert anyway. Anything going on there I should know about?'

'I don't think so. It's all about the village revitalization thing. I'm seeing that as life, in the broadest sense, rather than work stuff…though there'll be work involved, no doubt. But at least I get to spend a bit of time doing something with my fiancé, which makes a nice change.'

Annie was puzzled. 'What's Alexander got to do with it? I know Tude's been at it for weeks, collaring all and sundry, trying to give everyone in the village a chance to talk to him, Iris, and Marjorie, so they can speak up when they get a chance to do so with Stephanie and Henry, you know? But he hasn't said anything about Alexander.'

'That's why the get-together; Stephanie wants Alexander to do…something to do with buildings, is all I know so far, and he's asked for a sit-down.'

Annie tried to control Gertie, who had finally had enough of waiting about. 'Okay, well, keep me in the loop – Tude too. Talk soon. I'll just let Gert pull me home now.'

By the time Annie reached Sharon's shop she'd built up enough of a sweat that she was glad she hadn't bothered with a jacket, and was longingly thinking of Sharon's cooler cabinets. Yes, maybe a can of something fizzy was a good idea.

The little bell above the door tinkled as she entered. 'Alright if I bring Gert in, Shar?'

'As long as she's on her lead – but come through to the back so I can show you where Fliss and Felix went from, Annie.'

Annie walked through to the rooms behind the shop, past boxes and extra freezers, with Gertie sniffing like mad at absolutely everything. 'Oh, lots of smells, eh, Gert?' Annie kept going, and made sure Gertie didn't linger.

Sharon's head popped around a corner. 'The kettle's on, but let me show you where they were, then you can have a look around while I make a pot of tea. I'm guessing you fancy a cup?'

'Show me what's what, but I was thinking of something cold, to be honest.'

Sharon looked Annie up and down. 'Another flash? You're getting a lot of them. Aren't you getting to be the age where you should be past all that?'

Annie bridled. 'It's not a flash, it's just that it's warm and we walked fast…just so that you didn't wonder where I'd got to. You made it sound urgent on the phone, so here I am. Right then, where exactly were these Cypriot flamingoes of yours then?'

Sharon pointed to the far corner of what Annie would have called a scrubby strip of grass, if she were being kind, which ran down the side of a dilapidated shed. 'Right at the end, by the hedge,' Sharon said, moving to fill the teapot. 'I can see them when I'm upstairs then, as well as in the kitchen down here. Here are some photos on my phone – just scroll, you'll see.'

She shoved her phone into Annie's hand, so Annie scrolled and did, in fact, see…so many snaps of two wonky-looking plastic flamingoes. Having been left in no doubt – judging by Sharon's reaction to them having gone missing – that they meant a great deal to her, Annie chose her words carefully. 'So the one on the right is…?'

Sharon put the pot on the kitchen table. 'Aw, that's Fliss. Lovely, isn't she? See – she's got a different angle to her neck, much more graceful than Felix. He's a bit too…upright. There's a couple of close-ups there that'll show you better what I mean.'

Annie shared several of the photos with her own phone, for future reference. 'Any distinguishing marks?'

'I think there's a more pronounced line at the top of Fliss's eyes, a bit like eyeliner, you know? But, otherwise, no, not really. Other than the neck thing. I didn't write their names on them or anything like that, if that's what you mean.'

Annie sighed. On the off-chance that she might encounter an entire flock of plastic flamingoes – *was that the collective noun for flamingoes?* – she might be hard-pressed to pick out Felix and Fliss. 'On the basis that we get them back, Shar, maybe use one of those pens that show up under ultraviolet light to name them and say they're yours? You won't be able to see it when you look at them in daylight, but it could help if they're ever lost again. In fact, it's not a bad thing to do with everything that's precious to you – just in case, you know?'

Sharon took her phone from Annie and started typing. 'Now that's a good idea. I could maybe get some for the shop – put up a sign to make folks think of doing it for themselves. Oh look, twenty-five in a carton. There – ordered. They'll be here in four days. Thanks for that. It's always nice to have something new to offer people – and it would be a good crime prevention idea, wouldn't it?'

Annie observed, 'Well, not prevention, as such, but it could help if property is lost or stolen, then recovered.'

'Do you think someone's been into my garden and taken them then? I mean, that's the only thing that can have happened, isn't it? Carol did say I could do with a fence inside that hedge that leads to the lane up to Chellingworth, but fences don't grow on trees, do they?' Annie was about to reply, when Sharon burst out laughing. 'Listen to me. Fences don't grow on trees? Of course they do, if they're wooden. You must think I'm *twp*.'

Annie picked up her mug, 'Not silly, but emotional, I can tell. But you didn't hear or see anything odd overnight?'

Sharon shook her head and opened the tin which Annie knew always contained a delicious variety of broken biscuits; anything that got damaged in transit ended up in Sharon's tin. She offered it to Annie.

'Fancy a Jammy Dodger? Three packets went to bits when I dropped them. The jam helped to hold them together, but I couldn't sell them.'

Annie would have liked nothing more, but she was full of Bourbons, Garibaldis, and custard creams. 'Go on then, ta. But just one for me.'

'Take three bits, that'll be like a whole one.' Sharon pushed the tin right under Annie's nose. She took four pieces.

'You haven't got any clues about Marjorie's Kevin yet, have you? Something that might set you off on a trail to Felix and Fliss.'

Annie shook her head. 'Sorry, nothing yet. The problem is that no one saw or heard anything. Of course, just because nothing disturbed you last night, it doesn't mean that no one else noticed anything. I'll ask around. Again. Have you been asking whoever's come into the shop this morning? If so, tell me who you've talked to, so I don't waste time – mine, or theirs.'

Sharon sipped her tea thoughtfully. 'Marjorie, of course, she's always in early, and she was the first one I told, even before you. She reckons it's the same person who took her Kevin. Your Carol came in, and I asked her – in fact, she suggested I phoned you. Oh, and Janet came in from the tearooms. What did you make of her, by the way?'

Annie was circumspect. 'The Lamb looks quite different now, doesn't it? Have you been in?'

Sharon shook her head. 'Haven't got the time, with the shop. Besides, how can you do better than what I've got here – broken biscuits, and strong Welsh tea, with two sugars, and a drop of milk.'

'And every mouse in the world can trot on top of it, right?' Annie winked.

Sharon gazed into her mug. 'Tea and home, that's what makes me happy. Losing Fliss and Felix is a big hit. I like them. They make me smile when I look at them. It was a lovely time in Cyprus, that. Came back with an extra half a stone on me, and memories that'll be with me forever.'

Annie dared to ask, 'Holiday romance?'

Sharon blushed. 'That's a mug's game, that is, falling for someone you'll never see again, even if they promise they'll text.'

Annie's heart went out to Sharon, because it was clear she was speaking from bitter experience. She rose. 'Look, Shar, I can't promise anything, but I'll do me best for you, and Marge, of course. But sitting here drinking tea with you isn't getting me anywhere, unless there's something else you can tell me that might help. Is there?'

Sharon shook her head sadly, then bounced out of her chair as the bell in the shop tinkled. 'Talk about Pavlov and his dogs – that bell might not get me salivating, but it flamin' well gets me into that shop sharpish.' She shouted, 'Coming,' then ushered Annie and Gertie into the shop ahead of her.

Janet Jackson had her head inside one of the chiller cabinets.

'Can I help you?' Sharon sounded a bit snappish to Annie's ears – not like her.

'Paul didn't send enough squirty cream down from the Hall with the buns this morning. I always put it on just before I serve them, so the buns look their best on the plate. You haven't got any, have you, Sharon? I'm desperate.'

'Third shelf up in the next cabinet along, Janet. I think I've got three, and you can have them all if you want. I don't sell a lot of it.'

Annie said, 'Morning Janet. You didn't hear anything odd last night in the village, did you?'

Janet half-turned as she reached to the back of a shelf to get to the cans of cream. 'Nothing, except her. Again.' She nodded down at Gertie. 'Likes to bark, doesn't she?'

Annie felt slighted on behalf of Gertie, who was looking from Janet to Annie with a doleful expression. 'Gert wasn't barking last night. She's not a barker. Nor is Rosie.' Turning to Sharon she checked, 'I'm right that there aren't any other dogs around the green, aren't I?'

Sharon shook her head. 'There's a couple over by the duck pond, but if they were barking that would be buffered by the houses. Mind you, sound does travel strangely at night, doesn't it? Maybe your sense of direction isn't quite there yet, Janet. The village is all still so new to you, isn't it.'

'Sounded like it was right outside the Lamb, it did,' snapped the woman. 'There, yes, I'll have the three of these please.'

As Annie left, she could hear Janet expressing surprise at just how much three cans of squirty cream were going to cost her.

She commented, 'Well, Gert, we've all got to make a living, haven't we? Speaking of which, let's get going with asking everyone if they heard anything odd…again.'

Gertie yapped her agreement, and the pair took off to sniff out any information that might help Annie in The Case of the…*oh dear, I'll have to have another think about that one.*

# CHAPTER FOURTEEN

Upon arriving at the Twysts' private dining room, Henry was surprised to see the table laid for six. Uncertain about whom exactly he'd be hosting for luncheon, he decided it was better to stand at the window to admire the view than take his seat. It was a perfect September day – the sun was high in a clear blue sky, and the crowds in the gardens weren't too dense, now that the children were back at school. In less than a month Chellingworth Hall would close to the public, then he and his staff could get back to work on all the jobs that had to wait until there weren't hundreds of people tramping about the place.

Stephanie pushed Hugo into the dining room in his pram and parked him at the end of the table. 'I'm glad we agreed on transporting him this way, dear,' observed his wife. 'He's really quite a solid little chap, isn't he?'

Henry thought his son was getting to be rather chubby, but didn't like to say anything about that because Stephanie's role as Hugo's only source of sustenance made it a tricky subject. 'I'm sure he's as healthy as can be, which is what matters,' he replied cheerfully.

'He certainly is,' said his wife, cooing over the pram and its precious contents.

Henry dared to ask, 'We're having guests for lunch?'

Stephanie took a seat. 'I hope you don't mind – we all need to eat and I have a busy day. Christine and Alexander will be coming, as will Carol and Bob Fernley. I know it's not the norm for him to eat with us, but needs must. He's so terribly strapped for time, these days, and I hope we can come to some sort of resolution at this luncheon that might help everyone concerned.'

Henry had no idea how anything might help him in any way, but suspected he'd be putting his foot in it if he said so. 'You're always thinking of others,' was what he said. Stephanie's warm smile told him he'd struck the right note.

Edward announced the arrival of Carol, Christine, and Alexander. Just as they were helping themselves to cool drinks, Bob Fernley hustled in through the door that led from the kitchen, which Henry thought odd. What was even odder was that he immediately whispered something into Stephanie's ear, and she lost a great deal of her color.

Henry whispered to his wife, 'Is everything alright, dear?'

Stephanie sighed. 'Nothing I can do anything about at the moment, but I'll have to do something after this meeting.'

Certain that his wife would add no more, Henry replied, 'As you say,' and indicated to Edward that luncheon should be served.

Henry enjoyed the chilled tomato soup that was served with little rounds of buttered toast, as Stephanie encouraged everyone to eat, then talk. Bob got through his soup so fast that it looked to Henry as though he hadn't eaten for days, then he started talking about spreadsheets and schedules as if Henry knew what he was gibbering about. He didn't have a clue, though everyone else seemed to understand what was going on.

'I hope you don't all mind, but I need the paperwork next to me as I talk about it,' said Alexander hesitantly.

'It's a working lunch, feel free, Alexander,' replied Stephanie. 'Anyone else who wants to refer to materials, please, go ahead. I asked Edward to set places far apart for that very reason.'

As Stephanie mentioned it, Henry noticed that, indeed, the place settings were rather a long way from each other. He hadn't noticed before. At least it meant that everyone could read from sheaves of papers or, in Carol's case, a tablet thingy. Henry had no such papers, which he thought might explain why he didn't know what everyone was talking about. He felt better for having worked that out.

As numbers and dates were bandied about, Henry allowed his senses to enjoy the wonderful salad he'd been served. The Welsh trout season would finish at the end of the month, so he told himself he would enjoy it freshly smoked while he could. He also loved fennel, and there were shavings of it spiking the salad of chicory and other green leaves, moist beetroot, and crisp slivers of spring onion, all from Chellingworth's gardens, and all dressed lightly and fruitily with...well, he wasn't sure what, but it was delicious.

Then, suddenly, Stephanie was saying, 'That's right, isn't it, Henry?'

Henry's happy tummy flipped. 'I'm so sorry, I didn't quite catch that.' *Would he get away with it?*

Stephanie sighed. 'I said, we'll be incredibly grateful if Carol could find out as much as possible about this contractor that Bob dealt with. We've agreed that Alexander's rough estimate that it would cost twice as much as this Muggins suggests, makes the man sound…well, either inadequate for the task, or else as though he'll up the price after he gets the job.'

'I say, that's a bit harsh, don't you think?' Henry had to say something.

His wife looked puzzled. 'What's harsh?'

'Referring to him as a muggings. You know – as though he's put upon because he's a bit dim. Is he?'

Stephanie tutted.

Bob Fernley said, 'His name is Muggins, Your Grace. Art Muggins, from Cardiff. Came highly recommended. Has worked on some projects not dissimilar to what we're considering at the old school and the village hall. Though, as I admitted, I haven't had time to check into his references in any sort of detail, which is why Carol's on board.'

Alexander noted, 'I'm not saying you've made a bad choice, Bob, just that what he's quoted doesn't make sense to me. That said, I know the London area better than Wales, so maybe everything really is that much cheaper around here. And that's why I don't want to push myself into this role.'

Henry felt his back stiffen when his wife spoke firmly to their Estates Manager. 'You need to be honest with us, now, Bob. You're…you're having to add a great deal to what I know is an already full workload. The duke and I value your professionalism tremendously, as I hope you know, but we aren't sure how best to help you navigate these new directions we're pushing you to take. You have to tell us. Your professional input needs to go just this one step further, please.'

Henry tried to focus on the last morsels on his plate; he didn't think Bob needed to be stared at.

Bob spoke quietly. 'If I may speak freely?'

'Always,' said Henry, nodding at Bob between mouthfuls.

'Very well. Yes, I am feeling a little overwhelmed by these new tasks. I'm not a man who fears hard work, as I hope you all appreciate, and I believe I manage to keep all the plates spinning, as necessary. But these big projects you're wanting in the village will be on top of the normal maintenance of the fabric of buildings, which we all know is really something that Gwilym takes care of, but – as I'm sure you haven't forgotten – he's off with his new hip at the moment, and I can't see him being back to one hundred percent for a while.'

'New hips can be tricky,' observed Henry. 'Isn't that right, Mother?' When there was no reply, Henry looked up and realized he'd forgotten his mother wasn't present – she so often was when matters pertaining to the Estate were being discussed. Upon realizing that, for maybe the first time ever, significant decisions were about to be made not in the presence of the dowager, who always had an opinion, he felt a little nervous. 'Sorry, foolish of me. Mother's away, I know that, really. But, yes, hips can be tricky.' He hoped dessert would arrive soon.

'I'd be happy to walk through the buildings so I can provide a proper estimate of works,' added Alexander. 'Then we'd have something to compare and consider. And are you due to receive any more quotes, Bob? Other than this one from Muggins.'

'There was one due yesterday, but nothing's arrived, and another's due later today. Had three lots of them doing walk-rounds before we had the committee meeting, and all they needed to know was what we'd decided with regards to purpose.'

Henry was delighted when a lemon posset was placed in front of him. 'Any of those coconut shortbreads Cook Davies makes by any chance, Edward?'

Edward shook his head, looking grave. 'I understand there was an unforeseen shortage of desiccated coconut in the kitchen, Your Grace. Cook Davies has prepared brandy snaps instead.' He placed a plate of the glistening tubes beside the posset glass.

'Ah,' said Henry, trying to not sound too disappointed. 'Very well. I'm sure we'll manage admirably. I rather like Cook's brandy snaps…and we've not had them in a while. Thank Cook for me, would you please, Edward.'

'Indeed, Your Grace.'

As everyone else began to scoop up posset with their brandy snaps and crunch into them, Bob said, 'I'm more than happy to relinquish my management of the refurbishment of both the buildings in the village, if you'd care to take over, Mr Bright. Quite honestly, I'd be grateful for this to all be dealt with as a separate undertaking.'

Alexander nodded. 'Right-o, then. Carol – you and I can work on the numbers we have, if you can pass any more quotes through to us, Bob, we'll take them from there. And I'll have a walk around with…who would you suggest? Tudor? This afternoon. Or is there someone else who knows exactly what was agreed at the meeting? I wouldn't want to bother you, Stephanie.'

Henry noticed that Bob seemed to sit up straighter. 'Thank you. I have to meet the Hughes family at their house in the village today to get a full report drawn up on what needs to be done at the place before we can get new tenants in there; they'll be out before I know it, and I need to understand what's what.'

Henry thought Christine sounded excited when she said, 'The Hugheses are leaving? That's a lovely house they're in. Oh, I say, Stephanie, could we talk about that? I can't see how me, Alexander, and a baby are going to fit into the little apartment in the top of the barn. We'll be squashed together.'

Henry couldn't be certain, but he sensed that Christine had said something that made some people in the room grow tense. He could see that Alexander was giving his last brandy snap a great deal of attention, and Carol Hill was…well, it was quite unusual for Carol to look as pink in the face as she was at that moment.

Alexander almost whispered, 'We could look into buying something close to the village,' which Henry barely caught.

Carol's louder comment: 'Yeah, not all of us who could do with a bit of extra space are that lucky,' was much easier to hear.

Stephanie asked, 'Any progress on the matter of Mr Baker, by the way, Carol?'

Henry wasn't sure how she'd done it, but his wife's question seemed to have allowed the luncheon group to return to an even keel.

Carol nodded. 'A little, but I'm waiting for data to arrive that can't be hurried. He once had his own bakery, I can tell you that much…but it closed down, though it hasn't been wound up, as a business, yet. Which is odd, and which is why I'm waiting. I promise I'll let you know as soon as the picture is clearer. I know that the village revitalization is now a proper project for the WISE women, so if it's okay with everyone, I'll get back to my desk – well, to my dining table in any case – and get on with things. Can I give anyone a lift to the village?' Everyone shook their head. 'Thanks for a wonderful lunch. It's such…well, it's such a treat to have lunch served to me like this. Thanks, Stephanie, Henry, it was delicious and, look, I haven't even got to do the washing up. What a joy. I'll talk to you later, Alexander. Bye, folks.'

After Carol had left, Henry asked, 'Why does she work at her dining table? Where do they eat?'

Christine blushed as she replied, 'Carol works at home so she can be with Albert, and there isn't a space she can dedicate to being an office, so she uses the dining room, mainly. I think they eat in the kitchen.'

Henry recalled pleasant times when he'd done the same thing. 'There's nothing quite like the refuge of a kitchen, I feel. I used to eat in ours as a child, and the memories are always sweet. A place of calm, and order – and the smells! Ah yes, happy times.'

Stephanie rose. 'I'll let you take Hugo up to our rooms, dear, because I have to deal with a sticky situation concerning not only missing desiccated coconut but, apparently, also rosehip syrup down in the kitchen. I don't believe that your childhood memories of peace and stability hold sway at present there, dear. So, wish me luck.'

'Indeed,' replied Henry, hoping that nothing would stand in the way of dinner plans progressing smoothly.

# CHAPTER FIFTEEN

Mavis looked Althea up and down and said, 'I didnae think we'd need to change our clothing to such an extent for a stroll on the beach. We're no scaling the north face of the Eiger you know.'

Althea had kitted herself out in a pair of voluminous indigo cotton trousers that had pockets with toggled closures down the outside of both legs, teamed with a cream-and-pink striped blouson jacket that had almost as many pockets again. It looked to Mavis as though every single pocket was stuffed with…something. Althea was carrying a backpack, made of neon green nylon, which was almost pulling her backwards, and she was wearing a large pyramidal woven straw hat, tied under her chin, while her feet were encased in yellow socks, which poked out of the tops of sturdy walking shoes.

'You said a walk, Mavis, not a stroll. This isn't my strolling gear, this is my walking gear. There's a great difference. You should have been more specific,' whined Althea.

'Aye, well the hat will keep the sun off your face, and those shoes will stop the sand from being annoying.' Mavis looked down at her sandals and bare feet. 'For me? I like the sand between my toes.'

'That's a very surprising thing for a Scottish person to say,' said Althea haughtily as she headed toward the lift.

Mavis caught up with her and hissed, 'No need to play the wee madam when we're alone, dear.'

Althea dimpled. 'It hadn't crossed my mind to do so. Shall we?' She used both hands to pull open the door, stuck one of her substantial boots in front of it, then hauled open the noisy gate with a flourish. 'After you, dear.'

Mavis and Althea's arrival in the main reception area was heeded by almost no one, though Toni Conti waved cheerily as he rushed across their path, then he paused, stared at Althea, smiled again and carried on his way. Several people were sitting at tables or on lounge chairs on the terrace, making the most of the unusual warmth for the time of year. The pair nodded politely as they passed, planning to meander along the pathway which wound its way through terraced flower beds, toward the beach below.

'Good afternoon, ladies. And how are you both today?'

Mavis and Althea were both startled when Dennis Moore popped up from behind a rather large shrub.

Althea giggled. 'I say, Dennis, you'd better be careful back there. Those berberis can be horribly spiny. Is that a Harlequin?'

'It is indeed, Your Grace,' replied the gardener. 'Lovely colors on the leaves, aren't they? And the berries will come before long, too. It glows then.'

'Please don't Your Grace me, Dennis. It's Althea. I'm on holiday, remember?'

'Right-o, whatever you say. The guest is always right. On your way to the beach, ladies?'

'It's a lovely day for a stroll,' replied Mavis, doing her best to move Althea along.

'It's always a lovely day for something,' replied Dennis with a wink, which made Mavis grit her teeth.

Althea pushed Mavis's steering arm away and asked boldly, 'Have you heard what Frances died of, yet?'

Dennis leaned on the wooden end of whatever implement was hidden by the shrub. 'No one's told me anything. Not that they would. I'm just the gardener, after all. Are you keen on plants, Althea? You seem to know your berberis, if nothing else.'

Mavis watched in horror as Althea dimpled, and fluttered, and generally made a fool of herself. 'I know my lupins too…though I'm always keen to learn more. Do you grow any of those?'

'Given my name, you know I do. Though it's late in the season for them now, I do my best to extend them by deadheading all the time, and these are well-established plants. Want to see what's left?'

Mavis gave up. 'Take us to your lupins.'

Althea had given Mavis a detailed explanation of the way that sketches about a highwayman named Dennis Moore had been threaded through an episode of *Monty Python's Flying Circus*, with the scenarios becoming more and more ridiculous on each occasion – as though the idea that a man would hold people at gunpoint until they surrendered their lupins wasn't a bizarre enough starting point. Mavis had watched the whole thing online, too, and had to admit it was amusing. Thus, for once, she decided to indulge the dowager in her devotion to her comedic heroes. Mavis had to admit that Althea had been genuinely delighted to meet someone whose name really was Dennis Moore. And he was a pleasant enough man.

Winding their way to a bed that was protected from the sea winds by a hedge of stout and prickly berberis – which seemed to be a favorite of the gardener – Mavis saw spires of blue, white, mauve, and purple, with a few yellowy-orange ones dotted about. The display of lupins certainly bore testament to Dennis's ability to keep the attractive flowers blooming well into the end of the season. Althea twittered, asked about varieties, and took notes on a pad she extricated from one of her many trouser pockets with a pencil she pulled from a long, narrow pouch on the sleeve of her odd jacket. Mavis rolled her eyes until they almost fell out of her head, but Althea continued to generally treat the man as though he were some sort of saint.

'Was poor Frances keen on the garden?' Althea asked in such an innocent way that even Mavis was almost taken in.

Dennis, on the other hand, didn't seem to be fooled. 'You're very interested in a woman you never met, aren't you? Fancy yourself as some sort of Miss Marple, do you? Think she was bumped off? Well, here you go – how's about these lupin seeds for you? Grind those up and sprinkle them on someone's food, and they might get very ill, or even die. These aren't the edible sort, see? Though there are varieties grown specifically for their edible seeds. Very popular they are, these days, I hear. Not that I'll be planting any of them here any time soon – I prefer the beauty of the ones known for their blooms, not their seeds. But I don't think Frances was killed, I think she just died, like Toni said. Though…well, I don't like to speak ill of the dead – and I'm not really – but she was a bit nosey. Liked to know what was going on all the time.'

'There was talk, at breakfast, that she'd been asked to leave,' said Mavis, hoping Dennis might share some useful information.

His voice had a noticeable edge when he asked, 'Who told you that?'

Althea pounced. 'Siggy said...and Uma, and Sir Malcolm. Do you like him? I bet you two have long talks about the garden.'

Dennis looked puzzled. 'Why would I do that?'

Mavis and Althea exchanged a glance. 'Because he used to run a big chain of garden centers. Surely you two must have a lot in common.'

Dennis scratched his head. 'He's never mentioned that to me. What garden centers did he have?'

'Lee's. That's his name,' replied Mavis.

'Really? Sir Malcolm is *the* Lee, of Lee's? He's never said anything. Mind you, he prefers the beach to the garden, I've noticed. And you've talked to them all? About this business?'

Mavis nodded, while Althea said, 'We all got chatting over breakfast sherries, and they mentioned it. And they told us about all the strange things that happen here. You must know all about that, surely? The electricity always going off, the same thing with the hot water, mystery smells...and rats. That's why they said Frances had been asked to leave – she thought Mr Conti should be more proactive about trying to get to the bottom of all the odd, and inconvenient, things going on here, whereas he said she could shut up or get out. End of the month, and she was gone.'

Dennis laughed heartly. 'Hang on a minute. You've been here two minutes and you've got people talking to you, and to each other by the sounds of it, who have sat out on that terrace for months, nodding at each other like dogs in the back window of a car but never saying a word to each other? And drinking sherry at breakfast? Mavis, is this Althea of yours some sort of miracle worker, or what?'

Mavis tutted. 'She doesnae get out much, so she tends to over-socialize when she does, it seems.'

'I don't over-socialize. I have a charming personality.' Althea pouted.

'You're a wee scamp,' hissed Mavis playfully.

Dennis rubbed his chin. 'You're quite the pair, you two. I bet you're firm friends, really.'

Cross with herself that she'd spoken in a manner inappropriate for her assumed character, Mavis did her best to mollify the man. 'Her

Grace allows me more familiarity than others because, of course, I have to tend to all her personal needs.'

Dennis, sadly, didn't look convinced. 'If you say so, Mavis. But what I will tell you is that if you want there to be any beach to walk on at all, you'd best get down to the sands now – the sea will be up to the dunes before you know it, and that's hard walking. Not something either of you should be doing, however well-prepared for a hike you might be, Althea. Is that backpack of yours as heavy as it looks? What on earth do you have in there?'

Althea rolled her small shoulders. 'I'm afraid it's rather heavier than I'd imagined. I wanted to read on the beach, you see, so I brought a few books with me.'

'Looks like you've a shelf's worth in there,' observed the gardener. 'I'll happily carry it down to the beach for you, if you'll permit me to. I've time for a break.'

Mavis thought that was exactly what the man had been enjoying all the time they'd been chatting, but didn't say so, because she didn't have a chance to say anything, due to the fact that Althea was fawning all over him again as he removed her backpack and slung it over one of his shoulders, while offering her his other arm.

Mavis followed the pair down the last winding twists of the path between beds of plants onto the mounding dunes that led down to the beach. A wooden-slatted pathway had been laid, to allow for easier access to what turned out to be a beautiful little bay. This was bliss. Just the sound of the waves lapping onto the sandy beach was a delight, and she took a little while to allow herself to absorb the relaxing sounds and feelings.

'Mavis, Mavis – look what we've found!' Althea's voice invaded Mavis's quiet enjoyment, and she opened her eyes to see Althea standing over Dennis, who was on his knees poking at what appeared to be a mound of old clothing...or was it a large seal? *Did they have those around here?* No...it had an arm, and legs, and shoes on its feet. Mavis moved as fast as she could across the yielding sands until she reached the trio. Siggy Welbeck was lying on his side, on the sand, his face devoid of color.

'Stand back,' instructed Mavis. She kneeled and felt for a pulse. 'He's no' dead,' she observed.

Siggy opened his eyes and said, 'I know that.'

'You can talk. Excellent,' squealed Althea. 'What happened?'

Mavis bristled. 'Let's no' worry about that now, let me make sure it's okay for you to sit up, Siggy.'

Siggy sat up. 'It's perfectly alright for me to sit up – see? I didn't lose consciousness for more than a moment, I'm sure. No problem.'

Mavis snapped. 'I'll be the judge of that, thank you very much. You shouldnae move. There could be all manner of things wrong with you that you've no idea about. Of all four of us, there's only one who's a medical professional here, as far as I'm aware.' She glared at Siggy, Dennis, and Althea in turn. All looked suitably reprimanded.

Mavis asked Siggy questions, checked him over as far as she could…given they were in the middle of a beach, with the waves lapping ever closer. She finally allowed him to stand. 'You're a wee bit wobbly, Siggy, take time to get your balance.'

Siggy chuckled. 'It's the sand, that's all. Though I have to say I won't be sorry to get back to proper *terra firma*, and maybe have a snifter.'

'Good,' said Althea firmly. 'Now – what happened?'

Siggy said quietly, 'One moment I was watching the seagulls, the next there was a noise inside my head and a pain, then I was on the sand.'

'Were you hit?' Dennis looked concerned.

Mavis said, 'Let me take a good look at that head of yours.'

Siggy batted her away. 'I'm sorry, please let me be. I was not hit, I just…well, sometimes I take a bit of a turn. A problem I've had for a few years. Hence my early retirement. Can't drive, either. Not allowed. Stress doesn't help, they say. Another reason I live here. It would be hard to find a more peaceful spot.'

'Do you think Frances' death has set you off?' Mavis was deeply concerned. 'The shock? How well did you know her really? You weren't very forthcoming when we chatted about her at breakfast.'

Mavis held an arm toward Siggy's back as he straightened up and pronounced, 'Discretion is a trait I have always possessed, though not one about which I should boast. Shall we?'

As the men headed toward the path through the dunes, Althea scuttled along as quickly as she could to keep up, and Mavis felt herself torn – should she keep up with Siggy Welbeck, or hang back with Althea, who might easily trip in her haste. She stuck with Althea, and the pair followed behind Dennis and Siggy at their own pace…which was slow, due to the surprisingly steep incline of the path.

Once they reached the terrace – which took them both a great deal longer than either of them had imagined it would – Mavis could see that Althea was completely puffed, and she knew she wouldn't mind a sit-down herself. Fortunately, Dennis appeared with a jug of what looked like iced blackcurrant squash, and some glasses, on a tray, which he deposited on the table where Siggy had settled.

'Here you are. I rustled this up in the kitchen. Nothing fancy, but you all need some sugar.' Dennis made sure that Althea and Mavis were comfortably seated, and Mavis enjoyed the cool, refreshing, and surprisingly sweet, drink in short order.

'How are you feeling, Siggy?' She had to ask.

'Better for that. Thanks for your help.'

Uma Chatterjee wandered across to the table. She was wearing a surprisingly formal suit of pale pink jersey, and was carrying a lumpen tapestry bag beneath her arm. 'Hello, everyone. You look like you've been having fun on the beach. Good color you've got, Althea.'

'Siggy collapsed on the sand,' gushed Althea. 'It's because he misses Frances, isn't it, Siggy?'

Mavis spotted the way the ice in Siggy's glass tinkled as he blushed. 'I say, Althea, that's not at all what I said. It's what you inferred, but it's far from the truth. Which is not to say we don't all miss her, but not me more than anyone else, I shouldn't think.'

Uma said, 'To mangle the Great Bard, "Methinks he doth protest too much". She was the only person I ever saw you talking to, Siggy. You and her with those crosswords? You both loved your puzzles, and wordplay, and so forth, didn't you? You'll miss that, I know.'

Mavis looked at Siggy and wondered, not for the first time, what exactly he'd done at the Foreign Office. She suspected he'd never tell her, nor that she'd ever ask.

'Dennis, do they serve tea out here?' Althea appeared to have recovered from the long climb from the beach.

Dennis hovered uncertainly. 'I know they do, because I see folks out here having it, on occasion – but I'm not sure how that works, never having been a guest. Shall I ask…or maybe someone here knows?'

Mavis said, 'I'm sorry, Dennis. Althea's used to there being someone to do almost everything for her, so I'll go in and sort it out.'

Uma piped up. 'The menus are on the tables in the dining room, just tell the server in there what you want, I think it's Simon, and ask him to bring it here. If you're going to sit out, may I join you? It's not the sort of thing I do alone, though, honestly, I don't know why. Don't you think that having your tea outdoors is sort of…celebratory?'

Althea popped up out of her seat, startling Mavis. 'That's what we need – a spirit of celebration. Tell them to bring the works for five, Mavis. Dennis, you'll join us? As our guest, of course.'

Dennis shuffled. 'Kind of you to ask, but I don't finish for another hour, and I do still have a few things I have to get done today. I hope you don't mind. You all have each other now, so I'd better get back to it.'

Althea giggled. 'Those lupins won't deadhead themselves, I suppose, will they?'

'Indeed. Enjoy your tea. Oh, and look – you might be five after all, I can see Sir Malcolm heading this way. Bye for now.'

Mavis thought Dennis made his departure rather rapidly, and he was right, Sir Malcolm arrived at the table just a moment later. 'What are you all doing here without me? Do you have a sherry at teatime, too, Althea?'

Althea dimpled. 'I don't, but that's not a bad idea, is it, Mavis?'

Mavis put her foot down. 'Aye, it is. Teatime is for tea. Is there anything anyone doesnae want, or shall I just ask for tea for five to be brought out? Will you be staying, Sir Malcolm?'

'Excellent idea,' he replied. 'I shall. I loathe egg sandwiches; otherwise, I'll eat anything.'

'No eggy ones for me either,' said Uma, wriggling a hand in the air.

'I'll eat theirs, and swap anything with tomato in it,' piped up Siggy.

Althea said, 'You know me, Mavis.'

Mavis did her best to not roll her eyes when she replied, 'Aye, that I do.'

As she left, she heard a conversation about the horrors and delights of egg sandwiches breaking out behind her and headed toward the dining room, which was deserted. She wondered about pushing open the swing door that she suspected led to the kitchen, and dared to give it a go. About to call out to gain the attention of someone, she paused, when she caught the sound of musical laughter from a woman, and then a man said, 'Oh come on, you're not going to let me go without at least a peck on the cheek, are you?'

Mavis paused, one foot already in the open doorway – something about the exchange struck her as being…intimate.

The woman's voice replied, 'My darling Dennis, you know I can't be seen so much as hugging you.'

Mavis froze.

Dennis replied, 'I know. But it's not fair. You've got to tell him. I've been here long enough now. It's not fair on me – nor you.'

Mavis jumped when Simon's voice came from behind her. 'Anything I can do to help, Mrs MacDonald?'

Mavis allowed the door to close and snapped, 'Thank you, I wondered where everyone had got to.' She knew as she spoke that she shouldn't have taken the poor young man's head off – it wasn't his fault that she felt so ridiculously…disappointed. She forced herself to modify her tone, then made the teatime requirements of the group on the terrace quite clear. She placed particular emphasis on the urgent need for at least two pots of tea, then took herself off to rejoin the three residents and Althea, whose conversation had progressed to questions regarding the pleasant, and unpleasant, effects of seeds in jams. Mavis wasn't sorry she'd missed the bulk of that one, but was still feeling a surprising amount of internal turmoil about what she'd overheard in the kitchen. She told herself to stop being so foolish.

'I was saying to Mavis just this morning,' said Althea as Mavis took her seat, 'that I think it's terribly sad that no one here knew any of Frances' friends beyond these walls. Though you knew her when you were young, Uma, you say you still didn't know any of her more current circle?'

Uma pursed her lips and drummed her fingers on the table. It got everyone's attention, which was, assumed Mavis, just what she wanted.

Uma spoke quietly, 'I know I told you that I used to work for a newspaper, and that I was the receptionist-cum-general secretary there. Well, what I didn't mention was that I would often help the journalists when they needed a bit of a hand. Especially the younger ones. Oh, don't get me wrong, I didn't ever write the articles, or go out to interview people or anything like that. But they used to talk through ideas they had for stories with me, and we'd work through how they could find out what they needed to know – who to talk to, that sort of thing. And then, of course, I'd end up offering to do a bit of research for them at my desk, and I'd pass it along, then off they'd go to get their story. Some of them were quite generous if the story got picked up by the nationals, you know?'

Sir Malcolm leaned forward. 'You've been hiding your light under a bushel, Uma. Did you ever help with any really big stories? You know, those scandalous exposés in the Sunday papers?'

Uma shook her head. 'Goodness me, no. We were a local newspaper, when such things still existed, and a lot of the stories were of specifically local interest. Anyway, what I wanted to say was: I know who you are, Mavis, and I think I can guess why you're here. Yes, I knew Frances many years ago, and when we met up again, here, she told me that she had worked at the Battersea Barracks for years. You were the matron there, at the same time. You must have known Frances Millington quite well. So why did you lie about that?'

Mavis felt her head getting hot. Her brain kicked into overdrive. 'Aye, well—'

Althea interrupted, 'Mavis is now a private investigator. Frances came to her company for help, and we came here to do some undercover digging around with Frances, but when we got here, she was dead. And we don't think that's a coincidence.'

All Mavis could manage was a curt: 'Thank you, Althea.' She was livid.

'Are you even a real dowager duchess?' Uma's question was asked gently.

Althea nodded. 'As real as they come. I was the seventeenth Duke of Chellingworth's second wife, taken to provide a spare. Managed that, and added a daughter, at no extra cost. I used to be a dancer. I met my Chelly at the stage door, and that was that. I loved him with all my heart, and he loved me back. We were so happy, and I miss him terribly.'

'And are you're really a private investigator, Mavis, like Althea said?' Siggy sounded suspicious.

Mavis gave in. 'Aye, I am that. The WISE Enquiries Agency. There's four of us. All fully trained, insured, and a proper company. We have an office at a converted barn on the Chellingworth Estate, and I'm Althea's housemate, at the Dower House.'

As Simon arrived with a dizzying array of pots, plates, cups, and saucers, the five tablemates sat staring at each other, silently.

When the group was finally alone again, Uma and Sir Malcolm both spoke at once, each then deferred to the other, with it being finally agreed that Mavis and Althea should answer Uma's questions first.

Seeming to realize she was speaking on behalf of all three residents, Uma said, 'Please tell us why Frances asked you to help her?'

Mavis explained the history between herself and Frances, confirming Uma's research, then explained the less than helpful meeting with Frances at the barn. She even went so far as to explain about the trip that she and Althea had made in the dead of night to Frances' room, the contents of the spreadsheets she'd printed out, and the missing laptop.

'I saw a laptop in the office behind reception,' noted Siggy. 'There's never been one there before. Do you think that might be hers?'

Mavis shrugged. 'Frances was Toni Conti's secretary, so the laptop might have always belonged to The Lavender, rather than to Frances herself. That could be the one missing from her room, aye.'

'We should take a look at it,' said Siggy in what Mavis felt was a surprisingly matter-of-fact tone. 'But I want to see those spreadsheets first. Uma is right, Frances and I bonded over puzzles. And I have been known to indulge my love of codes and cyphers on occasion, too. I might be able to understand what sort of system she was using, so we could make some sense of it all.'

Mavis turned to Siggy and said, 'Ach no, I cannae have that. Did you no' take in the bit about me being a hired professional? This is no' a time for the involvement of the public, thank you. Even Althea's here under my care, so I'll take this forward myself. There's no reason why I cannae ask Toni Conti to let me have a look at Frances' laptop.'

'Don't talk to Toni about it,' snapped Uma. Everyone stared at her. Pushing a few stray strands of hair back into her bun, she added, 'Frances was adamant about there being someone behind all the weirdness that goes on here. I heard Toni shouting at her, *shouting*, that she should stop her nonsense. Said it was making his wife ill. I don't think you should ask him to let you have a look at Frances' laptop.'

Sir Malcolm chipped in. 'Tell you what, I'll come up with a plan for us to get hold of the laptop. Male-only sortie, I think. Would oh-two-hundred hours suit, Siggy?'

Mavis was stunned. 'This is no' *Five Go Sleuthing at The Lavender*, Sir Malcolm. This is no' your problem.'

'It's more ours than yours,' noted Sir Malcolm with a sniff. 'We live here. *This* is our home. We are the community directly impacted by all this. You two will be out of the place before you know it.'

Siggy said, 'He has a point, Mavis. Toni, and The Lavender, has taken us all in and given us a place where we can just *be*. I realize it's early days in terms of us all getting to know each other, but can't you sense the bond that already exists between we residents, as opposed to those who just visit, then leave? We are, as Sir Malcolm said, a *de facto* community.'

Mavis retorted, 'For all that that might be true, Siggy, we are – well, I am – trained to investigate. I have the resources of a whole team back at the office to call upon.'

Siggy snapped, 'I'm sorry to have to say it, Mavis, but while you might be a professional investigator, you have no client. Frances Millington is dead, so no one's going to be paying you. This should be something *we* do. We're the ones being inconvenienced, after all.'

Uma agreed. 'Siggy's not wrong, Mavis. With Frances dead, you don't really have any reason, or right, to be in charge of an investigation. We, on the other hand, have every right to poke about into what's making our lives a misery. And…dare I say it…even into Frances' death. Which, I have to agree with you, seems suspiciously convenient, given that she'd just retained you to investigate everything that's been going on here.'

Althea nudged Mavis, quite hard. 'Go on, this is what you're good at. Let's work as a team, and make a plan.'

Mavis knew that Siggy and Uma had made valid points. She sighed. 'In some ways you're right; Frances will no' be paying our company to investigate. But I owe it to her memory to do what I can. I cannae just walk away. And let's not forget that I do have experience in this sort of thing, whereas you don't. But, if you're all offering to help, *while I lead*, then let's see who can do what.'

Uma said firmly, 'Online research, for me. I'm good at that. And I've been told I'm good on the telephone too – not everyone is, you know.'

Siggy added, 'Like I said – codes, patterns, that sort of thing. I'm also quite good at languages. And I might have a few other tricks up my sleeve, should the need arise.'

Sir Malcolm tapped the side of his nose. 'I'm good at shifting stuff, and knowing where to get hold of…well, almost anything, really.'

Althea nudged Mavis. Again. 'See? We've got intelligence gathering, communications and codes, plus logistics management. We even have a Quartermaster, like James Bond had his Q. What more could we want? We're a team, Mavis. But we're not the WISE women…we're…'

Uma squealed, 'The Lavender Mob, like that film with Alec Guinness in it. But we won't be stealing gold, we'll be finding out what happened to Frances. All for one…' She flung an arm skywards.

'I'm not sure that the Four Musketeers thing will work,' said Siggy sadly. 'Nice try, though, Uma. And I rather like The Lavender Mob. And on loan to The Lavender Mob are our two honorary helpers, Mavis and Althea.'

Mavis felt as though she were being undermined, just a little.

# CHAPTER SIXTEEN

Annie was sitting at the main bar in the Coach and Horses watching the man she loved having a lengthy discussion with a couple from St Ives about the relative merits of a Cornish pasty over a Welsh one, and quietly losing the will to live. She admired Tudor's patience and couldn't imagine how the couple in question – who *looked* perfectly normal – had managed to develop such strong opinions about a mixture of meat and vegetables wrapped in pastry. She could tell that Tudor was relieved when they, reluctantly, agreed they'd try a Welsh one to be going on with, but that they'd share it, so they could compare notes. If they found it to be acceptable, they might have another before they began their drive home, following what had – apparently – been a lovely day out at Chellingworth Hall.

As they took their seat at a table far from the bar itself, Annie whispered, 'Want me to inject a bit of my hot sauce into that pasty before you serve it to 'em, Tude?'

Tudor's back was shaking with silent laughter as he disappeared into the kitchen. Annie was glad she'd made him chuckle – he deserved it. The weight of the world had been on his shoulders for weeks, no months. But they were…getting there.

The Coach was a lovely pub, there was no question about that, and it deserved to have the new life breathed into it that the Twysts had given them the chance to do. In all honesty, it wasn't that different to the Lamb and Flag, but it was more grand, because it had been built as a proper coaching house: the main bar was larger; the snug to the side was much bigger; and the kitchen and cellars were able to accommodate the extra resources needed for what would have been – at one time – a great deal more customers than they'd attracted so far. And there were the guest rooms, of course. That was what both she and Tudor hoped would make a big difference to the business, once they were ready to be occupied.

The work that had been carried out to renovate the pub had been a great success, even though Annie had wondered, at the time, if it would ever be finished. Built over five hundred years earlier, the thick stone walls with small leaded windows cut into them were now freshly plastered and limewashed, the massive inglenook fireplace had been repointed, and the flagstone floor properly cleaned and repaired. All the furniture was new, though in keeping with the age of the place, and made at the workshops at Chellingworth Hall from local wind-toppled or necessarily felled trees. Annie liked the way that nothing matched: there were large and small round, square, and rectangular tables; the chairs were made from different woods and were different shapes; the upholstered pads on the wooden seats and settles used several different fabrics, which were all modern interpretations of traditional designs. Everything felt fresh and welcoming; contemporary, and yet sympathetic to the pub's historic roots. The washrooms were absolutely modern, and Annie was delighted that the ladies' had three cubicles, plus there was a unisex cubicle beside the stairs specifically designed to be accessible for wheelchair users. The gents' was…well, Tudor had overseen that, being better placed to have an opinion, and he said it was fancy, by local standards.

Annie was still settling into the flat upstairs, and Tudor was still settling into the pub. Aled, on the other hand, had taken to the Coach like a duck to water. Annie knew Aled, of course, but didn't know him well enough to be able to put her finger on why he seemed to be flourishing to the extent that he was. She had her suspicions, which revolved around the amount of time Joan Pike seemed to be spending at the pub. As she finished her G and T, she could see that Aled was washing some glasses behind the bar of the snug, where she wasn't able to talk to him easily, but she determined to find out what she could, when she could.

'So, how's The Case of the Roaming Gnome going?'

Annie turned to see Sharon just behind her. 'Hello Shar, how are you? Those flamingoes of yours haven't landed back in your garden by any chance, have they?'

Sharon chuckled. 'I wish. What's the case called now, by the way?'

Annie sighed. 'I've been a bit tied up with asking all and sundry about what they might have seen, so I haven't got a new name, yet.'

Sharon looked disappointed.

Annie offered, 'The Case of the Fleeing Flamingoes? Though that makes it sound like they've absconded, rather than having been nicked, doesn't it? Don't worry, I'll come up with something. But look, while you're here – and while Tude's out the back – I did want to ask you about something. Oh, there he is now. Don't let me stop you ordering a drink.'

Tudor smiled broadly at Sharon. 'What'll it be for you?'

'I'll have a vodka and tonic, please, Tudor,' replied Sharon. 'I've earned it today. Loads of deliveries, and I've spent ages marking up the things with short dates on them. Hopefully that'll clear some shelf space for me. I'm trying to get in more long-life stuff these days – tins and packets, you know? I've noticed there's been quite a drop in demand for my fresh sweet and savory snacks since Janet opened up the Lamb Tearooms. Have you seen a dip in your business, Tudor? I heard about the pasty debacle.'

'The what?' Tudor sounded puzzled.

Annie could have kicked herself – or Sharon. She hadn't told Tudor about her conversation with Janet Jackson regarding Paul Baker making pasties up at the Hall for Janet to sell at the Lamb. She knew she had to own up, but didn't want to have the conversation in front of Sharon.

'When Tudor's served you, and you're settled in one of our nice, new, comfy chairs over there, him and me are going to have a quick natter about pasties – then I'll be over to ask you that question. Okay?'

Tudor handed Sharon her change and she gazed at her glass with what Annie reckoned was more lust than thirst.

Sharon didn't even glance at Annie as she replied, 'Lovely. I don't mind admitting that I've been looking forward to this drink for about an hour, so I'll just pop myself in that corner until you've got a minute.'

As Tudor cast an experienced eye across his domain, searching out those who might be about to order something, Annie apologized for not having told him about the fact that Janet was selling savory snacks at the Lamb, and that she had claimed to know nothing about any agreement that she would do no such thing.

His measured response of: 'I dare say there's been a bit of a breakdown in communication,' surprised Annie; she wasn't used to him being so calm about anything that might endanger the pub's chances of attracting customers. Then he added, 'I'm more worried about there not being enough tables and chairs outside in the beer garden, nor the pergola they promised us, to give a bit of protection from the weather when it turns, which it's bound to do soon. I'm afraid we've missed the boat in terms of building a reputation for a pub with good outdoor facilities, to be honest with you. I know it's the time of year when we might expect fewer people to want to sit outside, but Bob Fernley promised they'd get going out there pronto. With that out there, and those heaters he promised, we could extend our season, which would be wonderful. But there's no sign of any movement on that front.'

'Do you think that's one of the things Alexander will be looking into, rather than Bob, going forward?' Annie wasn't really clear about how Christine's fiancé was getting involved in all the changes planned as part of the revitalization of the village, because Christine had been vague, at best.

Tudor shook his head. 'There's such a lot going on, all at the same time, that I'm not sure, to be honest. I think another meeting's needed, with Alexander and Bob, so everyone knows who's doing what.'

Annie agreed. 'I might have another G and T to take over so I can have a catch-up with Sharon. But go light on the gin, eh? I need a clear head.'

Tudor chuckled. 'No problem – can't have you drinking all our profits, can we?'

Annie grabbed her glass and settled herself beside Sharon, who was staring into the inglenook fireplace as though it held the answers to all of life's mysteries.

'I wanted to ask you about dogs,' began Annie.

'Haven't got any, as you know. Not really going to work with the shop and everything, is it? Mind you, a dog would be a bit of company for me. I seem to spend all my evenings alone, nowadays. Since Mum...you know...left.'

Choosing to sidestep the knotty topic of the reasons behind Sharon's mother choosing to move away, Annie dared to say, 'Gert and Rosie are good company, I have to admit, but they're a responsibility, too. Still, at least with the two of them, they've got each other, so we don't mind leaving them up in the flat at times like this.'

Sharon didn't reply immediately, but Annie noticed she kept glancing across to the bar. She wondered for a moment if Sharon was keeping an eye on Tudor, then, when she saw the young woman sit up a bit straighter, the penny dropped. Sharon had been on the lookout for Aled, who'd just popped in from the snug to grab a couple of bottled tomato juices.

Annie's mind whirred. Aled and Joan? Aled and Sharon? Oh heck, Annie admitted to herself she'd never really considered Aled's situation, romantically speaking; she'd always thought of him as a boy. But, no, he wasn't – he had to be in his late twenties, about the same as both Joan and Sharon.

She asked, 'Do you prefer this bar to the snug, Sharon? Is it a bit too quiet in there for you?' With the lack of a 'crowd' in either area, Annie couldn't come up with a better way to ask Sharon a rather pointed question.

'Better company in here,' replied Sharon, suddenly smiling, and becoming quite animated.

*And Joan's in the snug*, thought Annie. 'Glad to be of service,' quipped Annie, deciding she wouldn't press any personal matters. 'So, about them dogs. You mentioned hearing dogs barking in the night, and Janet Jackson at the Lamb did too. I know she's new, so not really used to the way sound travels around the village, but did you really think it was Gert and Rosie doing the barking? You know what I mean…did it sound like them?'

Sharon laughed loudly, as though Annie had told a hilarious joke, then knocked back her drink, taking Annie by surprise. She announced, 'Let me have a think while I get another one of these,' then she was out of her seat like a shot and managed to cross the pub to the bar quicker than Annie had ever seen her move, where she asked Aled to refresh her drink.

As Annie watched, all the signs were there: Sharon kept touching her hair and face as she spoke to him, and while she wasn't quite fluttering her lashes, she was certainly making lots of movements with her head that made her appear coquettish, to say the least. And Aled was all smiles, too.

*A love triangle, in Anwen-by-Wye?* Annie laughed at herself as the thought flitted across her mind. *Focus on the job, Annie. Ask again about the dogs when she gets back...if she gets back.*

Aled was called to the snug bar, and Sharon brought her drink back to the table – eventually. 'Them dogs barking?' Annie prompted.

Sharon was looking a bit sullen. 'I don't know, Annie,' she snapped, 'I don't know what your dogs sound like, do I? They're dogs. Don't they all sound the same?'

Annie was tempted to try to explain how very differently Gertie and Rosie barked, or made any noise, really, but decided she'd probably be wasting her time trying to explain something like that to someone who'd never had dogs.

'They sound different to their humans, Shar, but I can't say more than that. It's just that neither Tude nor I heard them making any noise on either of the nights in question, and we've agreed that if one of them was making that much of a fuss – so much so that you and Janet would notice it – one of us would have heard them, too. Which is a puzzle, see?'

Sharon gulped down half her drink. 'If you say so. But what's that got to do with Fliss and Felix being stolen?'

Annie felt Sharon was far too distracted for her to make any headway with the matter, so replied, 'You're right, it's probably nothing. Dogs barking around here? Nothing unusual in that, really. But I am on it, Shar, really I am. Got feelers out all over the place, I have.'

She didn't, because she didn't actually have a clue about who to ask what when it came to locating a missing garden gnome and two flamingoes, but she wanted Marjorie and Sharon to know that, even if there was little she could do beyond asking folks if they'd seen or heard anything out of the ordinary, at least she was doing that much...in fact she'd already done it twice.

'Sometimes, I miss Cardiff,' said Sharon, out of the blue. 'Wendy Jenkins went down there a couple of days ago to see some friends, but I'm tied to the shop.'

Annie tried to lift her spirits. 'I bet Marjorie would look after the place for half a day if you wanted to sneak off, wouldn't she?'

Sharon chuckled. 'Yes, like a shot. But I didn't keep in touch with my chums there when I left, so all I know now is what's on social media...and they've all moved on. Proper boyfriends, fiancés, husbands, even children. Me? No change. Just the shop.'

Annie suspected a relationship-advice rabbit hole was about to appear at her feet, so was strangely relieved to see Janet Jackson come into the pub – with a man Annie had never seen before.

Janet had swapped her retro-style tearoom uniform for a retro-style lightweight dress, that harkened back to the 1950s, though Annie could see it was a modern take on the period. The man with her was tall and slim, wearing ripped jeans and a slightly baggy golf shirt, sporting a suspiciously black, glossy quiff, and unnaturally white teeth. He reminded Annie of...an off-duty Elvis impersonator.

She couldn't resist whispering, 'They're quite the couple. Who's that with Janet?'

Sharon looked around. 'That's Paul Baker. The new bloke up at Chellingworth Hall. Did you say "couple"? She's a bit old for him, don't you think?'

The lighting in the pub wasn't exactly dim, but it also wasn't stark, so Annie didn't get a proper look at Paul until he was walking past her toward the bar. Sharon was right; he seemed to be in his late thirties, or early forties, whereas Annie had put Janet in her fifties, though maybe the style of her hairdo and frocks were a bit ageing.

'Toy boy?' Annie winked and grinned at Sharon, then realized she might be putting a thought into the well-known gossip's head that she shouldn't.

All Sharon said was, 'Typical.'

Annie wasn't sure how to take that.

Janet twiddled her fingers in acknowledgement as she approached Annie and Sharon, then said, 'Hello you two. Mind if we join you?'

Annie welcomed the chance to chat a bit more about the sounds of dogs in the night, and reckoned she might be able to help out a bit with The Case of the Battling Baker, if only she could get something out of Paul about how things were going with Cook Davies up at the Hall.

She and her colleagues were proud of the fact that the WISE women always worked as a team, so whatever she might glean could be fed back to Carol and Christine, who could make of it what they would.

And so it went. Half an hour later, Annie was enjoying her third drink of the evening – her limit – as was Sharon, while Janet and Paul nattered on about how they were both settling in.

'Did you two know each other before you came to the area?' Annie had to ask.

'In passing,' said Paul, rather circumspectly thought Annie.

Sharon asked, 'What does that mean?'

Annie reckoned Sharon wasn't as used to three drinks in an evening as she was.

Janet replied airily, 'I ran a teashop at a garden center near Prestatyn – which isn't a million miles from Liverpool, nor Wrexham. Paul's company was one of our suppliers.'

Annie pounced. 'You had your own company, Paul?'

Paul did a little fidgety thing with his shoulders that gave Annie the impression he was trying to wriggle out of giving a straight answer. 'It wasn't just mine, there were a few of us involved. But I was the one with the baking experience. I left the business side of things to the others.'

'That'll teach you,' said Janet, which Annie saw made Paul flinch.

'Water under the bridge,' he replied, then he gave his attention to his drink.

Annie asked about the dog-barking that Janet had heard, and went around the houses in much the same way she had done with Sharon.

Sharon explained about her sad loss of Fliss and Felix, and both Janet and Paul expressed their concern.

Paul asked, 'Kids, you reckon?'

Annie was watching him carefully, and, to her eyes, Paul Baker seemed to be a perfectly pleasant man, and not the sort to go stealing anyone's currants, or supply of desiccated coconut, though – as Annie reminded herself – you never could tell what a person might do, under certain circumstances.

'There aren't that many kids in the village these days,' said Sharon thoughtfully. 'Those two Hughes boys have had their moments – but it wouldn't be them.' She and Annie had already agreed that Sarah Hughes's sons would not have taken Sharon's flamingoes – under threat of a massive backlash from their parents, involving access to their gaming set-ups, the most powerful deterrent possible, in their cases.

'Someone might have been passing through and took a fancy to them,' suggested Paul.

'They definitely went overnight,' said Sharon. 'However much they mean to me, I can't see someone who's been here on a day trip being bothered to come into my back garden in the dead of night to swipe Fliss and Felix. Besides, they were in my *back* garden, so no one passing through the village would even know they were there.'

'That's a good point,' said Janet. 'So…who would know of their existence?'

'Anyone who's been in my kitchen at any point over the past year or so,' said Sharon. 'Mam looked after the shop for me when I went away to Cyprus. That'll be –' she counted her fingers – 'sixteen months ago next week.' She sighed. 'I haven't had a proper break since then.' The slice of lemon in her glass hit her on the nose as she tried to drain the last dregs of her drink. 'And on that joyful note, I'm going home. Just as well I can walk from here, eh?'

Paul leapt to his feet. 'May I walk you across the green?'

Sharon looked amazed. 'That's very gentlemanly of you. But won't Janet's nose be put out of joint if you do that?'

Janet raised her glass. 'Nothing to do with me,' she said, and winked at Sharon.

'Ta, then. Yes,' replied Sharon. She then proceeded to make what Annie judged to be far too much of a fuss of loudly saying goodnight to Tudor at the bar – *maybe so Aled would overhear her?* – before she and Paul Baker left.

Annie observed, 'Paul's left a lot in that glass of his.' She knew he'd ordered one of the costliest Scotches Tudor kept.

'He'll be back soon. It's not far to the shop and back, is it?' Janet's tone was...hard-edged.

'I suppose not. So, tell me, Janet, why Anwen-by-Wye?' Annie had wondered that since she'd met the woman.

Janet stared at Annie for a moment then replied, 'Divorce is a messy business, Annie, and sometimes all you want to do is never see anything that can remind you of times past. Sometimes a fresh start is necessary, even if it's not what you want.'

'I thought you were widowed.' It was out of Annie's mouth before she could stop it.

Janet chuckled harshly. 'I wish! I don't know who's been spreading that story, but it's not true. And that's all I want to say about that.'

Later, as Annie and Tudor walked Rosie and Gertie around the green, with the pub safely locked up for the night, she recounted her evening's conversations, and asked questions – more of herself than of Tudor.

Tudor responded thoughtfully, as he waited patiently for Rosie to sniff out the perfect spot. 'So you reckon there's all this relationship stuff going on in the village, do you? Aled, Joan, and Sharon – and maybe Janet and Paul, or even Paul and Sharon? It sounds like something you'd see on the telly...though not the sort of thing I'd choose to be watching.'

'You must have seen it all over the years, from behind a number of bars, Tude,' observed Annie.

'You're right, there's not much I haven't seen – but Anwen's not the sort of place for all this sort of business. Are you sure you haven't picked up some sort of bug from Sharon? The gossip bug?'

Annie sighed. 'It's easy to go down that route, innit? So let's focus on work – all I got out of my time with that lot was that I can't honestly imagine Paul Baker swiping anything from Cook Davies's pantry. And I still can't imagine who'd be nicking garden ornaments...unless some sort of weird kleptomaniac is secretly walking a dog that barks a lot in the village in the small hours.'

Tudor laughed and gave Annie the hug she'd been hoping for. 'Let's get these two home, and get you a good night's sleep, eh? I bet you'll be much more positive in the morning.'

'I hope so.'

# 7<sup>th</sup> SEPTEMBER

# CHAPTER SEVENTEEN

Mavis momentarily felt a sense of *déjà vu* as she peeped out of her room into the dark corridor, then told herself she felt that way because she had, in fact, done exactly the same thing not twenty-four hours earlier. On this occasion, however, her target wasn't the room of the late Frances Millington, but a certain laptop in the office that was located behind the reception desk at The Lavender.

She'd made Althea promise that – under no circumstances – would she try to get involved in the sortie at all, and Mavis believed – hoped – she'd keep her word. But, unnervingly, as she crept along the corridor toward the stairs, Mavis felt someone was lurking in the darkness. However, though she listened and peered, she couldn't hear or see anyone. Once she reached the main reception area, she paused again; no, that wasn't breathing but there was…a presence.

Shaking her head, Mavis told herself to focus on the task at hand: find Frances Millington's laptop. She tried the handle of the door to the office and found it was locked, which didn't surprise her. Unfortunately, there was no handy-dandy key emblazoned with the word OFFICE hanging on the rack on the wall, though there was a bunch of keys labelled MASTERS, which confounded any concept of 'security' she had. Pushing aside her misgivings on that point, Mavis grabbed the keys with gratitude and tried several before finding one that unlocked the office door.

She silently thanked the person responsible for ensuring that the doors at The Lavender didn't squeak or groan when they opened, then stepped into the office and locked the door behind her, popping the bunch of keys into her pocket.

There were no windows in the office, so she turned on her phone's torch app and waved it around, trying to spot the laptop. Nothing. She checked the desk drawers – all of which were unlocked – and found a laptop tucked away in the largest one. She popped it onto the desk, opened it up and turned it on. When the thing came to life, she was surprised to see a familiar sight as the screen saver: a corridor with the personal cubicles known as 'Beddings' along one side, and tall windows along the other. The place had been part of her daily life for years at the Battersea Barracks.

As she stared at it, Mavis realized how important that building had been to her; she'd worked there for a good time, and she'd rarely known anywhere to have such an aura of certainty about it. Did she miss being a matron, especially in such a wonderful building? Yes, and no. Mavis smiled to herself. She was happy now, that was what mattered, and she was trying to help a woman – or at least respect the wishes of a now-deceased woman – who, back then, had helped make her own life run more smoothly.

Mavis was irritated beyond belief to discover that facial recognition was being used to secure the laptop's access. She angled the screen to see if there might be any clues to another means of getting into its contents when the thing opened up, all of its own accord, surprising Mavis so greatly that she heard herself gasp.

'It's because you look so very much like Frances,' whispered a voice behind Mavis in the darkness.

Mavis shot out of the chair and spun around, shining her torch into the face of…Siggy.

'How did you get in?' Mavis whispered as quietly as her fright and annoyance would allow. She felt the lump in her pocket. 'I have the keys with me.'

Siggy shielded his eyes with one hand. In the other he held up a slim, metallic instrument. 'Old habits,' he whispered, and she could see him grin, wickedly.

'So we'll add lock-picking to your abilities with codes and languages, shall we? That must have been a very interesting "low-level administration job" you did for the Foreign Office, Siggy. Maybe you'll tell me all about it, one day.'

'I've been asked to do much the same by people utilizing some exceptionally persuasive techniques, Mavis, and didn't divulge anything. But, you never know, maybe one day we'll have the time to swap old war stories. But now? Business. Have you brought something so you can download whatever's on that thing? Or were you thinking of taking it back to your room?'

Mavis held up a small but powerful external hard drive. 'I travel prepared,' she said, then added, 'take a pew, or have a hunt about for anything you might think could help with our investigation while I do this. I dare say I can trust you to leave no sign of your search.'

'No one ever knows I've been,' whispered Siggy enigmatically.

Mavis returned her attention to the laptop and busied herself transferring its contents to her portable drive. As she did so, she told herself off for having become so lost in reverie that she'd not heard Siggy pick the lock, nor even enter the room; she needed to be better at keeping up her guard than that. The downloading icon told her she'd have a wait of five minutes, then ten seconds, then four minutes, then ninety seconds – she lost her patience with it and turned her attention to the papers on the desk in front of her, allowing Siggy to deal with the rest of the room.

Invoices from suppliers were piled on the right, invoices to guests on the left. It was a simple system, but appeared to rely upon paper records, which she found odd, until she told herself she shouldn't be that surprised, because everything at The Lavender seemed out of step with modern times. A creak above the office made Mavis pause.

Another creak – heavier this time. *Someone getting out of bed?* She pictured the floor plan of the place in her mind's eye: above the office would be…the landing of the floor above, not a room.

Siggy whispered, 'I wonder if we made that much racket as we each crept along the corridor to the top of the stairs. Sounds like a baby elephant up there.'

Mavis hoped it wasn't Althea, but suspected the dowager didn't have enough heft to make such loud creaking sounds. 'Would a tiled and carpeted floor really make that much noise, even with a baby elephant on it?'

Siggy replied, 'Good point. No, it wouldn't. And that's what's above us, isn't it?'

Mavis replied, 'By my reckoning, aye.'

Siggy asked, 'Find anything?'

'A method of record-keeping which suggests that no one here likes to rely upon just computer records,' replied Mavis. 'You?'

'Only this, which is odd, rather than remarkable, I'd have said.' Siggy held out a brochure for a small bungalow being offered for sale by an estate agency with an office on the edge of Tenby. 'I can't see Maria and Toni Conti leaving this place for something like that.'

'Does anyone else use this office?'

Siggy was close enough for Mavis to see him nodding. 'The actual receptionist. She's been off since Frances died. Name of Pippa. Pippa Thomas. Nice enough. Yes, this might be something she'd be interested in – small, and inexpensive. I seem to recall her saying something about sharing a home with a sister before she moved in here, though maybe I'm misremembering.'

'I cannae imagine that's something you do a lot of, Siggy. Memory like a steel trap, I reckon.'

Siggy sighed. 'Once upon a time, dear lady. But no more, I'm afraid. Another side-effect of this blessed…condition of mine.'

Mavis's curiosity kicked in. 'A head injury?' She wondered if he'd say anything.

Another sigh. 'Since we're alone, and I trust your ability to be utterly discreet, no one's certain what's happened to me. I was in…another country…doing a bit of work, and those of us with desks at the same office came down with a wide range of seemingly unrelated symptoms, all at roughly the same time. None of us are able to function, professionally, any longer. Very sadly, one colleague of mine was impacted so adversely that he found it impossible to continue living the simplest of lives. He died by his own hand approximately eighteen months ago. All those of us who'd worked in that building, at that time, met up at his funeral; not one of us has received a satisfactory diagnosis, and we've all come to terms with our unique sets of symptoms as best we can. It's not something I can say more about, other than to add that there is, apparently, nothing anyone can do about any of it. At least, not that I'm aware.'

'Like those people in Cuba? That sort of thing?' Mavis had heard news stories about people suffering a range of distressing symptoms after what several governments had claimed – publicly, at least – might have been some sort of microwave, or soundwave, attack.

Siggy chuckled bleakly. 'It seems that you, too, retain information you've heard along the way, Mavis. Come on, let's get out of here. Don't want to push our luck, do we? Have you got everything off that?'

Mavis checked the icon. 'Yes, there it's finished.' She uncoupled the devices, turned off the laptop, and replaced it where she'd found it. 'Ready when you are.'

Mavis locked the door behind them, replaced the bunch of keys, and the pair set off upstairs. They didn't speak, until Siggy whispered close to Mavis's ear, 'That creaking wasn't coming from our floor – listen.' They continued climbing the stone staircase and, as soon as they got to their floor, they paused on the landing, close to where Althea had collided with the pot of orchids the previous night. Mavis caught the sound of a loud creak that seemed to be coming from the area close to the lift.

Siggy said, 'Incoming, Mavis. I apologize in advance for what I'm about to do, but needs must – cover story. Play your part, old girl.' He grabbed her in a firm embrace, pulled her bodily toward him, turned her head, and kissed her firmly on the cheek.

A voice seemed to boom out in the darkness. 'Siggy, is that you? And …Mrs MacDonald?'

Mavis felt herself being released, and she was able to turn to see Toni Conti, his mouth open, standing just a foot or two away. It seemed he'd exited the door she'd seen him pop out of when the orchid pot had smashed.

She gushed, 'Oh, Siggy, it's Mr Conti – whatever will he think?'

Siggy followed her lead and replied, 'I dare say that he'll be correct in his assumptions. But we're adults, Mavis, and Toni's a man of discretion, aren't you, Toni?'

Mavis suspected Toni's shifting of his weight from one slippered foot to another, and his unnecessary retightening of the cord of his dressing gown, meant he might also be blushing in the darkness.

He blustered, 'Well, I suppose so. I mean, none of us are children, are we? Though…in the corridor? Well, I dare say you'll both be heading back to your rooms…or, you know…wherever…um. Yes. Good night then.'

He turned on his heel and disappeared through the door – from which there then came a series of incredibly loud creaking noises.

Siggy whispered, 'That's what we heard downstairs, Mavis. Someone was either coming down, or going up, that staircase when we were in the office.' He stopped whispering when a gale of laughter could be heard from the floor above.

'Sounds like Toni's told his wife a really good joke. Probably about us,' observed Mavis. 'A convincing performance on your part, Siggy. Thank you for the warning, and for turning my head so you caught my cheek. Though I dare say I could have done without the "old girl" bit.'

'My apologies for that, and…my pleasure, Mavis.'

Mavis couldn't be sure exactly what Siggy meant. 'I'll get some work done on what I've got from the laptop, and report back in the morning.'

'I'd suggest that some sleep would do you, and – in the long run – the memory of Miss Millington a great deal more good. I look forward to breakfasting with you and Althea.'

Siggy reached for Mavis's hand, and she was so taken aback that she allowed him to kiss it, before he turned and headed along the corridor to his room in the wing that mirrored her own.

# CHAPTER EIGHTEEN

Henry was at a loss: his son was wailing; he feared that his wife was on the verge of pulling out her hair; and he was sitting at the breakfast table having a conversation with his butler that he could hardly believe.

'I don't understand,' he said, for what he suspected was the fifth time. 'One cannot lose that many kippers and there not be something fishy going on. And, no, I don't mean it in that way, Edward. Does Cook Davies have no explanation?'

'I regret to say she has only suspicions, which point in the direction Your Graces might imagine.'

Stephanie said bleakly, 'Cook believes that Paul Baker has stolen all the kippers?'

'Possibly moved them to a location where they cannot be immediately found.' Edward was trying to be helpful.

Henry was glad that Stephanie seemed to be rallying. 'Tell Cook we'll be happy to have an alternative – anything that can be managed. We'll start on the toast she kindly sent, won't we, Henry?'

'Toast is fine – to start with,' replied Henry sadly. He'd been rather looking forward to his kippers.

'Indeed, Your Grace. There was talk of sausages and bacon.'

'With eggs, that would be most acceptable,' said Henry quickly, his mouth moistening at the thought. 'Yes, most acceptable. Thank you, Edward.'

'Your Grace.'

With Edward gone, Henry dared, 'This situation in the kitchen seems to be gathering a dangerous momentum, my dear. Do we have any news that might help alleviate matters?'

Stephanie seemed terribly down. 'Carol has yet to report to me, and Christine made a suggestion that I haven't yet taken up.'

'That being?'

'She thought that an outsider might mediate between Paul and Cook. She suggested Val Jenkins. I thought it might work, but – of course – I wanted to consult with you, dear.'

Henry gave the idea some thought as he slathered glistening salt butter onto a triangle of toast. 'Val's a good choice. She's not just Hugo's godmother, but she has a well-deserved reputation as a woman who knows her foodstuffs – and she certainly understands how kitchens work. She was *The Curious Cook* on television, after all, and she's talked to all sorts of…foodie people. Yes, I'd say that's a good plan. She's an outsider who'd be respected by both a baker and a cook. Even Cook Davies, I'd have thought. But you've not approached her about this?'

'Not yet. I hesitated to get yet another person involved in what seems to be a matter that I, with a responsibility for the household, should be able to manage on my own. I've been so involved with the village revitalization business that I've taken my eye off the ball right here, in our home. Please forgive me?'

Henry was perplexed. 'You feel you've let me down in some way?'

Stephanie nodded, her eyes filling with tears.

Henry abandoned his toast and pulled a handkerchief from his pocket. 'My darling, please don't cry.' Henry never knew how to deal with a woman who was crying; it flummoxed him. 'You could never let me down. You are the reason my life is as wonderful as it is. I would rather lose Cook Davies than have you upset – and I think you know how both I, and my waistline, feel about Cook Davies and her abilities.'

Henry's heart soared when he saw a smile on Stephanie's face as she said, 'Thank you, dear. That means a great deal. But I hope things won't go that far. I'll phone Val after breakfast; maybe she could pop over today. And we might hear something from Carol about Paul later on, too.'

'I hope so,' agreed Henry, returning his attention to his buttered toast, upon which he heaped blackcurrant jam. *Oh, bliss.*

When Edward returned with a server and a variety of chafing dishes, he made sure that everything was as it should be, then approached Henry. 'Cook Davies asked me to deliver these…sheets.'

Henry looked at what his butler had handed him: scraps of paper, some stained with grease and other traces of indeterminate substances, had been scribbled upon. 'Thank you Edward. We'll see to ourselves.'

Henry passed the notes to his wife then headed to the food on the sideboard. 'I'll sort out a plate for you, but I think those notes are more up your street, than mine. I know you asked Cook to keep details of what she believed Paul Baker had been getting up to, and I suspect that's a list of all her grievances. Do you want mushrooms? They weren't mentioned, but have arrived.'

Uncharacteristically for his wife, she replied with a firm, 'I'll have a bit of everything, and two sausages, please, Henry. I need my strength for today. Forget my hips, I want a big breakfast.'

Henry was a little concerned about whether there'd be enough left for him; while they ate well, Stephanie had laid down the law about preparing too much food for meals – she hated waste. Which meant that if his wife had two sausages that would only leave two for him. *Ah well, anything to keep her happy.*

He delivered his beloved wife's plate with a flourish.

Stephanie completely ignored him, but said, 'This is most definitely getting out of hand, Henry. This is quite a list. Cook Davies is suggesting that Paul Baker has – and I quote – stolen kippers, which we know about, of course; has trimmed the rosemary and thyme that grow outside the kitchen door to a point that will endanger the plants' wellbeing; has "done something" to her eggs to make several of them go bad long before they should, and these are the eggs which are brought in fresh every day from our own chickens, by the way; and that he's "salted her unsalted butter", which, I have to say, sounds both a complicated and vindictive thing to do.'

'I say, it does rather,' agreed Henry, mounding his plate with all the remaining breakfast food. *Yes, just enough of everything, except sausages.*

Stephanie's phone pinged just as Henry retook his seat. He attacked his food with gusto, though he listened when she said, 'Carol wants me to phone her – she has news.'

'But we're eating.'

Stephanie's glare spoke volumes. She dialed immediately. 'Hello, Carol, it's Stephanie. We're in the middle of breakfast, but I'm keen to know what you've found out. Would you mind awfully if I put you on speakerphone and continued to eat while things are hot?'

Stephanie did so, so Henry assumed Carol had agreed.

'I won't keep you long,' said Carol, her voice sounding a little tinny. 'I thought you'd like to know that Paul Baker's references are all above board, though there's a gap between employers and I've found out why. He and two partners ran a company called *Sweet Everythings* for a couple of years. From what I've gathered, they specialized in highly decorated cakes for special occasions – you know, weddings, birthdays that sort of thing – as well as supplying retail outlets with a variety of cakes, pastries, buns, and bread products. The photographs going back a couple of years on their social media feeds show some spectacular cake designs, though I understand they were the work of someone, or several someones, other than Paul, who were never named. The business ran into financial difficulties and appears, according to comments made by creditors, to owe rather a lot of money to a great number of people.'

Stephanie asked, 'Did this all happen long before Paul joined us?'

'The company stopped doing business about nine months ago. Since then, Paul has been – as his references claimed – the head baker at a shop in Liverpool specializing in breads that use ancient grains, gluten-free recipes – the sort of items sold through niche outlets. They were extremely happy with his performance there, hence the glowing reference. However...'

Henry suspected that Stephanie's neglected food was probably getting cold as she stared at her phone on the table.

'Go on,' she urged.

Carol did. 'Paul's left the world of social media behind him, and I can see why. One of his ex-business partners has made some dreadfully personal comments about him where they can be read by the public. And he's even gone so far as to suggest that the failure of the business was due to Paul's inability to put in a full day's work on a regular basis – meaning that customers were let down. The man in question has openly threatened revenge on Paul Baker.'

Henry thought that Stephanie seemed much more interested in Carol's news than in the sausage languishing on her plate. He wondered if she might be too full to eat it.

His wife snapped, 'Oh, I say, Carol – do you think that someone else…like that man…could be doing the things that Cook Davies has claimed are being done by Paul himself, in order to undermine Paul?'

Carol's voice was drowned out for a moment by a child's scream, to which she responded with, 'Just a tick, Albert, good boy.' Then: 'Stephanie – that was my thought exactly. But the problem is – if someone else *is* doing these things, then how on earth are they getting into the Hall to do them? Can we talk – maybe a bit later, about your security arrangements there. Again. You see…access to the kitchens might be the crux of the matter.'

Henry was glad when Stephanie and Carol wound up their conversation by agreeing the matter needed some thought, and another chat later, then he watched – with a degree of disappointment – as his wife stabbed at her remaining sausage without mercy, and made short work of it.

It was a disappointing end to what had been a uniquely odd start to the day. Henry just hoped that normality would return sooner rather than later, and that, maybe, someone would track down those blessed kippers.

# CHAPTER NINETEEN

Mavis had hardly slept at all following her sortie to the office behind the reception desk, so it wasn't until Althea asked her a question as they were going in for breakfast that she really paid attention to the dowager.

The dowager hissed dramatically, 'Is that the Pippa Thomas The Lavender Mob were talking about? She's a...striking looking girl, wouldn't you say?'

Mavis looked toward reception and had to agree with Althea. The person standing behind the large desk was probably in her early thirties, with an unruly mass of long, copper curls exploding above and around a pinched, pallid face, and a figure that put Mavis in mind of a young Twiggy.

Mavis nodded. 'Striking? Aye. I wonder if she's always that pale, or if she's still no' feeling too bonnie.'

Taking their seats at 'their' table, Simon enquired about tea or coffee, then vanished, returning with two pots.

Althea smiled graciously as Sir Malcolm Lee entered the dining room wearing an entirely khaki ensemble. He took her greeting as a sign to join them, whereupon the trio exchanged pleasantries. Simon arrived with a cafetière for Sir Malcolm, without asking what was required.

Althea had barely begun her morning witterings before Uma Chatterjee joined them. Mavis thought she looked as fresh as the proverbial daisy in a lemon and white two-piece. When Simon arrived with a small pot of fragrant tea, it became clear to Mavis that the residents at The Lavender were used to at least their breakfast needs being known, and supplied, by the attentive staff.

Eventually Siggy Welbeck sauntered in. He looked haggard to the point that Mavis thought she should enquire after his wellbeing, which elicited a response from him that was curt enough to suggest she had overstepped some invisible mark.

'Sherries all round, or will it be just tea and coffee this morning?' Simon smiled wickedly as he brought another cafetière for Siggy.

'Just all this for now,' replied Althea airily. 'We'll get to the good stuff after we've lined our tummies, thank you, Simon.' When the server had left, Althea stared dreamily out of the window. 'He reminds me somewhat of a partner I once had, when I was a dancer on the West End stage.'

'You've lived an interesting life, I'd wager,' noted Siggy.

'Not as interesting as yours, I shouldn't think,' was Althea's enigmatic reply.

Siggy threw Mavis a questioning look, and she shook her head only slightly, to indicate she'd not shared his confidences with the dowager. To divert what she feared might be further inappropriate questions of Siggy by Althea, she asked, 'Shall we wait until we've been served our food to discuss any findings we might have come up with?'

General agreement was followed by small talk centering upon the fine weather, the amazingly good state of the flowering beds, and the quality of the light on the sea that morning – which allowed for racks of toast, and a couple of hearty breakfasts, to be delivered.

As Mavis crunched her toast, Siggy announced, 'I broke the so-called "code" that Frances used on those spreadsheets.'

Mavis was impressed, and said so.

Siggy demurred, 'It was easy for me, because I live here and witnessed most of the incidences of inconvenience she noted, and I'd also noted in my own diary what had happened on a few occasions. Once I was able to match up a few dates and times, it became evident she was using the first letter of the Latin word for her interpretation of the incident. For example, if there was an electrical fault she used an F, for *fulgur*, meaning lightning. For water problems, an A for *aqua*, and so on.'

Althea asked, 'What on earth did she use when the Wi-Fi went down? I can't imagine the Romans had a word for that.'

Siggy grinned. 'Good question, Althea. "Wi-Fi" is short for "wireless fidelity" and fidelity is rooted in the Latin *fidelis*. She used an F, preceded by a W – to differentiate from electrical problems.'

Mavis acknowledged, 'Frances was always good with medical terminology, and a great deal of that is from either the Latin, or the

Greek. A clever woman. And an excellent record keeper. Which is good for us. Was there anything else you found in those spreadsheets that was of interest, Siggy?'

Siggy leaned back and said quietly, 'Indeed there was. There was a period of about a week when there wasn't a single incident. Frances had noted the following about that week: Pippa Thomas, our receptionist, was away on holiday; Dennis Moore, our gardener, was off ill with a virus of some sort; and our host, the delightful Mr Conti, and his wife, had gone to visit a relative of his in the Swansea Valleys.'

'How long has Dennis been here?' Althea leaned forward as she threw out the question.

'Longer than any of us, I believe,' replied Sir Malcolm. Uma and Siggy nodded their agreement.

'And Pippa?' Mavis thought she'd follow through.

'Only about six months,' replied Siggy, sounding somber.

'Tell us about the dates in Frances' spreadsheets.' Uma also leaned in.

'They begin a little less than five months ago,' replied Siggy.

'That's interesting,' noted Sir Malcolm.

Mavis nodded. 'It is, indeed. And there was something I found in a note that Frances made on her laptop which related to Pippa, too.' She waited until Althea had stopped crunching before she continued. 'It would appear that Frances had managed to get hold of Pippa's references, which had been supplied to Toni Conti prior to her arrival. The references were no' on the laptop, but Frances had scribbled a note entitled PIPPA on a piece of paper, and had saved a photograph of the note, which turned out to be a very good thing, because the only folder accessible via her laptop was the one with her photos in it.'

'There are no documents on it at all relating to The Lavender?' Sir Malcolm sounded as surprised as Mavis herself had been when she'd discovered the fact.

'Someone must have cleaned everything else off it,' hissed Uma.

'They also deleted the photos,' replied Mavis, 'but they were in Frances' personal cloud, which was accessible via the laptop. I can only imagine she didnae store her other documents there, only her photos.'

Uma smiled. 'I do the same. My photos take up tons of space.'

Sir Malcolm looked surprised. 'Photographs?'

Uma smiled coyly. 'I just snap, always have. And I invested in a good phone with an excellent camera.'

'Interesting. I, too, enjoy fiddling about with photos on my phone,' said Sir Malcolm.

Siggy sounded overly patient to Mavis's ear when he asked, 'What did the note titled PIPPA say, Mavis?'

Mavis nodded, and kept her voice low. 'There was a list of addresses, some of which were hotels, and several of the places listed also appeared in Frances' photographs. There was also the name Dyggan Sales and Rentals. A quick internet search tells me that company is an estate agency, located on the outskirts of Tenby. Their website is full of, as one might imagine, lots of flats, houses, and cottages for sale. But it also suggests they're involved in the short-term lettings business, as well as the more traditional sales I mentioned, and long-term rentals.'

'What's "short-term lettings"?' Mavis noticed that Althea had jam on three of her fingers as she waved them in the air.

'It's what's ripping the heart and soul out of the seaside towns, and villages, of Britain.' Toni Conti was hovering just out of sight behind Simon, who was adjusting some chairs, and his angry voice carried across the now-deserted dining room.

Althea dropped her toast, and Toni had everyone's attention as he approached the table. He added forcefully, 'Bloodsuckers and leeches, the lot of them. They're turning communities into shells during the week, then into places that are overrun by marauding groups of drunken louts at the weekends.'

Althea shrugged. 'Oh, you mean bed and breakfasts. Gosh, I did have some rather splendid times at several B and Bs over the years. Especially when I appeared in panto in Brighton one winter, I recall.'

Mavis wondered why on earth Althea was wittering on so much about her dancing days all of a sudden, when she normally referred to them only rarely, but she didn't have a chance to wonder about that for long because Toni Conti was on a roll.

He loomed over the table and ranted, 'No, Your Grace, not bed and breakfasts, those have been around forever, and they don't do what I'm referring to. I mean those blessed set-ups that use various acronyms which all amount to the same thing: perfectly good housing stock is being removed from the marketplace to allow for one- or two-night rentals by people who want to feel they have the run of a place, and may do as they please while they're there. There's no oversight, no service is provided other than clean linens, and the places sit empty for about eighty percent of the time. It's a blight, I tell you. Don't you have perfectly serviceable country cottages in your neck of the woods that have been done up to appeal to folks with more money than sense? All they have to do is rent them out for one week in eight to achieve the same sort of income they'd get if they had full-time tenants. It's no wonder there's a housing crisis.'

'Hear, hear,' said Uma with feeling. 'The whole thing got going before I left the newspaper – or, I should say, before the newspaper closed down. You could see the estate agents telling people in their advertisements that something was "ripe for redevelopment into smaller units". And the planning people just let it happen. Don't people understand that *homes* are what create a community? Yes, it's the people who live in them that count, of course, but if there's no one there for most of the time, you're right, Toni – the heart is missing from a place.'

'We're fortunate that we have the say of who rents all our properties from our Estate,' mused Althea, 'and we're always mindful of what sort of folks those are.'

Mavis jumped in. 'Her Grace doesn't mean to imply that people are vetted against some sort of list of criteria, of course.'

'I do,' snapped Althea. Mavis couldn't be certain if Althea was play-acting her haughty-batty role again when she added, 'We've always thought most carefully about who we rent to. Everyone who lives in Anwen-by-Wye is there because they contribute something positive to the local community. The village is made up of wonderful, and historic, buildings, yes, but the people in them are what count, as you quite rightly said, Uma. The four guest rooms that will be opened again at the Coach and Horses will also allow for temporary visitors, but that will be run as a proper "inn", not as whatever it is you're referring to, Toni.'

'As it should be, I'm sure,' replied a slightly calmer Toni. He took a deep breath and asked, 'No sherries this morning?'

Althea dimpled. 'Not yet.'

'I see that Pippa is back at her post,' said Siggy. 'Feeling a bit more chipper now, is she?'

Toni nodded. 'Seems so, thank goodness. Maria's able to lend a hand, but we agreed when we opened this place up as a hotel that she wouldn't have to actually "work" here. This is our retirement, not just mine.'

'Was poor Pippa that badly taken by the death of Frances?' Uma smiled sweetly. 'Frances and I went way back. I didn't get the impression that she and Pippa were close.'

'You did? I had no idea.' Toni Conti sounded embarrassed to Mavis's ear. He blustered, 'I don't recall Frances mentioning that she'd known you prior to your arrival here. Did you and she…spend much time together?'

Mavis noted a distinct nervousness on the part of their host.

Uma replied, 'Her duties were only part-time, so she and I were able to enjoy chats, and strolls, and so forth. We met in school, though didn't keep in touch after we both left. Our lives took us in quite different directions. Then we found ourselves here, together, which pleased us both. I was…' Mavis noticed how Uma scanned the faces at the table before she continued. 'I was quite worried when you told her she might have to leave, Toni, though not as worried as she herself was.'

Mavis's side view of Toni Conti allowed her to see how his neck turned a mottled mauve color. Good, the man felt something about how he'd treated Frances, and it was likely that he was feeling guilty, which was even better.

His responded curtly, 'Yes, well…I'd better see if everything's going well with Pippa, now. We've got a new resident moving in today, so there'll be a bit of a kerfuffle, I dare say.'

'Anyone interesting?' Mavis asked, but Toni ignored her and disappeared into the main reception area.

'Brave of you to speak up, Uma, and quite right too,' noted Sir Malcolm.

'The chap couldn't get away fast enough,' observed Siggy.

'I miss Frances,' said Uma quietly.

Althea patted Uma's hand. 'I'm sorry, my dear — but we're here to help get to the bottom of this. So, what do you say, Mavis — should you and I visit this estate agency and find out how Pippa is connected to them? Which Frances' own note suggested she was.' Mavis could see the twinkle in Althea's eyes across the table. The dowager added, 'Since you'll be driving, there'll be no sherry for you, Mavis, but I'll just be sitting down all day…so where's Simon got to?'

# CHAPTER TWENTY

Aled was in the cellar, Tudor was in the kitchen, and Annie was fending off the 'help' being offered by Rosie and Gertie as she cradled the artistically tall, slender, varnished *papier-mâché* cat she'd collected from Carol's on her way back from walking the pups around the green. She finally set it on the floor beside the bar at the Coach.

'Tude, I could do with a bit of a hand out here for a tick, please,' she called.

Tudor emerged, and looked down at her prize. 'And that is?'

'Well, it's a cat. As you can plainly see. Someone gave it to Car years ago and it's been in the shed behind her house since she moved here. She's not that keen on it, and I asked if I could "borrow" it. She very kindly said I could have it.'

'Those two seem to think it smells interesting,' Tudor noted. 'I'm assuming you have a plan for it?'

Annie loved the way Tudor's face moved around when he was trying to work something out.

She replied, 'Well, it'll be a "them" before too long, because there's a pair, and I'm putting them outside in the beer garden, as bait. But they need cleaning up first.'

Tudor grinned. 'Bait? To tempt whoever's been stealing garden ornaments? I get it. And you're right, that thing's in desperate need of a good wipe-down, if nothing else…so maybe you could do that in the beer garden, rather than on my nice clean floor? I've already swept up, and we'll be open in half an hour.'

Annie looked at the bits of spiders' webs and remnants of grass clippings from earlier in the year – or, maybe, from even the year before – that had already dropped onto the floor. 'Yeah, sorry Tude, you're right. Tell you what, I'll leave it there for a minute, get these two settled upstairs, then I'll sort this one, and the other one, outside. But I could do with a hand with the ladder, please.'

Tudor stopped before he reached the door to the kitchen. 'Why do you need a ladder?'

Annie smiled her cutest smile. 'Cameras. I'm not going to sit looking out of the bedroom window all night on the off-chance that someone's going to take a fancy to this thing, am I? I'll put up a couple of cameras so we can see what's what. You're alright with that, aren't you? Up on the post that's got the sign on it, not on the pub itself.'

Tudor scratched his head. 'You know very well I'm open in half an hour...but I suppose Aled can hold the fort while we do that. However, I'll just say this: if I'm up a ladder installing a camera, which I will be, because there's no way I'm letting you do that, by the way, that's not exactly a secret, is it? And isn't that the point? That whoever is doing it doesn't know this is a trap.'

Annie had realized the flaw in her plan even as Tudor had started speaking. 'Gordon Bennett, Tude...sometimes I don't know what I'm thinking. You're right. We can't do it until after dark, can we? Okay, I'll shove this one and its partner outside and get them cleaned up, then we can install the cameras tonight, after you've closed. Good thinking, Batman.'

'You're welcome, Robin. Now, I'd better get back to my lamb stew. I know it's forecast to be another warm day, but I'm hoping a bit of stew will appeal to the visitors. I'll be serving it in a crusty loaf today, instead of a bowl. Well, it'll be a bowl, but an edible one. I got them from Paul Baker. It was an idea he put in my head last evening, and he's sent down a batch for me to try out today.'

'Nice one, Tude. And you and him and Janet are all sorted regarding pasties now, too?' He nodded. 'Thank goodness. I mean, she's got the only ice cream in the village – except for the few bits and bobs Sharon has in her freezer – so Janet can flippin' well keep her hands off the savories. Though I think you reached a good compromise by all agreeing she could do sausage rolls. Not a proper meal a sausage roll, is it? Not like a pasty.'

Tudor turned, and walked toward Annie, grinning. He wrapped his strong arms around her and kissed her. 'Annie Parker – I bet the woman you were a few years back could never have imagined the words you've just uttered coming out of your lips. I reckon I'd have loved her, but I know for a fact I love you.'

Annie spent the next hour or so washing down the large, grimy cats, then set about locating a properly flat bit of the beer garden. She deposited a few shovels-worth of gravel from the edge of the car park on the patch, to allow the cats to sit steadily on their wide bases. Then she popped over to Sharon's where she picked up a few pots of jolly yellow chrysanthemums which she wedged around the bases of the figures. She finished off the whole display by tying a large bow around each cat's elongated, narrow neck. She took some photographs, then popped next door to see Carol and show off her handiwork.

'Car, can I come in?' She knocked at the dining room window where she could see Carol's back, hunched over her two laptops. Carol jumped, turned, and nodded.

When Annie entered Carol's dining-room-cum-office she was surprised to see such a mess...for Carol. One look at her chum's face told her she shouldn't mention that Carol was surrounded by open folders, sticky notes, and – of course – Albert's toys, as well as Bunty's. It was all a bit...well, Annie was glad that Gertie and Rosie had always been rationed to one toy each at a time.

'Busy, Car?' As Annie said the words, she had a feeling she'd said the wrong thing.

'Busy? Am I busy? I'm still going down deeper and deeper rabbit holes as part of the background check I'm doing on Paul flamin' Baker for Stephanie; I'm up to my armpits with the research into what are looking like a couple of extremely dodgy firms of building contractors that Bob Fernley was thinking of using for various jobs around the village; David's away for a day or so at something where he's giving a keynote speech – which means I'm really proud of him, of course, but I've got this one to look after on my own; and Bunty's chosen today, of all days, to have one of her tummy upsets. Look at her – she's been draped across the cushion there for the past hour looking like she's about to give up the ghost. And we all know that the nearest vet is, what, an hour away? Oh, and I've just been sent two urgent requests for background profiles for job candidates at my old place in the City, which means they need them turned around fast, because they do, after all, pay us a lot of money for that privilege.'

Annie could see the stress in her friend's eyes. 'If I could drive, I'd take Bunty to the vet, but I can't. Maybe I could help with the profile-building work? I know you're faster, but Chrissy could help me, maybe; she's not as fast as you, but she's a lot faster than me. And, well…'

'Hold that thought, here's Christine on a video call now,' said Carol. 'Hi Christine, Annie happens to be here with me. What can I, or we, do for you?'

Annie stuck her head in front of the camera. 'How are you, Chrissy? Is our Pregnant PI feeling alright today?'

Christine smiled weakly. 'Thanks, I'm good, but our client Stephanie isn't too grand. It's all going to pot at the Hall, it seems. Cook Davies hasn't walked out, but she has lots of complaints. And I believe Stephanie's taking up my idea of bringing in Val Jenkins as a mediator. However, I think we need to actually *do* something while we wait for more news about Paul Baker from you, Carol.'

Annie saw Carol's back stiffen as she replied, 'I'm doing the best I can, given all the jobs I'm trying to juggle.' Carol sounded totally defeated. 'I can only chase people for information so often before they start to ignore me altogether. I've already told Stephanie that Paul has a questionable past with failed baking company, and I'm hoping I get a phone call back from one of his partners who openly criticized him on social media, but I don't know when that might be.'

'Paul's not backwards in coming forwards when it comes to using the kitchens at the Hall to do an extra bit of business,' Annie offered. 'He made some loaves for Tude to use as bowls for his lamb stew and delivered them to the Coach this morning.'

Christine looked into the camera and said, 'That's very…enterprising of him. And I have to say that I haven't been able to form an opinion about him as anything other than a decent baker. See, what I was going to suggest was that we install some cameras in the kitchens, overnight, then we can have a look at what's going on there. But Stephanie thinks that might be the last straw for Cook Davies; that she'd think she was being spied on. So we'd have Stephanie and Henry's permission, but it could end up throwing a spanner in the works. What do you think? It's a decision we need to make as a group.'

Annie replied, 'I'm going to be using a couple of our cameras to keep an eye on a trap I've baited in the beer garden of the Coach – all to do with the Case of the…oh heck, I still haven't got anything to pull gnomes and flamingoes together, but that case. But there'll still be some cameras left over, Chrissy. I reckon we should do what we think is – professionally speaking – the best thing to solve the case. And cameras could help us do that at the Hall, as well as in the village. Right, Car?'

Carol nodded. 'As long as you don't need me to help install them, I'm fine with the idea. And it's just us three doing the decision-making for this one, right? Mavis is off with Althea on the coast doing their thing, and – by the way – not taking the time to keep me, or us, informed about what on earth they're getting up to there…which could be just as well, I suppose, because then I'd end up having to type up notes and distribute them, so I suppose I'm pleased about that.'

'You okay, Carol? You sound a bit stressed,' observed Christine.

'I'd be a lot better if everyone would stop asking me if I'm alright,' snapped Carol.

Christine settled her chin into her upturned palm. 'Tell me about it. I can't pick up a kettle without Alexander asking if I'm doing too much. He'll be the one helping me to install the cameras; heaven forbid I'd suggest climbing a ladder.'

Annie chuckled. 'We're lucky we've all got partners who like to look after us, right, girls? Not that we're not capable of doing everything we let them do for us. I'm an independent woman who knows how to accept help – you too, Chrissy…and you three, Car.'

Christine sighed. 'You're right. I'm doing my best to work out the difference between independent and stupidly headstrong, and nothing about that judgement is to do with me being a woman…it's all to do with using my brain. So – cameras it is. I'll sort that with the Twysts and Alexander. Thanks – glad we talked.'

Carol said, 'Hang on there a moment, Christine, I have something I want to ask. Stephanie said she'd look into whether it's possible for someone who doesn't live at the Hall to be able to access the kitchens overnight. Yes, I think the cameras are a good idea, but we need to at least narrow our potential suspect pool. Has she said anything to you about that aspect?'

Christine nodded. 'Well, you might be surprised – or not – to discover that, despite the amount of money they've spent on that security system at the Hall, there are ways around it.'

Annie and Carol shared a look of amazement. Carol said, 'Haven't they learned their lesson? And didn't those people they've had in there doing that huge inventory-taking exercise tell them they needed to tighten the system up?'

Christine chuckled. 'All I can tell you is this: because of various historically necessary reasons for all sorts of delivery people and so forth to be able to access the stores in, and leading off, the kitchens, there've been lots of keys given out over decades – or maybe hundreds of years – for the main door to the place. And before you ask, no, they can't change the lock, because it's protected, being historically significant. You've probably never seen it, but I have, and it's the sort of thing you'd expect to see on the door of an ancient church; the key is massive, and each one they've had made has had to be crafted out of iron. The solution, it seems, would be to affix some sort of secure secondary door, or even a barred gate, inside the kitchen itself, but – again – there are problems with doing that, due to the listing of the building. It seems the kitchens are in the oldest part of the building, and date back to the late 1400s.'

Annie said, 'But they've got a great big refrigerated room there – it was mentioned in the notes that Cook Davies made.'

Christine nodded. 'All made to measure, and fitted within the shell of the original building, so not attached to the fabric.'

Annie sighed. 'I remember all the fiddle-faddle about the special plaster they made us use when we were having the main bar at the Coach renovated…the listing people are really strict about all that stuff.'

Carol acknowledged, 'It's important to keep what we have that represents our history, but it brings its own challenges. So you're saying there are possibly dozens of people who can come and go, at will, via the kitchen door, right, Christine?'

'Well, no, it's not that bad, to be fair. Yes, Stephanie doesn't know how many keys are out there; Bob Fernley says there are records in the Estates Office of who's been given one, and when, and he'll get them out when he can. But, the main factor is that, although anyone with a key can get in, not everyone has the code for the alarm. The kitchen door is alarmed, you see, and there's a pad when you come in through that door. So whoever is doing this, has that number.'

Annie asked the question she suspected she might not like the answer to. 'And how many people have that code, Chrissy? Do we know that?'

Christine sighed. 'Um, Stephanie's not sure – and I suppose she's resigned to never being able to be certain. Because of what the code is.'

Annie dared. 'And that is?'

Christine grinned. '1485. Battle of Bosworth, when Henry Tudor won the crown...aided by the Twyst who he then made the first Duke of Chellingworth, as a thank-you.'

Carol shook her head. 'Of course it is.'

Annie laughed. 'Yeah, so almost anyone who knows, or bothers to find out about, the Twysts, could make an educated guess. Excellent.'

# CHAPTER TWENTY-ONE

The afternoon sun was low in the sky when Althea and Mavis arrived at Dyggan Sales and Rentals on the road leading into Tenby.

'Odd place to be if you want to sell houses,' said Althea as Mavis helped her out of the car.

'I agree, though maybe they have their reasons. Less expensive to be here than in the town itself?'

'No passing trade though – well, except for all the cars whizzing by. Chelly and I used to enjoy strolling about towns and cities looking at the homes for sale in estate agents' windows, when we traveled. Then we'd imagine ourselves living in the ones we most liked the look of. We spent many a happy dinner chatting about what our lives would be like if we lived in a different place.'

Mavis had to smile. 'With Chellingworth Hall all yours, and the house in London, and the place in Scotland…there were places you fancied the look of better than them?'

Althea looked a bit misty-eyed. 'Not "better" but certainly different. To live in a nice little cottage overlooking the sea, where it would be just we two, alone, with no one to bother us, for example.'

'And where you'd do all your own fetching, and carrying, and cooking and cleaning, you mean?'

Althea dimpled. 'There are services one can access for those sorts of things, dear, though I would say that I used to be a half decent cook, when I had to be. At least, when I used to sneak an electric ring into a B and B so I could heat up a tin or two, with the windows all open, you know? Girls in the chorus line didn't get paid much back then. I dare say they still don't, comparatively speaking.'

'Moving on…can you no' get into character for this job now, dear? Remember – you are the batty you, and you're thinking of buying something as an investment in these parts – something that will earn you a rental bob or two – like we agreed, right?'

Althea swooshed her voluminous scarf around her neck. 'Yes, I remember my brief, Mavis, you don't need to fuss. And you're my humble nursey, correct? And don't forget the humble bit.' She winked at Mavis then tottered toward the glass door painted with large letters proclaiming that DYGGAN WILL DIG OUT YOUR NEW HOME.

Mavis allowed herself a quick eye roll as she followed the dowager inside, and steeled herself for what might befall. But nothing happened. The office was completely deserted. There were two abandoned desks, a closed door that said STAFF ONLY, a telephone ringing, and even a mobile phone sitting on one of the desks pinging away to itself.

'It's like the *Marie Celeste*,' whispered Althea. 'They need a little bell, like Sharon has at the shop in the village. Hello-oo. Anyone here?'

The door opened and a male head popped out. Its hair was tousled, and it was attached to a tall, slim body encased in a suit that appeared to Mavis to have shrunk in the wash. The man was in his thirties; it appeared that the 'my hair just got out of bed' look was intentional; and as for the suit? It baffled Mavis that the man had to yank his jacket around his spare frame to be able to button it, and that she could see at least three inches of his yellow-and-purple striped socks.

'Ladies, pleased to meet you. I'm Gerry Dyggan. How may I help you this fine day?'

Althea surprised Mavis by addressing the man in Welsh.

'Ah, you'll need my colleague, Bethan. Just a tick, I'll fetch her. She's copying some details in the back office. Sorry, I am local but I never learned to speak Welsh, see?'

'Never fear, I speak English perfectly well,' snapped Althea. 'I'm Althea, Dowager Duchess of Chellingworth. This is my right hand, Mavis. I want to make some money and I hope you can help me do it.'

Mavis suppressed a smile as the man stared at Althea, then Mavis. She was convinced he was trying to decide if Althea was joking; her chosen get-up for the visit – a powder blue knitted suit which drowned her, an emerald scarf which all but enveloped her, and stout walking shoes – did make Althea look as though she might be a bag lady who'd left her bags outside, beside the road.

'Her Grace is interested in acquiring some property she can rent out, to produce an income,' said Mavis, hoping this would get the man to accept them as potential customers.

His shark-like smile told her she'd hooked him, and he waved to the two chairs across one of the desks – the one with the mobile phone that was still pinging. 'Please, do make yourselves comfortable, ladies…um…Your Grace. I'll just set this aside, and let's see what we have for you. Did you have a budget in mind?'

Mavis wasn't surprised that the subject of money had come up immediately; she'd have asked the same question.

'No more than a million,' said Althea curtly.

Once again, Gerry looked to Mavis for confirmation. 'Aye, that's what she said, and what she means. Though you did say you'd consider a bit more, if the income potential was good, is that no' right, Your Grace?'

Althea dimpled. 'Indeed. Mavis. Do you have anything?'

Gerry Dyggan rubbed his chin. 'Just let me see what we have that might suit. Would either of you care for some refreshment while I check? This isn't the sort of thing we'd put on display for members of the general public, you see – more the sort of thing we keep tucked up our sleeves for special clients.'

'A pot of tea would be most welcome,' said Althea. 'Not a mug with a tea bag. A proper pot. And a cup and saucer, please.'

Once again, the man looked toward Mavis for confirmation. Mavis smiled and added, 'With milk and sugar.'

Standing and rebuttoning his jacket – sitting down had necessitated its unbuttoning, it was so tight – Gerry said, 'Just one moment. I'll have a word with Bethan, and I'm sure she'll be able to rustle something up.'

As soon as he disappeared through the door, closing it behind him, Mavis nipped around the desk and started scrolling through lists with photographs of properties beside addresses and general descriptions on his computer screen. She snapped with her phone, noting as she did so that these were not houses, nor even blocks of flats, but large properties and imposing homes, some looking historically significant. She was thrown a little when she saw a picture of The Lavender, but kept scrolling and snapping until she reached the end of the list. She scampered back to her seat and was looking out of the window in a carefree manner when Gerry emerged, looking a bit pink, and with an apologetic expression on his face.

'Bethan and I have checked everywhere, but we don't have a pot. Terrible oversight on our part, of course. Is there something else I could offer you?'

Althea snapped, 'A property with which I can make some money.'

Gerry smiled, showing lots of even, white teeth. 'Of course. I do have one here that could be of interest. Currently being developed into sixteen dwellings, one bedroom each. Used to be a hotel, in Tenby. Not a bad spot.' He turned his screen so that Althea and Mavis could see it.

'Here's the proposed floor plan, the exterior, as was, and the proposed new façade. And a mock-up of one of the dwellings. Completion should be three months from now. As you can see, the one-bedroom format could easily accommodate a couple. Should rent for…oh, let me think…' Mavis stared as he played with his phone, then he held it up to show a figure on the screen. He played with the pad again and added, 'Of course, if you were to consider each of the units as a short-term let then you might clear this much per month, instead – and that based on just eight nights' accommodation being booked.' He held up his phone again, and the number shown was almost triple what it had been the first time. 'Rather an attractive proposition, wouldn't you say? And none of the sort of bother that goes along with long-term tenants who sometimes like to linger when you'd prefer them to get out, or complain about rent increases.'

'Would you be able to email that to me? Her Grace doesn't have an account.' Mavis smiled as simperingly as she could, and Gerry bared his teeth at her. Mavis held up her phone displaying her email address, which he noted.

He pressed a few keys. 'There, all done.'

'And could you add details of any other properties you have of a similar type, please Gerry?' Mavis asked sweetly. 'Large properties, currently being, or soon to be, renovated to allow for multiple tenants, with locations that might prove appealing to the short-term market.'

Mavis thought Gerry's teeth might burst into flame they gleamed so brightly at her. 'But of course. Would you like to wait while I do that, or...?' He allowed his question to hang in the air even as he scrolled and typed.

'Thank you, we'll wait,' said Althea.

He typed fast.

'I think that's it,' he leaned forward and attempted what Mavis suspected was his most earnest expression. 'I hope you find something appealing within the list I've just sent, but – please – if there's nothing there that fits the bill, don't hesitate to check back with me. We have new properties becoming available all the time...indeed, we're working on a very special project at the moment. But that may take some time to come to the market, so yes, please give some thought to what you have there.'

Althea piped up. 'If I see something I fancy the look of when I'm out and about, that doesn't have a sign saying it's for sale, would you be prepared to go to the owner to see if they could be persuaded to sell, for the right price?'

Mavis was surprised by Althea's question; they'd not discussed any such thing during their journey, though she had to admit it was a good one to ask.

Mavis thought Gerry's face might split in two, and she almost rolled her eyes when he actually rubbed his hands together. 'But of course, Your Grace. The owner or owners would never even have to know who was interested in their property. Please, do consider us for any role whatsoever concerned with the acquisition, or even disposal, of property.'

'And you'd know folks who could make any changes and renovations that needed doing, would you?' Mavis thought she'd follow where Althea had led.

Gerry adopted an air of earnestness. 'We have access to a range of trusted general contractors and subcontractors. Firms we've dealt with on many projects.'

'Would one have heard of them?' Althea used her snootiest tone.

For the first time, Gerry looked uncertain. 'Possibly. Though maybe not. Would you like a list of them, too?' He glanced at Mavis, who nodded.

'We'll wait. Again,' said Althea.

Now Mavis could see the panic on Gerry's face. 'Just a tick – I don't keep a list, as such, you see. But let me create one for you...umm...would it suit if I just gave company names and locations, rather than actual addresses?' Mavis nodded. 'Excellent, I can do that much from memory. Just a tick.'

As he typed, he licked his lips a great deal.

Eventually he said, 'Those would be half a dozen I would have no hesitation in suggesting. Sometimes timing means you have to use whoever's available, right?'

Althea stood. 'No, young man. One has to use the best, and turning to whomever is available often means they're not in use because they are not the best. Good day. My best to Bethan, who seems to be taking an inordinate amount of time getting that copying done.'

Althea held her little chin as high as she could as she waited for Gerry to open the door, then gave the same performance as Mavis opened the car door for her. Once they were about half a mile away, Althea giggled like a schoolgirl and insisted upon making whooping noises every moment or two.

'Aye, it was fun, and you did an excellent job, my dear, but would you no' make that noise anymore? Thank you. It's terribly distracting.' Mavis could see the dowager pouting, but managed to keep her eyes on the road. 'You've no' been told off, so wipe that look off your face. We got some excellent information, and I bet those lists will be helpful. Ach...who's that sending me things making my phone ping? I thought I'd turned off all my noises. You never know when they're going to go off. Could you please take a look for me, Althea?'

'No dear. After the mess I made of trying to type while you were driving last time, it's fifty-fifty that I'll do something wrong, then it'll all be my fault if I cut someone off, or delete something important, and you said you didn't want to be distracted, so let's wait until we get back to The Lavender and you can see for yourself then. We won't be long.'

Mavis had to agree that Althea made good points, so she didn't see the string of texts from Siggy until they'd pulled into the car park at their temporary home. 'Good heavens,' she said as she read the various messages.

'What?'

'Hang on…good grief.'

'What!'

'It seems Siggy's been using the time we've been off-site, as he calls it, to get some digging of his own done. And given what I saw on young Gerry's computer, and maybe what we'll find in the list of properties he's sent us, I think we have something.'

'What…what…*what*?' Mavis could see that Althea's little fists were clenched.

'The places listed in Frances' note about PIPPA, and the photographs of hotels and so forth that she had in her cloud storage, were all places where Pippa had worked over the past five years. *And* I just saw several of them listed as available for sale, now, in Gerry Dyggan's office.'

Althea sounded puzzled. 'How did Siggy find out so fast about where this Pippa person has worked? I don't think even Carol could manage that, this quickly. And Carol's exceptional.'

Mavis smiled. 'Ah yes, but Carol didn't once have a so-called low-level admin job at the Foreign Office, did she? I wonder what sort of favors Siggy is actually able to call upon. He's quite an interesting chap.'

'And not bad-looking, in a certain light – though not a patch on Dennis of course, who's rather ruggedly handsome, don't you think? Those green eyes of his, so unusual, and quite startling.'

Mavis tutted, thinking about the conversation she'd overheard between Dennis and an unknown woman in the kitchen. 'That Dennis has an unsettling air about him. Besides, looks are no' the point in any case. It's what's on the inside that matters. And *we* should be getting inside now. It's time to change for dinner.'

'Excellent,' squealed Althea, 'I have a lovely lemon chiffon thing for tonight. I picked it up at my favorite charity shop in Brecon.'

Mavis dreaded the thought.

# 8th SEPTEMBER

# CHAPTER TWENTY-TWO

As soon as Annie got out of bed, she opened her laptop to check on the two bait-cats she'd placed in the beer garden. With mixed emotions she saw they were still where she'd left them. 'Drat.'

'What's wrong?' Tudor was already dressed for the day, and had taken Gertie and Rosie out for a quick walk around the green. 'You okay?'

'The cats. They're still there. My plan didn't work.' Annie was disappointed.

Tudor gave her a welcome hug and a kiss. 'I know – I saw them there myself. Never mind. It's early days. And we had a laugh putting up those cameras last night, didn't we?'

Annie chuckled as she recalled the way it had taken them an hour to get the job done; it had been a cloudy night, completely pitch black, and they'd discovered that trying to erect a ladder, get up it safely, and attach two cameras to a massive pole, while avoiding a swinging pub sign, hadn't been as easy in practice as it had sounded in theory. Annie was only glad that Tudor had done all the climbing and reaching for her.

She asked, 'Is your back alright this morning?'

Tudor rolled his neck. 'Not too bad, considering. I'm not as young as I once was.'

'Not yet sixty, Tude. A good age. Besides, maybe the thief gave them cats the once over during the night. I'll check the recordings from the cameras in any case. Right after breakfast.'

'Fry-up?'

'Nah. And maybe you should think about something not dripping with fat, too. How about we both have some cereal, and toast? There's a bit of that loaf that needs toasting.'

'As long as we've got enough Marmite, I'm up for that.'

Following a pleasant interlude where Gertie and Rosie enjoyed toast-crusts, Annie and Tudor reached a few conclusions about the décor for the guest rooms, and two pots of tea were consumed. Annie kissed her beau before he descended to his domain in the pub, while she sat at the table and watched the recordings from the cameras the previous night. With no luck.

Annie was just deciding whether she should phone Carol or Christine first, to check on general progress with cases, when her phone pinged. It was a text from Sarah Hughes, which surprised Annie – she wasn't even aware that the woman had her number. As the text requested, Annie phoned Sarah, who hadn't wanted to interrupt Annie if she was busy.

'Hello Sarah, Annie here. What can I do for you?'

'My flying pigs have gone, and I know you're helping Sharon and Marjorie, so I thought I should tell you.'

Annie stared at the feed paused on her screen. *Fat lot of good you two did*, she thought as she stared at the two cats. 'How about I pop over? Twenty minutes?'

'Lovely, ta. It's all a bit chaotic here, because we're packing, so you'll have to take us as you find us.'

'No worries. See you soon.'

Annie made sure the girls were settled to be left alone; Gertie enjoyed the attention she got, and Rosie took the chance to grab both stuffies the dogs had been snuggling with, and place them on her bed.

'Share nice now, girls,' said Annie as she looked up the stairs before she shut the door. Tracking down Tudor in the snug – where he was rearranging a few tables and chairs for what she knew was the umpteenth time – Annie told him where she was going. 'No idea when I'll be back, but I will be. The girls are set, and I've got my phone.'

'You know where I'll be,' called Tudor as she headed out of the pub and toward Sarah's house.

As Annie entered the Hugheses' garden, she realized she'd never been into the house before, and acknowledged that she quite liked seeing how people lived. However, the piles of cardboard boxes stacked inside the porch, and in the entry hall beyond the front door, which was wide open, suggested this wasn't exactly how the Hughes family always lived.

'Hello-oo,' she called, not wanting to venture in without being invited to do so.

Sarah's head popped out of a doorway. 'Come on through, Annie. If you don't mind, I'll carry on attacking these kitchen cupboards while we talk.'

Annie entered Sarah's large kitchen, which was – as promised – in chaos. Even so, Annie's comment of, 'What a lovely house and kitchen,' came from the heart.

The place was massive and – if it weren't for all the boxes – it would have been a stunning kitchen. The house was one of the newer ones in the village – she reckoned it had been built in the 1930s – large, by local standards, and had obviously been modernized relatively recently. She couldn't imagine why anyone would need six rings on a gas stove, but that's what the Hugheses had, and she was impressed by how clean Sarah managed to keep the stainless-steel doors of her appliances. Annie had only been having to deal with such things since she and Tudor had moved into the flat at the Coach, and they were driving her to distraction already; you couldn't touch them without leaving a mark, she was finding.

Sarah was on a two-step stool so she could reach the top of the cupboard she was obviously emptying. Annie offered, 'Do you want to pass things down to me and I can put them on the counter for you to sort out?'

Sarah nodded. 'Thanks. The box is for what we're taking, the plastic basket thing is for what's going out. I've got to be honest and say I don't even know what's up here, though I suspect it's been there since we moved in. It's all well and good having cupboards that go up to the ceiling, but all I've done is shove stuff in them I never use. So what's the point of keeping it?'

Annie sympathized. 'You don't have to tell me, doll – just been through it all myself, moving to the Coach. And the cottage was tiny compared to this place. You tell me about these pigs that have gone, and just say box or basket and I'll do my best down here.'

'Thanks. Box. The flying pigs used to be up on the wall in the porch. Basket. No, box. But along with everything else, they had to come down. Definitely basket. Steve did that because he put them up there. Box. Box. Basket. His mother gave them to us when we got married, because she reckoned he'd never tie the knot. Box. Box. Been with us ever since. Basket. No, box. No…go on then, basket. They're only plastic, but they mean something to us. Box. He'd left them on the floor in the porch ready to be packed. Well, washed, then packed. It wasn't till he got them down that I realized how dirty they were, and I don't want to pack dirty things. Basket. Basket. Box. And only two of them have gone, after all. Box. I found one of them over by the hedge. The biggest one. So the two smaller ones have gone. Box. Box. Box. Good grief – I don't even know what this is for, so basket for that. The big one's over on the kitchen table, so the others are exactly the same but there's a middle-sized one, then a baby one. Like three flying ducks. You know…like Hilda Ogden had on her "murial". Remember that, on *Coronation Street*?'

Annie chuckled. 'Who could forget? I loved her and Stan.'

'Everyone did. Basket. Oh, go on…box. And that's all I can tell you, sorry Annie. Steve put them there last evening – about nine, I should say. At it all hours he is, after work, with me doing my best through the day. I'm dropping the boys at their new school, then coming back here to do this, then driving to pick them up again at the end of their day – it's over an hour each way, but we all agreed that at least they needed to start the new school year properly. Unlike me, as you can see. It's all a bit of a nightmare; it sounded like a good idea for the last headteacher to stay on for the start of the year to help with the handover, but, because we couldn't find anywhere to rent to live in until next week, we couldn't move until then, so she's actually doing the job on her own at the moment, when she really should be enjoying her retirement. But I have to be there next week, or the education people will blow their tops. They've been very accommodating.'

'I should think they're only too glad to have you. I keep hearing that teachers are leaving the profession faster than they can be trained up. At least, that's what they said on the news.'

Sarah rolled her eyes. 'You don't have to remind me about that. But it's all I've ever wanted to do. And, yes, I've been a hard worker all my life, but there's also been a bit of luck involved, like the headteacher before me knowing the people who had been renting the house we're moving to. I...I don't know how we'd have coped without somewhere local to live. But now? Well, as you can see, there's still a lot to get done.'

'Have the boys been much use with it all?' Annie suspected she could guess the answer.

'Surprisingly, yes. Once I told them that if it wasn't in a box by the end of the week it was going out, they finally got going. Box. Box. Box. Oh my word, Annie, I am so sick of boxes. Basket. Is there anything you've found out about everything else that's gone missing yet?'

Annie explained that no one had seen anything useful, and explained about the cat-trap that hadn't proved as tempting to the thief as Sarah's flying pigs.

'Good idea, though,' said Sarah, finally coming down the couple of steps. 'There, that one's empty at least. She looked at the box and the basket. 'Oh heck, I haven't really got rid of that much, have I? Oh well, maybe I'll think better of keeping things when we get to the new place. It's not as big or as nicely done up as this house, but it'll only be for a while. We're looking to buy, when we can find something we can afford.'

'Think you'll be stopping there, then, in Abertillery?'

'It's a good school, and I hope that when I'm in charge I can make it even better. It's what I've always wanted; I enjoy the management and all that, as well as the teaching, you know? But now? Yes, this'll be it for me, I should think. I wouldn't want a bigger school, with more pupils than this one. So we thought it was the best thing to do. Not that it's easy, of course. There's not a lot of choice out there, so the estate agents keep telling us, and needing three bedrooms is – apparently – what everyone wants. And I don't want a long drive to work, if I can avoid it. And there's Steve to consider, too. We don't know how long it'll take us to find the right place, so we could be renting for a while yet. But we'll manage. It'll be a bit of a squash, of course. Owain and Rhys are already whining about having to share a bedroom. That'll probably be our biggest headache, to be honest – they're so used to their own space here. Still, as long as World War Three doesn't break out every day, we'll manage. It's funny, I've become very attached to this place, though I hated it when we first moved in. The house is called *Tŷ Mawr*, which means Big House in Welsh, and it felt like we were rattling around in here at first. Of course, the boys were much smaller then, and they've accumulated so much stuff over the years. As have I…and Steve, of course. This move should force us to clear out…well, a bit, at least. How are you finding the Coach?'

Annie chatted about getting used to new appliances, decorating plans for the guest rooms, and how Gertie and Rosie were taking to the place happily. 'But, Sarah, lovely though it is to catch up – and it is nice to see this place before you go – I'd better get on. I'm guessing you'd have mentioned seeing or hearing anything odd last night – but, just to be clear – anything? Nothing?'

Sarah shook her head. 'No. I asked Steve, and the boys, too. I think all of us are sleeping like the dead at the moment because we're wiped out by the time we go to bed…though that doesn't stop my mind whirring with lists of things I've got to do. But, no, nothing out of the ordinary. Though I'm glad to hear that your dogs are settling in alright. They've been a bit disturbed of late, haven't they?'

'You're the third person to mention that. Dogs barking at night, right?' Sarah nodded. 'Yeah, and it's not Gert or Rosie; Tude and I haven't heard a thing. It's weird that.'

'Well, dogs will bark – I wasn't saying it's been a problem.'

Annie shrugged. 'Ta, yeah, I get that. But we know it's not our two. Ah well, just another mystery to solve, I suppose.'

'I think Sherlock Holmes sorted that one, didn't he?'

Annie winked. 'Careful now, you're talking to a trained investigator here who likes her fiction to be criminally good – which means I've done my fair share of Holmesian reading. That one's called "Silver Blaze" and the clue that helps him solve it is the dog that *didn't* bark in the night, suggesting it was familiar with the person who stole the racehorse in question. But…yes…the dog barking? That might be something. Quick question – the two pigs that went, just how much smaller were they than this one here?'

Sarah used her hands to suggest body lengths.

Annie checked, 'And they were flattish, like this one, to sit snug against the wall? But not as fat?'

'Yes. About two inches deep, I'd say.'

Annie grinned. 'Thanks, Sarah. Right-o, off I go. I've got to check something with Marge, then I'm off to do my best to sort out The Case of the…nope…gnomes, flamingoes, and now pigs with wings still aren't getting me there. But I will do my best for you. When do you leave, by the way?'

'Four days' time. So – no panic, you know. Besides, I dare say we'll pop back, now and again. Just knowing they're safe would be enough. You know, them being from my mother-in-law.'

Sarah waved at Annie from the porch, and Annie took herself off to see Marjorie Pritchard to enquire about the thickness of Kevin's neck and pointed hat.

# CHAPTER TWENTY-THREE

First thing that morning, Carol had sent messages to Stephanie, Christine, Alexander, Annie, and Bob Fernley, requesting a video conference at eleven. Everyone had replied, and only Bob had declined to attend, which was fine by Carol, because she really didn't want to possibly embarrass the man; she didn't have good news about the building contractors from whom he'd requested quotes.

She'd tidied up the part of the dining room that would be on camera, which meant that at five to eleven she was sitting staring at heaps of toys, and a son who was at least enjoying the chaos she'd created as he scrambled through mounds of stuffed animals and giant building blocks. He was having a whale of a time, whereas Carol was envisaging several ideal-but-not-yet-invented storage solutions that would actually clear a room for you. She was convinced that Heath Robinson would have had some excellent ideas on that one.

'You look like you're miles away, Car.' Annie's cheerful voice announced her arrival at the virtual meeting.

Carol snapped back to reality. 'Sorry – not much sleep. Albert was fussy, and Bunty wanted attention too. She draped herself across David's half of the bed all night, while he no doubt had breakfast delivered to his room at the hotel where his conference is being held.'

'How's poor Bunty feeling today?'

'A bit better, I think, but she's still not herself. Ate all her food, though, which is a good sign. I gave her the fancy salmon-flavored one she loves this morning. And I spoke to the vet last evening. Bless her, she phoned me back a long time after her normal hours. She likes Bunty, and Bunty likes her, which is always good, of course. We both reckon it's nothing serious; she just probably ate something she shouldn't have done. Maybe something – or too much of something – that Albert dropped from his highchair. He thinks it's a game to feed her that way. Goodness knows how many bits of his food she actually gets when I turn my back for two minutes. I've been thinking he's been doing well with his meals…but now I'm not so sure.'

'Give Bunty a gentle cuddle from me, and Bertie a snuggly one,' said Annie. 'Bunty's like these two here – Rosie'll take whatever she can get that drops from the table, if Gertie doesn't get it first, which she usually does. Mind you, it's handy having two dogs to lick our two plates clean when we've finished with them, before I put them into the dishwasher…but I dare say it's different for cats.'

Carol agreed. 'Oh yes, cats are quite different. As my life would be if I only had a dishwasher. Hello Stephanie, how are you today?'

Carol admired the way that Stephanie's hair was always just so, and that she was always dressed nicely – never with any food stains on her clothes – then told herself off for being just a little bit jealous; she didn't have dozens of people to do everything that needed to be taken care of around a house.

'Mustn't grumble,' said the duchess – a sentiment with which Carol heartily concurred…still thinking of the staff at the Hall.

'Hello folks, sorry I'm last to the party, as usual,' said Christine cheerily. 'Alexander and I are at two desks at the office – grand, there he is. Excellent, that means I wasn't last after all.'

Carol was struck again by the perfection of Alexander's looks – his even smile, wonderful teeth, the gold-flecked light hazel of his eyes, and felt a gut-wrenching pang as she realized how very much she missed the sight of her husband's face around their home. She'd been counting the hours until he'd return since the moment she'd waved him off for his conference.

With a squeal, Albert announced his presence in the room. 'Obviously Albert is here with me,' said Carol, 'and I dare say Hugo's with you, Stephanie, so let's all get on, shall we? I have information to share pertaining to both The Case of the Battling Baker and The Case of the Revitalized Village, which is what Annie and I have agreed should be the name for the investigations into the potential building contractors to be used for various projects around Anwen-by-Wye. Any preference for where we should start? Stephanie, you're our client for both cases, so it's your choice.'

'Which one's got most information to share, Carol?' Carol reckoned Hugo must be asleep, because the duchess spoke quietly.

'Revitalized Village. That one first, then?' Stephanie nodded. Carol clicked to the appropriate screen on her second laptop. 'Okay, here we go: I'll share my screen with you when I need, so don't worry if I disappear, I'm still here really – but speak up if you want, because I might not be able to see you. First off – Muggins…'

Carol showed photographs of previous projects the contractor had been involved with, and shared her findings of the pitiful record of the man who was running what was now his fifth general contracting company. It didn't make for easy listening. Nor did the information she'd gleaned about the other outfit that had quoted on the work needed in Anwen.

She continued, 'The third company Bob Fernley approached didn't even put in a quote, and when I talked to someone named John there, he swore blind he'd never heard anything about our village, let alone the work needed. He admitted that his partner might have been the one who walked through the old school and village hall with Bob, but then told me they barely spoke any more, which, frankly, doesn't bode well, I don't think. So, there you have it – dodgy, dodgier, and dodgiest, in that order, I'd say. Did you gain any insights, Alexander? I know you were going to ask around about these three specific companies.'

Alexander shook his head. 'No one I know has ever heard of any of them, but, as I said when I made the offer to get involved, that's not surprising because most of my contacts are in London. However, what I do have is a proper estimate for works that I've put together, with input from subcontractors I trust, and who I know I could rely upon. Christine – can you share that for me, please? Sorry – I'm not sure how to do that on this computer – I'm used to doing pretty much everything on my phone, these days.'

'Email it to me from your phone, Alexander, I'll share it for you,' said Carol, 'then I'll have it where it's needed, at the comms hub.'

Annie chuckled. 'Oh, listen to you: comms hub? Fancy.'

Carol smiled. 'Center of the universe, me. Got it, and here it is, folks.'

Stephanie said, 'That's still twice as much as Muggins quoted, Alexander, and even more than the other company suggested. Not that I'm criticizing – but could you explain why that is, maybe?'

Carol knew that the main part of her job on this particular case was behind her, so allowed herself to keep a keen eye on Albert as Alexander talked about what would need to be done to allow for people who would be renting spaces to be able to pay for only the utilities they used, rather than everyone paying a fixed rate. Carol tuned out a bit when he began to talk about roofs because she got it – it was basically spend more now to save down the line and help the planet, or spend less now and face having to do things again and the climate be damned. She reckoned she knew what Stephanie would say.

'Thanks for that, Alexander. We'll go with your proposal. Including the new roof. I've learned here at Chellingworth Hall how incredibly costly it can be if a roof fails. When can you start?' Stephanie had spoken, and Carol zoned back in.

'Today, if you want.'

Alexander's words surprised Carol, so she asked, 'Really? *Today* today?'

Alexander laughed. 'Yes, Carol. *Today* today. It's all good timing really: roofers are in great demand at the moment – good weather, with winter on the way, and all that – but there's a company I'm working with down in London who've just been told they can't get onto a site they'd planned to be working on for the next two weeks; the bloke who runs the company rang me about an hour ago practically begging for work. The supplies he has on hand are exactly what I'd have proposed for the old school, and he's got access to as many solar panels as we might need, more in fact, because the job he's not doing now would have been bigger than this one. I say let's grab him and his team while we can.'

'Then let's raise a roof,' said the duchess, grinning. 'Want to take a break to phone your man right now, Alexander?'

'I'll text him…have texted him. There you go – I told you he'd be pleased: he'll be on his way in an hour, with all the supplies he'll need.'

'What an excellent start,' Stephanie said. 'Now that's in hand, what's next?'

Carol said, 'If that's all on that case then, can we move on to the other things I've been doing?' She hadn't meant to sound as much like

Mavis when she spoke, but knew she had done. Albert was trying to fit a giant plastic block into his mouth, which was distracting her.

'By all means,' said Stephanie. 'I've spoken to Val, by the way, and she's coming to the Hall this afternoon, so maybe with more information at hand, she and I can get things sorted regarding the situation in the kitchens. Over to you, Carol.'

Carol clicked on her other file of case notes. 'Okay – Paul Baker? There might be an issue there. I finally managed to talk to one of his ex-partners at the baking company that three of them ran together. This is the situation: when the three men started the company, the one I spoke to – his name's Patrick – gave personal guarantees against the leases for the baking equipment Paul said was necessary for the set-up. When the company stopped trading – and they haven't wound up legally yet, by the way – this Patrick discovered that he's on the hook with the lease companies to pay the full value of the equipment, or else continue to pay the monthly fees – which is what he's choosing to do at the moment.'

'And is Paul definitely the reason they stopped trading?' Carol could hear the anxiety in Stephanie's voice.

'So Patrick says. His side of the story is that Paul was incredibly gung-ho to start with, and they all thought they were going to be quids in because he managed to get the business rolling in. Loads of orders, more than they could cope with – so they took on more staff, and the turnover grew nicely. Then Paul started showing up late, then not at all; Paul said he reckoned the other people they'd hired could do the job without him. Next thing Patrick knows, Paul's working at the bakery that gave him his most recent reference – the one you know about, Stephanie, where they made niche products with ancient grains and no gluten, that sort of stuff. If you recall, they were really happy with him because – once again – he brought a great deal of new customers to them.'

Annie chipped in, 'Paul did them special loaves for Tude, and I know for a fact he'd talked Janet Jackson into doing sausage rolls *and* pasties at the Lamb Tearooms. So maybe this is his pattern? He gets to a new place and can't help but build more and more business for himself?'

Stephanie looked uncertain. 'It's an odd behavioral pattern. Especially if he then reaches a point where he's attracted so much business that he can't cope, or just decides to go somewhere else to do the same all over again.'

Annie asked, 'Are we thinking that he's going to sabotage Cook Davies's work in the kitchens at the Hall just so he looks better? Is that what this suggests? That he's a bit of a narcissist?' She chuckled. 'When I saw him in the pub, the first thing that went through my head was "Elvis wannabe". Might that suggest some sort of...I don't know...personality disorder? Do you want me to run this past my counsellor? She might help; this in't my area at all. Anyone?'

Carol thought it wise to say, 'Stephanie – you're our client, this would be your call.'

Stephanie seemed distracted, and Carol suspected that Hugo was doing something that had caught her eye. 'Come in and sit, Henry, dear. And if you could rearrange Hugo's blanket, that would be lovely.' Returning her full attention to the camera, the duchess added, 'I'm not sure. To be honest, I don't think any sort of psychological diagnosis would help, even if that might explain the reason he's doing these things, if he is. I think what we really need is evidence that he is, in fact, doing them or – if not him – then who is. I honestly don't believe that Cook Davies is making any of this up – but there are now counterclaims being made by Paul. So this might not be as straightforward as we think. Or, maybe, he's "acting against himself" so we won't think he's doing it.' She sighed heavily.

'The cameras might help,' offered Christine. 'We've discussed it, Stephanie, and we all agree that would be the best course of action. But, obviously, we can't install them without your permission...and we respect the fact you haven't formally given it yet.'

Henry's voice sounded far away, but Carol distinctly heard him say, 'For your sanity's sake, dear, say yes.'

Stephanie stared straight into the camera. 'Get the cameras in tonight. I'll speak to Edward – he's the only person other than myself and Henry who needs to know about this. The fewer who know, the better. And I'll hope that the meeting with Val this afternoon will at least pour some oil on troubled waters.' There was a muffled sentence in the distance, then Stephanie turned and said, 'Yes, Henry, I'm sure the kippers will be discussed. And please take Hugo's foot out of his mouth, dear. Thank you.' Into the camera she asked, 'Anything else?'

With a shaking of heads all round, the duchess thanked everyone and said goodbye. Once she'd gone, Carol said, 'Hang on for a second everyone else, please,' Annie, Christine, and Alexander all stayed where they were. 'Look, I haven't heard anything from Mavis – have any of you? Should we be worried?'

'She texted me to ask if I knew anything about a whole list of building contractors,' said Alexander. 'I don't know what's going on with you lot at the moment, but all your cases seem to involve buildings, or property. Anyway – I said I'd ask around, and I have done.'

Carol replied, 'Thanks for that, Alexander – but I can't help but think of that as odd. It seems like Mavis is bypassing the rest of us and choosing to work completely on her own. She and Althea took off, and that's all I know – not a dickie bird from either of them, except this, via Alexander. I'm going to get in touch with her, if I can.'

Annie said, 'To be honest, Car, I haven't been able to worry too much about Mave and Althea, I've got my hands full of gnomes, flamingoes, and now flying pigs…and not even a nibble at your cats, Car.'

Christine was waggling at the screen. 'Slow down, Annie – and please explain.'

Carol snapped, 'Look Annie, you tell Christine all about The Case of the…whatever you're calling it now, but I really need to go. Albert needs some of my time, too – so I'll let you all know what I hear from Mavis, okay? Bye.'

Carol clicked off and leaped out of her chair – just in time to stop Albert from shoving Bunty's tail up his nose.

# CHAPTER TWENTY-FOUR

Mavis and Althea were heading to the dining room for lunch when Mavis realized that the dowager had fallen behind. Then she heard Althea's voice ring out across the reception lounge.

'Mr Conti, have you ever thought of selling this place?'

It was clear to Mavis that Althea was using her assumed persona of a batty and slightly annoying dowager – at least, she hoped she was.

Toni Conti's indulgent response was immediate. 'I have not, Your Grace. I fell in love with The Lavender the second I set eyes on it, when I was a boy. From that moment, I wanted it to be mine. It was a foolish ambition to harbor at such a young age but, yes, I admit it. And, after I did purchase it, I spent a great deal of time and money to restore it to its original glory – as you see it now. As you know, it's been my home for many years. Inviting guests to share it with me and my wife during my retirement from my business life has turned out to be a decision not without its challenges, but I don't regret it. It's how I come to meet so many wonderfully engaging people, like yourself.'

Mavis watched Althea watching the man. When she pressed with: 'Not at any price?', Mavis wasn't surprised by Toni's curt answer of: 'No!'.

Mavis smirked as Althea flounced off, leaving Toni Conti staring after her. As he passed Mavis she whispered, 'Thanks for that, Mr Conti, Her Grace thinks she can get anything she wants, when she wants it. But I dare say many people feel the same way about The Lavender that you once did – that they would like to possess it. Are you approached about selling it very often?'

'Only every week,' he replied with a smile, 'and yet, here I am. Some things mean more than money, you know, Mrs MacDonald.'

'I understand, Mr Conti.'

Mavis joined Althea and Uma Chatterjee at what was rapidly becoming their usual table, beside the window.

'And how are you this fine day, Uma?' Mavis liked the woman, and felt sorry for her, because of the loss of her old friend.

Uma smiled broadly and replied, 'It is a lovely one, isn't it? Again. Funny that it's this warm, this late in the year. However, truthfully, I'll tell you that I'm not enjoying it very much, thank you for asking, Mavis. There's still no news about exactly how Frances died, and there's this terrible thing in the pit of my stomach that won't go away. I know we've all been chatting about her, and sort of around the topic of her death and so on, but…well, you knew her too, Mavis; don't you miss her?'

Mavis considered her response. 'I didnae know her like you did. We all always know a slightly different version of everyone we meet, don't we? I met a well-organized mature woman who was utterly professional, perfectly polite, but not…warm, exactly. Which is no' to say I didnae like her. I just didn't…connect with her often enough to really go beyond that. Tell us about the Frances you knew, Uma.'

Uma stared out of the window. 'She was brave. When we met, in our local, small school, I was the only girl who didn't have lilywhite skin in our class, and she shouted down the bullies, more than once. She stood up for me when our English teacher said I couldn't read the part of Desdemona aloud in class when we studied Othello; he said I couldn't do it because Othello talks about how white Desdemona's skin is just before he kills her. But Frances said that the boy in our class who was going to read the Othello part aloud was white, so why couldn't I be Desdemona? That was brave. She didn't like injustice.'

'Aye,' said Mavis. 'Until now, I'd forgotten about an occasion when Frances stood up for a nurse being accused of administering an incorrect dosage of a medication when it was a doctor who'd written it down wrong. She was good with details, too. Is that why you think she went to Toni Conti with her concerns about this place?' A thought struck Mavis. 'Was someone being blamed for everything that was going wrong here, and mebbe Frances thought it wasnae them?'

Uma shrugged. 'I don't know, Mavis, because she didn't tell me. That was one of her faults, I suppose – she was so secretive, in many ways. But I do happen to know that Toni's had several companies in and out of here checking into things like the electrics, the plumbing, the Wi-Fi, and so on.'

Althea slapped the table, making Mavis and Uma jump, then hissed, 'I wonder if someone's making all these things go wrong to make money for the companies who come to put them right. They could make a lot of lolly out of Conti that way.'

Uma shook her head. 'They're always different people, different companies – I haven't seen the same vans here twice.'

Althea sighed sadly and pouted. 'So that wouldn't work then, because Toni would be paying different people every time, so there's no advantage to any one company or person.'

'He's just told us, in no uncertain terms, that he'd never sell this place,' said Mavis. 'But what if all the things that have happened here had happened to someone who wasn't as attached to a place as he is to The Lavender? Might that lead them to sell, do you think?'

'You make a good point,' said Sir Malcolm nodding at each of the three women as he dragged out a chair and sat down. 'I've been having a look at everything we've pulled together between us, and I think that what you were just talking about is exactly what's been going on.'

'What's that?' Siggy joined the group.

Before Sir Malcolm could answer, Simon arrived to take the luncheon orders.

Once he'd gone, everyone leaned over the table, and Sir Malcolm continued quietly, 'We've found out that Pippa Thomas has worked at several places that have subsequently ended up being redeveloped to be suitable for lucrative short-term lettings. And they're all available for sale through Dyggan's. Those are the common denominators – Pippa Thomas and Dyggan's. What if she's sent into places to work *by* Dyggan's, just so she can make all these annoying things happen, meaning the owner throws in the towel and sells up to the estate agent?'

'What an idea,' said Althea, looking scandalized.

Sir Malcolm looked suitably grave. 'I'll grant you that a worn-down owner might, in fact, sell up to a developer, but they, in turn, could be tied to the estate agent, and maybe the Dyggan lot are doing all the buying, and the eventual selling. I've bought and sold a great deal of property in my time: the problem with garden centers is that they need a lot of land, you see, and buildings that are fit for purpose, so I've rarely been able to buy up existing buildings – I usually had to buy land and then we had to build. And when you do that often, you realize it's all a small, interconnected world. People know each other, and there are more than a few sharks out there.'

Uma sounded skeptical. 'So we think Pippa gets a job at a hotel or whatever, then plans and implements a program of sabotage, to get the owners to sell to developers that the Dyggan lot have in their pocket?'

Siggy spoke thoughtfully. 'Sounds like a possibility. And we know that Pippa's been employed by a good number of the places where that's exactly what's happened. Though I have to say that Pippa doesn't strike me as the sort of person who'd be equipped to interrupt the flow of electricity, or hot water, or whatever.'

Mavis couldn't help herself. 'You can never tell by just looking at a person what they're really capable of, Siggy, can you?'

Siggy nodded his agreement, with a raised eyebrow.

'And don't think she couldn't do all those things because she's a woman,' added Althea. 'Women can do anything they set their minds to.'

Everyone's head nodded.

When Simon had delivered the lunches, and plates were being oh-ed and ah-ed over – the kitchens did an excellent job at The Lavender, thought Mavis – the conversation turned to less knotty topics, but Mavis wasn't surprised when Althea brought the subject up again.

'How can we prove it's Pippa? Or prove it's not her, if it's not?'

Uma offered, 'Search her room? We might find something incriminating.'

Sir Malcolm shook his head. 'We can't go breaking into her room.'

'We could,' said Siggy quietly. Mavis glanced at him across the last of her buttered broad beans, but didn't comment.

Althea mused, 'When Mavis got into Frances' room, she was able to do it because the key was behind the reception desk. If we were going to get into Pippa's room when she's at work, do you think she'd bother hanging her key on the hook right behind where she's standing? I'd just keep it in my pocket, or wherever.'

'There are ways around that,' said Siggy.

Mavis decided to hold her tongue.

'What would we even hope to find?' Sir Malcom looked puzzled. 'I might have a good idea about many things, but I've no idea what tools and so forth you'd need in order to…do whatever it is that needs to be done to make things like the hot water, or the pipes stop working. An assortment of wrenches at least, I should imagine.'

'I might have done a bit of research on that front,' said Uma.

Mavis allowed her surprise to show. 'And why would you have done that?'

Uma tilted her head coyly. 'I'm curious by nature?' She smiled. For the first time Mavis noticed that the woman had one dimple: not quite up to the dowager's standard, but getting there.

'Clever Uma,' whispered Sir Malcolm.

'Indeed,' agreed Siggy.

Mavis had her suspicions that Siggy himself would be able to turn his hand to any task required to make things stop working; maybe 'sabotage' had even been a part of his job description, once upon a time. She asked, 'Your research, Uma – was it all online?'

Uma nodded. 'I never leave The Lavender.'

Mavis pressed, 'So are you saying that there are online resources that could show a person what to use, and what to do, to make the hot water stop working, make the Wi-Fi drop, cause noxious odors, and so forth?'

Uma nodded as she pushed away her plate. 'Oh yes, you can find out how to do almost anything online. There are videos for most things, and they're quite specific – you know, meaning specific to whatever system you'd be trying to nobble. Though they're all really "fix-it" videos, all you have to do is the opposite of what they say then you've "un-fixed-it", if you see what I mean.'

Siggy mused, 'So Pippa's browser history might tell us something.'

Mavis could tell that she and Siggy were thinking along the same lines. 'Aye,' she said, 'but if it is Pippa, and if she's been doing this at various locations for years, she'd no' have been looking up generalities like which bit of something to hit with a hammer. No, she'd have been checking specifics, wouldn't she? Researching the exact systems that are used here. So we'd also need to find out what systems are in this place in order for anything she'd been looking up online to be matched.'

'They might be quite common systems, for a place this size, or for a hotel in general,' said Sir Malcolm. 'Again, from my own experience, similar structures had similar heating, air conditioning, and electrical requirements.'

'But you were dealing with new buildings, as you said,' observed Mavis. 'Old places like this? They might have less common systems. So, yes, there might be something we could get on her – if we could see what she's been searching for, probably starting soon after she got here.'

Althea said, 'So a history of looking things up on her computer about how to scupper specific systems – that's a good start. Then possibly some specific tools. It might be worth scouting around her room, after all.'

'As I suggested,' said Uma quietly.

'In that case,' said Sir Malcom with authority, 'we'd have to start by coming up with a way to make sure she's out of her room for some time – which we know she is when she's on duty at the reception desk…but we'd also have to be certain that she didn't just pop back to her room for something.'

Uma said excitedly, 'A lookout, and a warning system.'

Siggy suggested quietly, 'Maybe something more concrete? A way to ensure she can't pop back because…she's not at The Lavender?'

'I could tell Toni Conti that I need her to accompany me…somewhere…for some reason.' Althea dimpled as she spoke. 'I can be quite persuasive when I need to be. But where? And why?'

'Into Tenby, for some reason?' Sir Malcolm looked vague.

'Got it,' snapped Althea. 'Mavis – you'll have to come over poorly, so you can't drive, and I'll be desperate to get something in Tenby. I'll pretend it's some sort of medication – she'll have to drive me to a chemist. How about that? It would be a real emergency. Toni would be bound to let her help me then, wouldn't he?'

Mavis panicked. 'I'm no' sure that's such a good idea.'

Uma sounded shocked. 'But you couldn't do that, Althea. You'd be putting yourself at the mercy of a potential murderer.'

Sir Malcom bridled. 'Surely we're not thinking that Pippa killed Frances, are we? I mean, have we even been told – or decided – that Frances was actually murdered?' He whispered his last word so quietly that he almost merely mouthed it.

Everyone stared at him, and chorused, 'Of course.'

He blanched. 'You really think Pippa Thomas – that young woman standing over there, not thirty feet from us – is a cold-blooded killer? Because I can't see that myself. Maybe she could manage a bit of underhand sabotage, yes. But taking someone's life? I can't begin to imagine her doing that. I mean – how would she have even done it? There's nothing of her…she couldn't have overpowered even a small woman, like Frances.'

Uma sat very upright and cleared her throat, gaining everyone's attention. 'I've met three murderers in my time, Sir Malcolm, and every one of them had a family, and friends, and even work colleagues…none of whom could believe they'd done what they'd done. But done it they had. If we could look at a person and truly know them, life would be so much easier, wouldn't it? We'd know who was lying, who was telling the truth, and who we shouldn't trust, however much we might want their words to be true. But life's not like that.'

Sir Malcolm looked taken aback. 'How on earth have you managed to meet three murderers, Uma?'

Uma sighed. 'I worked for a newspaper, you know that. Local murders usually involve local people, and when you know the people in an area you meet all sorts. Including killers. Like I did. One of them was an older woman who frequented a café I also enjoyed using – we'd nod as we sipped our cappuccinos, that sort of thing, though we never talked. It turned out that she'd killed another woman – a girl, really, because they'd both been teens at the time – in a knife fight in a nightclub, many years earlier. They got her for it when technology allowed the small blood sample the police had to be enough to get a DNA profile. Another was a man who walked his dog in the park where I used to jog…in my younger days, of course. I knew him passingly well. His dog, too – a lovely Cardigan corgi. He killed his wife. Then he killed his second wife. No one knew until he married for the third time, and she went missing. Then it all came out.'

Sir Malcolm asked, 'Was he the jeweler with a shop in The Lanes, in Brighton? They found the third wife locked in the vault, didn't they?'

Uma nodded. 'He hadn't reckoned with her mother, who more or less bullied the police into taking notice of her concerns about her daughter.'

Sir Malcolm, appeared – to Mavis's eyes at least – to be considering Uma in a fresh light.

He asked, 'And you knew him?' Uma nodded. Sir Malcolm shook his head sadly. 'So who was the third murderer you knew?'

Mavis noticed Uma's fists clenching before she spoke. 'My brother's best friend, who was my boyfriend, at the time. He killed my brother. It's…it's not something I talk about. Usually. It's…it's something I carry with me every moment of every day. He and my brother did everything together. Then, for some reason – and he never said why, not even in court – Dickie turned on my brother and pushed him off a bridge, into the river below. My brother couldn't swim. Not that he'd have stood much of a chance in any case; the river was running fast and deep. As I said earlier – the world would be a very different place if we could truly know other people when we look at them, but we cannot.'

Mavis felt enormous sympathy for Uma, but wasn't sure what to say, so allowed the silence around the table to remain undisturbed.

Mavis wasn't surprised when Althea said, 'I'm so sorry, Uma, my dear. As I'm certain we all are. I expect the pain never goes away. Is all this talk of murder now – you know, the Frances situation – upsetting you?'

Uma looked up, dry-eyed. 'Not really. You're right, it never goes away. But it happened over thirty years ago, and I've obviously got on with my life since then. Though I never did marry. However, I do have a different perspective on killers, their victims, and those left behind, I think. You see, I understand – on a deeply personal level – that bringing a killer to justice means very little. It might mean they don't kill again, of course, which is a good thing. And robbing them of their liberty is a punishment I believe they've earned. But, in all other respects, there can be no return to so-called "normal life" for anyone connected to the killing – on the victim's side of it, nor the killer's side of it – in any way. As I said, I've got on with my life, but I've lived a completely different one than I'd have lived if my boyfriend hadn't killed my brother. That being said, I do believe in justice. As a concept. And it's worth fighting for – worth doing something, anything, to make sure it's delivered. And that works both ways: it's only fair to work just as hard to prove a person innocent, as to prove they're guilty. Which is why I believe we should investigate Pippa's role in all this; not just because we want justice for Frances, but also because – if it's not Pippa doing the sabotage, and if it's not Pippa who killed Frances – then we should know that, too, and find the culprit, or culprits.'

Mavis could hear the passion in Uma's voice.

Siggy nodded gravely. 'We need a plan.'

'Mavis could become ill, overnight,' suggested Althea. 'And I could need my tablets in the morning. You could get into Pippa's room then.'

Mavis sighed. She had a feeling she knew what everyone would say next.

# 9th SEPTEMBER

# CHAPTER TWENTY-FIVE

Annie couldn't sleep. At least, she didn't believe she'd been asleep, though the hours did seem to have passed since she'd gone to bed. Tudor was making the usual noises beside her, as were Gertie and Rosie on their beds in the corner of the room; it was quite a cacophony between the three of them. Yet she was still aware of the quiet of the night through the bedroom window, which was open just a little; it still wasn't too chilly to allow for a nice bit of fresh air in the place, to help clear the remnants of the decorating smells.

Convinced she wouldn't settle again, Annie rolled out of bed as gently as she could, and tiptoed past the dogs. She closed the bedroom door after her, and thanked her lucky stars she hadn't disturbed anyone. Of course, it did occur to her that the fact that neither Gertie nor Rosie had even twitched an ear at her passing meant they couldn't be relied upon to provide an alarm should anyone try to break into the pub at any time. But that wasn't why she and Tudor had them; they loved them, and that was that.

Annie sat at the kitchen table in the dark, listening to the ancient timbers and walls of the pub make their noises, and thought she heard the wind picking up a little, rustling through the still fully-laden branches on the trees outside. She wondered if – out there, in the dark – someone was plotting another excursion into Anwen-by-Wye to steal some sort of garden ornament or other. If they were, she hoped it would be the two cats Carol had kindly loaned her that had cameras trained on them.

Realizing she wouldn't settle at all unless she took a look at what was going on outside the pub, she flipped open her laptop and accessed the screen which showed her the feed from the cameras.

Camera A gave a general view of the approach to the pub with a wide-angle lens; it gave good coverage of almost one hundred and eighty degrees in black-and-white images. It took in the front and side of the pub, including the road which approached the green, as well as part of the green itself. Camera B was directed toward the cats, giving a tighter angle and better-defined color images. If the camera captured an image of someone nabbing those cats, Annie wanted it to be good enough to allow for identification of the thief. Both cameras used infrared lighting, invisible to the naked eye, to allow for good quality recordings.

The cats were still sitting upright, surrounded by the potted flowers she'd stuffed around them, which was good. Annie fancied they looked rather smug, sitting there with their paws neatly arranged, their long, curvaceous necks slightly tilted, and their half-closed eyes suggesting their superiority. She tutted at herself; what was she thinking? They were made of varnished *papier-mâché*, they weren't real.

In the distance, Annie heard the atmospheric sound of a fox – that half yelp, half screaming-bark that it had taken her many weeks after her arrival in the village to get used to hearing. She'd seen foxes in London, but she didn't reckon they sounded the same there as they did out in the Welsh countryside. Annie smiled to herself as she realized that, now, this village was most definitely her home, and that the foxes – and all the other wildlife in the area – were her neighbors, every bit as much as the humans who lived around the village green.

The Coach and Horses pub was – by Annie's calculation – her eighth home, if she didn't count the places she'd lived in with her parents as a child. And there'd been quite a few of those. She'd always thought of the places she'd lived as temporary – the way a hermit crab might think of one of its many different shells, rather than as a snail might do, having only one. The peripatetic nature of her life had never bothered her before, but now she hoped that she and Tudor might be able to settle into this place for some time.

As Annie thought of each of the buildings around the village green, she realized she knew every single person who lived in every single home. And not just by name, but as a person with a life story, and with a clear understanding of their place within the community of Anwen. The insight came to her not as a shock, but as a revelation: she'd grown roots. She, too, was a villager. Like them. How had that happened? It had never happened to her before. She'd hardly known the people on the same landing at her last flat in Wandsworth, let alone anyone on any of the other floors.

Was that because it was a village, not an urban setting? Or was it because of the way the homes here all nestled around the central green? The heart of the place. Maybe it was just because the majority of the homes looked directly at all the others, so you always – whether you wanted to or not – had a sense of all the comings and goings there. Which was good, and bad. Did community mean no privacy? Annie had always valued her privacy. Did privacy mean no community?

Of course, clearly not *everything* that happened in the village was seen, because, otherwise, there'd be no mystery about who'd stolen Kevin, Fliss and Felix, and now Sarah Hughes's flying pigs. Unless someone *had* seen something and was choosing to keep quiet about it – which Anne thought highly unlikely. They were only garden décor items, with no real value except for the sentimental attachment felt by their owners.

She sighed, padded to the loo, then padded to the window. It was a mainly cloudy night, and the brilliant orb of the almost full moon only peeped through the clouds occasionally, meaning it was deeply dark across the green. There were no lights – that had always been the way in Anwen-by-Wye, she'd been told; outdoor lighting was not allowed, thereby keeping the village truly dark – meaning folks could see the stars, when they were not obscured by clouds. She liked that.

There weren't many truly dark places in London. She'd grown up when the streetlights had still been yellow, not the bright white they were these days, and everything had glowed in the dark. She'd liked that light, shining through her curtains at night, as a child. But she preferred the dark...like this.

A loud bark made her jump. It was across the green somewhere. Had that been a fox? She didn't think so. It didn't sound right. There it was again. Not a yappy little dog, but not a thunderous large one, either; a middle-sized dog, with a middle-sized bark. Annie gave her head a shake – what was she thinking? She chuckled at herself; before she'd had Gertie in her life, she'd never have been able to think of dog barks as something so distinctive. But being a dog-owner had allowed her to develop an appreciation of the unique voice each animal possessed.

Straining her eyes to make out anything in the darkness, she hoped she'd get a better idea of what was going on by looking at her screen. She settled herself at the table, and watched the feed from both cameras, simultaneously. Nothing. No movement anywhere.

Then she saw it: something walked…no, *loped* across the corner of the frame of the wide-angle lensed camera. Then it disappeared. What was it? It…it didn't seem to move like a dog.

Annie's mind raced; all those stories she'd read over the years about big cats roaming the British countryside were myths, weren't they? There weren't really panthers living in the wilds of Wales, were there? No…it couldn't be…

Another flash caught Annie's eye, in the same area. Something zoomed across the line of vision of the camera. She couldn't make out what it was, but it was big, fast, and on the edge of the camera's ability to capture its image.

'You're up,' said Tudor. His voice cracked with sleep. 'Why are you sitting in the dark?' He turned on a light.

'No, turn it off,' shouted Annie, too harshly.

'Sorry.' He turned the light off again.

'Oh no, you might have frightened it off, now.'

'Frightened what off?'

Annie didn't take her eyes off the screen. 'I don't know. It was something…I couldn't make it out.'

'Something? A person?'

'Some sort of animal.' Annie was willing whatever it had been to return.

'Elephant? Hedgehog? Something in between?' Tudor was behind her now, and peering over her shoulder at the laptop. 'Those cameras are good, aren't they? That one pointing at the cats themselves has a surprisingly sharp image. Was that where you saw it?'

Annie pointed the other camera's image. 'No, there. Just for a second. Definitely an animal. It loped, then ran really fast.'

She heard the telltale sounds of Gertie's claws pattering on the wooden floor. 'Gert's up now,' she said, without looking away from the screen.

Tudor laughed. 'How can you tell it's Gertie, not Rosie?'

'Gertie's always almost-running. Rosie plods more.'

'You're weird,' said Tudor. He kissed the top of her head. 'You going to sit here staring at that thing all night? Don't you think you'd be better off getting some sleep, then watching the recordings in the morning, when you're a bit better rested? I mean, it's not as though you're going to be able to do anything about whatever it is you see on that, is it? The point of the cameras is to capture an image, isn't it? Not to let you go flying down the stairs to try to nab whoever, or whatever, might approach those cats. That is right, isn't it? That's the plan? That's what you said. No running off to intervene – just record and watch, right?'

'Yeah.'

'So what's the point of sitting here, then?' Tudor leaned close to Annie. She could feel the warmth of his body on her back.

She sighed. 'I'm still wide awake, and you sound anything but. Why don't you and Gert go back in, and I'll just sit here till I feel sleepy.'

Tudor reached over Annie's head and closed the laptop. 'Come on, you won't get sleepy staring at that, and you know it. Then you'll be useless in the morning. It's gone four. You really need some rest. You had a heck of a day, yesterday – all go. And tomorrow – well, today – might be the same. You know I worry about you.'

Annie sighed. 'You won't go if I don't, will you?'

Tudor chuckled. 'Correct. You know me so well, Annie Parker. Let's all get some sleep. The recordings will be there when you wake, and we can watch them together over breakfast, alright?'

Annie sighed. 'Yeah, Tude. You're right.'

She stood and petted Gertie, whose fur was so warm and soft that Annie wanted to snuggle into it. She got a lick on the face, then said, 'Come on, Gert – back to bed.'

Gertie trotted prettily toward the bedroom door. 'And some people say I haven't got any control over her. What do they know, eh Tude?'

'Bed, Annie. Get some sleep.'

The next thing Annie knew, her alarm was going off, and she cursed the hours she'd lain awake the previous night as she forced herself to get out of bed. Tudor was already making noises in the kitchen, and she popped her head out to see what he was up to. He had three frying pans on the stove.

'Just cereal for me today,' she called.

Tudor's shoulders drooped. 'No fry-up?'

'Nah. Maybe we could save that for special occasions? You're so good at it that I don't want to take it for granted, you know?' Annie didn't want to hurt Tudor's feelings, but she also didn't want to spend all her mornings feeling completely stuffed – then miss lunch, then be starving and eating naughty things all afternoon. She loved it, but knew she shouldn't do it.

'Well, I fancy a bacon sandwich now. Just seeing the bacon, I've got my mouth in shape for it. Want one?'

Annie relented. 'Go on then – but only two rounds of bread, right?'

'Brown sauce and hot sauce?'

'Pope, Catholic. Ta. Bathroom.'

Freshly showered, and dressed, Annie munched her delicious sandwich as she scrolled through the night's recordings. She picked up where she'd left off and fast-forwarded until about the four thirty mark.

'Look – we've got him!' Annie dropped her sandwich in her excitement, and it landed on her lap, oozing sauce. 'Oh, Gordon Bennett, look what I've done.' She grabbed the sandwich, dumped it onto her plate, and stood to wipe herself down, pushing one leg of her chair against Gertie's paw. Gertie yelped, and leaped out of the way, then promptly skittered over Rosie, who'd been laying on her side, half asleep. Rosie also leaped up and darted around to Tudor's side of the table, almost tripping him up as he was carrying a mug to the table from the coffee pot.

Tudor didn't drop the mug, and Annie managed to wipe off most of the sauce with a napkin, then headed into the bathroom to put her jeans to soak so that the stains wouldn't set. It wasn't until about ten minutes later – when both she and Tudor were settled again at the table, with Gertie and Rosie beside their respective humans, at their feet – that Tudor was finally able to say, 'Right – show me whodunit.' Annie turned the screen so he could see what she could see. 'You can see for yourself.'

They both stared at the screen which showed a mottled gray blur race across the wide-angled lens, then a rump came into sharp resolution for about a second on the tighter shot, showing the cats – then the picture flared white, then, when it came back into focus, and color, one of the pair of cats had gone.

Tudor stared at Annie. 'What happened?'

Annie sighed. 'I can only think it was the moon. It was cloudy last night, but the moon was almost full. When it peeped through the clouds it was almost like daylight out there. Those infrared cameras have a filter on them: it opens at night, so the camera can gather as much infrared light as possible, giving excellent night vision. But the filter covers the lens during the day to make the colors more natural, and to block excess light from entering the lens. A flash of bright moonlight beat the equipment, by the looks of it. It might have been at an angle that meant it shone right into the lens when it popped out from behind a cloud. You can see that the camera's mechanism reacted, but just not quickly enough. And in that moment, that's when the thief acted.'

'On purpose?'

'I don't think so. See – it approached fast, up here –' Annie pointed – 'and we see it leave, but only in that tiny corner, there.' She pointed again. 'Then it's gone. As is one of the cats. Sod's Law, rather than intentional, I'd say.'

Tudor scratched his head. 'I couldn't even begin to guess what that might be, from what I saw. Except to say it's not human. Right?'

Annie nodded. 'Yeah. Not human.'

'Dog? Or – and I can't believe I'm about to say this – you know those old wives' tales about big cats?'

Annie sighed. 'Yeah, I know the ones. My thinking was in the same place yours is now at about four this morning, Tude.'

Tudor attacked the last mouthful of his sandwich. 'So, one of the bait-cats has gone, and we're none the wiser. What now?'

Annie smiled coyly. 'Well, you aren't sharing a breakfast table with an amateur, Tude. Properly trained professional, me, as you know. So, up inside each of those two hollow cats, I stuck one of those little devices you can track. Like we were talking about using for Rosie and Gertie's collars? So look, if I check the app on my phone, I might not be able to tell you who, or what, nicked that cat, but I can show you on a map where it is.'

She held the screen toward Tudor's smiling face. 'You're a clever woman, Annie Parker. Now, I suppose, you'll be wanting a lift, eh?' Annie kissed him.

# CHAPTER TWENTY-SIX

Althea was almost in tears as she explained her quandary to Toni Conti. And he was buying her sob story, which made her glow – internally only – with delight. She managed to make her chin quiver, just the way her grandson Hugo's always did before he bawled, and that, she was sure, would be that. But she didn't want to leave anything to chance.

She pressed some more. 'I'm sure that Mavis will get over her migraine quite quickly, if only she stays in her room, in the dark. But I cannot wait for these tablets, I'm afraid, Toni. It was terribly foolish of me to not bring enough. I must have miscounted. But at least I have a prescription for more with me. All I need is for Pippa to drive me to a chemist, and everything will be tickety-boo. I wouldn't steal her away for long, I promise. She looks as though she'd be a very good driver, and I am something of a particular passenger.'

Toni Conti looked down at Althea and smiled, hesitantly. 'And you're sure she couldn't just collect them for you – or could someone else do that? I'd hate to lose her, even for a couple of hours. It means I'd have to ask Maria to cover for her, you see. What about Dennis – could he take you instead? I wouldn't miss him from the garden as much as I'd miss Pippa from reception.'

Althea stuffed a hankie against her mouth and sobbed pitifully. 'I'm afraid not. It has to be me who gets them. In person. And I have to be driven by a female.'

Toni looked unsure. 'We don't have anyone due to check out today so, if she were willing to do it, could you be back before, say half one? We do have two new guests arriving today, but not until after two.'

Althea knew she'd won. 'But of course, Toni. So – the sooner we go, the better, eh?' Althea tried to hide her delight – she didn't want to appear to have recovered from her distress too quickly.

Toni nodded. 'I'll speak to Pippa now. I'll find you in the dining room. I presume you'll be having breakfast before you go.'

Althea beamed. 'Indeed, Toni. Most important meal of the day. See you in a moment, then.'

Althea wanted to punch the air with delight, but restrained herself, and took a seat at the window table for which she was developing quite a liking. Simon delivered tea, and she took a few moments to contemplate the day ahead.

It had been decided that a migraine was just the right malady from which she should say Mavis was suffering: they came on at the drop of a hat, and at unpredictable times, were quite debilitating, then disappeared just as surprisingly. The perfect cover story. They'd both agreed it would be highly unlikely that anyone would be so rude as to ask Althea what type of medication she needed so urgently, so they hadn't bothered with a detailed background for that side of things, but Althea felt confident, now, that their plan would work.

When Siggy arrived at the breakfast table, he appeared to be genuinely concerned about Mavis's condition. Althea was impressed, but not surprised. She'd had him pegged as MI6 since he'd first mentioned his job, so expected him to be a jolly good actor. And he was. He was also rather an appealing man, with the remnants of what she was convinced had once been dashing good looks, and very good hair and teeth.

They were joined by Sir Malcolm and Uma, who arrived together. Well, not *together*, Althea, told herself – there was no way they were a couple. Completely unsuited to each other. In fact, the only potential alliance for which Althea could see a possibility was between Mavis and Dennis. Althea had really taken to Dennis, and that wasn't just because of his name, nor his lupins. He had a bit of go in him, and she very much wanted Mavis to have someone like that in her life. She deserved it. She certainly deserved more than sitting in the Dower House with Althea every evening.

She'd have to Do Something About That. Yes, Dennis Moore.

'So it's all set, I hear,' said Sir Malcom, addressing Althea.

She pulled herself from her reverie. 'Indeed,' she replied. 'I was never in any doubt, of course.'

The Lavender Mob all nodded and agreed that, of course, she was bound to have been able to get it all to work out. She accepted their congratulations with what she hoped was humility. 'I think the hardest part of all this will fall to poor Mavis,' she added. 'She's not one to let others do the work, as a rule. But she agreed that, since her incapacitation is my reason for needing Pippa's help, she cannot be seen leaving her room, at all, during my absence. You will all do a good job for her – for Frances – won't you? Make a thorough search, but ensure Pippa never has a clue you've been there?'

Althea took the nodding heads of Sir Malcolm and Uma to be a signal of intention only. It was Siggy's response that intrigued her most. He said, 'She'll have no idea we've been there.' Althea had no doubt that, if he had anything to do with it, that would most certainly be the case.

Breakfast was a relatively swift affair, as the entire group was keen to execute its plan, and to find out if Pippa was hiding anything that might either prove, or disprove, their suspicions about her. All of which meant that it wasn't much past nine when Althea allowed herself to be led by the young redhead toward the car park. Once she saw Pippa's car she feared for her comfort; Mavis's ancient Morris Traveller had its moments, but Pippa's car looked like a toy. It was tiny, had only two seats, and looked as though it had been designed by a child who'd entirely forgotten to provide the back half of the vehicle.

Althea was rather glad she was a compact person as she buckled herself into the passenger seat, and was most grateful that Pippa herself was as slim as she was pale, because there wouldn't have been room for two people with well-rounded hips in the seats which, to be fair, weren't as uncomfortable as Althea had feared.

Althea could immediately tell that Pippa lacked a winning personality, which she found odd in a person who'd been retained by Toni Conti as a receptionist.

'Do you like him?' Althea realized as soon as she'd spoken that her driver wouldn't have any idea what she was talking about.

She was greatly surprised when Pippa replied, 'Toni's not the worst boss I've had, not by a long chalk. He cares about the guests, and the people who work for him. Thoughtful, but not very...professional.'

'Well, he's not really running a business, as such, is he?'

'S'pose not.'

Althea thought she'd chat while the chatting was good. 'He really does seem to like having people around to interact with.'

'Except he doesn't really interact much with the residents – you know, like the three you've got pally with. They're all very quiet. Reserved. No, he's never mixed with them much. It's like he's…I don't know…just given them a quiet refuge?'

'I say, that's terribly perceptive of you, Pippa,' said Althea. She was genuinely impressed by the young woman. 'I dare say your experience as a receptionist must mean you meet all sorts, and have the opportunity to size people up. Do you enjoy that aspect of your role?'

Althea felt that, since she was going to be spending time with Pippa – albeit as a ruse to keep her away from her room – she might as well do a bit of digging of her own.

'I do,' replied Pippa thoughtfully. 'Though, sometimes, I'm quite wrong about them.'

Althea said gleefully, 'Oh, do tell.'

Althea saw a strange smile on Pippa's face. 'Like you, for example. When you arrived – well, when I first met you, in any case – I thought you were a phony.'

Althea bridled. 'Why so?'

'You're just a bit too batty to be real. The way you dress, for example. A bit OTT, isn't it?'

Althea considered what she was wearing: a yellow chiffon skirt, pink blouse, and a green scarf. 'I always dress like this.' She felt a little wounded, and let it show.

'Really? Why?'

Althea considered her response. 'I like to be comfy. Besides, who cares what I look like? I'm old. And no one would criticize me openly, in any case. I'm rather surprised you even mentioned how I dress. What if I were to complain to Mr Conti about you being rude? Aren't you worried that you might lose your job?'

Pippa chuckled. 'No. I won't be there long, anyway. You can even tell him that, if you like. No skin off my nose.'

Althea was surprised by the turn the conversation had taken. 'You were quite badly affected by the death of that woman, Frances, weren't you?' Toni said you needed a couple of days off to recover. Is that why you're leaving?'

'How d'you mean?' Pippa's tone took Althea aback – it was quite sharp.

She cooed, 'I suppose you knew her well. Was she a nice person?'

'S'pose so. Bit of an old fusspot, if you ask me. Stuck her nose in where it wasn't wanted.'

Althea pressed. 'How do you mean? I thought she was Mr Conti's secretary. Wouldn't that mean she'd have a role to play in quite a lot of what goes on at The Lavender as part of her job description?'

'She reckoned.'

Althea was intrigued. She knew The Lavender Mob would be casing the joint, back at the hotel, and couldn't help but wonder what they might find in Pippa's room. How could she help them?

She dimpled, and said, 'My son, the duke, says I meddle. I don't, I'm just old and don't have the capability to get involved in much these days, so I like to know what's going on around me. It helps pass the time. Maybe she wasn't meddlesome? Just taking an interest in her surroundings? I understand that lots of little things have been going wrong at The Lavender over the past several weeks. Indeed, the electricity's gone off a couple of times while Mavis and I have been staying, as has the Wi-Fi, and the hot water wasn't hot at all when I went to bed last night. Was that the sort of thing Frances was worried about?'

Pippa checked both ways before she turned at a T-junction. 'You and that Scottish woman, you've got yourselves very cozy with Uma, Sir Malcolm, and Siggy, and they're a right odd bunch. Never even talked to each other before you two turned up, now they're hardly ever apart. That's another thing that's made me wonder about you. That's not normal. The temporary guests at The Lavender usually keep themselves to themselves.'

Althea didn't want to be drawn on that topic. 'As I said, I live a small life on the Chellingworth Estate, so to be out and about in the world is quite exciting. I said so to Mavis just the other morning, when I knocked over that orchid – which I still feel badly about.'

'What orchid?'

'The one at the top of the stairs.'

'I wondered where that had gone – you knocked it over?'

Althea said, 'I'm afraid so. I didn't see it in the dark.'

'Why was it dark?'

'It usually is at half-three in the morning, dear.' Althea was losing her patience a little.

'What were you doing out in the hallway at half past three in the morning?' Pippa managed a slight turn of the head, and Althea noticed her eyes narrowing.

*Drat! She'd almost given herself away.* 'Apparently, I wander. Mavis heard me and came to get me. It's why I came to The Lavender. My doctor suggested the sea air.'

Even just one side of Pippa's face was enough to tell Althea that she wasn't impressed. 'Well, that's a load of old guff. Doctors don't say that sort of thing these days. It's all pills and tests, if you can get to see one at all, that is. Got a posh one, have you?'

Althea was miffed. 'He's in Harley Street, if that's what you mean.'

'Whatever,' said Pippa dismissively.

Althea was cross with herself. The young woman seemed to be getting a lot of information out of Althea, when it should have been the other way around. 'So did you know her well? Frances?'

'Sort of.'

Althea was starting to get really annoyed. 'How did she die? Have they said yet? All Mr Conti said was that it wasn't something catching.'

Pippa laughed aloud and slapped the steering wheel. 'Yeah, he would say that. Never annoy the guests, right? I don't know what she died of. Besides, why do you care?'

Althea shouted, 'Cat!'

Pippa flinched and the little car swerved. 'What are you on about?'

Althea pointed behind them. 'There was a cat at the side of the road. I thought it was going to run out in front of us. Sorry, dear, I didn't mean to alarm you. It was a lovely black one – which they say is good luck. You know, if it crosses your path. But I don't think it would have been very lucky for us if it had done so. You have good reactions,

Pippa. Well done. And you kept your cool, too. Mavis would have been telling me off for shouting at her by now. Poor thing.'

For some time after that, Althea did her best to come up with remarks about the countryside, or how unexpectedly smooth the ride was – but Pippa did nothing but grunt by way of a reply.

Eventually, Pippa asked, 'Why is Mavis a poor thing?'

Althea took the chance to natter. 'Migraines. She's a martyr to them. So thank you for this. By the way, is the chemist's shop much farther? We seem to have driven a long way, and Mr Conti gave me to believe the place wasn't that far.'

'I've made a little detour. Someone I've got to see. I hope you don't mind. Since I had to drive you toward Tenby, I thought I'd take the chance. We're nearly there – then we'll stop at the chemist on the way back.'

Althea's tummy clenched as Pippa pulled up to the curb outside the windows of Dyggan's estate agency. Althea tried to slide down in her seat, with little success: the car was small, but, for all that, the seats were quite upright, and the windows were large. She rearranged her scarf to hide as much of her face as possible, and hoped Pippa wouldn't notice.

Pippa unbuckled herself. 'I just need a quick word with my sister. She works here. I'll be back in five minutes. You okay here?'

Althea waved and smiled. 'Just tickety-boo, thank you, Pippa.'

As soon as she was alone, Althea wondered why Pippa had brought her here. Who was her sister? Maybe the phantom photocopier, Bethan, who'd been hidden in the back room when she and Mavis had visited the day before? Althea couldn't think of anything else.

She rued the fact she'd put her handbag at her feet, because it meant she had to unbuckle to be able to reach down, so she could get her phone to text Mavis – who would most certainly want to know of this development; it seemed that The Lavender Mob had been onto something...Pippa and her sister...yes.

Althea's head popped up, she had her phone in her hand, and she was about to settle back to type a text when her car door opened, and she almost fell out.

Standing over her, leering, was Gerry Dyggan himself. 'Well, hello again, Your Grace. Two visits in two days, eh? We're honored.'

Althea felt flummoxed. 'Oh, I haven't come back to see you. Pippa brought me here. I'm just a passenger.'

Pippa was standing behind Gerry, as was another woman – younger than Pippa, but with the same copper curls. It had to be the sister, thought Althea.

The sister said, 'Come on in, Althea. Like I said to Gerry, we'd be happy for you to have a cuppa while we talk about cats.'

Althea was both confused, and nervous. The young woman's tone was unmistakably threatening. She forced her dimples into play. 'You all take as long as you want, I'll sit here. It's a lovely day for it.'

Gerry pulled her arm. 'Really, I insist.'

Althea tried to wrench her arm from his grasp, but he just grabbed on tighter, which hurt. She didn't like how her situation was making her feel, and not just because her arm was sore.

'I don't think I should,' she said, waving her free hand in front of her face. 'I don't feel quite myself.'

But Gerry didn't fall for it. Instead, he put his arm around her shoulders and all but pulled her bodily from the car. 'All the more reason to come in for a proper sit-down, Your Grace.'

Pippa and her sister steered Althea into the estate agent's shop, and flipped the sign on the door to CLOSED.

# CHAPTER TWENTY-SEVEN

Christine had been promising herself a bit of a lie-in for days, and had finally taken the chance to have one. When she eventually dragged herself out of bed, she was dismayed to discover that it was already gone ten, and she knew she'd be behind for the whole day.

Alexander had left a note beside the coffee maker, and he'd ground beans for her before he'd left at…gracious, before seven. She knew he had his work cut out for him with all the jobs being done in the village, but she hadn't foreseen that he'd be so…hands-on with the whole thing. His note said he wanted to make sure that the roofers were getting on well at the old school, and that she should text him when she was 'with it'.

Showered and dressed, Christine finally settled herself with a mug of coffee and her laptop on the sofa in her flat. Although the office was just down the spiral staircase, she didn't fancy working down there in the yawning space; she was cozy upstairs. She opened her laptop and retrieved the feed from the cameras that she and Alexander had set up in the kitchens up at Chellingworth Hall. She hoped that she'd see something useful, then couldn't help but chuckle to herself as she watched an empty kitchen, at night, from four different angles. Until…

She hit the pause icon, and replayed the recording again. Yes, there was a shadow moving on the wall. But what was making the shadow? There weren't any lights on in the kitchen. Christine played it again. Someone with a torch? Yes, the light source was moving, as well as the figure. She watched at real-time speed as the shadows moved, but no actual figure came into the camera's field of vision. One camera was pointing at Cook Davies's pantry, another into the baking kitchen, another had a wide-angled view of the main kitchen, and the fourth caught the chill-room door and entry from the main kitchen.

Finally, a figure appeared. It was wearing a tracksuit, with a hooded top. The figure was waving a tiny torch, using its free hand to open cupboards and drawers. It was moving items from one drawer to another, and from one cupboard shelf to another.

*That's got to be really annoying when you're looking for something,* thought Christine.

Paul Baker wasn't a large man, so it could be him. He was slim, and this figure wasn't fat. The figure didn't have a pronounced bosom, but there wasn't any real reason it couldn't be a woman. Cook Davies? It could be, though Christine wondered if the movements were just a little too fluid for it to be a person in their sixties, which Cook Davies was. So more likely to be Paul. But…but this figure didn't move like a man. It…it walked daintily.

Christine wished she could see the figure's feet – then rationalized that big feet didn't necessarily mean a male owner, as Annie was always pointing out. If she was lucky, and watched carefully, maybe the figure would show its face to one of the cameras.

As she watched, Christine noted down time codes and camera identifications so she could go back to the parts of the recordings where she might stand the best chance of enhancing images to get a better idea of the person's identity.

Over the next half an hour or so, Christine made a list for further reference, but, sadly, at no time did the figure show its face to any of the cameras. At one point she got a good side view, but it was clear that the figure was masked – with a scarf or kerchief, worn the way cowboys in old Westerns on TV used to do.

When the figure disappeared, she fast-forwarded to see if it returned, but it didn't. However, she did see the arrival of Paul Baker, then of Cook Davies, and then the other members of the kitchen staff.

And then the fireworks started; it was clear that the activities of the shadowy figure had borne the fruit the saboteur had hoped for. Paul Baker emerged from his baking kitchen, and the chiller room, waggling a box of butter in Cook Davies's face, and she, meanwhile, was pointing a large knife at him, which she'd pulled from a drawer. Christine had seen the figure put it in there, having taken it from its sheath which hung in pride of place above the ancient butcher's block. Christine knew that putting a good knife into a drawer with other sharp-edged items was a big no-no, so Cook Davies's reaction wasn't unexpected, though it looked quite alarming on the screen.

Rather than wait for any more developments, she thought it best to phone Stephanie straight away.

'Hello Christine,' answered Stephanie, sounding frazzled. 'Tell me you have some news. Please. The atmosphere here is becoming really quite difficult.'

Christine recounted everything she'd seen.

Stephanie's reaction sounded to be a mixture of panic, and relief. 'Of course, I wasn't privy to the scene in the kitchen this morning, but – according to Edward – the waving of the knife led to accusations being made on the part of Paul Baker that became quite personal in nature. I had wondered if Paul had been overreacting, but with you describing what happened, I can quite see why the man might have felt truly physically threatened.'

'Have things settled down now?' Christine hoped they had, because she was still at a loss to know how reports of an unidentified figure might help: both Baker and Davies could still, if they chose, point the finger of blame at the other, with no clue as to the saboteur's true identity.

'Somewhat,' said Stephanie. 'I took Hugo down there and stood them both in the middle of the kitchen and forced them to shake hands. I'm not sure how much good it did, but at least they each retired to their own corner and got on with the day, in a manner of speaking. Luckily, they don't have to interact much down there, and they aren't within each other's sight if Paul's in the baking kitchen, and Cook Davies is in the main one. I just hope neither needles the other.'

'I'm assuming that things didn't go well when Val Jenkins visited you yesterday then?'

Stephanie sighed heavily. 'To be fair to Val, she did a wonderful job. And I thought that we'd reached at least a truce in the kitchen. But this morning's events made everything flare up again, and with more vehemency than before. It's...quite worrying. Henry and I have discussed sacking Paul Baker – because, of the two of them, he's the one we could more easily replace. Though we'd have to make some sort of arrangement to ensure that the supply of baked goods to the Lamb Tearooms was sustained while we recruited someone new.'

Christine replied, 'I'm going back to the recordings now, and I'll capture the best images of the figure that I can. If I send them to you, could you take a look at them? Maybe you can tell who it is – or even be more certain than I am of who it isn't. Then…well, would you like me to come over to ask Baker and Davies where they were at the time in question? At least now we have something to show them, proving that someone is doing the things they claim are being done by the other. And we can show them the lengths that person has gone to just to ensure that they aren't easily identified.'

Stephanie thanked Christine. 'By all means let me see the images, because you're right, I might be able to spot something you can't. I'll let Henry have a look too. Now, is there anything else I need to know? Or shall I let you get back to sorting out some good images for us to look at?'

Christine gave her answer some thought. 'I'll get on, and I'll email them to you as soon as I can – and I'll text you to let you know I've done that.'

'Thanks, Christine. It's not a solution, but I feel we're on the right path. Talk later.'

Christine was as good as her word, and within an hour or so she had three sharp images of the mystery figure, one a full-body image, showing the figure in motion, another close-up of the masked side of the person's face, and a third showing them crouching to reach for something down low, which showed how flexible they were. She emailed and texted Stephanie, then took the time to write up her report for her colleagues, and sent them the images being sure to cover all her bases.

# CHAPTER TWENTY-EIGHT

Mavis suspected she was feeling more frustrated than at any previous time in her life. And that was saying something. She'd been stuck in her room at The Lavender all morning, without the faintest idea about what on earth was going on, anywhere. It was making her cross, and all she could do was scream silently at the walls.

She'd sent texts galore to Siggy Welbeck, and to Sir Malcolm Lee, and to Uma Chatterjee – with no response from any of them. She'd have expected them to have searched Pippa's room by now, but they still hadn't sent word of their findings – which they'd promised to do as soon as they were able.

And where the devil was Althea? Mavis was conflicted about that. She reasoned that if Althea came back, it meant that Pippa had returned. Which, in turn, meant that if something had stopped The Lavender Mob from getting into Pippa's room when they had planned to, they might be found out. So, theoretically, the longer Althea kept Pippa away, the longer there'd be to search her room.

Mavis stared at her watch. Everything should be over by now. Surely.

She jumped at the sound of a loud rapping at her door.

'Aye, who's there?' Mavis feigned a weakened voice, just in case it was someone who needed to believe the migraine story.

'It's us,' said Siggy's voice.

Mavis pulled open the door, to find herself facing Sir Malcolm, Siggy, Uma…and Toni Conti. She stood her ground, and did her best to look pathetic.

'I think you have some explaining to do, Mrs MacDonald,' said Toni Conti, stepping forward so he stood just a few inches in front of her. He glared down at her upturned face.

'I'll do no such thing.' Mavis also stepped forward until her whole body was touching Toni's. The immediate shift in his expression told Mavis she'd won; he stepped back, looking embarrassed.

'We all need to come in, Mavis. He caught us at it,' said Siggy, sounding resigned to the situation.

Mavis stood aside and watched as everyone managed to find themselves a spot to sit. The bed hosted Uma, Siggy, and Sir Malcolm; it didn't sag too much. Toni took the seat at the little desk, leaving Mavis with the armchair beside the window.

Toni began curtly. 'I think I have a right to ask why four…no, five of my guests – because I dare say the dowager is in on this too, which I am amazed about – have conspired against a member of my staff. Three of you have lived here for some time, and I have to say that I'm shocked. That you have dragged Mrs MacDonald and the dowager into this…mess…is unforgivable. I demand an explanation. My staff have every right to their privacy.'

Mavis looked across the room at Siggy, whose expression was stoic. He said, 'There comes a time in a campaign when one has to decide that the only way for the goal to be achieved is for the initial strategy to be shelved, and an alternative one adopted. This, in turn, demands that different tactics be employed. My suggestion, in this instance, would be to invite our host to join our team, and furnish him with the facts to date. How say you all?'

Mavis said, 'Aye.' Uma nodded.

Sir Malcolm cleared his throat and uttered a begrudging, 'Hmm.'

Siggy said, 'Mavis – over to you to kick things off, I'd say.'

Mavis was at least pleased that Siggy recognized her role, so she told Toni Conti everything that had happened, beginning with the visit made by Frances Millington to the offices of the WISE Enquiries Agency. She was pleased that the man didn't interrupt. Not once. He just stared.

When she'd finished, Mavis said, 'I wonder if you'd tell me what's happened this morning, Uma, Siggy, Sir Malcolm.'

Toni Conti finally spoke. 'Yes, please do…right up to the point when I found you in Pippa's *private* room.'

Uma began. 'We decided that Sir Malcolm would be our lookout, so he took his position in the lounge, where he could see anyone coming or going – Pippa, or you, Toni. And I was second lookout, along the corridor from Pippa's room, in case anyone came that way. Sir Malcolm would text me, and, if the danger he'd spotted came closer, or if I spotted one myself, I was to text Siggy. Siggy was assigned the task of entering Pippa's room and undertaking the search.'

This time, Toni did interrupt. 'This sounds like a military exercise. Who came up with this plan?'

Uma and Sir Malcolm both looked at Siggy, but said nothing.

Mavis noticed that Toni Conti raised one eyebrow and looked…unsurprised. 'Go on,' he urged.

Sir Malcolm said, 'I have to say I feel I contributed very little to the whole operation. I understand that my role was essential, but since Pippa didn't return, and you obviously managed to get upstairs without using the main entryway, or staircase, Toni, I fell at the only hurdle on the racecourse, it seems. Sorry.'

'I didn't go up, I came down,' said Toni. 'I'd been upstairs, sorting out a few things in our apartment, because – with Pippa gone – Maria stood in for her at reception.'

Sir Malcolm looked relieved, judged Mavis. 'At least I didn't mess that bit up,' he said.

'But I did,' said Uma. 'I was watching the stairs, and I didn't pay any attention to what was happening behind me. I know you have your own stairs down from your floor that come out beside the lift, Toni, but I didn't realize there was another set at the far end of the corridor. Hence my not looking behind me. But, still, I feel I have to answer for this.'

'Not your fault,' said Siggy. 'If I'd closed the door to Pippa's room properly, Toni wouldn't have spotted me in there. All down to me. An error worthy of an amateur. I feel…terribly despondent about that. I must be slipping. As my superiors suggested.'

Toni Conti snapped, 'I really don't care too much about the ins and outs – what I want to know is what the devil you were doing there in the first place.'

Mavis replied rather tartly, 'I just explained the basis for our suspicions, Toni; I laid out our whole theory about Pippa, and the role we fear she's played over the years in making owners of properties ripe for redevelopment more ready to sell because of their buildings being beset by problems she's caused. I even explained what Siggy would have been looking for in her room. Did you no' get that?'

Toni looked affronted, and Mavis wondered if she'd gone too far.

He snapped, 'Yes, I got it, but I still don't think that breaking into someone's private dwelling – which is what Pippa's room is – is acceptable.'

Mavis ignored him. 'What did you find, Siggy? Anything useful?'

Siggy nodded and pulled out his phone. 'I took photos. Maybe Toni would like to see them, while I explain.' The phone was passed, like a parcel; there was no music to accompany its journey, but it stayed in Toni's hands when it arrived there. Mavis watched as he stared at the screen and scrolled, as Siggy explained. Mavis listened intently, as did both Sir Malcolm and Uma. Various exclamations left the lips of all four members of Siggy's audience at various points. Mavis was in absolutely no doubt whatsoever that Siggy was loving every moment of being in the spotlight.

When Siggy sat back, with a smile of satisfaction on his face, Mavis nodded her appreciation.

She summed up, 'So you found electrical and plumbing plans for the entire building, a small but comprehensive toolkit, a totally illegal stun gun – useful when applied to Wi-Fi routers, no doubt – and a collection of nasty insects and rodents, all dead, and kept in Pippa's personal refrigerator's little ice box.'

'And a cat,' added Siggy. 'Somewhat timid, but it did have a bit of a go at me when I went near Pippa's bed. Decent set of claws on the creature.'

'And a cat,' acknowledged Mavis.

'Cats are forbidden here,' said Toni heavily. 'Maria's horribly allergic. Pippa must have…well, I suppose she kept herself well-groomed, so that Maria wasn't sneezing all the time, which was decent of her.'

Mavis allowed her surprise to show. 'That's what you're taking from all of this?'

Toni's neck reddened. 'No. But you know what I mean. Pippa's…crossed some lines, I think that much is clear.'

'Crossed some lines?' Mavis couldn't believe her ears. 'She's orchestrated a campaign of massive inconvenience for you and your residents, for some months. Do you no' see that, Toni? Any evidence of a concrete link to the Dyggan outfit, Siggy?'

Siggy smiled slyly as he nodded. 'Indeed. She had an email account on her personal laptop – which I, um, managed to access – with no emails sent or received. That's an old one: two parties have password-protected access to an email account which is never used to send emails, thereby eliminating an actual email trail. All each party has to do is write an email, save it as a draft message, then the other party checks the draft messages and – hey presto – they're talking to each other. Detailed communication in the draft email box between her and one G Dyggan – the Gerry you and Althea met with yesterday, I believe – and someone named Bethan T. All their plans for the sabotage are there. And this isn't the only property they are targeting. There's a B and B on the seafront in Tenby itself where someone named Otterlie Bowen is doing what Pippa is doing here. This Otterlie took up a position as a cleaner at the B and B two weeks ago, so it's early days for that campaign, it seems. It's also clear that this is something they've been doing for some time. The dates of the draft emails go back at least four years.'

Mavis noticed that Toni was sagging as Siggy spoke. He said weakly, 'But it doesn't necessarily mean that Pippa...um...you know...' Toni wasn't able to finish his sentence.

Mavis stepped up. 'Did you find anything to suggest, or prove, that Pippa did, or did not, kill Frances Millington, Siggy?'

Siggy stood. Uma and Sir Malcom almost toppled off the bed. Siggy approached Toni and held out his hand. 'If I may? My phone, please.'

Toni relinquished the phone and Siggy scrolled. As he did so he said, 'To my eyes, there's been a struggle in Pippa's room. I've taken photographs of scratches on the walls – the wallpaper's been hit by something sharp, leaving dragging cuts – see, here?' He passed the phone to Mavis.

'Aye, I see what you mean. Something hard's hit it there, then bounced off, or fallen down. Broken...pottery? Glass?'

Siggy took his phone back and pocketed it. 'Never having seen the room before, I don't know what might be missing. A vase? A bowl of some sort? Maybe a framed photograph? That sort of thing did this, in all probability. If there was an altercation, it's unlikely anyone would have heard it.'

'Why so?' Mavis was puzzled.

Uma sounded extremely glum when she said, 'Pippa's room is at the end of the corridor. The only room adjoining hers was the one used by Frances herself.'

Mavis checked, 'Is that it, Siggy?'

Siggy nodded.

Sir Malcolm sounded dreadfully disappointed when he said, 'So we can prove that Pippa's the saboteur, but we still don't know what happened to Frances.'

'It might have something to do with the cat,' said Uma quietly.

Mavis felt her brow furrow. 'The cat? Why the cat?'

Uma was nibbling her thumbnail. 'Frances had a fierce dislike of cats. She was almost smothered by one, when she was a baby. Those stories about cats sitting on a baby's face, and the baby dying? Well, Frances' mother took her, as a babe in arms, to visit a friend of hers. Her mother put Frances onto the friend's bed for a nap, and the friend's cat sat on her face. Apparently, Frances was blue by the time they went back to have a look at her. Frances used to have nightmares about cats when she was young – when I knew her at school. Unsurprisingly, she couldn't abide them.'

Mavis put her brain to work. 'What if...what if Frances worked out what we worked out about Pippa and did the same thing – you know, somehow got into Pippa's room and then the cat went for her...no, that won't work.'

Siggy urged, 'Go on, Mavis.'

Mavis focused. 'Frances was found dead in her bed, in the morning, that's correct, Toni – yes?' Toni nodded. 'And we don't know what she died of, yet...'

Toni waggled a hand. 'I got through to someone at the hospital. I've been dealing with them, because Frances didn't have any family.'

'You're wrong, Toni,' said Uma sharply. 'We were her family. The Lavender was her home...and you threatened to make her leave.'

Mavis pressed, 'What did the hospital say, Toni?'

'All they said was what the paramedics said – a heart attack. I said she was as healthy as a horse, but they said she was taking tablets for arrythmia, which I have to say I knew nothing about. Did you know, Uma?'

Uma nibbled her lip. 'I knew she saw the doctor once a month, but she didn't say why. And she certainly took tablets regularly, because she'd go to collect them. And she took statins, of course. Well, everyone does, don't they?'

Mavis was surprised when everyone else in the room nodded.

She asked, 'Any marks on her body, Toni? Did they say?'

Toni shrugged. 'They didn't give me chapter and verse. I'm not a relative, see? Just the next best thing, I suppose – and I was doing my best to get information out of them because…well, so many people keep asking me about her. Marks? I didn't ask, and they didn't offer. Though you'd think they'd mention something like…a wound. Is that what you mean, Mrs MacDonald?'

'No, I was thinking more of two small marks, about an inch or so apart,' mused Mavis.

Siggy pounced, 'The stun gun! If Frances had heart problems, maybe being zapped with a stun gun could give her a heart attack? I'm no medical professional – so, what do you say, Mavis?'

Mavis almost chuckled. 'In all my years of nursing I learned one very important thing: the human body is a wondrous instrument, and – generally – it works in predictable ways…until it doesn't. You'd be hard-pressed to find any truly knowledgeable medical professional who would tell you that the human body will *always* act in a certain way, or can *never* act in a certain way. Unless they're naïve, of course. But I still cannae put this together in my head. Toni – has there been a post-mortem? Did they *tell* you that she died in her bed? Did they give you a time of death?'

Toni smiled. 'There's been a post-mortem, and they said she'd died where she was found – which was in her bed. And they said she died in the early hours of the morning of the fifth of September. The day you arrived. That was the time of death according to the post-mortem.'

Mavis said, 'Now that's something – we know when she actually died. And where she died, which they'd have worked out due to lividity, and so forth.' She looked up. 'All know what that is?' Everyone nodded except Toni. She explained, 'When you die, the blood stops pumping around your body. It settles. Depending on the position you're in when you die, it'll settle in different places. It's gravity at work. If you died sitting there, at that desk, Toni, the blood would pool in your feet, ankles, and lower legs, your hands and lower arms, and the undersides of your thighs, and your rear end. But if you'd died in bed, laying on your right side, the blood would pool accordingly. So they'd know if Frances had died elsewhere and had then been moved…unless she was moved almost immediately, that is.'

Sir Malcolm asked, 'I don't understand why that's important, Mavis. Can you explain, please?'

Mavis smiled indulgently. 'We know that Frances suspected Pippa of the sabotage. Did Frances go to Pippa's room to try to gather evidence against her – as we did? Or maybe even to confront her? There are possible signs of a struggle in Pippa's room. Pippa has a cat. Pippa has a stun gun. To me that offers a possible scenario wherein Frances dies in Pippa's room. But—'

Sir Malcolm interrupted, 'But Frances was found in her own bed, not in Pippa's room, Mavis. And I can't be alone in believing that Pippa's probably not capable of moving Frances' dead body.'

'What if she had help?' Uma's suggestion startled Mavis.

Mavis acknowledged her point. 'Aye. But if Frances died in Pippa's room, and she was moved, with help, after her death – that help had to come fast, or they'd have seen signs on the body.'

Siggy said, 'An accomplice? Here, at The Lavender, you think?'

Mavis shrugged. 'You know everyone here much better than I do. What do you think?'

'I wish we could ask Pippa herself,' said Uma testily. 'Where on earth is she? And Althea, of course.'

Mavis looked at her watch. She felt an unpleasant tinge at the nape of her neck. 'They've been gone far too long. This cannae be good. I'll ring her again, though she's no' answered any of my texts.'

# CHAPTER TWENTY-NINE

Annie couldn't believe how the world seemed to be conspiring against her. She'd been champing at the bit when she'd got up that morning, eager to go to the location where the tag she'd attached to the missing bait-cat was blinking on her app.

Carol had taken Albert for a planned doctor's appointment, which meant she wasn't able to drive Annie out into what appeared to be the middle of nowhere. Christine hadn't replied to her texts with more than a: 'Sorry, a bit tied up for now'. Mavis was still away in Pembrokeshire. And Tudor? He'd said he'd drive her there when Aled arrived, but they'd had an early rush, the two of them had been busy, and she was still waiting for a lift. She noted that it was almost lunchtime, and feared there'd be another rush soon. She promised herself she'd have another go at the driving lessons, soon, because this not being able to get about under her own steam was doing her head in.

Eventually, Carol texted to say she was back from the doctor, and asked if Annie still wanted a lift. Annie texted back that she did, grabbed her stuff and managed to give Tudor a peck on the cheek as she raced out of the pub to her friend's house next door. She knocked at the kitchen door and waited until Carol let her in. Albert was fast asleep in his father's arms.

'He's worn out,' said Carol. 'Look at him. Comatose. Lovely.'

David smiled at Annie, and whispered, 'He's at his most perfect, right now. Look at that face.'

Annie did. It was squashed against his father's shoulder. She didn't know why David had bothered whispering – it looked as though a brass band playing in the kitchen couldn't have woken Albert.

However, Annie thought it best to follow suit so whispered, 'Smashing. Lovely boy.'

'The best,' agreed David quietly.

Annie raised an eyebrow toward Carol, who said, 'David's on duty now. Let's get going.'

The journey was…interesting. By watching the screen on Carol's dashboard, and the app on her own phone, Annie finally got the hang of the differences between the two, but when she looked up, reality didn't seem to be closely related to either of them. However, the little dot showing where the tag was located was, most definitely, getting closer – at least, they were getting closer to it.

Half an hour later, they were facing a massive field, that was semi-vertical, surrounded by tall hedges in full leaf. They stood looking over a metal gate that was sturdy, and heavily padlocked.

Carol stood firm. 'I know the app says the tag is in there, somewhere, but I'm not climbing over this gate, Annie. Not in this frock. I didn't change before I left home, and this is one of my good ones. It's not stained. And it fits nicely. I don't want to go pulling it all out of shape or catching it on things.'

Annie could feel her frustration building. 'It's there – out there. In that field somewhere. That mystery animal I saw on the camera must have some sort of lair, or whatever, and we're this close. Come on, Car. I'll give you a leg up. There's no one around. Just pull your frock around your waist and have at it. I won't look.'

'It's all well and good for you to say that – you're in jeans.'

'Fetch one of Bertie's blankets from your boot. I'll hold it up like a changing towel at the beach. No one will see your ninnies.'

Carol harrumphed a bit, but Annie knew her chum would do it. Eventually. And she did. They left the blanket draped across the gate as they orientated themselves in relation to the dot on Annie's phone.

They started to move up the hill, toward one of the distant hedges.

'There's a house up there,' said Carol, pointing even farther up the hill. 'I wonder if they own this field, and if they can see us wandering around it like two lost souls.'

'We're not lost, Car, we're heading in the right direction. It's just that what this is saying in't making much sense. Look, according to this, that cat of yours should be there. Right beside that hedge. But there's nothing there at all.'

'There's a sort of hole at the bottom,' said Carol. 'And, no, I'm not crawling through it, Annie. So don't even think that. Besides, look at the diameter of that gap – and look at me. Not going to happen, is it?'

Annie hugged Carol. 'Nah, not really, doll. However, I am, as I have always said, sort of tube-shaped, with a sticky-outy bum, so if I try to keep that down, I might make it. Though I don't think this blouse will. Ah well – it lived a good life. And this is for Marge, Shar, and Sarah…so, here goes. Hold me phone, Car? Ta.'

Annie got down onto all fours, relieved that the ground was relatively dry for the time of year, and crawled toward the hole. 'It's not a hole, Car,' she shouted. 'Well, it is, but there's a hollowed-out bit under here, a real dip…yay – the cat's here. And Kevin, and Fliss and Felix, and the pigs, and…oh, I think that's a stuffed porcupine toy, and some – ugh, I don't know what that is. This is like…like some sort of a nest. There's so much stuff here, Car, you wouldn't believe it. Oi, stop kicking me.'

Annie guessed that one of her feet was still poking out into the field where Carol was standing, because otherwise Carol wouldn't have been able to reach her to kick her.

Carol's voice bellowed from behind Annie. 'Something's coming, Annie…fast. It's an animal. It's big…it's…oh my!'

Annie didn't have time to register fright before something was looming ahead of her blocking out the light. Then it was right in front of her face…big eyes, a snout…and a tongue. Then it was licking her. She screamed, which was a mistake, because she knew the thing's tongue made contact with hers, which made her retch, so she slapped her hand over her mouth and screamed that way, stuck under a hedge, atop some sort of weird nest filled with garden ornaments being licked by a…greyhound?

Just as she recognized the animal, she heard Carol call, 'Don't panic – it's only a greyhound.'

Annie wasn't panicking, and finally understood why the creature she'd seen on the camera had appeared to lope rather than walk…greyhounds had a very different way of moving than Labradors, she knew. But she was still generally puzzled…and unable to move.

'Someone's coming,' shouted Carol. 'On one of those four-by-four thingies. They're driving angrily – if that's possible. I think they've come from that house up on the hill. Here they are. Are you going to come out of there, Annie?'

The dog was still licking Annie, so the last thing she wanted to do was take her hand away from her mouth. But, at the sound of an engine stopping, the dog disappeared, so she was able to use both hands to help herself reverse through the hole in the hedge, until she finally pulled herself up to her feet beside Carol.

Carol looked her up and down, and Annie could tell she was trying to not laugh aloud. So, when Carol said, 'You know that saying about being dragged through a hedge backwards…?' Annie thumped her.

'And who are you, then?' A light, sing-songy female voice carried from the other side of the hedge.

Annie could just see over the top of the shrubbery, but realized Carol couldn't see a thing, so said, 'I'll start,' then stepped forward, stood on tiptoe and shouted, 'Annie Parker and Carol Hill, from Anwen-by-Wye. We tracked down some lost property from our village to what looks like a hidey-hole under this hedge. We think…well, we think your dog took it. That your dog's been taking things from around the village for a few days, actually.'

The voice said, 'I'm Josie, and this is Dandy – short for Dandelion – but I didn't think she'd been out and about lately. Hang on, let's have a look.'

Both Annie and the owner of the voice knelt down, and they introduced themselves to each other again under the hedge. Josie couldn't believe what she could see, but appeared – to Annie – to accept it quickly.

Sounding a bit put upon, Josie offered, 'I'll pull the stuff out this side and dump it onto the back of my vehicle. If you come around to my place, we can talk properly there. It's on Lovelorn Lane. It's called Houndsville. Only house around. You can't miss it. I'll put the kettle on. See you when you get there.'

As they trudged down the hill, heading for Carol's car, Annie accepted her colleague's congratulations for her idea of using the electronic tags, and the trap she'd set for what appeared to be a greyhound with a penchant for collecting random garden ornaments.

Annie clambered over the gate first, they did the 'modesty' thing for Carol again, and Annie even managed to brush off the worst of the mess she'd got herself into before she got into the passenger seat.

When they arrived at Josie's home, they saw a massive sign showing the outline of the house itself – which was quite striking, with tall chimneys at each end – as well as the silhouette of several greyhounds' heads. The place was, apparently, a sanctuary for retired racing greyhounds.

Josie herself opened the front door of the squat, stone-built house. 'Thanks for coming up. Come on in. I hope you're both alright with dogs. There's a few of them about.' She laughed when Annie and Carol immediately began to pet the two animals who were boldest in their approach to the newcomers.

'They'll be smelling my Gert and Rosie on me – we've got two Labs,' said Annie. 'And I bet they'll smell Bunty all over Carol.'

'Calico cat,' explained Carol.

Josie replied, 'As long as you're alright with that, then. I've got about half a dozen of them in here at the moment, the rest are outside. We've got a fenced paddock, and they like to do their zoomies out there, then they come and go as they please through the house. And, boy, can they sleep. Anywhere, and everywhere. But Dandy's our escape artist, isn't she?' Josie ruffled the head of what Annie believed was the dog with whom she'd made…contact. She wiped her mouth with the back of her hand at the thought.

'She likes to stray? How did she get out?' Annie thought Dandy looked lovely – a bit shy, if anything, with a wonderfully marled coat of browns, grays, and creams. And terribly sad eyes. Then she noticed that many of the dogs had much the same doleful expression, so put it down to the breed, rather than the dog. Gertie and Rosie looked as though they were forever smiling – these dogs? Not so much.

'I check the fences every day,' said Josie, 'and I haven't noticed any holes, but that's all I can imagine has happened. I have kennels in the barn for them all and they're usually very happy there, but this one's always been a digger. She'll have got out somehow, I dare say. But Anwen-by-Wye's a long way from here. Got to be a couple of miles.

That's a long way for a greyhound – they like to sprint, not go for long walks. I wonder what drew her there.'

'I bet that's quite a sight, that many dogs,' said Annie.

'Want to come and meet them all? They like visitors.'

Carol shrugged. Annie said, 'How about we let the cat woman here sort through the stuff you brought up in your vehicle, while the dog woman comes to meet your pups?'

Carol and Josie agreed, and Annie followed her host – and half a dozen inquisitive and excited greyhounds – through the house, along a sort of fenced-in corridor, and into a massive barn. Inside, both long sides and one short end were fitted with partitions that created small stalls, each kitted out with a couple of squishy dog beds, with leads hanging on hooks, toys scattered about, and a name carefully painted onto a little board on the wall above each stall.

'Gordon Bennett, Josie…you've got one heck of a lot of dogs here. How much food do you get through in a week?'

Josie laughed, 'Oh, ask, Annie. This lot get through a ton of it, not to mention the supplements some of them need. And the vet's bills? It mounts up quickly, which I knew when I set up the charity, but I didn't realize the fundraising would be so difficult. When everyone's tightening their belts and watching the pennies, old greyhounds are a tough sell.'

Annie was adoring all the wet noses being pressed against her hands, the tentative licks, and all the truffling noises. 'Aw, they're lovely, in't they? How did you get into greyhounds, then?'

Josie smiled sadly. 'My dad raced them when I was little, so we always had them around, and I loved them. But when I asked him where they went when they couldn't race any more, he said "away", and it took me a long time to find out what that meant. Some of them went to friends and family I know, but some…well, you can imagine. As a result, I've been doing this since I turned twenty. Almost ten years, now. Dad died suddenly and, ironically, the money I made from selling his house in Caerphilly got me this place. I know it's a bit pie in the sky, but I want to offer a home to any greyhound that hasn't got one. A bit ambitious, I know, but there you are. I…I just love them.'

Annie grinned. 'It's their eyes, innit? A bit sad, right?' Josie grinned and nodded. 'Yeah. But…it's a lot, Josie. And it's just you?'

Josie laughed. 'Just me? Oh no, I'd never sleep. There are a few volunteers who give me a hand here, and then some other folks who help with the fundraising, too. But it's a lot, you're right. Some of these dogs will go to homes with families, and I need to check them all out – I'm very selective. See, here, they don't need walking, as such, because they get to run around in the paddock, but anyone taking on one of this lot needs to be prepared to do a lot of walking – and, unless they've got fenced land too, the dogs always need to be on a lead. They'd run, you see. Well, they would, wouldn't they? Bred and trained for it. And, while they're here, we have to make sure they remain socialized to humans as well as each other, so the volunteers come to play with them really, rather than walking them. And sometimes…well, they have different personalities, see? Like Dandy, for example. You'd think this was Colditz the way she likes to try to escape. Silly girl. Everything she really needs is here.'

'Except a comprehensive selection of garden ornaments,' said Annie with a chuckle. 'Quite the variety she'd stuffed under that hedge. What's all that about then?'

Josie shook her head. 'I love dogs, and I understand them to a certain extent. But this? No idea. I mean look at her area – that's it, over there. It's full of soft toys. I know she loves to snuggle them, but what I pulled out of that hollow was…well lots of it was hard plastic stuff…not the sort of thing I'd have imagined her liking at all. And to bring them all that way back with her? Well, to be honest, I can't explain it at all. Of course I'll do my best to keep her in, and I hope everyone she's inconvenienced will be alright about it, now that it looks like you can return what they lost. But I'm most concerned about her being out there, on the roads, on her own, at night, to be honest with you. That's not safe for her. Not at all. Not for any of them. They've got a big run attached to the barn for their overnight…requirements, but she shouldn't be taking off like that. I'll maybe have to think about refencing the run…or maybe even the whole paddock. Bury the fence deeper, I suppose.' Josie sighed. 'Another thing for the list.'

Annie didn't want to go down that road, so asked, 'So what was this place before you got it? Sheep?' She knew that most of the local farms had sheep.

Josie nodded. 'Indeed, and some quite posh ones, at that. They had a special line of sheep here that they exhibited – Royal Welsh Show, that sort of thing. And horses. Just a few. You should see the stuff they left behind when they sold up – loads of fancy animal transporters just outside, in the yard. See? Through that end of the barn?' Annie looked, and nodded. 'Handy for when I need to collect or deliver dogs, of course, and some of them are lovely – really old-fashioned.'

'I was just going to say that – is that one there all white? It looks like…I dunno, it looks almost bridal, in a way.'

Josie smiled. 'I did that. And I fitted it with electric hook-ups. Want to see it?'

Annie nodded; the two women, and about a dozen greyhounds, strolled to the end of the barn.

Annie was quite taken by the trailer. 'It's lovely. Why did you do all this to it?'

'I use it at local fairs, agricultural events, that sort of thing, as a little shop and information booth. We've got some merchandise with our logo on it, leaflets to give out, that sort of thing. It wasn't that hard to do – just some paint, and a few off-the-shelf units so I can hook it up to power…and one heck of a lot of elbow grease. But that's free, right?'

Annie said, 'Oh…you've got lots of transporters. Big ones, too.' Josie nodded.

When Annie finally joined Carol at her vehicle, the hatchback section was full of the stuff to be returned to Marjorie, Sharon, and Sarah, and Annie was glowing with excitement.

'What's up with you? You look like the cat that got all the cream,' said Carol as Annie buckled up.

'Well, I've solved the Case of the Grabby Greyhound…yeah, I'm going with that…and I've had a great idea for a birthday present for Tude. One he wouldn't see coming in a month of Sundays.'

'Oh yes, that's coming up soon, isn't it,' said Carol starting the car. She turned to Annie, her eyes round. 'You're not getting him a greyhound, are you? Isn't the Coach full enough with you two, Gertie and Rosie?'

'It's a surprise, and...yeah, I might need a bit of help from you to pull it off. You up for driving me here now and again over the next couple of weeks? Drop me off for a few hours? Then help me deliver something to Tude on his big day?'

Carol drove down the hill toward the main road. 'Go on then...tell me what you've got up your sleeve.'

Annie did, at length, then they chatted about how lovely it would be to see Marjorie Pritchard's face when she got her Kevin back. Annie hoped she wouldn't mind the teeth marks on his tall, pointed hat...he really was in pretty good shape, other than that. She also hoped Sharon wouldn't be too upset that both Fliss and Felix's long, shapely necks were now both scarred, too. One was a bit worse than the other, but she knew she'd have to wait until she presented them to Sharon to be sure which had sustained the most damage...she really couldn't tell them apart, though she agreed with Carol that it made sense for her to do her best to not admit that, at the time.

# CHAPTER THIRTY

Christine and Stephanie stared at Henry, but said nothing. He was standing beside the fireplace in the small private sitting room at Chellingworth Hall. He stuffed his thumbs into his waistcoat pockets, which always helped him feel more in control of things.

Finally, he puffed out his chest and said, 'Showing Cook Davies and Paul Baker those photographs of a grainy figure, in the kitchen, in the dead of night, will not achieve what you want. Even if I were that person's parent I might not recognize them from that. It's a hooded blob. That's it. And I am quite convinced that at least Cook Davies will not take well to the idea that we've given permission for cameras to be installed in the kitchens, without her knowledge. Had the cameras captured a more useful image, then I'd have agreed with you. But, under the circumstances, I cannot.'

His wife pleaded, 'But Henry…what should we do then? Just wait? Hope the cameras do a better job of it tonight? This could go on for days. And you heard all about the situation down there this morning.'

Henry had. He sighed. 'I do see that a delay might prove harmful…'

His wife pounced, 'Maybe even more harmful, in the long run. How much more of this do you think Cook Davies will stand, dear?'

Henry wished his mother was there – which was something he rarely found himself thinking. Despite the fact that she liked to meddle, there were times when her longer tenure at the Hall was useful. As her face popped into his head, Henry told himself that his mother had as much right as anyone to a little break. She'd not left Chellingworth for even a night since…well, he couldn't recall when. And the general consensus was that sea air was good for one, so he decided to put thoughts of his mother to the back of his mind, and focus on the matter in hand.

However, he couldn't help but wonder what his mother might have suggested at this juncture. 'If we're to confront them with this evidence, such as it is, and ask them to account for their whereabouts at the time – though I would hope you have a plan to couch that in different terms, so it doesn't sound so officious – then we shouldn't force them to do that in front of each other. Where a person might be at three in the morning is, largely, I'd have thought, a person's own business.'

After he'd spoken, Henry sighed. He'd capitulated, and now had to face the ramifications of that. There'd be interviews, and possibly some wringing of hands…but he hoped they could make some headway toward restoring normality at the Hall. His nerves were frayed.

'I think Cook Davies first, don't you, Henry?' He heard a warmth in his wife's tone again, which relieved him, because he'd thought she sounded quite harsh earlier on when he'd not agreed with her.

'Indeed. I'll…I'll leave you two to it, then. Shall I take Hugo to our rooms, dear?' He hoped he'd be able to escape.

'I really think you should be here, Henry,' replied Stephanie hurriedly. 'We need to present a united front.'

Christine agreed. 'Oh yes, Henry, I think we should all be here.'

Henry sighed his agreement. 'I'll ask Edward to invite Cook Davies to join us, then.' He didn't relish the prospect. At all.

Twenty minutes later, Cook Davies bustled into the sitting room. She was pink-faced and looked about as eager to be there as Henry himself felt. But there they both were.

He looked toward his wife and felt relief wash over him as she spoke. 'Thank you for joining us, Cook Davies. We won't keep you long. We're aware that your day has already been impacted by recent developments. We wondered if you'd be prepared to look at some images we have of the person we believe is responsible for…everything.'

Henry noticed that Cook Davies addressed his wife, not him, when she replied. 'Well, I will, of course. But how do you mean – "images"? How have you got these, then?'

Henry held his breath.

Christine said, 'As a professional investigator, I find it useful to keep an eye on the scene of a potential, or past, crime. As such, the duke and duchess gave permission for cameras to be hidden in the kitchens. At approximately three o'clock this morning, the cameras captured these images of someone in the kitchens. These are shots I have taken from the recordings. The person I am about to show you is the one I saw remove your knife from its protective sheath and place it in a drawer.'

Henry knew this was a critical moment. He held his breath. Would Cook Davies explode because they'd had the audacity to position cameras in her kitchens?

Cook Davies stared at each of them, in turn, then focused on Christine. 'You actually saw someone – this person – take my knife out of its sheath and dump it into that drawer where anything could have happened to it? That knife has been with me since my first day of training. It was a gift to me from Mam and Dad. I have cared for that blade every day of my working life. So, yes, let me see who dared to endanger it.'

Henry breathed out. No explosion. He watched as Cook Davies studied the photographs.

Eventually she looked up. Her face was crimson. 'Could be anyone, that. What's the point of robbing me and my team of any sense of privacy just so you can show us this sort of thing?'

Henry felt the knot in his tummy immediately tighten. The danger hadn't passed.

'We felt it necessary,' said Stephanie quietly.

'Have you heard about Marjorie Pritchard's Kevin going missing, in the village?' Christine surprised Henry with her question, and the seemingly unconnected topic.

Cook Davies chuckled. 'Show me someone who hasn't, and I'll show you a person who's just come back from Timbuktu. Of course I have.'

Christine continued. 'The WISE Enquiries Agency also installed cameras to observe the site of a potential future crime in that instance, and I've just received news from my colleagues Annie and Carol that the surveillance has brought that case to a successful conclusion. No one's been snooping on you, Cook Davies, we simply wanted to use the best tool for the job. Something with which I am certain you are professionally familiar.'

Henry couldn't take his eyes off Cook.

She tilted her head a little, her shoulders unhunched a tad, and she spoke grudgingly, 'Yes. Well…I suppose you make a good point. The cameras won't be recording during the working day, will they?'

'From now on, not while the kitchens are in use, no. The saboteur wouldn't strike then,' said Stephanie.

'Right-o then. So you'll be doing this tonight again, will you? If so, you can rely upon me to not utter a word about it. If everyone knows, that would mean the cameras would be pointless, wouldn't it?'

Henry felt his breathing return to normal.

'We'll be asking Paul Baker to take a look too,' said Christine.

'You'll do no such thing,' snapped Cook Davies. 'How would he know who that is? He's only been here two minutes.'

'It could be someone who's targeting him, not you – possibly someone from, or sent by someone from, his life prior to him coming here to work,' said Christine rapidly. 'And I'll also be asking him where he was around three this morning – as I am asking you now.'

Henry's tummy did a somersault. At least, that's how it felt. He feared Chellingworth Hall was about to lose the woman who made all his favorite dishes. He suspected that if Cook Davies had lasers in her eyes, Christine would – at that very moment – have been cut in two.

'How dare you ask me such a thing. Not that it's any of your business, but I was where all God-fearing single women would be at that time – in my own bed, alone. And I've seen enough of those things on the telly where people are asked for a witness to their alibi to be able to add that no one can vouch for me. But, after all my years of service to this family, I'd have thought that my word would be good enough.'

Stephanie stood and approached Cook Davies. 'Of course it is. Please accept our apologies for the question having to be asked.' She shook Cook Davies by the hand then hugged her. 'You're the world's best cook, Cook Davies. I don't know what we'd do without you. Thank you for being so understanding.'

Henry was flabbergasted. He'd never seen anything like it.

Cook Davies's reaction suggested to Henry that she was as shocked as he: she leaped away from Stephanie as though she'd been scalded, then she turned and mumbled, 'Thank you', and left quite hurriedly.

'I say,' said Henry when the door had closed, 'that was a bit extreme.'

Stephanie grinned. 'I once hugged the chief financial officer of a multi-billion-pound organization to give him enough of a shock that he didn't fire our PR firm. At least, not at that meeting. Hugging disarms people – literally and figuratively. Now, shall we get Paul Baker in?'

Henry was rather taken aback to think that his wife might be adept at such underhand tactics, but he at least regained his composure as he waited for the arrival of the baker, Baker.

Upon his arrival – clad in a horribly floury apron, smeared with jam, and what Henry assumed was chocolate – Paul Baker took the photos from Stephanie, swore he had no idea who the figure could be, and hesitated only slightly before answering Christine's question about where he'd been at three that morning.

'You're not the police, so I won't answer you.'

It wasn't the response Henry had been expecting.

Christine said, 'I'm aware that a firm of private enquiry agents isn't the same as the police, but we're hoping you'll take the chance to help us understand why this figure couldn't be you, Paul.'

The man laughed. 'Me? That? You're kidding. Look at the size of that person, compared to me. I'm much taller. They're a good six inches shorter than me.'

Stephanie asked, 'I'm sorry, Paul, but how can you say that? There's not really much context in these still shots, is there?'

He replied sharply, 'The photo where they're side-on, when they're next to that table? Look where the table is, in relation to their body parts. Now look at this photo of me standing by the table in the main kitchen.' Paul held his phone toward Christine and Stephanie. Henry didn't stand a chance of seeing it. 'Look at where that table is in comparison to my body. Nowhere near the same place. That person's smaller than me. And I'm still not going to tell you where I was last night, because it involves another person.'

Henry was agog.

Christine shrugged. 'Janet Jackson, I presume.'

Henry was even more agog.

The baker snapped, 'How do you know that? Who saw us?'

Henry stared at Christine, waiting for her answer.

Christine smiled sweetly. Henry knew she didn't do that often. 'No one saw you, Paul. But someone's mentioned to me that the two of you were in the Coach and Horses together the other evening, and I thought I'd take a chance…and your response is my confirmation, thank you.'

Paul tutted loudly. 'I don't want word getting about. It's not fair on Janet. I don't want her hurt. She's too good for that. Gossip can be terrible in a place like this. We've had to move on before now because of it. It's the age difference, I reckon; for some reason it seems to bother people.'

'You're a couple?' Henry couldn't help himself.

Paul turned toward him and did one of those upside-down smile things with his mouth that always confused Henry – they could mean so very many things, especially when the person also nodded, then shook their head, as Paul was doing. *Unfathomable.*

'Not in the broadly recognized sense of the word, I suppose,' said Paul, illuminating nothing as far as Henry was concerned.

'But of course,' said Stephanie, rather annoyingly.

Christine asked, 'Many years?'

Paul shrugged. 'Quite a few. Off and on. Here and there. She's moved around a bit. Even got married. We met when I was only twenty. She's a good few years older than me, as I dare say is obvious. It shouldn't work. We…we just don't seem to be able to stay away from each other for very long, even when one of us says they've had enough and, you know, storms off. Don't know how many fresh starts we've had, between us. It is what it is.'

Henry thought the entire thing sounded most unsatisfactory.

'Love's a strange thing,' said Christine quietly.

'Indeed it is,' said his wife, with more feeling than Henry felt the situation required.

Christine added, 'So she'd corroborate, if asked discreetly?'

Paul nodded, then asked, 'You going to keep those cameras

recording tonight, too? I'll keep this shut, if so.' He mimed locking his lips and throwing away the key. 'Does "she" know too?'

'If you mean our valued member of staff for many years, Cook Davies,' said Stephanie firmly, 'she does. And she's also promised to not let the cat out of the bag. So, if you would kindly keep your promise to remain calm today…to do your best to allow peace to reign…then we'll see what we'll see in the morning.'

Paul nodded his 'Your Graces' and Henry could see Edward hovering beyond the door when the baker opened it to leave.

Edward entered and whispered, 'Might I have a word, please, Your Grace?'

Henry was unused to his butler asking such a question, but nodded.

'It's about Cook Davies, Your Grace.'

Henry's tummy was feeling as though someone was churning it again. 'Oh dear. Stephanie, Edward has news about Cook Davies.'

His wife and Christine looked toward the butler expectantly.

Stephanie said, 'What now, Edward?'

Edward closed the door and spoke softly. 'Cook Davies mentioned that you asked where she was at three this morning. I was up and about at that time myself; a touch of dyspepsia, nothing more. Cook Davies has a room across the corridor from my own. Speaking confidentially, of course, the way she…um…snores means it's easy to tell when she's asleep. I can attest that she was sleeping – quite loudly – at that time.'

Henry saw the light. 'Splendid, Edward. A snorer, eh? That must be difficult for you. Thank you for telling us. Mum's the word, eh?'

'Indeed, Your Grace.'

'Thank you, Edward,' said Stephanie. 'I wonder, would you take a look at these photos and tell us if you recognize this person.'

Edward took no more than a moment to scan the pictures. 'I'm sorry, Your Grace, I cannot say that the person looks familiar.'

When the three were alone again, with Hugo still sleeping soundly, Stephanie said, 'So it's not Paul, and it's not Cook Davies. Rinse and repeat tonight, Christine?'

'I'll get up early to spot anything on the recordings as soon as I can,' said Christine.

# CHAPTER THIRTY-ONE

Mavis was worried. She was doing her best to not let it show, but the fact that Althea hadn't answered her phone, hadn't texted, nor had she returned to The Lavender after an absence of almost four hours, had Mavis on pins. Toni Conti had phoned and texted Pippa, and she wasn't responding, either. Mavis MacDonald and Toni Conti were pacing the main lounge together, but in opposite directions, each clutching a mobile phone, when Siggy Welbeck approached.

He said, 'Sighting of Pippa's car on the A477 heading east. ANPR picked it up an hour ago. Three hours prior to that? On the A478 heading toward Tenby. Don't ask how I know. I won't tell.'

Mavis thanked Siggy. 'A favor owed to you, no doubt,' she observed. She peered at her telephone's map app. 'Thanks for using it up for this. Why would Pippa be there, heading that way, an hour ago? That road's way past this place. Heading toward Tenby not long after they'd left here? That makes more sense.'

Sir Malcolm sprung out of the seat he'd been occupying for the past half an hour. 'ANPR? That's the system they use to read number plates, right?' Siggy nodded. 'Was Pippa alone at the time?'

Mavis was cross with herself that she hadn't asked the very same question.

Siggy replied, 'Only one occupant in the car an hour ago, as far as could be seen. Two occupants when it was heading toward Tenby, earlier. I have the earlier location here, on my phone.' He held up his screen and Mavis peered at it.

'That's no' so far from where Althea and I were the other day. If Pippa's connected to the Dyggan lot, that would be my guess for where she was headed. But, if she's in the car alone a couple of hours after that, then where's Althea? We should head to Dyggan's, ourselves.'

'Would you drive us, Mavis?' Siggy sounded more energized than Mavis had ever heard him.

'Try to stop me,' she said. 'Anyone else coming?'

Toni Conti replied, 'I'll stay here. Our guests, you understand.'

Mavis nodded. 'Of course.'

Uma waggled her fingers. 'I'd like to come, too, please.'

'We won't all fit – not if the aim is to extricate Althea from some sort of…situation,' said Sir Malcolm forcefully. 'I'll drive everyone in my car. Much bigger.'

'It's a Rolls Royce,' hissed Uma to Mavis. Mavis had seen a large vehicle in the car park enveloped by one of those tarpaulin-like covers, so assumed that must be it.

'Dennis keeps it ticking over for me,' explained Sir Malcolm as he headed for the stairs. 'I'll just get my keys. Don't keep them in my pocket, as a rule. Back in five minutes-ish.'

'I'll find Dennis and ask him to uncover the car,' said Toni Conti.

'I'll just get back to my…contact, to check on any further sightings,' called Siggy.

Mavis followed Sir Malcolm to the stairs. 'I'll need a few things from my room, too,' she said. 'Let's all meet back in reception in no more than ten minutes.'

When the foursome exited The Lavender, Dennis Moore was standing beside what Mavis thought had to be the most exquisite vehicle she'd ever seen. Attached though she was to her beloved Morris Traveller, the gleaming, infinitely black beauty that Dennis had just revealed took her breath away.

She all but whispered, 'A Silver Cloud III, probably 1965. The housing for those double headlamps has the little RR monogram – and they didnae bring that in until late in '64. And they stopped making them in '66.'

Sir Malcolm gushed, 'You know your cars remarkably well, Mavis.'

Mavis smiled. 'For a girl who comes from a market town in southwest Scotland, you mean, Sir Malcolm? Young girls can dream, too, you know. How long have you had it?'

'Bought her when I sold the business. I hardly get to drive her at all nowadays, of course. But that's my choice. Fit for purpose, you'd say, Mavis? For tracking down a missing dowager duchess.'

Mavis chuckled. 'Aye, Althea would be pleased. She gets about in her old Gilbern.'

'Not a Gilbern!' Sir Malcolm sounded delighted. 'I'd love to see that one day. The only car ever manufactured in Wales, I believe. My grandparents might have come over from Hong Kong, but I think I've got "Made in Wales" stamped through my middle, like a stick of seaside rock. But first, let's find her, eh? Come on – everyone in.'

Dennis tapped Mavis on the shoulder. 'Althea's gone missing – is that what Sir Malcolm said?'

Mavis hesitated; something they'd discussed about Pippa needing help to carry a body from one room to another was niggling at the back of her brain – if that was what had happened. 'You could say that,' was the answer she felt best fitted the bill.

Getting into the car with its luxurious cream-leather interior, walnut finishes, and so much space, was a joy Mavis suspected she'd never get the chance to repeat, so she allowed herself to take it in for just a moment...even though Althea's safety was, in reality, uppermost in her mind.

'She'll make short work of the trip,' said Sir Malcolm confidently, 'so, if everyone's ready, I'll get us going.'

Mavis and Uma sat beside each other in the rear seat; both compact women, they could have easily fitted within one half of the seat but, instead, Mavis pulled down the dividing armrest and they each splayed themselves across their generous portion of the car.

Uma winked at Mavis. 'Look at these,' she whispered, pulling on the chrome handle of a walnut-veneered table set into the back of the driver's seat. 'So posh.'

'No GPS on this old bird, Siggy, so I'll let you direct me. Off toward Tenby, correct?'

'That's it.'

Mavis tried to stop imagining scenarios that might explain Althea's absence, because none of them were particularly uplifting. For all that she was capable, and generally healthy, Althea was over eighty and not used to being out and about in the modern world on her own.

Of course, Mavis told herself, Althea encountered, and even got to know, an impressively wide range of people while fulfilling her duties as a dowager, and because of her support of so many, varied community and outreach programs. But – as Mavis was only too well aware – Althea rarely did any of those sorts of things alone; for the past year or so at least, it was unusual for Mavis herself to not be by her side.

Mavis told herself she should never have agreed to Althea's suggestion – that she should never have let her go off alone with a possible killer. What had she been thinking? She'd allowed herself to be carried along by a wave of foolish enthusiasm on the part of a group of amateurs. She could have kicked herself.

As though he'd heard her thoughts, Sir Malcolm said, 'Never fear. Mavis, we'll find her. None of this is your fault, nor Althea's. It's all about Pippa Thomas. Entirely because of her inept sabotage at The Lavender. But she won't hurt Althea. She wouldn't dare.'

'I thought we suspected her of killing Frances,' said Uma, which ratcheted up Mavis's stress level no end.

Mavis did her best to watch the Welsh countryside as it flashed past; the Rolls purred along magnificently, making her feel as though she were on a magic carpet. And yes, she really could hear the clock ticking. Pulling herself back from a moment of blessed reverie, something Sir Malcolm had said earlier struck a chord. She pulled out her phone and said, 'About how long before we get to Dyggan's?'

Sir Malcolm said, 'Twenty minutes, or so?'

'About that,' agreed Siggy.

'Good – I'll just catch up on a few things back here and I'll be ready for action when we get there,' said Mavis.

Uma peered across the armrest. 'Anything I can do to help?'

Mavis spoke quietly, 'Thanks, but no thanks. I got an important email from the office this morning about a case we're handling at Chellingworth Hall that the rest of the team are dealing with. I've no' had the mental capacity to respond until now. However, now that I know we're on our way, I should take care of that.'

Uma said, 'I miss being part of a team. That's one of the things I loved most about working at the newspaper – we were a team.'

'I know what you mean,' said Siggy. 'Ah, there you go – pinging in is the news that Pippa's car's been spotted on the M4, west of Cardiff.'

Mavis tried to filter out the ongoing chatter as she texted madly to Carol – who'd just got back to her desk following an outing with Annie, apparently. Mavis didn't ask to be told about what they'd discovered, but hurriedly told Carol about Althea, typed a list of questions that she made plain were of critical importance, then waited for the summarized replies she'd requested. She knew Carol was good, and fast, and she didn't think she'd asked for information it would be difficult for Carol to get hold of...and had a feeling she knew some of the answers in any case. If she was right about things...

'Not far now, Mavis,' said Siggy, pulling her away from reading the messages Carol was sending. 'Five minutes or so. Do we have a plan?'

'Full frontal attack,' said Mavis. 'Park outside, you and me through the front door Sir Malcolm, you and Uma around the back, Siggy. Okay?'

'Around the back?' Uma sounded a bit panicked.

'Good plan, Mavis,' said Siggy, 'I'll take care of you, Uma. You can rely upon me, Mavis.'

'I shall,' said Mavis.

'Here we are,' announced Sir Malcolm. The incredible vehicle sighed to a halt, in much the same spot that Mavis had used when she and Althea had visited Dyggan's. She immediately noticed the CLOSED sign showing through the glass of the front door, though she could see Gerry Dyggan inside – as well as someone else, a young redhead.

'I think I see Pippa, inside,' she hissed, 'which makes no sense if her car was spotted on the M4. Come on, Sir Malcolm, let's go.'

Mavis marched to the front door and rattled the handle. Gerry Dyggan turned at the noise, saw Mavis and Sir Malcolm, blanched and shook his head, pointing at the sign on the door. Mavis hammered on the wooden surround of the large plate of glass bearing the name of the company. 'Open up...now!'

Gerry looked quite alarmed, and started making shooing motions at the pair at the door.

'I'll no' go until you open up,' shouted Mavis, hammering as hard as she could. 'Come on, Sir Malcolm, help me out here. Put those fists of yours to good use.'

'I'm afraid I might break the glass,' he said timidly.

'Don't hit the glass, hit the wood,' Mavis instructed.

He made a few attempts that Mavis judged as feeble, then she shouted, 'Okay, I've stopped being nice, now – if you don't open up, I will break this glass. You've a crowbar, or some such, in the boot of that very attractive beast of yours, I dare say, Sir Malcolm?'

He stammered, 'I-I wouldn't have thought a crowbar. You mean something heavy…metal?' Mavis nodded. 'I could look.'

'You do that, then bring it here. Thanks.' Sir Malcolm left, and Mavis shouted, 'He's gone for something that'll break this glass. Or you can let me in. Now.'

Mavis watched Gerry stare at Sir Malcolm as he headed to the Rolls, his eyes widening. Sir Malcolm opened the boot, pulled out large chrome spanner, then he turned and looked straight at Gerry, waving the tool above his head. Gerry flinched, and all but ran to open the door.

Mavis pushed her way inside. 'Thank you for seeing sense, Gerry.'

The man grunted something. He stepped back a couple of feet when Sir Malcolm entered.

Mavis's opening gambit was stronger because of what Carol had been able to email to her, as a result of some swift online digging. 'Is Bethan here, by any chance? Bethan who was in the back room doing a bit of photocopying the other day when I visited with the dowager duchess. Bethan Thomas, who bears a striking resemblance to her older sister Pippa Thomas, who works as a receptionist at The Lavender. That Bethan.'

Gerry looked shocked. 'How do you know who Bethan's sister is? And no, she's not here. She's…off today.'

Mavis stepped forward. 'May I take a look in the rear of the building, Gerry? I think I might find a chum of mine there.'

Gerry stepped back, barring the door with the STAFF ONLY sign. 'It's private. Sensitive information kept there. Not for the public to see.'

'Not a place where a little, old, lost dowager might hide out, then?' Mavis smiled sweetly.

Gerry stared at Mavis, then at Sir Malcolm – who was shifting his weight from one foot to the other, still clenching the spanner – then back at Mavis.

'If you don't let me through, you'll be sorry,' warned Mavis.

The door opened, and a young woman entered the office. She looked very similar to Pippa, but they weren't twins. This one was taller and less angular, more willowy; her hair was less wild than her sister's, and she was heavily made-up. Mavis held up her phone and snapped a photo with the flash on, then hit a few keys on her phone with her thumb. She asked, 'Are you Bethan?'

Bethan screwed up her eyes, momentarily blinded by the flash, and nodded at Mavis. 'You're Mrs MacDonald, aren't you? I hope you got a nice snap of me there. For an album you're putting together, is it?'

Mavis nodded at Bethan. 'I am, and I'm sure you know why I'm here. It's no' a photo album I'm interested in, it's the whereabouts of my friend that concerns me. She got into your sister's car at The Lavender this morning, and hasn't been heard of since.'

Bethan's eyebrows rose. 'My sister Pippa? Oh no, I hope nothing's happened to them. I should check the hospitals – they might have had an accident. Mightn't they, Gerry?'

The young man jumped. 'What? Oh yes. An accident. Do you want me to phone…um…'

'The local hospital, Gerry, yes please. Would you be so kind?' Mavis smiled sweetly. Again.

The young man looked at Bethan, then Mavis, then Sir Malcolm and his spanner…then pulled his phone out of his pocket. 'I'll just get the number,' he said, tapping and scrolling.

As he worked on his phone, the two women stared at each other; it felt to Mavis as though even the clock on the wall had stopped ticking…then Siggy burst through the door behind Bethan.

'I've found Althea. She's fine, not hurt. Behind a locked door. I've contacted…people who can help. Who's got a key for that door?'

'Bethan will have that, I should think,' said Mavis. The young woman didn't hesitate, she shot past Mavis, eluded the grasp of Sir Malcolm, and ran out of the shop and around the side of the building.

Siggy followed, Sir Malcolm stood agape, Gerry flopped onto on a chair, hard. Mavis said to Sir Malcom, 'Keep him there. Sit on him if you have to,' then she ran to the back of the building where Uma was talking to Althea through what Mavis hoped was a flimsier door than it looked.

'Stand back, Althea, Uma and I are going to break down the door,' called Mavis.

Althea's voice replied quite calmly, 'No dear, don't do that, you'll hurt yourself. I'm perfectly alright, I can wait until you find a key, or get a locksmith here. It's a bathroom. I have water, somewhere to sit, and any facilities I might require. There's nothing to worry about.'

Mavis and Uma smiled at each other.

'She's been saying that since we found her,' said Uma. 'She really does sound as though she's alright in there. They didn't hurt her. She told me that.'

Siggy appeared. 'She got away. I managed to get a photo of her car. I've sent it to those who need to know.'

Mavis nodded. 'I believe her sister Pippa made her escape earlier, and now Bethan will follow. However, we have a more pressing problem, and I lack the skills to solve it. Skills I happen to know you possess. Would you be so kind? It's not a difficult lock for you to pick, I shouldn't think.'

'You can pick a lock, Siggy?' Uma's tone suggested a mixture of shock and delight.

'I can neither confirm nor deny that,' said Siggy, fiddling at the lock with something he'd pulled from his pocket.

'I'm free!' Althea burst out of the little washroom looking as healthy as she had done when Mavis had foolishly allowed her to go off with Pippa that morning.

'What happened, dear?' Mavis performed a visual inspection of the dowager. 'They've no' hurt you, have they? No lumps or bumps anywhere?'

'Didn't touch me, except for pulling at my arm a bit. But...I heard things, and I made notes.' Althea held up a long strip of toilet paper, upon which she had scrawled in red felt-tipped pen. 'I had a pen in my handbag,' she said proudly holding up a capacious tapestry satchel, 'and improvised when it came to something to write on. So, listen up while I tell you everything: Pippa's sister, Bethan, is the ringleader. That Gerry's a bit dim, and I think he's afraid of Bethan. Pippa seems to be, too. They both did what Bethan told them to. Pippa's driving to Cardiff to fly...somewhere that I couldn't hear. But they have a place there, that they own. Bethan said she'd meet her sister there, then Gerry would go too. They were going to clear out of this place. And they had a big row about someone called Roger: Bethan was most insistent that Pippa was not to go back to The Lavender to collect him. We haven't met a Roger there, have we, Mavis? I was a bit confused about that, but I also gathered that Bethan was angry with Pippa because of something to do with a cat – which is what set Pippa off in the car.'

Althea looked up from her notes, and scratched her head through her scarf. 'It was very strange...I saw a cat about to cross the road when we were driving to the chemist, so I told Pippa to look out for it, of course, and she acted most peculiarly after that, and drove us directly here. Then I heard them talk about a cat again, twice, though I cannot imagine why a cat is so important. In any case, they blamed everything on the cat – which makes no sense. I mean Frances – they blamed Frances being dead on the cat. At least, that's what I think I heard. "It was the cat's fault." See? Nonsense. You should ask Gerry. Is he still here? Gerry knows all about it. I could hear Siggy saying that Bethan got away, too. These walls? Terribly thin.'

Mavis reached out and hugged Althea. 'Oh, my dear, what shall we do with you?'

'Well, I'm rather peckish. They didn't feed me.' Althea's expression was pathetic.

Siggy said, 'Sir Malcolm is watching Gerry – let's have a word.'

They all re-entered the office where Sir Malcolm was looming over Gerry, who was sobbing.

Althea asked, 'Mavis, what's going on?'

'Have a wee sit, dear – on a chair, for a change. We'll wait here until the police arrive. I'll swap a couple more messages with Carol.'

Althea pounced 'Carol? What's she got to do with all this? I thought you said she was terribly busy with background checks for those people in the City of London.'

Mavis spoke as she typed. 'She has been, dear, and she's helped Annie out, and Stephanie at the Hall, but she's been able to get information to me in a timely manner, too. Information critical to allow me to understand if a theory of mine holds water.'

'Do you know who killed Frances Millington, Gerry?' Sir Malcolm sounded quite intimidating, thought Mavis.

'It was an accident,' sobbed the young man. The words tumbled out of him. 'Honest, just an accident. I never met that Frances, ever, but she worked out what Pippa was up to at The Lavender and went into her room and confronted her about it, and Pippa's cat jumped at Frances and she had a funny turn. Pippa thought she was dying…had a heart attack or something, because she was holding her chest and she was out cold. Bethan said Pippa should use this stun gun thing she had to zap her. Like they do with those paddle things they use on the telly? But it didn't work – she just died. And Pippa was in a right old state and didn't know what to do, so Bethan said she had to put Frances into her own bed, so no one would know she'd died in Pippa's room. See? It was an accident. And Pippa tried to save her. Then she said that you –' he nodded at Althea – 'told her in the car that you knew about the cat, so she brought you here and Bethan said we had to keep you here, and Bethan sent Pippa off to get away to Cardiff airport, and I dare say that's what Bethan will do too now she's gone, and there's only me left and I had nothing to do with any of it at all.'

Gerry drew breath, and sobbed again.

Mavis had no sympathy for the young man. 'Aye, well, you can tell that to the police when they get here. And I dare say they'll be wanting a lot of details about the scheme you've cooked up to "persuade" property owners to sell up to you after a sustained campaign of inconveniences and irritations. All implemented by Pippa, or other people you've managed to get on the inside, elsewhere, with Bethan no doubt orchestrating matters from behind the scenes. Or were you the brains of it all, Gerry?'

Gerry looked up at Mavis, with tears running down his face. 'Me? No way. I love Pippa, and she can't help but do whatever her sister says. Bethan wouldn't even let Pippa get her cat, Roger, from The Lavender before she sent her to the airport. I…I want to be with Pippa, no matter what. But Pippa didn't kill anyone. Frances died because of Pippa's cat. None of us know why, but she did.'

'Frances was terrified of cats,' said Uma quietly. 'Poor Frances. I didn't know a person could actually be frightened to death.'

Mavis leaned down to Gerry. 'What time did all this happen, Gerry? Did Pippa say?'

Gerry nodded. 'It was about half seven at night. She phoned Bethan. We were both still here in the office. I said I'd go over to The Lavender to fetch Pippa, but Bethan wouldn't let me. Bethan said Pippa had to put the dead woman in her own bed, so it would look like she'd died there. Pippa phoned back about an hour later to say she'd managed to do it. They were only next door to each other, and she put the body into a wheelchair they keep in the storeroom in case anyone needs one at the hotel in an emergency, and wheeled her from one room to the other. That bit only took a minute, she said. But she had to…oh dear, she had to undress her for bed. Pippa was a right mess afterwards, said she couldn't stay at The Lavender any longer…but Bethan made her. Said the place was worth it…worth a fortune, if we could get it. I love Pippa, and now…now I might never see her again.'

Althea patted the young man's hand. 'There, there.'

Mavis said, 'Aye, well you might be right there. You see, Gerry, poor Frances didnae die until the early hours of the next morning. She wasnae dead when Pippa put her into her bed. She could have been saved, even then, if only Pippa had called an ambulance, instead of trying to cover it up.'

Gerry looked up, horrified. 'No, Pippa was quite sure. She couldn't find a pulse at all. Frances was cold to the touch. Not breathing, she said. And she did want to phone for an ambulance, but Bethan said to try shocking her with the zappy thing, and when that didn't work, to put her into her bed. Pippa…Pippa always does what Bethan tells her to.'

Mavis felt a terrible sadness for her old colleague. 'Ach, poor Frances. I hope she didnae regain consciousness before she passed. As for you, and Bethan, and Pippa? You'll all have a chance to explain this to the police. I believe they'll be gathering up Pippa and her sister as we speak. And they'll be here for you momentarily.'

Gerry sobbed, Sir Malcolm shuffled, Siggy was texting, and Althea was unwrapping a boiled sweet she'd pulled out of her handbag.

Mavis put her arm around Uma, whose tears were flowing silently. And they spoke quietly of the woman they'd both known, who had died alone.

# CHAPTER THIRTY-TWO

Henry checked his watch. Tea was never late. But there was no Edward, and there was no tea. Stephanie was attending to Hugo, who was fast asleep in his crib. They'd elected to have tea in their apartment that afternoon, and had both agreed that something simple would be more than adequate.

He ventured, 'Do you think something's happened?'

His wife replied distractedly, 'Well, something must have happened, mustn't it? But let's wait for Edward to come to tell us about it. We don't need to go hunting for any more disasters, do we?'

Henry thought Stephanie sounded quite snippy, but didn't say so. He knew she was correct about not seeking out disasters.

A moment later, Edward knocked at the door. Henry could tell immediately that something, was, indeed, wrong.

'Out with it, Edward,' said Stephanie. 'What's up?'

Edward cleared his throat. 'I'm sorry to report that Cook Davies is packing. She has stated her intention to leave the premises forthwith. Also, Mr Baker is packing, having said he is of the same intent.'

'What's happened now?' Stephanie's voice was full of dread.

Edward cleared his throat again; Henry wondered if he might be coming down with a cold. 'Cook Davies and Mr Baker have fallen out over the arrangements for their shared use of the baking kitchen. Mr Baker...ahem...refused to allow Cook Davies to work alongside him, when she felt it necessary to bake for tomorrow, for Your Graces' requirements.'

Stephanie stood. 'This has gone too far. Edward, please ask both parties to meet with us downstairs in the small sitting room. As soon as possible. Henry, let's get Hugo sorted out, then let's deal with this.'

Edward left, and Henry helped to get Hugo settled into his carrying basket, wondering all the time how any of this could be made to work.

Henry bleated, 'Soon there'll be no one left to cook for us, nor for the tearooms in the village, nor for the public tearoom here at the Hall. It's...it's a dreadful mess.'

Stephanie nodded. 'I'm aware. I've allowed this to fester for too long. I'm sorry, my dear.'

As they were about to leave their rooms, Stephanie's mobile phone rang in her pocket. She pulled it out quite irritably, then took the call.

'Yes Mavis, what can I do for you?'

Henry listened as his wife listened.

'Of course I'll speak to her, but why didn't she phone me? Oh, I see. How did she manage to lose it? Oh…oh, good heavens. Is she alright? Well, yes, of course I shall. No, I won't let him worry at all.'

Henry was fit to burst. 'Has something happened to Mother? Is she alright?'

Stephanie said, 'Hang on a tick, Mavis. Yes, Henry, your mother is perfectly well. She and Mavis are taking tea with some acquaintances they've made at The Lavender, and will be back at the Dower House later this evening. Meanwhile, your mother is about to speak to me. She's lost her phone, that's all.'

Henry felt a little better, but something told him he wasn't getting the full story.

Stephanie said, 'Good afternoon, Althea. Mavis says you have something to tell me? Oh, to tell *us*? Very well, I'll put you on speakerphone.'

Henry was unusually delighted to hear his mother's voice. They exchanged rather abrupt pleasantries, then Althea said, 'Mavis was sent some shots taken from recordings made overnight in the kitchens there. By Christine. Someone lurking in the dark. Well, I saw them, and it's quite clear to me who they show. It's Cook.'

Henry and Stephanie shared a worried glance. Henry said, 'No, Mother, it's not. Edward assures us that Cook was asleep in her room at the time.'

There was a pause, then his mother said, 'How on earth would Edward know that?'

'Her room is opposite his, Mother.'

'No, it's not.'

'Yes, it is.'

'Don't be ridiculous, Henry…oh…*your* Cook. Cook Davies. Yes, her room is opposite Edward's. Always has been. I see what you mean. But I meant *my* Cook.'

Henry was utterly confused. 'Sorry, Mother – what do you mean, exactly?'

'It's my Cook in the photos. Mary Wilson – my cook. She has quite a distinctive walk.'

Henry felt completely exasperated. 'Mother, they are photographs, one cannot tell how someone walks from a photograph.'

His mother sniped back, 'I saw the photos that Christine sent, then Mavis kindly asked her to send some of the moving film, so I saw that, too. And it's Cook. My Cook. Cook Wilson. In your kitchens. At the Hall. Though what on earth she would have been doing there at that time of night I couldn't imagine. So I asked her.'

'Pardon?' Henry was struggling.

Althea sighed. 'I saw the photos. I saw the film. I phoned Cook Wilson and asked her what she was playing at. I wasn't overly cross with her, I don't think, but I asked her directly. And she dissolved. Cried her eyes out. Said she's sick of me. Never thought that working for a dowager would be so boring. I was flabbergasted, as you might imagine; I've always thought she's been very happy. She's been with me for about ten years. But it seems that I do not present enough of a challenge for her. She'd set her heart on moving up to a more fulfilling role at the Hall. Her one last chance to achieve her potential, she said. Hence the campaign against Cook Davies. I have been understanding, as one might imagine, and told her she can stay with me, or go. If she stays, she must apologize to both Cook Davies and Paul Baker. We can't have anyone acting that way toward our valued staff, can we?'

Henry didn't know what to say, so thought it best to say nothing.

Stephanie said, 'You've fired Cook Wilson? What – on the telephone? From Pembrokeshire?'

'Not at all.' Henry thought his mother sounded quite wounded. 'I've left the choice up to her. I said she'd get a good reference from me if she decided to go, but made it plain that I'd prefer her to stay. I like Cook Wilson. I'm not being spiteful. Just decisive. I'm too old for a lot of fiddle-faddle. If she goes, well, I'll have to find someone new.

Apparently, any number of adequate cooks could meet my needs, which are unchallenging, it seems. As you know, I do my best to eat as many of her baked goods as possible, because they are rather wonderful, but Mavis and I are only two people, after all, and it's not as though I receive visitors often. And that's the problem – she's feeling underutilized, it seems. I thought I should let you know, in case it helps with what Mavis tells me is called The Case of the Battling Baker.'

'It does,' said Henry, feeling relieved. 'Edward's just told us that Cook Davies is packing. Maybe this will allow her to change her mind, and stay.'

Stephanie said, 'I don't know, Henry; while Cook Wilson's actions might have lit the blue touch paper, the fireworks between Cook Davies and Paul Baker are now – by the sounds of it – completely out of control. I fear things have gone too far, so that, while we're grateful for the information, Althea, I believe it might have come too late to make a real difference.'

'Well, I've done what I can,' said the dowager. 'I could pop over to you in the morning to have a chat with Cook Davies – if you think she might be persuaded to wait for that? Cook Wilson has at least agreed to not leave the Dower House until tomorrow at the earliest, which is good. Mavis and I should be back for dinner. I'm relieved to say that Cook – my Cook – has promised duck, which I shall enjoy tremendously. She relishes cooking duck, it seems. Not something she's mentioned even once during the past decade. I'll admit that our conversation was far from normal.'

Stephanie said, 'You know what, Althea – I'll do what I can to ensure that both Paul Baker and Cook Davies at least agree to stay on until you can have a chat with them both tomorrow morning – if you'd be so kind.'

Henry almost laughed aloud when his mother giggled – it was a sound he'd grown up hearing, and it never failed to amuse him. She said, 'But of course, dear – that's what mothers, and mothers-in-law, are for. I shall come for elevenses. Now, I must go; Mavis is getting rather irritated that this is taking so long. See you tomorrow.'

When his mother had disconnected, Henry and Stephanie took their son and headed toward the small sitting room. At least now they had some ammunition to use in their battle to hang on to what they both admitted were an excellent cook, and a highly sought-after baker.

# CHAPTER THIRTY-THREE

Mavis knocked again at the connecting door between her room and that of the dowager; she had no idea what the woman was up to – they were late for tea, and they'd already had to make arrangements for it to be delayed for them in any case.

'Can you no' come back to finish packing after we've had our tea, Althea?' Althea opened the door. Mavis could see that the bed behind her was, quite literally, covered with clothes, but chose to say only, 'Right, let's be going. They'll all be waiting for us.'

Althea nodded, and the pair headed for the noisy little lift in silence. A silence which continued as they descended toward the main reception area. Just as Mavis was grappling with the annoying gate, Althea said quietly, 'Although I'm pleased I've been able to identify the person doing those dreadful things at Chellingworth Hall, I have to say that I am worried about what it all means.'

Holding open the heavy wooden door so the dowager could exit the cubicle, Mavis replied sharply, 'It means that Cook Wilson has no' taken any of the chances she had to tell you she was feeling unfulfilled, and has chosen a particularly spiteful method of trying to make someone so unhappy in their job – at which they excel – that they end up walking away from it.'

Althea smiled tiredly. 'I suppose you're right.'

'I am,' affirmed Mavis. 'Now, let's make the most of our chance to have a proper goodbye with the people we've spent time with here.'

Althea straightened up and stuck out her chin. 'Of course, dear; this will be an important leave-taking. Though I hope not a permanent one.'

Mavis didn't have a chance to reply, because Toni Conti rushed to meet the women, his wife at his side. 'Your Grace, Mrs MacDonald, Maria was just saying that you've not been formally introduced, and now here you are about to leave us. A terrible oversight on my part. Would you mind if she joins us all for your farewell tea? I've had a word with Simon, and there's going to be Welsh Rarebit all round.'

Althea clapped her hands. 'Oh excellent. You can't beat a nice Welsh Rarebit…as long as good cheese is used.'

'Welsh cheddar, of course,' said Maria Conti, 'and even Welsh mustard, too. We get it from a farm just along the coast. Sharp, but rich – both the cheddar and the mustard.'

Mavis was surprised by the woman's voice – it was deep, and rich. She realized in that moment it wasn't the first time she'd heard it. This was most definitely the person she'd heard talking quietly with Dennis Moore, the day he'd been skulking in the kitchen.

Mavis felt her mouth dry up. *An affair then. With the owner's wife.* Mavis acknowledged Maria Conti's good looks: a trim figure; well-cut silver hair, just grazing her shoulders; and just enough make-up to emphasize her full lips, excellent cheekbones, and sparkling green eyes.

Althea said, 'Lovely to meet you, Maria – we've heard a great deal about you, and we've seen you about the place, of course. I say, you've got eyes just like Dennis Moore. How extraordinary. Have you any idea just how rare truly green eyes are?'

Mavis wasn't surprised when Maria's entire neck flushed red, quickly followed by her prominent cheekbones turning pink. What did surprise her was the fact that Toni Conti looked equally uncomfortable. *He knows about the relationship!* Mavis sighed as she realized that Althea had, yet again, waded into someone's private affairs – quite literally, on this occasion.

Mavis was completely taken aback when Maria stared at her husband and snapped, 'I told you, Toni – there's no point in us trying to hide it. It's obvious to lots of people. You should let us be us. He's been here for years, now, and I've had enough of it all.'

Mavis was immediately worried that a major marital disagreement was about to break out between the Contis, so she grabbed at Althea, ready to steer her toward the comparative safety of the dining room.

'Oh, I see,' said Althea, winking comedically.

Mavis sagged, the wee woman had no clue. 'Come on, dear, this isnae any of our business,' she said firmly.

Althea tutted loudly, then spoke directly to Maria Conti. 'You're very much alike, the two of you. It must be nice to have Dennis around.

Though I dare say your husband doesn't like the guests to think you're consorting with the help, eh?'

Mavis finally gave in. 'Honestly, Althea, the way people choose to run their lives is no business of ours. Come away now, and let these poor people have their privacy.'

Toni Conti took his wife's hand in his and said, 'I'm sorry, my love. I know you're right, really, but…well, I do think it's a bit much, if the two of you are seen to be, you know, joshing about. You know what you're like, once you get going. There's no stopping you.'

Mavis struggled with her emotions; the way some people chose to view their marriages left her completely flummoxed. *The man's being so open about it all. Accepting, even. He doesnae seem at all worried about what his wife's getting up to with Dennis Moore, just that they shouldn't be seen to be doing it by the guests.*

Maria Conti grasped her husband's hand tightly. 'My darling, I love you more than words can say, but I've really had enough of this…denying my true nature. You said that, if you opened the place up to guests, it wouldn't affect the way I live my life. Well, it is, my darling. I don't mind putting in a few hours around the place to fill a staffing gap here and there, but I want to be able to be open about Dennis. He's my big brother, Toni…of course I want to be able to give him a hug when I see him, or give him a thump if he deserves one. This not being able to be ourselves? It's getting to be a real strain, especially when there are so many other stressful things going on here. So it's either you letting us be us, even when there are guests around, or I put my foot down and that's the end of all the guests.'

Mavis whispered, 'Dennis Moore is your brother?'

Althea said, 'Of course he is – look at them, so alike. Not just the eyes, but the nose, too.'

Mavis gave herself a moment to reassess the conversation she'd overheard between Dennis and Maria in the kitchen. She tutted at herself. *How did I no' see that? Jumping to conclusions…you're a professional investigator, Mavis!*

She sighed. 'Aye, you're on the ball as usual, dear. More so than me, in any case. Now, will that cheese on toast no' be getting cold?'

Althea smiled. 'Quite right, dear – and a cold Welsh Rarebit is not pleasant…just greasy. Let's go; you must come too, Maria, and why not invite your brother to join us? Rip off the sticking plaster: tell your residents about who he is, though you might discover they've all guessed in any case. We're none of us quite as good at hiding the truth about our feelings toward another person as we'd like to think we are, eh, Mavis?'

Mavis had no idea what Althea was wittering on about, so ignored her last comment, and steered the dowager toward 'their' table in the dining room.

Uma Chatterjee, Siggy Welbeck, and Sir Malcolm Lee were already seated, though, of course, the gentlemen rose as Mavis and Althea approached. Toni and Maria Conti joined the group, and Dennis Moore eventually strolled in from the garden – where announcements about his relationship to Maria Conti were met with almost no reaction, other than for Uma to whisper to Mavis, 'I didn't know it was even supposed to be a secret,' which just made Mavis feel even more inadequate as an investigator.

As she sat there listening to the chatter ebb and flow, congratulations being passed from one person to another, and the general camaraderie that was evident within The Lavender Mob, Mavis marvelled at how rapidly one became accustomed to a temporary group of companions, and residence, feeling the wrench of leaving so keenly after just a short time.

She told herself that, in this instance, the emotion of experiencing some sort of loss was heightened by the true loss of Frances Millington, whose death was only now seeming to become real to Mavis, because the cause of it had been discerned.

Siggy confirmed that both Pippa and Bethan Thomas had been apprehended at Cardiff airport, prior to them being able to get on a flight to Barcelona, and that one Otterlie Bowen had been picked up at a bed and breakfast in Tenby, which allowed Mavis to feel a sense of closure concerning The Case of the Secretive Secretary, until the various court cases might be held. But she still had a nagging feeling that these people she'd met, this place she'd come to rather like –

despite, or maybe even because of, it's completely outlandish Gothic flourishes – wasn't quite done with her yet. She realized she'd missed something when Althea kicked her ankle under the table.

'Earth to Mavis,' said Althea pointedly. 'I said we'd be delighted to have Sir Malcom, and Uma if she wants, come to visit to see my Gilbern, wouldn't we?'

Mavis nodded absently.

Dennis, who was sitting to Mavis's right, asked, 'What's all this about a Gilbern?'

Mavis replied, 'Althea has a Gilbern. The late duke gave it to her as an anniversary gift, some years ago. It's an interesting vehicle.'

Dennis nodded. 'As is Sir Malcolm's Roller, which I very much enjoy keeping ticking over for him, and your little Morris Traveller's a gem, isn't she?'

Mavis asked, 'You're interested in cars, Dennis?'

The man smiled his delightful wrinkly smile. 'A fair bit. You must be too, to be bothered to keep yours on the road. How does Althea manage with her Gilbern?'

Siggy, who was sitting to Mavis's left, jumped in. 'I bet there's someone local to Chellingworth Hall who's able to keep it on the road, eh? It doesn't just need passion to keep old vehicles healthy, but technical know-how too. As is true of life, of course.'

Mavis was just about to reply with a pithy response, when Althea rose, lifted her cup of tea and said, 'To The Lavender Mob. Mavis and I have had an interesting time here with you, and we wish you all the very best for your future together, here, at your lovely home. Cheers!'

The group joined in, with bone china being carefully chinked across and around the table. Mavis finally felt things at The Lavender had reached their natural conclusion, and hoped she and Althea would be able to get back to the Dower House before darkness fell, and in good time for dinner.

# 10<sup>th</sup> SEPTEMBER

# CHAPTER THIRTY-FOUR

The heavens had opened at about one in the morning, according to the weather reports, and Mavis had insisted that she and Althea should be driven to Chellingworth Hall from the Dower House when they left for elevenses. Mavis had noted, with some satisfaction, that Althea put up only a half-hearted fight to be allowed to walk, so Ian was collecting them at half past ten.

Even Mavis was looking forward to getting away from the Dower House, and they'd only been back at the place – awake – for a few hours. But what hours they'd been.

Of course, the first thing that had happened upon their return the previous evening was the great fuss that had to be made of McFli, and the great fuss that McFli had to make of them. Mavis hadn't minded that so much. Indeed, seeing Althea's happy little face had lifted Mavis's spirits considerably. However, with McFli still yapping at their heels, and Ian still carrying bags from Mavis's car, Cook Wilson had chosen that moment to announce, haughtily, that she'd just prepared her last duck for the dowager – which Althea had not taken well.

Mavis had been impressed by Althea's resilience – she'd endured threats and incarceration that day – and Mavis had no doubt that Cook Wilson had no insights about Althea's experiences. But she was only too well aware that the woman had been heaping insult upon injury when she'd made her announcement about the duck just a few moments after the two women had crossed the threshold. Even so, Mavis had still been shocked by Althea's response – which was to tell Cook Wilson to stay in her room until she left, which was to be first thing the following morning.

Mavis knew she'd gone out like a light when she'd repaired to her room, and could only imagine that the same must have been true for Althea – the wee woman had to have been exhausted.

When Mavis had opened her curtains to the gray, wet morning, she'd seen Ian Cottesloe helping Mary Wilson load her car with her bags; the cook had left the Dower House before Althea had even emerged from her room.

A breakfast of toast with jam and a pot of tea, that wasn't quite right, was served by Ian, who was now the only member of staff left at the Dower House – if one discounted the 'loaned' gardeners, cleaners, and maintenance staff. It was a situation both Althea and Mavis agreed couldn't continue for very long.

And now they were waiting for Ian to drive them to the Hall, where Althea had promised she'd intercede with Cook Davies and Paul Baker on behalf of her son and daughter-in-law. Mavis couldn't help but feel that the dowager, doughty though she was, was taking rather too much upon herself. But Althea would not be swayed – a promise was a promise, she'd said. So off they went, with McFli sitting on the dowager's lap in the Gilbern, which Ian nursed through the lashing rain to the Hall itself. They were greeted by an umbrella-wielding Edward, who ensured they weren't soaked to the skin in the few moments it took to ascend to the side entrance, which wasn't used by the members of the public. Not that there were many of them about on such a dreadful day.

Stephanie and Henry, with Hugo in his pram, Althea and Mavis, with McFli always within six inches of his mistress, Christine and Alexander – Mavis had no idea why he was there – were all gathered in the duke and duchess's private sitting room when Paul Baker and Cook Davies joined them. They were invited to sit and take tea; both sat, but declined refreshments.

Althea took center stage by sitting very upright, and clearing her throat dramatically. She explained her conversations with Cook Wilson, which surprised and saddened Cook Davies, if Mavis was reading her shifting expression correctly.

'And now she's gone,' concluded Althea quietly. 'I honestly had no idea that she was so unhappy. Had I known, I'd have invited her to move on to a position where she'd feel her talents were better utilized. I shall give her an excellent reference, of course, which I hope you both understand. I don't think such a unique set of circumstances would be likely to ever prevail again, so I have no doubt she'll never resort to such sabotage in the future. I just hope you both feel you can – well…' She giggled. 'I dare say "kissing and making up" isn't quite on the cards, is it?'

Mavis noted the sour look Cook Davies had on her face before Althea giggled, then saw it soften. A little.

Mavis watched as Cook Davies shook her head sadly. 'I don't understand what Mary did. I thought we were colleagues, in a way. Her down at your place, me up here. I'd never suspected jealousy on her part. And to covet my position? To try to get me to walk away from my life here by making me unhappy? Well, Your Grace, you're a more forgiving soul than me if you're giving her a good reference.'

'Maybe the reverend might consider a sermon on forgiveness, one of these Sundays,' said Althea quietly. 'But, while you're considering that, Cook Davies, will you please stay? The duke and duchess – my son and daughter-in-law – would miss you greatly. I think they hope you'll be here to host little Hugo in your kitchen when he's old enough to be taught to mix the dry ingredients for Welshcakes, and roll out dough ready for cutting.'

'Please stay,' said Stephanie, rather meekly for her, thought Mavis. She noted that Henry just nodded.

'And will he be staying, too?' Cook Davies looked at Paul Baker with the sort of venom usually reserved for cartoonish baddies with waxed mustaches.

Mavis was surprised when Althea asked slyly, 'Paul – do you, by any chance, cook as well as bake?'

Paul Baker shrugged. 'I can, and have done in the past, at a small restaurant I once worked at. I'm not good at fancy stuff.'

Mavis stiffened as Althea tilted her head and dimpled. 'Do you think you could manage three meals a day for two women who prefer old-fashioned, plain food? If so, I might know of a vacancy. It wouldn't keep you very busy, I've been led to believe – but there'd be a kitchen at your disposal where you'd have the run of the place, so you could bake for the Lamb Tearooms there. The Dower House is just as much a part of the Chellingworth Estate as is Chellingworth Hall, so there's no reason why you couldn't work there, the way you were going to work here.'

Mavis could see the twinkle in Althea's eyes. *The little minx.*

Paul Baker grinned, and Mavis could even see Cook Davies perk up a bit. 'Now that, Your Grace, is the best idea I've heard in a long time. Thank you. I'd be pleased to accept your offer – though I reserve the right to renegotiate my contract with the Estate, in light of my extra duties.'

Mavis noted how quickly Stephanie and Henry nodded their agreement.

'Now come along,' said Althea to the two culinary experts. 'No kissing maybe, but at least shake hands, will you? Please.'

Paul Baker and Cook Davies shook hands.

'He's not getting my recipe for seed cake,' sniffed Cook Davies. 'If Your Grace wants one, I'll make it myself and have it sent over.'

Althea lowered her voice to a conspiratorial level. 'That would be wonderful. In confidence, Cook Wilson's was never a patch on yours.'

# 22nd SEPTEMBER

# CHAPTER THIRTY-FIVE

The village hall was alive with activity, and Carol Hill was exhausted. She flopped onto a seat beside her husband, who was bouncing Albert on his knee. 'I never thought he'd stay awake this late,' he said, speaking loudly enough that his wife could hear him over the jollity surrounding the trio.

'Maybe he'll sleep through tonight, if we're lucky,' replied Carol, popping a second dish of *cawl* in front of David. 'Don't stuff yourself, *cariad*, that *cawl's* very filling.'

David grinned. 'I love it. The lamb's so soft. And the veg? Fantastic. I don't know what they've put in this, but it's like silk.'

'It's just leeks and potatoes, and some carrots. I make *cawl* all the time…well, not through the summer, but I'll get going with it again now. Is this better than mine, then?'

David laughed. 'Not at all, but it's the first I've had in a while, and the change in the weather this past week means it's welcome tonight. Lovely harvest service in church this morning, wasn't it?'

Carol nodded as she made sure she got as much gravy from her faggots mixed in with her mashed potatoes and peas as she could, loading her fork. 'I've never been any good at making faggots. Cook Davies up at the Hall has done us proud here tonight, bless her. And yes, it was a lovely service, and the church looked wonderful. That bread wheatsheaf that Paul Baker made, for the front of the altar? Amazing. A work of art in its own right, and a proper harvest service icon.'

'It looked too good to cut up and eat, as I said at the time,' said David, 'yet here I am dunking a slice of it in my stew. What a day.' He gazed at his son. 'He's been as good as gold. He's settling into his new room alright, isn't he?'

Carol mopped up the last remnants of her tasty dinner with a hunk of bread. 'He is. I know he's young to have his own room, but with both doors open we can still hear him if he needs us. I still can't quite believe it, if I'm honest: it only took us a week from the time Stephanie phoned me and asked if we'd like to move into *Tŷ Mawr*, once the Hugheses had gone, until we were in.'

'We couldn't have done it without Tudor, the social committee, and all our neighbors,' said David, smiling. 'I'll never forget the entire thing, and I know you took loads of photos for Albert to see one day. Everyone coming into our house and taking a box or a piece of furniture – or even part of a piece of furniture – and carrying it across the village green to our new house? What an amazing thing to see, and for everyone to do. Marjorie Pritchard with that wheelbarrow she borrowed…with all your pots and pans in it? What a sight. And then that lovely Josie you've got to know, from the greyhound place, coming along with the horse box, to shift the big stuff. Wonderful. All done in a day. One day. And now we're in…and almost unpacked.'

Carol pushed away her plate. 'All I've got to do now is remember where I've put everything. Especially in the kitchen. Mind you, the new one is so much bigger than our last one, I'll have to buy twice as much stuff as we've got now to fill it all.'

David kissed her on the cheek. 'Oh no you won't. Let those cupboards breath, my love. Time will fill them, no doubt.'

'No doubt. I won't even have to make an effort.'

David grabbed Carol's hand. 'I know it's been a lot of work for you, making two hundred Welshcakes, to bring tonight, but everyone's pleased about it.'

Carol smiled. 'Yes, it was a big job…but I wanted to do something to say thank you to everyone, and – besides – it was such a joy to have that massive counter to do the rolling out – and did you see how many I had cooling, all at once? Life-changing that kitchen's going to be, and the rest of the house, too. We'll have a whole room each, just for our work stuff. A real luxury.'

'Not to mention that dishwasher, eh?'

Carol grinned. 'Oh yes, the dishwasher. You know what, *cariad*, I always pined for a dishwasher…and now that I've got one, I was right

– it's changed my life.'

Annie was standing beside Tudor at the makeshift bar – in other words, one end of the counter at the large opening between the kitchen and the hall. 'The harvest decorations look lovely, Tude. Good job all round.'

Tudor grinned. 'Had to make a bit of an effort, didn't we? I mean look at the place anyway – you can hardly recognize it. Before Alexander and his lot got in here, there was paint peeling off all over the place, the lights for the stage didn't work half the time, and the seating had to be the most uncomfortable you could imagine. But now? These tables and chairs are wonderful, and they fit lovely into the space under the stage when they need to be out of the way, now that's all been cleared out. Everything's been fixed, and freshly decorated. And have you seen the loos? Put ours at the Coach to shame, they do. Gleaming.'

Annie passed a glass of lemonade to one of Sarah Hughes's sons – she couldn't remember which one it was. 'Nice to see that your family came back for this,' she said to the boy. 'Settling into your new school, and house, alright?'

A hasty 'Yeah' was thrown her way as the boy hurried back to his brother, who was hiding some sort of electronic handheld device under the tablecloth.

'Kids these days, eh?' She laughed. 'Gordon Bennett, listen to me, Tude, I sound more like my mother every day.'

Tudor hugged her. 'Not the worst thing in the world.' He kissed her cheek.

'And that's for?'

'Everything. You haven't stopped, Annie. All that work you've been doing? Your "secret mission" up at Josie's place? Best birthday present ever, that was. That's a real novelty – everyone says so. There's not a lot of pubs have a swanky horsebox, with fairy lights, that serves drinks beside a posh gazebo with its own heaters, like we've got now at the Coach. That photo in the paper? I nearly burst my shirt buttons with pride when I saw that. A giant cake shaped like a foaming pint, thanks to Paul Baker; a horsebox decorated to the nines and set up to accommodate a keg of beer or two; and a newspaper photographer coming to take pictures of it all, and give the Coach a lovely bit of publicity…all on my birthday, and all thanks to you – you're quite the woman, Annie Parker.'

'I love you, Tude, and we're going to make sure the Coach is a roaring success. Now listen – try to get the recipe for this stew from Cook Davies over there, because there's a flavor in it that I can't put my finger on, and I don't think it would be a bad addition to your lamb stew, for the pub.'

'It's parsley.'

'No, it can't just be parsley.'

'I've already asked her. And you're right, I am going to try it – though my lamb stew is a thick stew, whereas this is traditional *cawl*, with a thinner broth, so it might not work as well; mine's heavier – the flavor might get lost. But I'll give it a go. I might also talk to her about her faggots. I know I get them in from a butcher a couple of villages over, but hers are better, and we might get a better deal, since she'd be making them on the Estate. She might say yes.'

Annie smiled. 'Love a good plate of faggots, I do – good idea, Tude. But, come on then, tell me – who's helping Aled over at our pub tonight? Joan Pike? Or Sharon Jones? I haven't seen either of them here at all.'

Tudor shrugged his shoulders. 'My lips are sealed as to who it was that he invited to give him a hand, but I'll put money on them both being there, in any case. There may be trouble ahead for poor Aled. Men are in short supply in Anwen-by-Wye, especially young ones.'

'Yeah, and in any case all the good ones are taken, however long in the tooth they might be,' said Annie playfully.

'Have you no' had enough of that stuff, Althea? You'll be up all night.' Mavis stared in horror at the plate in front of the dowager.

'I adore *bara brith*, and Paul Baker's made a very good one. Well, he's made a very good couple of dozen loaves of it. It's being very well received, given it's been made by an Englishman. He's settled in quite nicely with us, don't you think?'

'Only because he and Ian share the serving, and because you indulge him. But, yes, he's doing a good job. And the Lamb Tearooms are doing well too, I hear. Tudor's got that horsebox thing outside the Coach, and now Janet Jackson's got the new awning installed at the Lamb Tearooms so folks can sit at those few tables outside even if it's raining a bit – and the village looks…I don't know, just more inviting. But not in a twee way – just a proper way. Ach, I'm rambling. I must be getting old.'

'Oh no you're not,' said Althea, dimpling. 'You're not dead yet. I happen to know you're an attractive enough woman that you've *two* men showing an interest in you. How are Siggy and Dennis, by the way? I'd expected The Lavender Mob to have visited by now – using an interest in my Gilbern as useful cover, no doubt. Have you put them off?'

'No' exactly, but it seems that Sir Malcom has rediscovered the joys of motoring, so he's off out and about in his fancy car taking everyone with him, before the weather closes in for the winter. Siggy cannae drive himself anywhere, as you know, and Dennis doesnae even have a car, just a bicycle, so I'll no' see either of them unless I pop down to The Lavender myself.'

'And when will you do that, dear?'

Mavis shrugged. 'Uma Chatterjee is organizing a memorial gathering for Frances Millington there in a couple of weeks. Would you like to come, too?'

Althea waved a hand airily. 'If I'm still the right side of the grass, dear, I shall.'

Mavis grinned. 'Ach, you'll outlive us all, you wee scamp. And stop talking about me and men. I'm no' interested in men. Aye, that Dennis is a healthy enough specimen, and I find Siggy's brain fascinating – he'd have made a good administrative worker for the Foreign Office, I'm sure.'

'I'm sure he did, dear. You should tend to that friendship – Siggy could be a useful contact for a firm of private investigators.'

'Ach, Althea, you're a conniving wee thing.'

Althea bit into a slice of *bara brith* she'd mounded with glistening salt butter, her eyes closing with contentment.

Mavis tutted. 'Like a heart attack on a plate, that. Let this be your last piece, please?'

Althea nodded and nibbled. 'Looking lovely, isn't it? The village hall. I hear they're making great progress with the old school too, though that was a much bigger undertaking, of course. The stage here is so much more…stagey, now, don't you think? It always looked terribly amateurish, and rather sorry for itself. Now? I can almost see myself up there, treading the boards as I did in my youth. I do so hope it gets used.'

'Isn't Iris Lewis's granddaughter Wendy looking into how this hall can be used to host various performance arts?' Mavis recalled that was what she'd heard at the committee meeting.

Althea nodded. 'Yes – she has all those contacts from her time studying music in Cardiff. The right young woman for the job. But what I meant was that I hope it's used for something that's more about building community from within. Look at us all here tonight, for example. We've all enjoyed a good harvest service in church, though I always think it's such a pity that we only get to belt out "We plough the fields and scatter" once a year, at that service, don't you? I thought that the reverend gave an excellent sermon about the redemptive power of forgiveness, I must say, and now we're all here. With all this lovely food. No, what I meant was something like…oh, I don't know, like back in the good old days. A panto – something like that.'

Mavis sighed, and tried her best to not roll her eyes. 'Aye, well, I dare say you'll get your way, whatever it is that you want. You usually do.'

'Really?' said the dowager, dimpling.

'Higher…a bit to the left…there,' said Christine to Alexander, who was holding a large mirror against the wall in the entryway to their new home, which they had jointly decided to name Honeysuckle Cottage, because they'd both been blown away by how wonderful the scent of the honeysuckle growing around the front door had been on the evening when they'd come to view the place. That had been Christine's second visit to the cottage – she'd been there once when it had belonged to Mair Jones, Sharon's mum.

During her original visit she'd registered that the cottage was far from anywhere, on the edge of fields, and cozy, with a wonderful garden and large front windows that really allowed the outdoors to feel as though they flowed into the sitting room. When she and Alexander had come to look at it as a potential place to live, the cottage had already been stripped of anything Mair Jones owned, so it was a blank slate – which she was now delighted to have the chance to make her own.

*Their* own.

She'd already brought a few key pieces from her flat in Battersea, and from her parents' home in London, and she had plans to use the considerable talent of her friend Nat Smith, the renowned wallpaper designer and muralist married to Alexander's business partner, Bill Coggins.

'This is so exciting, Alexander. We're the luckiest couple in the world.' She kissed her fiancé, and he kissed back, with passion.

'Hang on a minute,' she said, pulling away and giggling, 'we both know how that ends up and we've got to get back to the barn at a reasonable hour tonight, because I've got some reports to finish up for Carol, by ten tomorrow.'

Alexander carefully balanced the mirror against the wall. 'So let's get going now? I know it's not that far, really, but you're right, I've got an early start tomorrow, too. Up to London, meetings with Geordie at three building sites. He's doing all the heavy lifting for my London projects at the moment, and he needs a bit of support. The teams in Anwen at the old school are getting along nicely; I can afford to leave them to it for a couple of days. You remember we said I'd go tomorrow – back Wednesday?'

Christine arched her back. 'Of course I do. In fact, Mammy'll have a box for you to bring back with you, if you don't mind. I know there's hardly any room in that car of yours, so I guarantee it's a small box. And we'll have to think about that, too: your car.'

Alexander headed toward the rear of the cottage, to check that the doors and windows were secure. He called, 'My car is my car. When our child needs to be transported, our child can go in its mother's car, thank you very much. Though I hate calling it "it". We need a way to refer to our child, while it's still in there.' He gently patted Christine's midsection when he reached her.

Christine held him close. '"Our child"? It doesn't seem real, does it? None of this seems real. Will it feel like it's truly my life again, one day?'

Alexander leaned back and looked into the eyes he loved. 'No idea, but – if this isn't real – then I'm all for unreality. Bring it on.'

Henry lay in bed contemplating the ceiling. 'It all went off terrifically well this evening, don't you think? Good turnout. Happy faces. All that sort of thing.'

Stephanie was at her dressing table brushing her long, chestnut hair. 'It did, and you're right, everyone was in good spirits. It's funny, you know, harvest really is the turn of the year, isn't it? We've all sort of had enough of summer, and we're looking forward to pulling on a sweater, and snuggling in front of the fire with a mug of hot chocolate. Well, I am anyway.'

'I didn't think you cared for hot chocolate, dear. It's one of my most favorite flavors, as you know, but I thought you didn't have it when I do because you don't like it.'

Stephanie joined her husband in bed. 'I like it, Henry, but it doesn't like me. I always feel as though my teeth have been carpeted after I've drunk it, and then I get the most dreadful sugar crash an hour later. It makes the drinking of it hardly worth the after-effects.'

Henry harrumphed a little as he turned onto his side to go to sleep. 'Hugo was a cracking good boy tonight, wasn't he? Not a peep out of him. And so many people cooing over him that I thought he'd wake and make a fuss.'

Stephanie sighed. 'He was an absolute angel, dear, just like his father: one can count on the Twyst men to act correctly in company even when they're infants, it seems. That was our first big community event in the refurbished village hall, and it was a good way to start, I think. I hope when the old school opens up that it brings some fresh blood to the village…I'm sure it will.'

Henry cleared his throat. 'Fresh blood? I'm not sure that's the most appealing term, dear. It makes it sound rather…murdery, and gruesome.'

'Not my intention, Henry. But you know what I mean.'

'Indeed.'

# *ACKNOWLEDGEMENTS*

Writing a book is a solitary experience…until it isn't. My editor, Anna Harrisson, has helped me make this a better book, and my copy editor, Sue Vincent, has helped to polish it. We've all tried to make it the best version of this story that it can be, and I thank them for their help. I'm also grateful for every blogger, reviewer, librarian, bookseller, friend on social media and anyone who's supported my work and helped to get the word out – it's a big world and there are lots of books, so it makes a huge difference when a lone author's voice is amplified. Finally, thanks to you for choosing this book, and to anyone who helped you find it. I really hope you enjoy/ed spending time with my chums in Anwen-by-Wye, and from farther afield, as much as I do.

*Cathy Ace*
*June 2024*

# ABOUT THE AUTHOR

CATHY ACE was born and raised in Swansea, Wales, and migrated to British Columbia, Canada aged forty. She is the author of The WISE Enquiries Agency Mysteries, The Cait Morgan Mysteries, the standalone novel of psychological suspense, The Wrong Boy, and collections of short stories and novellas. As well as being passionate about writing crime fiction, she's also a keen gardener.

You can find out more about Cathy and all her works at her website: www.cathyace.com